DEAD THIN

Diana Brahams

HeathView Books

*To my dear husband Malcolm without whom this
book would never have been published.*

CONTENTS

FOREWORD

DEAD THIN is a work of fiction and Forsyte International Pharmaceuticals plc and all other companies and characters featured in the plot are entirely imaginary as is the formula for Reduktopan. The search for a safe and effective and safe slimming pill continues in reality.

The main action takes place in the 2000's when mobile phones were simpler. Faxing was a common method of transmitting documents over a long distance. It relied on the recipient having an ample supply of paper to allow them to be printed out. Alternatively they could be saved on disks and posted as electronic messages in this way, but smaller items could go out in emails as well.

In 2004 the role of the Medicines Control Agency (MCA) was expanded and it was reconstituted as the Medicines and Healthcare products Regulatory Agency (MHRA) with responsibility for medicines, medical devices and blood components for transfusion in the UK.

The Middlesex Hospital in Mortimer Street, central London, closed in 2006. The distinctive red brick building was demolished and has been replaced with apartment buildings. The medical and nursing staff were transferred to other hospitals.

I would like to express my gratitude and thanks to Ms Eleanor Jane Turner PhD, FRCS and her colleague Dr Corinne Stannard MBBS, FRCA who read the medical chapters. For any mistakes that still remain I apologise and I take full responsibility! My thanks also to Barbara Jackson, artist and art teacher, whose sinister photograph inspired the painting on the front cover.

PROLOGUE

Cambridgeshire, England. 31st March 2001.

It was dark and raining heavily when David drove out of the flood lit but deserted Flat Acres car park. He had not been sleeping well for weeks. Yet, somehow he had been able to continue working, quite efficiently, if you made allowances for the occasional catnaps at his desk. He had forgotten to lock his office door yesterday and guessed that Reiss had seen him slumped over his files before slipping quietly out. The last thing he needed was Reiss poking around in his affairs. He really needed to get away. If the patient trials of Reduktopan were not due to start in four weeks he would already have been applying for jobs abroad. He could let out the house or sell it depending on how things worked out. He fancied a move to the States.

In the full beam of his headlights the rain looked like a wild waterfall as it tumbled over the windscreen. Fortunately, the hard top of the convertible was securely attached; the ageing canvas leaked in several places and was best kept for dry weather. Through the frantic motion of the wipers he negotiated the private narrow road to halt at the barrier where the guard was seated in his cabin surrounded by CCTV monitors. Waving to David, he opened the electric gate and raised the heavy bar to let him out. Now eager to get home, David rapidly circled the war memorial and was passing the sodden Village Green when an image of Lara came into his mind so clearly that it felt as if she was really with him inside the car. He glanced sideways but the passenger seat was quite empty of course. An illusion but still troubling. She was dressed as she had been the morning when she reached her target weight; she was wearing one of his striped office shirts over black lacy underwear. She was reaching out a ghostly hand to his knee when he heard once again his former mentor's reproving voice:

"David, what have you done here? You are not a sculptor modelling a lump of clay. You are having a sexual relationship with this young woman? A woman who was your patient? Is your patient? You must end it at once."

Easy to say. Not easy to do. Too late now. Far too late.

As the car leapt forward, skidding round the sharp bends, David took a hand from the steering wheel to rub his aching eyes, glad that the rain had reduced to a fine drizzle. It was then he realised that the brick wall that should have been on the left side of the road was racing straight towards him.

CHAPTER ONE

1st April 2001.

The phone by his bed was ringing. Reiss snatched it up.

It was Marcus Pomeroy who sounded stressed. "Why aren't you in the office? It's after nine o'clock."

Reiss snapped, "I must have overslept. I was up for half the night, after all."

"I know that. Look, you'd better get over there and deal with it, A.S.A.P. I've told Alan to get everyone who can make it into the Barn for a ten o'clock meeting. They need to hear about this directly from you, Raymond. What's left of David's stupid little sports car is lying in a heap at the side of the road and the rumour mill is going wild."

Reiss was already out of bed. He shaved and dressed quickly in a dark suit and tie and took his Barbour jacket from the peg by the front door. He should have left it to air. The unpleasant scent of the fire and smoke from the crash had permeated the fabric and was in his nostrils. He saw that people were standing around in groups, their heads bent and voices low; many of them wore white laboratory coats with lanyards, some furtively smoking.

Marcus was right: the news of David's death was obviously spreading fast. Reiss quickened his pace along the path leading to the "Farmhouse" where he and David had adjoining first floor offices. Externally, the Farmhouse looked much as before, but inside it had been completely rebuilt. His large room had a double aspect with one row of windows facing to the front where the small executive car park was divided by a tall electric fence from Pemberton Manor Health Farm and its grounds.

Through the smaller side windows there was a view of the modern laboratory block. He would need to allocate some time with Tim Scott, with whom David had worked closely on Reduktopan and which would now be his responsibility to take forward.

Sinking down at his desk and feeling unpleasantly under pressure as well as weary, Reiss switched on his computer as an email came in from Alan Michaels.

Good grief: the man was offering to organise a memorial service for David? It was common knowledge all round Flat Acres that two men had disliked each other. Dislike and distrust had erupted into a full scale row when Michaels had insensitively served David in person with a written warning on the first day he returned to work after his adverse drug reaction.

Reiss had heard them shouting through the partition wall, but decided not to intervene.

"I'm not a fucking junior lab assistant, Alan! I'm the deputy Medical Director here, and I'm senior to you, so what the Hell do you think you're doing giving me this?"

Alan had bawled back, "David, I am the compliance officer here, and you didn't comply with company procedures, did you? You put yourself and the company at risk when you do that! Our insurers won't pay out if procedures aren't followed to the letter and then we get a black mark and pay bigger premiums. This warning will run for six months and you're lucky I didn't make it a year!"

Reiss responded promptly to Alan's email, discouraging him, saying it was too soon, and he would in due course prefer to deal with this himself. His own relationship with David had not been without its challenges, but overall, they had worked reasonably well together. Reiss had respected David's autonomy to take responsibility for his own projects, leaving it to his deputy to update him as needed. They had worked in a complementary fashion; David's sudden death would leave a gaping hole that would not be easy to fill.

With this preying on his mind, Reiss went next door into David's room and glanced around gloomily. It was a little smaller than his own with a single set of windows that faced to the front. David's framed prints of six Oxford colleges included a view of St Catherine's, where he had won a scholarship from his Leeds grammar school aged seventeen. On the adjacent wall was a wide angled group photograph in which he and David sat beside one another in the centre of the front row. It had been taken soon after Reiss left his consultant post to become Medical Director at Forsyte International Pharmaceuticals plc, more conveniently referred to as Forsyte or FIP.

Reiss gave a tug at the handles of the desk drawers and then the filing cabinets. They were all locked. He was not surprised by this; David had been obsessive about security after the break-in and attack on his car by an animal rights group last year. And as he now had all David's keys in his possession, this would not pose a problem but he decided to leave the task of trawling through David's desk and cabinets until later. After his return from the morgue where officialdom apparently required him to formally identify the body. Yet he had been the one to certify David was dead at the side of the road last night in the presence of the police, the fire brigade and paramedics who had arrived late on the scene.

Explaining that David's keys were needed for the company's offices, the police had released them to him in return for a receipt.

Reiss checked his watch. He had five minutes in hand. He switched on the computer, that was networked into the system like his own and was annoyed to discover that David had changed the password without informing him; another breach of protocol. He rang the head of the technical support team who promised to come and "sort it today".

He walked across the landing to speak to Linda, who had been their shared secretary for eighteen months. She was sitting hunched in her chair with tears trickling down her powdered, plump cheeks.

"I can't believe he's not going to walk through that door any minute. But he is really dead, isn't he?" Her voice was not much above a whisper.

"He is, Linda. I am so sorry. I can ask someone else to type up his tapes if hearing his voice will upset you too much?"

Linda sniffed, dolefully, "No, I'll do them. I owe him that, the poor man. But it's so sad, Dr Reiss, so sad."

He agreed and suggested she make herself a cup of tea then find him the contact details for David's married sister.

Back at his desk, feeling time before the meeting fast draining away, Reiss jotted down the key points he would need to make and then tried again to phone his wife. Sally's mobile was off and she was not in the staff room; most probably she was taking her morning seminar. He left a message for her with the College secretary before ringing Beatrice to let her know that his planned two day visit to Stockholm next week would be postponed along with all his other non-urgent appointments.

Beatrice, however, responded by saying she would be coming to London to take someone else's place. She would be speaking at a conference, but it would be just a day trip. Unless her daughter, Steffie, stayed over with a school friend for a night? Perhaps they could meet up then?

His spirits a little raised by this possibility, Reiss emailed Dr John Stannard, the Chief Executive of A.C.E. to let him know he would taking over David's role as well as his own in the short term. A.C.E. was the independent contract organisation that FIP was paying to coordinate the multicentre outpatient trials of Reduktopan in different parts of the UK over the next months. A.C.E. also ran most of the company's "animal" studies if they were not conducted in-house at Flat Acres.

Stannard replied by return with the usual condolences, adding, "We're both going to miss him a lot, Raymond. He's going to leave a gap in your team, isn't he?"

This comment, prompted Reiss to phone human resources at the company's Head Office.

"I'm in urgent need of a medically qualified assistant. How about that guy who was a registrar at St Ursula's? Isn't he due to start soon?"

"You mean Dr Bill Ryder? We've given him a six month trial contract. You approved his C.V. three months ago for a job in Head Office, Dr Reiss. He starts there tomorrow."

"Head Office will have to wait. Tell him to report to me here at ten fifteen tomorrow morning and let them know at the barrier that he's coming, will you?"

It was a few minutes before ten. Reiss walked the short distance to the Barn, so-named because it had been erected on the same site as its dilapidated predecessor. Though externally vaguely similar, it was much larger and accommodated a lecture theatre on the ground floor and a library and conference rooms above. Beyond the Barn, the old piggery sheds had been rebuilt to house the staff canteen and kitchen with the remaining scattered outhouses used for storage purposes. Beyond these buildings, and sited closer to the electrified fence which divided Flat Acres from the extensive grounds of Pemberton Manor, was the animal block and the incinerator.

Alan Michaels was waiting for Reiss by the podium. He was a stocky, pear shaped man with heavy lidded eyes and the misshapen ears and flattened nose of a former rugby player.

"Do you think David was over the limit? He did that road ten times a week."

Reiss frowned at him."Let's not speculate. We'll know for sure after the P.M."

Alan Michaels cheeks were flushing. "I was just wondering, that's all."

He, and half the audience gathered there, no doubt.

Reiss ascended the platform and stood holding his notes while he waited for latecomers to find a seat. These included Tim Scott, looking a bit flustered, with petite Dr Ayesha Patel in his wake. Her head barely reached to Tim's tall shoulder. She had been recruited last autumn: an attractive and intelligent young woman whom, he noticed, was now twisting her head round to chat with Molly Owulu, the company's very capable "nurse monitor". They, like everyone else there, looked sad and subdued.

The three young scientists who worked directly under Tim were now squeezing up to Ayesha as Reiss tapped the mike. It squealed and the hall fell silent.

He spoke well and had the gift of making each member of his audience feel that he was speaking to them individually. His personal sadness and regret were reflected in his expression and tone of voice as he provided an edited account of events. The local police had rung him at eleven thirty last night to alert him there had been a serious car crash. As, fortuitously, he had been staying over in the Cottage at Flat Acres and was close by, he could reach the scene more quickly than emergency services with an ambulance expected to take forty-five minutes.

But after racing to the accident spot with his medical bag, there had been nothing he could do until the fire brigade had arrived and put out the blaze and cut the twisted wreck open to remove David's body, by which time he was dead.

As a few people were now openly sobbing, Reiss hurriedly reassured them that David had died immediately on impact. His neck was broken. "He wouldn't have known anything about what happened after he hit the wall at speed."

He did not tell them that while he stood helplessly watching, the car lay on its roof like an upturned beetle in a blazing pool of oil and petrol while David's body seemed to be writhing around in the heat and flames. He had not known for sure then that David was dead and the image would haunt him for years to come. But he gave no hint of this now.

Instead, he told them of David's intellectual achievements and how he had won a series of scholarships to get to medical school. That this had been all his own doing as his family were not in a position to ease his way. "He was driven by his own ambition and his brilliance. His death was a great blow, but we owe it to him to see that his work continues here and I will do my utmost to see that happens. I'm sure we all will. Thank you."

They stood for a minute's silence.

As the rest of the room filed quietly out, Reiss gestured to Tim Scott and Dr Jim Menzies to remain behind with Alan Michaels. Jim, who was employed one day a week as FIP's occupational physician, was volunteering to help with Reduktopan. This would be useful as he was a general practitioner in the area.

Reiss updated them about the expected arrival of Dr Bill Ryder and asked Tim to call an urgent department meeting for nine o'clock the next day.

"Do you want me there, Raymond?"

"No need, Alan. Thanks, anyway."

Reiss left them heading for the science block and walked back to the Farmhouse, listening impatiently to a rambling message on his mobile. It was Dr Otto Wengler from Zurich commiserating in German at the terrible news. Wengler had heard about it from Dr Schindler. Then it was Carl Ohldssohn ringing from Stockholm. Beatrice had let him know. Bad news travelled fast.

The next message was from Jerry Evans, the forensic pathologist in Cambridge. "I'll be doing the PM at one. Can you be here by 12.45? You can identify him before I start."

Back again at his desk, Reiss wrote an affectionate but carefully worded email to his youngest daughter, Mandy, who was travelling with two friends around India for a few months. She went most days to an internet cafe. Mandy had got to know David quite well as at her request he had (successfully) coached her for her entrance exam to read Medicine at his old Oxford College.

He was on the point of leaving when Sally rang sounding more upset than he had expected; she could only have met David three or four times at company events and once when she came with him to visit him in hospital.

"That's so awful, Raymond. He was only forty! Mandy said he

was brilliant and that he helped her a lot."

Reiss, a little jealous, responded, "Yes, I know. She told me."

Mandy's postcard had been prominently displayed on David's mantelpiece. It had a picture of a snake charmer sitting cross legged. On the back she had scrawled a brief message: *Having a wonderful time. Thanks so much for all your help and good advice. x M.*

Sally said, "Will you write to her? We don't want her hearing about this on the grapevine."

"I already did, Sal. Now, I'm off to the mortuary. Can't wait."

"Oh, Raymond, I'm so sorry. How horrible for you."

"I'll leave you to tell Joanne, but she won't be bothered too much. She hardly knew him." Joanne was twenty and in her second year, reading natural sciences at Durham. She was fair and looked more like Sally; Mandy on the other hand resembled her father, with dark hair, blue eyes and dimples when she smiled.

Sally changed the subject. "Will you stay over again at the Cottage, tonight?"

"Yes. Most of this week. I'm overwhelmed here. But I might make it back on Thursday."

Sally responded, "I have a college meeting that night. I'll be home after ten thirty."

Reiss retorted, "I'll see you on Friday, then."

CHAPTER TWO

On the way back from his unpleasant visit to the mortuary and still with the smell of formalin mingled with the fire in his nostrils, Reiss braked at the Flat Acres barrier . He waited for it to rise and then for the gate beyond to swing open and allow him through. Opposite was a large sign. It was identical to one fixed to a post at the point where the private road reached the cross roads leading to Pemberton Village. Their purpose was to discourage any intruders or unwanted or casual visitors from approaching Flat Acres as was clear from the wording.

FORSYTE INTERNATIONAL PHARMACEUTICALS PLC.
PRIVATE PROPERTY - ADMITTANCE IS RESTRICTED TO
AUTHORISED PERSONNEL AND AUTHORISED VEHICLES:
PASSES MUST BE SHOWN.
GUARD DOGS ON PATROL AT NIGHT.

The guard in the hut waved him through and a few minutes later Reiss parked once again in his reserved bay close to the Farmhouse.

At his desk, Linda brought him a welcome cup of tea and a plain biscuit along with David's sister's name and address. "Was it awful, Dr Reiss?"

Reiss nodded. "Yes, Linda. it was. And I'm not being insensitive, but I'm going to have to clear his room of all his personal stuff today. I'll take it to his house when I go there tonight to collect the company's property. I'm getting a new young doctor in tomorrow to assist me with some of the work and I want him in that room where I can keep an eye on him."

Linda nodded, dolefully. "I understand. H R has provided us with a couple of boxes and a roll of bubble wrap. Do you want me to help you clear it?"

"Best if I do that myself, but thanks, anyway."

Reiss finished his tea and went next door. He took David's six framed prints down first and packed them quickly in one of the boxes. Then, using the bunch of keys that had survived the inferno with just the fob burnt, he unlocked the desk drawers. In one he found a selection of pens, still in their presentation boxes which included the expensive one he had himself given David for his fortieth. There was also a spare pair of reading glasses in a case, some pencils, stationery, two quirky staplers and a hole puncher. In another drawer were a few clothes kept for emergencies or convenience: a sweater for when he worked late, a clean shirt folded in its laundry pack, a silk tie, a pair of socks, running shoes and some toiletries. David's modest personal possessions barely filled the two boxes.

The other drawers contained only a note pad (empty) a spare box of paper for the printer and a couple of novels that he might have bought at the airport when on a trip somewhere. With the dictating machine, were boxes containing cassettes and floppy disks, all carrying FIP's logo and emanating from the firm's stationery supplies.

Reiss moved on to tackle the filing cabinet, pulling out the metal drawers and riffling quickly through the paperwork that he would need to check properly at a later date. He was on the point of slamming back the bottom drawer when he noticed a thin file that had slipped sideways. He pulled it out to replace it and glanced inside and frowned and pondered for a minute as if perplexed before lifting out the top sheet of paper and replacing the file in the drawer and locking everything up once more.

Reiss took the two boxes of David's stuff downstairs and loaded them into his car and drove again down the narrow, bumpy road to the barrier flashing his headlights and tooting his horn gently as he approached. This time, Jim, one of the guards, came out of his hut.

Reiss lowered his window. "Is something wrong?"

"No, sir. I wanted to tell you how much we all appreciated

what you said about poor Dr Devereaux. I heard it over the loudspeakers when I was having my break in the canteen."

Reiss mumbled something appropriate as he waited to leave the compound which was bounded by tall electrified steel fencing that divided Flat Acres from Pemberton Manor Health Farm the whole of which had once formed only a part of Lord Pemberton's family estate.

Forced to sell when his father (the fifth earl) had died, Cecil Pemberton was reduced to owning only the Dower House and a few hundred Forsyte shares. And even the Dower House was reputed to be heavily mortgaged.

At the cross roads, Reiss turned towards the Village and circled the war memorial, where a black spaniel was lifting his leg over a wreath of faded red paper poppies. He drove slowly along the high street, where a few people were meandering along and glancing in the shop windows. Most would be on their way to or from the Pemberton Arms or the Rose Cafe' whose heavy wooden signs were now swaying on creaking chains in the chilly April breeze.

With the Village green now behind him, Reiss turned off to sweep past the low-rise post-war housing estate, where Linda lived with her family, and took the turning leading to the industrial estate where the company's administrative headquarters and storage depots were located. Pomeroy's office was in the largest of three white flat-roofed buildings.

Reiss signed the attendance book and took the lift to the third and top floor where Pomeroy's secretary, Julie, was waiting for him. She was a slim young woman wearing a lot of shiny lipstick, a skimpy black dress and very high heels. She spoke with a local country accent.

"Good afternoon, Dr Reiss. Mr Pomeroy is expecting you."

Notwithstanding, she rapped on Pomeroy's door, to announce his arrival.

"Come in!"

Pomeroy striding forward met Reiss halfway across the thick blue carpet. They were a similar height, close to six feet, but Pomeroy was in his late fifties and unlike Reiss, had the physique of a man who spent most of his time in meetings or behind a desk.

They shook hands briefly.

Given the unattractiveness of the building's exterior and its location, Pomeroy's penthouse suite was remarkably pleasant. It had pale lemon walls, white ceiling and woodwork and light oak custom-built modern furniture. From the expanse of plate glass windows there was a sweeping vista of farmland to one side and the distant Village from the other. This afternoon, as rain was splattering down, Pomeroy had half-closed the vertical blinds and the room was artificially lit.

"Thanks for coming in, Raymond. I know how busy you must be. It's strange, but I still can't get my head round the fact that David's dead? That he's never coming back?"

Reiss retorted bitterly, "You'd believe it if you'd seen him naked on a slab like I did a few hours ago. Poor guy looked and smelt like a lump of barbecued meat."

Pomeroy muttered, faintly, "Shut up, will you? It's different for you, you're a doctor. You're used to that sort of thing, I'm not."

"David was my close colleague, Marcus and I prefer my patients to be alive. I found the whole thing utterly sickening. Frankly, I could do with a drink." Reiss sank down on to one of four small armchairs that were cosily arranged around a circular glass topped coffee table. "It's been a hellish day. But I have one piece of good news. David wasn't over the limit when he hit the wall. He was stone cold sober."

"So what happened?"

"My guess is he was tired, lost concentration and misjudged the bend, which he took much too fast. The police reckon he was doing at least sixty.

Pomeroy poured a good measure of Glenfiddich into two cut glass tumblers. He handed one to Reiss and sat down opposite.

"I suppose there'll have to be an inquest?"

"Yes."

David had called Pomeroy a grey man of industry. He was a

15

solicitor but had left active legal practice ten years ago. It was a fair description given that Pomeroy's hair and eyes were grey and he wore steel rimmed spectacles. He favoured grey suits too, but today, as a mark of respect, he was wearing navy like Reiss.

"Did you stay there while they did the autopsy?"

Reiss nodded, "For most of it. There were no obvious abnormalities visible in his gut but I asked Jerry to send off some bowel samples to the lab. If the findings are negative, it will strengthen our position with regard to our nervous American suitors. I will be sending the results to the MCA and FDA as well in due course. I have to do that, Marcus."

Pomeroy gnawed his forefinger. "Why did he break his neck? Didn't the car seats have head restraints? Wasn't he wearing a seat belt?"

"Yes and yes. He hit a solid wall at high speed. It was the force of the impact. If the head violently jerks forward and back it can snap the spine like a judicial hanging."

Pomeroy muttered, "Awful."

"Yes, it was. Look, I spent a few minutes going through his room earlier and I found this. I thought I should show it to you." He passed a sheet of paper to Pomeroy, who looked at it uncomprehendingly.

"But we shelved Dyspeptic last year? Why run a toxicity study on it, now?"

Reiss retorted, sharply, "This compound isn't Dyspeptic, Marcus. It is R/P."

Pomeroy's jaw dropped in dismay. "Are you quite sure?"

Reiss nodded. "Yes. I am. He hid this new study under a false name."

"He was probably over budget on R/P and there was a little cash left in the Dyspeptic account?"

Reiss replied, irritably, "Marcus, this is primary animal work. It's a study on rabbits. We're years past that. In four weeks we're starting multi-centre trials on two thousand human patients. It makes no sense - unless he got scared that we've

16

missed something?"

Pomeroy groaned, "The man was obsessive and he was ill after he tried R/P on himself, remember?"

Reiss said, "That was over a year ago. This is way down the line from that. It bothers me, that he's done this."

Pomeroy leaned forward, conspiratorially, "Have you told Alan, yet?"

"No. Not yet."

"Does it show anything new?"

"Not so far. I think we should close it down. Now."

"I agree. Backdate the letter and close it down in David's name. Then lose the file. Permanently."

Reiss stared at him. "And not tell Alan?"

"What for? It can only start a hare running?"

Reiss shrugged. "All right." He replaced the paper in his briefcase and instead dangled David's large bunch of keys in front of Marcus with their burnt MG fob. "I plan to take David's personal stuff from his office to his home and collect our equipment and paperwork during the same visit. Best if I go there before his sister Anne arrives from Yorkshire. H.R. have been in touch with her already, but I'll phone her myself later as well."

Pomeroy nodded. "Yes, clear our stuff from his house and go through it when you've got it all back at Flat Acres. We don't want any loose threads lying around when that American journalist woman comes to Pemberton in a couple of months."

Reiss banged down his glass."What American journalist woman?"

Pomeroy responded, quickly, "It was Marlon Strelitz' idea and David agreed. The plan is to impress her so she gives Pemberton Manor and R/P a blast of good publicity in the USA. Marlon thinks it may pressure the FDA to move forward more quickly and if our share price goes up in anticipation it's all to the good."

"Who exactly is this woman?"

"Sarah Goodwin. She's a feature writer with The New York

17

Globe, apparently, with a big following. We've offered her a short free stay at Pemberton Manor about three or four weeks after the trials have started."

Reiss shook his head. "I should have been consulted about this. If I had been I would have said, 'No'. I don't want some nosy journalist hanging around and getting under my feet. You'll have to put her off."

Pomeroy hissed urgently, "It's too late for that. And we need the promotion in the USA, Raymond. The FDA are sitting on their hands and Oribo and Sion are offering us lousy terms because they know we're so financially weak and borrowed to the hilt. With a good write-up our shares will rise and with it the purchase price for our collaboration. Win-win for all of us, here. Including you."

"I want you to put her off, Marcus."

"I can't, it's too late. She's been invited to do a feature on Pemberton Manor and the Health Club. She'll be surrounded by two hundred patients who are losing weight. If they want to talk to her, let them. Cecil's dead keen on the idea; as you know he still owns a few shares in the place. If we refuse he'll just ask her to stay with him at the Dower House as his guest. That would be much worse; he's a complete idiot and we'll have no control over the rubbish he'll tell her."

"You could stop him if you put your foot down. He's only a minority share-holder. And his house is in terrible state. It's practically falling down."

"He's on our Board, Raymond. If you try and block this woman from coming he'll be your enemy for life and so will some of the others. They're all for it. Pemberton has cost us a fortune and it needs high occupancy to make a decent profit. Meanwhile, people like *you*, Raymond, get to use the pool and the golf course and the gym for free. If you don't want to rock the boat, keep your mouth shut on this one is my advice."

Lord Pemberton's former estate had been bought for a knock-down price from the mortgagees. The extent of repairs and building works needed had, however, been grossly under-estimated along with the time needed to obtain planning approval for the two new residential annexes in the health farm (where the trial patients would be staying). Then the costs of refurbishing Pemberton's "Pavilion" had escalated. The Pavilion comprised a cluster of buildings with a series of domed roofs that covered the state of the art sports and treatment complex, various indoor courts, the Orangery and a 25 metre heated swimming pool that Reiss used when he had a gap in his day or stayed overnight at the Cottage in Flat Acres. "Cecil will demand we withdraw free staff privileges if you don't cooperate with him on this. He's a pain in the neck, but he's still got a bit of influence and he's got sympathisers on the Board."

Reiss muttered, "Oh, all right, let her come, then."

CHAPTER THREE

The Viennese carriage clock on the mantelpiece had chimed seven times when Reiss sat down in the Cottage's small and chintzy sitting room to phone Anne, David's married sister, who lived in North Yorkshire with her husband and two teenage sons. The phone was answered by a lad with a strong local accent. "Mum's making dinner, then she's going out straight afterwards this evening."

"Tell your mum that I phoned. I'm Dr Reiss (not RICE, he spelled it out, letter by letter), your Uncle David's friend from work. Tell her I'll telephone her again, tomorrow morning."

He did not leave his number for Anne to call him back. Instead, he plugged in his mobile phone to charge and slowly climbed the narrow stairs. The small house was the only survivor of a meanly built row of dwellings originally intended for the estate's farm workers. Finding the others virtually derelict, Forsyte's builders had knocked them down, leaving the Cottage to survive on its own. It had been cheaply renovated but had efficient central heating and plumbing, new windows and the double bed was comfortable. Reiss's use of it was exclusive and it conveniently saved him the long commute back to Cambridge mid-week.

He had originally intended to drive straight on to David's house after his meeting with Pomeroy, but a wave of tiredness had swept over him so he had diverted to the Cottage for a shower and a change of clothes first. Reaching the small landing, he went past the closed door of the box room (he had refused the offer of a bed in it as he did not want visitors staying) and stripped off as he entered the bedroom. He was glad to stand under the comforting warm spray, which reminded him agreeably of his first meeting with Beatrice. They had met at a conference in Prague eighteen months ago.

Beatrice was an attractive, ambitious and athletic young doctor in her late thirties who worked at the Karolinska Institute in Stockholm. He had met her several times since; fortuitously, FIP had an on-going development program with a Swedish company called Zastro, with a view to producing an improved NSAID.

As he dressed in the casual clothes he had left in the cupboard, Reiss was pleased that his trousers seemed a little looser round the waist. He had cut down on carbohydrates lately and exercised more regularly. But there were more crows' feet around his blue eyes that now needed glasses to decipher small print and his dark hair, with its engaging widow's peak, was flecked with silver, as if someone had taken a sugar shaker to it. Downstairs, in the small kitchen, he ate the sandwiches and an apple he had taken from the Orangery and dropping his phone in his pocket, left for David's house.

Outside, the Flat Acres complex was quiet and floodlit, with few people walking around, though some, Reiss knew, were still at work in their laboratories and offices in the science block. With a sense of déjà vu, Reiss drove his dusty Range Rover towards the Village, passing through the electric gate and under the raised barrier before heading past the War memorial and took the turning that led towards David's house. Slowing down as he approached the concealed sharp bend where David's car had rammed into the wall, he saw the wreck had been removed, though the car's headlights picked up glints of metal here and there. The brick wall was blackened in places and a few bricks had been broken or dislodged and lay scattered by the side of the road.

Sighing, Reiss turned the car into the private development where David's house was located about five miles from the Village. A second phase of "24 luxurious detached homes" were now under construction. David's house was half way down the new private road. Reiss backed the Range Rover onto the drive to make it easier to load the computer and printer into the boot later on. A bright security light beamed down while he fumbled with the bunch of keys, the two boxes from Flat Acres at his feet. There was a twitch of a curtain in the house opposite. Having opened the front door, he hurried inside and dropping the boxes under the hall table, carefully keyed in the code the alarm company had provided to him.

That done, Reiss looked around, curiously. David, unusually forthcoming soon after Reiss's arrival at Flat Acres, had shown him the brochure, explaining he had bought the show house, as he liked the furnishings and fittings there and it would be less bother for him.

The kitchen was functional and smart with white cupboards and charcoal work tops. Opening the fridge Reiss noted that it was stocked with fresh food. Not compatible with the actions of a man who intended to kill himself by driving a car into a wall.

An empty whisky bottle stood on a window ledge. Reiss put it by the front door to take with him; David would not have wanted his sister to see it.

The living room was L-shaped with the bland furnishings left behind by the developer. Neutral carpeting and floor to ceiling stone-coloured pinch pleat curtains were drawn closed. On one wall, there were shelves David had filled with books, photo albums, a hi-fi system and CDs and cassettes. A large television had been fixed to the facing wall, which Reiss correctly deduced had been installed by the developer.

Pushing past the pair of brown leather sofas and the upright Steinway piano, Reiss, mildly curious, took down the pile of photograph albums. He flipped quickly through a succession of holiday views, friends' parties, what looked like university gatherings and reunions, and a series taken with a gloomy grey stone house in the background which was surrounded by open country. Merrivale Farm, he supposed, where Anne, David's married sister lived with her family. And indeed there was a snapshot of David pulling a face as he petted a large sow who was suckling her many piglets.

A wedding album showed a younger David in a top hat and morning coat standing next to a pretty, slim, smiling bride. The marriage had not lasted long. David had been divorced for ten years.

The most recent photos, however, were not in an album but were in a plastic packet. They had been taken at Forsyte's annual summer party last July. Reiss remembered David passing his camera around so that he would appear in some pictures himself and he had obviously selected some to be printed off. There were a few group photos which included Reiss and Sally and Marcus Pomeroy and his wife Mary along with members of the Flat Acres R & D team sipping champagne. In several of them, Sylvie and Tim Scott, then newly married, were larking about near the refreshment tent. The last three, however, were of his younger daughter, Mandy. She was kneeling down and picking daisies in a secluded spot, evidently at some distance from the main gathering. She was looking up at the photographer a little uncertainly, half smiling. An expression that Reiss knew very well; it was the look she had when she needed a favour. More help from David with her Oxford application, he supposed.

These three photos could be of no interest to David's sister, so Reiss slipped them into his pocket with the negatives before replacing the packet with the albums on the shelf.

Upstairs, there were four bedrooms. The two facing front had a bathroom between them and were simply furnished as occasional guest rooms; the cupboards contained only spare bedding. Opposite, in the main bedroom, the double bed was tidily made and the curtains pulled closed. There was a large framed print of Edward Leighton's "Flaming June" which Reiss guessed had been left by the developer along with more beige carpeting and curtains. A row of plain white fitted wardrobes extended along one wall and matched with the white night tables standing on either side of the bed. One was bare, with empty drawers. On the other, presumably the side David had slept on, was a telephone, a digital bedside clock and a biography of Charles Darwin with its dust cover turned over to mark his place.

Idly, Reiss opened the wardrobe doors, glancing in at the rail of suits, trousers and jackets, noting that a bunch of empty hangers had been pushed along to one side. Several of these bore the name of shops selling only women's clothes. Curiously searching for a clue to the woman's identity, Reiss felt through the pockets. In a dark suit, there was a folded note in David's cramped left-handed script:

Funeral 2.30 pm 16.3.01. Golders Green Crematorium. Hoop Lane, London NW11. Northern Line. 10 min walk from tube station.

Reiss now recalled that David had taken the day off, saying he had to attend the funeral of a friend in London. He had come in late the following morning, looking tired and a little depressed. There had been the hint of alcohol on his breath.

Bending down, Reiss saw there were two black plastic bags leaning against the back of the cupboard. He lifted them out and tipped the contents on to the bed. A woman's clothes, most of which looked quite new. Some still had their price tags attached. He held up a pair of jeans against himself; they would only fit a very slim and not very tall woman. She had small breasts; the black lacy brassiere had size A cups, like his daughters had worn when they were fourteen. But who was this woman who had shared this bedroom with David? Why had he kept her existence a secret? Was she already married? And why had she not taken her clothes away with her instead of leaving them behind for David to bag up? Had he been expecting her to return for them? Or had he known she would never come back? Had it been her funeral on 16th March?

But whatever the explanation, from the few comments David had made about his sister, (who came from a place where fields were broad and minds were narrow), Reiss knew David would not want Anne to find this woman's clothes in his cupboard. It would be kinder to take the bags away with him and see if he could discover her identity to return them.

With this in mind, Reiss pulled out David's night table drawer. In it was an unsealed envelope which contained two photographs of two very different young women. One had dark hair in a pony tail. She was overweight and wearing leggings and a shapeless top. The other had short bleached blonde hair and was very slim and very pretty. She was smiling radiantly at the photographer. And wearing what looked to be the fitted white jeans and red top with a low V neck that were right now lying on the bed beside him.

Frowning with puzzlement, Reiss put on his reading glasses to study the photograph of the pretty young woman more carefully. She was leaning over the railing of Waterloo Bridge in London. In the background the trees were in full leaf so most likely it had been taken the previous summer. He turned the photograph over. There was an undated note on the back written in a round feminine hand. *To my darling David, my miracle worker. All my love for always and ever, Lara 49.9 Kgs!!!*

He laid the two photographs side by side on the night table and stared at them with a dawning realisation: it was the same young woman, but the transformation was remarkable. Indeed, Lara had thought so herself: she had described David as her *miracle worker.* But how had this miracle been achieved? The possibilities were making Reiss feel very uneasy. The trees in what he mentally labelled Lara's *Before* photograph showed spring blossoms, perhaps taken some two months earlier? Had Lara shed all the weight by diet and exercise in such a short time? Or had there been another factor at work?

Had Lara been a client at the Pemberton Manor slimming clinic? Given her appearance in the *Before* photograph, Reiss thought it unlikely; treatment there was very expensive and she did not look as if she could afford it. But she may have been employed there in some capacity? However, Reiss, a frequent visitor there, did not recognise her face and he noticed pretty women.

Well, if Lara had ever worked or stayed at Pemberton, the system would find her even using only her first name. He was about to push back the drawer when he noticed a small torn scrap of paper that had become wedged in the back corner. The scrawled writing was in Lara's round hand:

It's 3.20 am and I've been awake since 1.15. Vomiting and the runs and cramping pains. I've taken 3 temazepam because I'm so tired and they'll help me sleep. I threw up the one you gave me earlier. I was stupid to refuse the jab. If I am still asleep when you get up please don't wake me. T G I Saturday and neither of us has to go to work. x L.

Reiss, unease mounting horribly, read the note through a second time before stuffing it into the envelope with the two photographs of Lara. He checked the contents of the wall cabinet and the vanity unit in the ensuite bathroom but found nothing you could not buy over the counter. There was no pethidine, no morphine, no stematil, no prednisalone, no temazepam or even co-codamol. David had disposed of it all.

The "family" or visitors' bathroom cabinet held a box of blister plasters, a bag of cotton wool balls and a tube of Sensodyne toothpaste.

Reiss dithered on the landing beside the two black sacks he had refilled with Lara's clothes. The symptoms Lara described could have been caused by a severe bout of food poisoning or an attack of IBS, but as David had offered Lara a *"jab"*, it suggested a recurrent problem he had anticipated. Had he written out a prescription for a chemist to dispense? Or raided the dispensary? Or had Lara's GP prescribed the medication for David to administer? Reiss thought this unlikely and Lara had referred to David giving her temazepam so he had obtained it for her.

But why waste time speculating? David was an obsessive note-keeper. All the answers would be on his computer.

CHAPTER FOUR

Entering the study Reiss felt David's presence keenly. It was obviously the room where he had spent much of his time when alone and he had invested more of himself in it. There were floor to ceiling custom built shelves filled with books and journals on the wall which included some medical texts but also reflected his interest in medical informatics and computer technology. However, after briefly glancing about him, Reiss went over to the work station where David had connected FIP's loaned IBM Pentium III computer to a fast laser jet printer that he had also requested. Beside them, his land line telephone was plugged into an old-fashioned answering machine that was flashing with one message indicated. Perhaps Lara had called David? To arrange a time to collect her clothes?

Reiss sat down with a thump on David's black leather and chrome swivel chair and pressed the playback button, drumming his fingers as the tape wound itself briefly back. He had a shock when a loud, angry and accusing woman's voice, said: "Dr Devereaux? Are you there? Or are you out somewhere playing God, again?"

Not Lara, evidently.

There was a short pause for taking breath and Reiss heard the muted hum of voices in the background, then the woman, her tone very aggressive, asked: "Did you read that report I sent you? You really wanted to see it, I know you did. How did it make you feel, Dr Devereaux? Jane said she loved you, but that you didn't love her anymore. If you ever did love her, that is?" Another brief pause for breath (with more ambient noise), then, "Jane never had much luck with men, poor girl! Or *Lara,* as she called herself, lately. She thought a new name would change her luck? I think like all the others you got tired of her and wanted to end it, didn't you? Poor Jane or Lara, whatever, she couldn't deal with that, but you didn't care? You *must* have known the state she was in? You are a bloody doctor, aren't you? Well, I'm not finished with you, yet, Dr Devereaux!"

Reiss, chewing his lip, listened to the tape a second time.

What report was this woman referring to? A psychiatric report? Was Lara locked up in a secure psychiatric ward having become manically depressed and suicidal? Unlikely, and the woman had referred to Jane/Lara in the past tense. This suggested she was dead. Had she taken her own life? Was the report an autopsy? Was it Lara's funeral that David had attended? The timing of it would fit. This angry woman would have to be a close relative to have been provided with an autopsy report: Lara's mother or sister, perhaps?

If Lara was dead, it explained why she had not come back to collect her clothes and why David had bagged them up with a view to disposing of them. He could check the names of people who had been cremated on 16th March in Golders Green to see if there was a match.

Alternatively, he might try to ring back this angry woman? Reiss fingered his chin, uncertainly. She had left neither name nor number and her hostility was discouraging, but if he told her that David was dead, she might be willing to talk to him. He dialled 1471 and then dialled the inner London number the it provided only to get the flat tone of an unobtainable line. The operator advised him it was a public call box in King's Cross Station that was not programmed to accept in-coming calls.

Reiss ejected and pocketed the cassette tape from the answering machine and turned on the computer. It booted up and bleeped, inviting him to enter his password. A problem he should have certainly foreseen. With little hope, Reiss keyed in the two he could remember David using in the past in the office. They were summarily rejected. He must have kept an aide-memoir somewhere, but Reiss, with a sinking heart, knew he would never find it. There would have been clues on his mobile phone which had been destroyed in the car fire. Perhaps some cryptic notes in the little black pocket diary that David kept with him at all times and which had been burned to cinders. Reiss wasted a few minutes rifling through the drawers and paper files, but to no purpose.

In a locked cupboard, opened with his bunch of keys, he found David's emergency medical bag. It contained only standard contents and there was not even a faint indentation on the prescription pad.

Reiss sat down once more at the computer and hesitatingly keyed in "Merrivalefarm".

As if insulted, the computer bleeped furiously, then to his dismay, a warning message flashed on the screen:

You have failed to enter the correct password three times. If you are not certain you can enter this within the next 60 seconds SWITCH OFF THE MACHINE IMMEDIATELY AND REBOOT LATER WHEN YOU HAVE IT AVAILABLE. FAILURE TO ENTER THE CORRECT PASSWORD WITHIN THE NEXT 60 SECONDS WILL CAUSE ALL THE DATA TO BE REMOVED PERMANENTLY FROM THE HARD DISK MEMORY.

Reiss swore and turned it off, defeated.

David had been a member of an elite group specialising in medical informatics that met monthly at the Royal Society of Medicine in London with FIP paying his subscription. He was capable of designing and modifying sophisticated programs and he had made sure nobody could read his private notes without his permission. Reiss shouted in frustration. He went to the shelves and dragged an armful of books and journals off the shelves and flicked through the pages, but found nothing. No scraps of paper with a password on it fluttered out. He crammed everything untidily back on the shelf and swore softly as he began disconnecting the computer and printer to take them back to Flat Acres.

Under the beam of the security light from the porch, Reiss

loaded everything into the car, uncomfortably aware that some of the neighbours were watching him from behind their curtains. One woman even opened her front door to stare at him before retreating inside.

Reiss, jammed everything into the Range Rover's large boot including the whisky bottle, the two black sacks filled with Lara's clothes, the company's computer and printer and a box of the company's disks, a few office files and all David's computer literature in the hope it might hold a clue to breaking his codes.

After re-setting the alarm and double-locking the front door he passed yet again under the raised barrier and through the electric gate into Flat Acres. He parked and made straight for his Farmhouse office to search the system for Jane Lara. It took only a minute: her full name was Jane Lara Bucknell, her DOB 2.2.73 and her occupation: *Teacher (English).* She had taken part in the very first healthy human volunteer trial of Reduktopan that David had run. The address she had provided for that purpose was a rented flat in Cambridge from which she had evidently moved. She was recorded as *Lost to follow up: mobile number unobtainable.*

At the start of the trial she was obese at 69 Kgs. She had lost 7 Kgs in three weeks achieving a base weight of 62 Kgs and was *Delighted.* With David's help later on, Lara who had regained some of the weight lost in between, had lost some fourteen kilos to weigh in at 49.5Kgs and it was this which had prompted a shopping spree with him in London.

With this startling news to relay, Reiss telephoned Pomeroy at his home. Pomeroy's mobile went straight to voicemail so he rang the landline. Mary answered saying they were "in the middle of a bridge game" but she would call Marcus if it was "really important".

"Well, what is it?"

"Marcus, I'll be in meetings most of tomorrow. Can you come and see me at the Cottage in the evening? But before that, there's something you need to do. You must do it yourself. Do not, I repeat, do NOT leave it to Julie. It's confidential. Check if a woman called Jane Lara Bucknell was cremated at Golders Green Crematorium in London on March 16th this year. Have you got that?"

In the background, Reiss could hear Mary Pomeroy calling indignantly, "Marcus, make it snappy. We're all waiting for you. Come back and play your hand now, will you?"

"Marcus. This is really important."

"I've got it noted."

"See you tomorrow evening."

CHAPTER FIVE

The department meeting overran the next morning, because Tim Scott arrived half an hour late. Apologising, he explained that his wife, Sylvie, had slipped in the bathroom and banged her head and he could not leave her. She still had severe morning sickness he whispered to Reiss. Fortunately, as the baby was due in August, the multi-centre Reduktopan trials would have all been concluded by then their data collected and analyzed by Tim and his team. Meantime, he was under a lot of pressure and it was starting to show.

With the meeting finally over, Reiss hurried back to the Farmhouse where Linda had provided Dr Bill Ryder with a cup of coffee while he waited for his new boss to return. He rose at Reiss's arrival and they shook hands firmly before Bill followed him into his office where Linda had left Bill's C.V. printed out on his desk.

Reiss reviewed it quickly. "You're thirty-three?"

"Yes, Dr Reiss."

"You have useful recent clinical experience, so I'm diverting you from Head Office to assist me with these trials on Reduktopan. Are you happy with that?"

Bill nodded. "Yes, I am. More than happy, Dr Reiss."

"It is a temporary job. You will report directly to me here, but depending on how you shape up, it could lead to something more permanent. You will be sitting in Dr Devereaux' room but you are not taking over his role."

Bill said he positively understood that he would not be taking over Dr Devereaux' more senior role. He understood it was a more junior position. But he would do his very best to help fill the gap his death had left.

They went next door into David's old office where the computer was once again accessible and had a new password that Reiss had noted in three places. Stripped of their Oxford prints, the walls looked a little bare.

"You can use the existing hooks to put up something of your own." He then escorted Bill across to the main laboratory block to introduce him to Tim Scott, who was busily checking the latest data sent in by A.C.E. Tim would tell Bill that the medical and science team (other than his late deputy and Alan Michaels) all called Reiss, "Chief".

Reiss enquired: "How is Sylvie? Is she feeling any better?

Tim's long thin fingers twitched over the computer keyboard. "Bit tired and washed out, but she insisted on going to work, later."

Reiss grunted, "If you're worried, you can ask Jim Menzies to see her? There'll be no charge."

Tim flushed, "Sylvie doesn't want people here getting involved. But thanks, anyway, Chief, I appreciate it."

Reiss left Tim explaining the interaction of Reduktopan's remarkable triple compound to Bill and walked back to the Farmhouse where there was a message from Marcus Pomeroy on his office phone. "It *was* her. You've made me curious. I'll see you about nine at the Cottage."

Reiss, a little saddened by the confirmation of Lara's death, studied her photographs once more. According to the mystery woman caller, Lara had not tired of David, but he of her. If she had jumped from a high window it would have made it into the local newspapers. More likely she had cut her wrists or taken an overdose and died quietly and it had been discreetly hushed up.

Reiss stared down at David's former parking space that was now Bill's (he drove a blue Ford Escort) and then turned his head to glance through his side window. He and Tim Scott were leaving the main laboratory building together and heading for the Barn. They looked to be deep in conversation. Bill, shorter and stockier than Tim, was in a suit and tie. Tim, who had removed his white coat, was dressed casually in a sweater and chinos. He was bespectacled, lanky and thin and remarkably well informed about everything that went on at Flat Acres. He would show Bill the rest of the R & D compound including the grim barred animal houses, discreetly located behind the incinerator stack.

Reiss did not favour keeping research animals at Flat Acres, but the ambitious and cost-effective breeding programme had been in place when he took up his post. The animals were well housed and cared for at Flat Acres and would not benefit from a move to a contract organisation like A.C.E. or P.P.L. Unfortunately, however, their presence had attracted protesters, who distributed unpleasant leaflets and yelled abuse over megaphones or from loudspeaker vans until they were escorted off the company's private road. Last year, a violently militant group had actually broken into Flat Acres causing a lot of damage. They had smashed windows and daubed angry slogans on the walls in red and black spray paint and set fire to David's car (left on site while he was abroad on company business). He had replaced his sensible Honda with the scarlet vintage MG in which he had died.

Unlocking the filing cabinet, Reiss took out three files for Bill to read and left them on his desk.

CHAPTER SIX

In preparation for Pomeroy's visit that evening, Reiss took out a new bottle of single malt but did not break the seal. He would do that when Pomeroy arrived. In his head he could hear the voice of his late father, Professor Dr Rudolf Reiss, who, in his Viennese accented German, was reminding his son to drink less than his enemy.

Reiss replied aloud in German, as if the old man were actually present, "He's not an enemy, Papa, but I don't altogether trust him. That's why I'll be recording our conversation, tonight."

Reiss locked the Art Deco walnut cocktail cabinet that had come from the living room of his late parents' Highgate flat. He continued the imaginary conversation with his father, aloud in German, "I may need it to protect myself in the future."

"Be careful where you store it, then. In the wrong hands this tape could be a double edged sword, Raymond."

Reiss nodded, "You're right. Papa. But I'll be careful, like you say. Keep it at home in Cambridge in future. Not here."

He placed the small recording machine in his open briefcase under the coffee table and, to humour his father's ghost, put on a reissued recording of Fritz Kreisler playing Beethoven's violin concerto in 1928, when he was at the peak of his career. His father had maintained there was no violinist who surpassed Kreisler at his best and whose playing was filled with joy and charm. But, sadly, Kreisler's skill had declined in later life, not helped by his deafness and a road accident and his lack of enthusiasm for practising before a concert. His father, though, had remained loyal throughout; he had heard Kreisler play in Vienna before the war. Before Hitler, who had killed and ruined so many people and whose vile politics had prompted Kreisler to hurriedly leave for America. He was not Jewish himself but had deplored and opposed Hitler's regime. He was a rarity as while on the surface the Viennese were charming, below the veneer, sinister and evil currents flowed freely.

Reiss sat down to catch up on some reading while he waited. The bell rang at five minutes to nine. Reiss turned on the recording machine, then opened the door.

Marcus Pomeroy, still in city mode, looked immaculate in a crisp white shirt with chunky cuff links, a grey chalk stripe suit and a Dior tie. He told Reiss about his meeting in London with Forsyte's city solicitors. Unusually, Marlon Strelitz, the company's key American lawyer, had flown in from Washington and been present as well. Reiss knew that, as Marlon had telephoned him to demand he come to the USA in May to present Reduktopan's credentials to the FDA to speed up the licensing process. It should be after the patient trials had started in the UK. They had settled on a date in late May by which time the Pemberton and A.C.E. multi-centre trials would have been running for several weeks and the (hopefully enthusiastic) New York Globe article would have been published.

When Reiss again expressed his unease about having an American journalist visiting Pemberton, Strelitz had laughed. "Don't worry, I'll take care of this. My New York law office experts are drafting the confidentiality agreement which Sarah Goodwin, the Globe's journalist, will have to sign."

Reiss had asked him: "What's Sarah Goodwin like?"

Strelitz had retorted, "I've not met her. But she writes well and she has a big following. You just have to be nice and charming and keep her sweet when you meet her, Ray."

Pomeroy sat down on one of the pair of chintzy armchairs. "The meeting went pretty well, today, Raymond. Marlon seems confident we'll get FDA approval soon, provided there are no unforeseen hitches, obviously. He's looking forward to meeting you in person when you go to Washington."

"He told me. But right now, Marcus I want to talk to you about Jane Lara Bucknell. She was one of our first healthy volunteers over a year ago. And, as you discovered today for yourself, she's now dead."

Marcus asked anxiously, "It wasn't from taking R/P was it?

"Not as far as I know. But I'm worried." Reiss held up the two photographs. "Lara called David her miracle worker. Here's why. She went from that to this? Lost a lot of weight very quickly. She looks pretty here, doesn't she? When she was David's girlfriend."

Marcus snapped, "I don't like where this is going. David's messy private life is not our business, Raymond."

"If David did give Lara a load of R/P, I think I've worked out his supply route."

Marcus groaned, "I don't want to know any more."

"He substituted something for the batch of sub-standard R/P capsules he personally signed off to be incinerated. He could easily have kept back that whole batch for his private use. He would have handed over a sealed bag and it would have gone straight into the burners."

"But you said those pills were sub-standard? If he gave them to her, that's terrible, Raymond."

Reiss shook his head with a faint smile. "They were only sub-standard in terms of their sugar coating. Something went wrong with the process; instead of being a smooth, shiny orange, they looked a bit misshapen and dull. I remember handling some at one of the first meetings I attended after I arrived at Flat Acres. It was about eighteen months ago. A new batch was ordered to replace them and it was that batch that was used in the healthy volunteer trials. That David ran himself. Well, he ran all the R/P trials, didn't he? If he hadn't killed himself last night, he would have been in charge of the A.C.E. trials as well as our residential one at Pemberton next month. He used half a dozen from the new batch on himself before he collapsed on the office carpet."

"Which happened on your watch, Raymond."

"How was I supposed to know what he was doing in secret? And, as he pointed out in his own defence, he could have qualified as a healthy volunteer if he had signed himself up officially to take part. His diabetes was well controlled; he was not insulin dependent. We excluded all diabetics after his ADR, but not before that. It is quite common for scientists and doctors to try experimental stuff out on themselves before they give it to other people. They're acting from the best of motives as I'm sure he was, then. He didn't need to lose weight himself. On the contrary. You could argue that it showed he had confidence in the product, I suppose. But he was out of order. He broke the rules."

Pomeroy said, gloomily, "Yes, and more than once by the sound of it."

"There were around a thousand pills in the defective batch. That's quite some private supply and it's a no-brainer that he gave some of them to Lara. One a day is routine for someone of her weight but it can be as many as two or even three for a limited time for a morbidly obese candidate. I'd guess he gave Lara a course of treatment and it worked pretty well. By the end of it, she was, as we can see here, very slim. She looked great and they were both thrilled with her transformation. But something definitely went wrong later. At some point in the nine months between her death and the miracle moment."

"Love affairs can go sour, Raymond. Perhaps David became bored with her? He was a difficult guy and I doubt he was easy to live with. And she may have been a pain, who know? But, frankly whatever happened between them, it's really none of our business."

"Even if he gave her a load of our pills, Marcus?"

"You don't know for sure that he did. This is wild speculation on your part. You didn't find any pills at his house, did you?"

"Well, no, but he would have been careful to keep his stock hidden. They might even have been in his car and been destroyed in the fire. Or he could have run scared and genuinely incinerated the remaining ones. Who knows?"

"Raymond, you've told me that officially David sent all the sub-standard pills to the burners eighteen months ago. Let's leave it there, shall we?"

Reiss laughed, softly, "I take it you don't wish me to raise any of this with Alan Michaels?"

Pomeroy snapped, "Are you mad? Of course not. The last thing we need is to have rumours zooming round Flat Acres that David went *off piste* a second time with some secret girlfriend who then topped herself. Do you have any idea of the damage this could cause to the company? And it won't do *you* any favours, either. You were David's boss. If he went rogue and you didn't notice, you'll get stick for it. And the poor man is dead and can't defend himself."

"I know all that, Marcus."

Pomeroy's voice became more measured and a little coaxing. "Raymond, Lara did not die from an overdose of R/P, did she? So even if David was a little bit naughty, and he gave her a course of pills that she took under his supervision, is that really so terrible? It speeded up her slimming and turned her into a beauty; we know from the back of this photograph she was very happy about it. She bought herself a new wardrobe of pretty clothes that I'm guessing David paid for. What he did with Lara is no different from what thousands of other patients will be doing over the next few months. Two hundred plus under your supervision instead of David's. And as Lara was a healthy volunteer we know she was in excellent health when she started, whereas some of these people won't be. Look at it this way."

"That is true."

Reiss pursed his lips. Silence hung between them.

Pomeroy snapped, "They're both dead, Raymond. End of story. We close this chapter and we move on, now."

Reiss persisted, obstinately, "Marcus, David was involved in a sexual relationship with a young woman whom he met as her doctor, yet he encouraged me quite deliberately to believe he was a closet gay last summer. Until the fiasco at his birthday party made it very clear he wasn't."

Pomeroy stood up decisively. "Well, whatever he got up to in private, we move on now. This is not a medical matter for you, but a policy issue for me. I say we leave well alone. We don't go stirring the embers. I suggest you divide up Lara's stuff into smaller bags and drop them into different clothes bins when you're next in London; don't scatter her stuff around here."

Reiss massaged his aching neck; the pain was spreading; invading his shoulders and upper back. "It's not all wild speculation, Marcus. There's more. I found this note from Lara in David's night table drawer."

He handed it to Marcus who read it then screwed it up and pocketed it. "So she had a bit of tummy trouble. She had a bad night. So what?"

"David offered her a pain killing injection she wished she had accepted. That means he was expecting trouble. I need to know why that was."

"No, you don't. This note wasn't meant for you to find."

Reiss muttered, "There will be a post mortem report somewhere. David obviously saw it, but he must have destroyed it but not before he would have noted the findings on his computer. If I could only access his notes we'd have all the answers."

Marcus shouted, "Leave it alone, I tell you! Have you at least called off that rabbit study?"

"Yes. I typed the letter myself. I back-dated and sent it off in David's name."

Marcus rose to his feet. "Thank God for that. Well, I'll be off home, then. It's getting late."

Reiss muttered, now also standing. "Marcus, I have his computer - well the company's computer - in the boot of my car. I need to access his files so we know for sure what went on."

Pomeroy replied, fiercely, "For the last time, Raymond, David's private notes made in his own time, are not company business and I don't want them to become company business. If he kept records they were for his own private use. They were not made for the company or in the course of his employment."

"I'd agree if he'd used his own equipment but he was using ours. And the R/P was ours, too."

Pomeroy began agitatedly pacing around the small sitting room. "Raymond, you must drop this. Draw a line under it. Your priority is to get R/P licensed by the regulators, as soon as possible So that millions and millions of obese people can take it safely and lose weight and live their dream and at the same time enjoy healthier, happier and longer lives."

"Spare me the spiel, and stop prowling around like a caged tiger, will you?"

"Raymond, please. We're the major employer in this area and we're borrowed up to the hilt. We're already in serious danger of a hostile bid. If that happens a lot of people who now work for us will lose their jobs. I don't mean you and me: we will find other places to go. But there are people working here who won't and who will be on the dole. This is an area of high unemployment. And when people lose their jobs, other people's businesses suffer. The tea room and the pub and the shops will have fewer customers with less money to spend. It's a downward spiral."

"And your bonus would be smaller as well?"

"That's beside the point. The commercial reality is that FIP urgently needs a return on its investment. Stay focused on that. Don't get derailed by wild conjectures about what David may or may not have got up to. Get rid of Lara's clothes. And if you can't do it yourself get an outside firm to remove the hard disk from that computer. Then run that lumping great Range Rover of yours over it half a dozen times before setting fire to it in a metal bucket. Do I make myself clear?"

CHAPTER SEVEN

Ten days later, on a bleak, wet and windy April day, David was buried in his native Yorkshire soil. His sister, Anne, had made it clear to Reiss that the local church was *very* small and the family wished the funeral to be a largely private one. Could he limit FIP's staff attendance to himself and one other close colleague?

"Yes, of course. It will just be myself and Tim Scott in that case."

"Thank you. I appreciate your understanding."

After the traditional service and a short address and a reading by David's sister and a boyhood friend, they made their way to the graveyard with Reiss and Tim staying near the back of the small cortege. Tim was wiping his eyes, but Reiss was not sure if it was the drizzling rain or if he was shedding a tear. He muttered, turning his head so that Reiss could hear him above the sound of the wind and the rain. "It's such a stupid, bloody waste. David had so much to give the world. That he would have given the world. He was so brilliant. Such a shame. Cut down and gone at forty."

Reiss responded softly, "Golden girls and boys all must, as chimney sweepers, come to dust."

Tim blew his nose. "What was that you said?"

"Nothing. You're right. It is awful, what happened."

But instead of the countryside around him Reiss was seeing, for a few moments, David's flaming red sports car lying on its hard top with his body twisting around inside, arms flailing as if he were trapped alive and in agony. As the wind and the rain beat against his face, Reiss forced himself back to the dismal present, squelching through the muddy and saturated grass to reach the grave where brown water was sloshing around at the bottom. The vicar intoned, but Reiss, distinguished only the words:

" ... ashes to ashes and dust to dust... " as a gust of wind blew against them.

It was a plain, pine coffin that was being lowered now. Inside, David's body would be wrapped in a shroud, but instead, Reiss visualised again, his scorched and twisted corpse laid out on the mortuary slab. The stench had caused him to gag even behind a mask; he had apologised and left the room at a run at the sound of the electric saw and stood outside till he was ready to return.

Years ago, when he was in his teens, his father had tried to comfort him at his mother's funeral, telling him that when a person died their spirit departed, leaving the body in the same way as a snake shed its skin. But it was not convincing then. Or now.

On the journey back, Tim had remarked, "It's a shame David had no kids."

"He never said he wanted any, Tim. Speaking of which, how is Sylvie doing?"

Tim had muttered, "Not being sick in the mornings at least, but her blood pressure's gone up."

"Have they found any protein in her urine? "

"Sylvie's a very private person. She doesn't want people at Forsyte getting involved, so I can't discuss it with you; I would otherwise, believe me."

"Fine. Sorry I asked."

Tim had then mumbled dismally, "But it's not fine, that's just the point. I'm not happy with the way it's being handled by those bossy midwives. Sylvie and I had a bit of a row about it only last night. But she won't listen to me, and she gets upset, so it's best I leave it for now."

Reiss had glanced sideways, noting the strain lines in Tim's thin face.

"Give it a little time and let's see how it goes."

After David's funeral, the days seemed to have rushed by and April was at an end. It was the penultimate day before Pemberton's in-house residential trial was due to begin as well as some of the A.C.E. outpatient ones in other parts of the country.

Looking at Tim, who still wore a tired, strained expression, Reiss wondered if he should send Jim Menzies over to have a word with him in his capacity as the company's occupational physician. But Tim's work was beyond reproach. He was conscientious and thorough and such an intervention might cause offence and could be counter-productive.

There was a long agenda to get through that morning; Reiss found his concentration drifting as Molly Owulu read out the list of diverse activities and competitions that had been devised to keep the resident patients amused for two months until the trial ended on June 30th.

Even before the meeting ended, Susie who was on the Pemberton reception desk, had called to tell Molly that the first patients (including all three Americans who had shared a cab from the airport) had arrived. By now they would be unpacking their cases in the two large modern annexes to an extent concealed behind trees at the rear of the original Manor House. Or they might be taking a gentle and exploratory stroll around the grounds?

Reiss shut his eyes for few seconds. He had not been sleeping well since the crash. He suffered from a recurrent nightmare which took different forms, but each time it began with the phone ringing by his bed. It was the local police to tell him there had been a serious road accident. They recognised the car. It was his colleague's. Could he come at once with his emergency bag as the ambulance would take forty minutes to get there.

This morning there had been a new variation: Reiss was trying to hurry but he could not find his medical bag, and then when he did, and he opened it, he found it empty. He drove like mad to reach the accident site, but when he reached it, the red sports car was ablaze. He could still smell the smoke and the burning flesh even after he woke up and opened his eyes. Even when he reached out to touch Sally's warm sleeping body.

He scraped back his chair, noisily. The room was too warm. He went over to the window to open it wider and stared out. From the first floor of the Barn's conference room, there was a view of not just Flat Acres but also Pemberton Manor House. From a distance, the Dower House, surrounded by a small garden, looked pretty, but close up you could see it was very neglected. But everything looked better in the warm spring sunshine and it was a truly glorious day. In the brilliant blue sky a few puffy small clouds drifted lazily past allowing the sun to shine down on the hastily planted tubs of geraniums, whose petals were opening and attracting a few bees to investigate them. Further away, in the shrubbery, rhododendrons were blooming in vibrant shades of mauve, pink and red. A massive bush filled with white blooms, dropped petals on to the azaleas beneath, that flamed in startling purple and yellow. Beyond them, the three magnolia trees were poised to flower shortly. Completing this rural English idyll, was a small flock of goats and sheep, who peacefully cropped the abundant and very green grass.

Reiss turned round to stand with his back against the wall, beckoning to Molly to continue as he faced his "team". It included a couple of in-house medics he would not have included, had he any choice. However, that said, most had come along quite well with the extra training, and Bill Ryder was competent. So, after some quite intensive instruction, the motley group was bonding and would be able to work reasonably well together. Reiss was allowing only two days to clerk-in all the trial participants; the final numbers would be known then. They had to allow for the inevitable drop-outs or no-shows, but if unexpectedly, they had a full house, extra accommodation would need to be found.

Checking everyone in would be a tedious process and Reiss accepted, that senior or not, he would have to do quite a bit of this, himself; he could not just swan about handing out orders, even with the help of the three in-house doctors dragooned out of their desk jobs at headquarters. Jim Menzies, too, was coming in for a few hours and they had recruited two extra nurses for the trial's duration: two tall, bronzed Australians, Jessica and Harriet. Jessica, who was a natural blonde with blue eyes and a tip tilted nose, would work primarily with Bill, while her friend, Harriet, who had long dark hair and who played a keen game of golf, apparently, would assist him as needed. Reiss hoped they would be as efficient as their references suggested.

The protocol required all two hundred and six patients to be interviewed, then physically checked with the detailed findings recorded and analyzed. But the next few days would not just be taxing for the clinicians. As an inducement, patients were being encouraged to invite a relatives or partner to spend the day at Pemberton when they could enjoy the splendid facilities there. There was the possibility they would be allowed to visit every so often during the trial, which made it more likely that more patients would stay the course.

At a quarter to seven Reiss closed the meeting. In a stampede for the door, the Australian Amazons collided with Tim and his three science clones, whose names all began with a J, and whom Reiss could never separate out. Within minutes, the room was empty save for himself and Bill. "Is there anything more you need me to do now, Chief?"

"No." Reiss rose and stretched, "I fancy a swim. Then, if I've got the energy, I'll work out in the gym." He flashed Bill a grin. "Those two Australian nurses look pretty fit. Can't have them thinking all Pom doctors are flabby bastards, can we? Do you want to join me? The pool's usually quiet around seven when most people are stuffing themselves in the Orangery. But they go on serving there till nearly nine."

"Yeah, Chief. I'd like that."

In the dusk, beyond the electrified fence, the bright lights of the Pavilion's domed glass and metal buildings twinkled across the grass. In addition to the pool and "fitness centre" and the Orangery, there were showers, saunas, a cafe', shops and a hair dressing salon. During the trial, however, most of the examination and treatment rooms had been commandeered for Reiss and his medical and nursing team.

At the Pavilion, Reiss and Bill stripped off in the communal changing room. Reiss noted that Bill had an old appendectomy scar and little body hair. He moved with the enviable, easy grace of youth. Reiss felt himself stiff and ponderous by comparison as he stepped into his swimming shorts. But the impression Bill had gained was of a physically powerful mature man with abundant but not excessive body hair. In his late forties, Reiss was still handsome. He had regular features, keen blue eyes and dark hair that was flecked with silvery lights. The gossip at Flat Acres, that had already reached Bill via Tim, was that Reiss had a young, pretty mistress somewhere abroad. She must know he was married as he wore a thin, gold wedding ring that he was said never to take off. Sometimes he plucked at it or twisted it, abstractedly, as if he found its pressure on his finger irksome, but he was never seen without it.

He spent several nights each week in the Cottage to save himself the long commute to his home in Cambridge. Bill had seen the photographs of Reiss's wife and daughters displayed on his desk. Sally Reiss, whom Bill guessed to be in her mid forties, was still an attractive woman and he was sure she would have been lovely twenty-one years ago when Reiss married her. Now, however, she looked a little faded, and with a husband like Reiss, Bill thought Sally would do well to take more trouble over her appearance.

Bill had discreetly questioned Tim on that first morning when Tim had shown him round the compound.

Tim had replied in a conspiratorial whisper, "I probably shouldn't be telling you this, but at last year's summer party at Pemberton, I saw Mandy and David Devereaux together. They were standing on their own and he had his arm around her shoulder and she was leaning against him. I'm not sure what was going on there, and I didn't hang around to find out. But I can tell you that if the Chief had thought there was something between those two he'd have gone *ballistic*. He and David didn't get on particularly well and David was old enough to be Mandy's father." Tim continued quickly, "But, whatever they were talking about, and it might have been her application to read medicine at his old college, Mandy left the country to go travelling round India as planned. She's been away for a few months now. She sent David a postcard from India; I saw it on his mantelpiece."

"It's not there now."

"Reiss cleared the room before you arrived. Their other daughter, Joanne is nice as well. She looks like Sally must have done at that age. But I don't know either of the girls very well."

Bill thoughtfully splashed after Reiss through the disinfectant foot bath and followed him into the pool area. Unseasonably warm evening air wafted in through the open sliding doors which led out on to the terrace, where some people were being served drinks and bar snacks by the Orangery staff. Inviting blue water lapped gently over the parallel black swimming lanes, gurgling as it drained away into the filters.

Reiss made for a vacant white plastic table with two chairs and threw down his towel as did Bill, who unhooked his watch strap and glanced across at Reiss, who had already removed his, and was now slowly and rhythmically massaging his neck with the tips of his fingers.

"I've seen you do that before. Do you have a problem with your neck?"

"It plays up sometimes." Reiss changed the subject. "I gather your three East London ladies have arrived? I allocated them to you because you're nearer their age; I thought you'd be the better person to deal with them."

"Thanks. I'll take that as a compliment, shall I?" Bill blew a raspberry.

Reiss grinned, "Come on, I allocated myself all three Americans. You should see Herman Orloff's medical notes?"

"Herman Orloff wasn't abused by his father, raped at twelve, put in care and raped again before going on the game and taking drugs by the age of fourteen. That's Sharon. Two abortions before the legal age of consent. But she's finding her way back, apparently. She's a care assistant at an old people's home these days. So why the P.P. and red sticker? Why do you think she may still be a problem?"

Reiss said, seriously, "I'm worried she may be helping herself to the old people's Valium. She'll need watching. Make sure you're properly chaperoned for any consultations."

Bill shook his head, "Why did you take these three? They'll be bored stiff out here in the sticks; they won't last two weeks, let alone two months."

Reiss retorted irritably, "I didn't choose them, I inherited them. Like I inherited Herman Orloff and the American journalist woman along with the whole damn trial. It was David Devereaux who was supposed to run it not me."

"Well, why did *he* take them, do you think?"

Reiss sighed, " I think he liked a challenge. He didn't come from a privileged background himself; I think he wanted to give people who were struggling the opportunity to change their lives for the better."

Had it been the challenge that had prompted David's relationship with Lara? The challenge to transform her into the slender and beautiful young woman in the photograph, who had called him her darling and her miracle worker? For whom he had bought a wardrobe of pretty clothes and sexy underwear? The clothes that Reiss had deposited in charity bins during his last trip to London.

"A challenge? Fantasyland, if you ask me!" Bill retorted, then dived neatly into the water. Reiss stood for a few moments before following him, his mind uneasy.

He had made no progress with accessing the information on David's computer. He had tentatively approached four different computer firms. None felt able to help and all of them agreed that it would be a time consuming task with no certainty of a successful outcome. The last man he had spoken to over the phone had warned Reiss: "I wouldn't be surprised if the guy who put these codes on hasn't added a timing device that wipes the hard drive if the computer is dormant for too long. Let's say, six months? This isn't a problem for a conventional programme analyst, what you really need is a hacker. But one you could trust. That's a difficult combination, particularly, if as you say, this material is sensitive. The best hackers are teenage boys, weird nerds or crooks."

Reiss exclaimed bitterly, "If I just knew the password."

The man gave a contemptuous laugh. "Oh, there won't just be one, you can be sure of that. This guy is much too smart for that. There'll be files with passwords and sub-directories with passwords. But he must have kept an aide memoire. Can't you find that?"

"If I could, I wouldn't be asking you, would I?"

"Do a deal with him. Most people have their price.

"He can't use money where he's gone. He's dead."

"Oh, I didn't realise...I *see*." The man paused and thought for a moment. "You could try the classified ads using a box number: *The Times* or a computer magazine, but my guess is *Private Eye* would be your best bet."

Reiss drafted something the next day for *Private Eye: Computer challenge: super hacker sought to beat complex anti-tamper device. Generous remuneration to successful applicant. Lawful and confidential. Apply to Box ...*

Unfortunately, he had just missed an issue. It would not be out for another two weeks.

He had said nothing to Pomeroy.

He climbed out of the pool and dabbed himself dry and then stood, massaging his neck as Bill came over. His hazel eyes assessed Reiss, clinically.

"How long have you had this problem?"

"I'll be all right in a moment. I'll go back in. Another swim will do me good. "

Bill persisted, "I've got some lineament in my bag. I can rub it in for you, later - or you could take a Valium, as a muscle relaxant?"

"You're off duty, now, Dr Ryder." Reiss smiled, however, to show that he appreciated Bill's concern.

Bill, Reiss had decided, was a sociable fellow unlike David. No girlfriend at present, he had confided to Tim, as his last relationship had gone "pear shaped". Tim had relayed this nugget to Reiss, who now eyed Bill thoughtfully. He was growing to like this young man and was glad he had joined his team.

CHAPTER EIGHT

May 1st

Reiss had allocated himself and Bill the two largest (and conveniently communicating) sets of rooms on the ground floor close to the Pavilion's reception. Both had small outer chambers for their nurses. The set of two smaller rooms with a shared sluice room upstairs would be used by Ayesha and Jim Menzies. The three company medics, who were only here for the first and last two days of the trial to assist with clerking in and out, had been given the poky rooms behind the steam baths.

Reiss, who had stayed overnight at the Cottage in Flat Acres was at the Pavilion by seven thirty, inspecting all the suites. He checked that the computers and other equipment was working and that the medical supplies had been delivered to the dispensary there which now had a second heavy padlock to secure its metal shutter. His first appointment was not till nine so, with a little time in hand, he took a walk around the nearby grounds, leaving a track over the dew spattered grass. Reaching the Manor House he passed through the open heavy oak doors into the lofty hall. This was echoing with the clatter of feet and the buzz of conversation. A few people stood around, evidently waiting to be allocated their bedrooms by the harassed clerks at the reception desk. Others he saw were heading for the trestle table where Molly Owulu, crisp in her nurse's uniform and Tim Scott, wearing his usual white coat, formally registered them into the trial, with Tim tapping their details into a computer terminal. Molly smilingly handed over clinic appointment cards, the day's meal and drink vouchers, lanyards with name badges, saying cheerily each time she handed one out, "Please do read these information packs as soon as you can. It is really important."

On the walls hung a series of framed energetic posters. Beaming middle aged men and young women, wearing brightly coloured sweaters, swung golf clubs or enjoyed jolly country walks. In others, sporty young men and women vigorously wielded tennis, squash and badminton racquets, swam enthusiastically in the pool or worked out energetically in the gym. Pretty girls in leotards (available from our shop) did aerobics or perched in cocktail frocks on high stools as they swigged vegetable cocktails. (Try our barman's special at happy hour).

Reiss, having waved discreetly to Tim and Molly, walked briskly past the Orangery where they were busy serving healthy breakfasts, snacks and drinks. Visitors had to pay menu prices, but participants, where appropriate, could use their vouchers.

In the Pavilion, the farm produce, gift and sports shops had flung open their doors. Marilyn, at a temporary reception desk, fluttered her false eyelashes and told Reiss his three Americans had arrived. Frank Miller (much too early) had been persuaded to go for a stroll, but Mrs Dora Shane was changing and Herman Orloff was ready and waiting for him in his robe.

Reiss went into his suite, removed his jacket and buttoned on his white coat. Frowning, he lifted down Orloff's three bulging folders of medical notes. Orloff should never have been included. He was sixty-seven and he had a long and complex medical history; over the years he had taken a cocktail of drugs. What had David been thinking when he enrolled this man? But he was here now. Reluctantly Reiss pressed the buzzer.

Orloff's complexion was putty coloured and his flabby cheeks and jowls quivered like jelly each time he moved and spoke. Nothing that Reiss said would dissuade him from taking part in this trial.

"It is the reason I came to England. I'm paying over a hundred dollars a day for my accommodation here so I can take your miracle drug. I can eat celery and drink carrot juice in Florida for a third of the price. I made real progress this last year under Dr Devereaux, but it's not enough. I *have* to reduce further." He waggled his cane, to emphasise his point.

"I agree that you need to lose more weight, but you are already taking a lot of other medications and they can interact and..."

Orloff interrupted, breathily, "No buts, Dr Reiss. No more buts, please! Listen, I been on a hundred diets! A thousand diets. I *starve - I eat nothing -* and I lose very slowly. Very, very slowly, maybe a pound a week. Then I get discouraged, and when that happens I start eating again. I want to lose forty pounds while I'm here! I *need* to lose more weight. I'm still over two hundred pounds and I'm not tall like you are: I'm five feet six."

"Height 1 metre 167.6. Ninety-one kilos. "

"I like it better in kilos. It sounds less."

"You say you understand the risks, and I know you've signed all the forms. But you see, while you're staying here, I am responsible for your medical care and for starters I'm not happy with your steroid levels; they're far too high; I can see that just by looking at you. Your doctor's letter confirms it, along with her many attempts to reduce them. But we will have to do that while you're here, Mr Orloff. You're Cushingoid and your skin is thin and flaky. The steroids may be affecting areas inside that we can't see and touch. I need you to work with me to reduce your steroids from now on. Do we have a deal?"

Orloff admitted, unwillingly. "I know I have a problem. I bruise too easily. The least knock and it's a bruise."

Reiss nodded. "That's partly the steroids. We have to reduce them, starting today."

Orloff shook his head, and panted agitatedly, "My doctor back home tried reducing them, but she had to put them back up. I couldn't breathe when she did it. I gasped like a fish for air, like this." Orloff gasped and waved his hands dramatically.

"We'll do it very gradually, you won't even notice, I assure you."

"I couldn't breathe. It was frightening." Orloff repeated, then coughed and wheezed pathetically, waggling the cane again.

Reiss said in a steely tone, "This the deal. You allow us to help you cut down, or you don't come into this trial. You needn't worry, I won't let you suffocate."

Orloff protested feebly and then capitulated. He climbed up the steps to lay on the couch. Reiss then performed a thorough physical examination, took a blood sample and showed Orloff to the door, "Let us know of any new symptoms, immediately, please."

"What kind of symptoms?"

Reiss hesitated. Orloff was obviously highly suggestible. "Severe headaches or nausea, persistent thirst, cramping abdominal pains, a major change in bowel habit, but allowing for the fact you've just travelled a long way and you're having a change of diet. Difficulty peeing. Anything unexpected. You're not in great shape and I need to know as soon as possible of any problems. You have the medical on-call number. We provide twenty-four hour medical cover here during the trial."

"That's great. Really comforting to know, thanks a lot, doctor."

Mr Orloff shuffled out, leaving the door ajar so that the voices from the ante-chamber were clearly audible. Reiss hovered out of sight. Dora Shane, as yet unseen, exclaimed forcefully, "Herman! You're white as a sheet! What did he do to you?"

"He took blood. I always feel dizzy when they take blood. Psychological, I guess, but I have to sit down, I feel a little nauseous."

Harriet's Australian brisk voice said, "Sit down for a moment, Mr Orloff. Would you like a glass of water?"

"No, I'll be okay in a minute."

Mrs Shane bellowed, "He took blood off you? The nurse took some already! How much more do they want? An armful?

I don't want him taking it blood from me! I'm terrified of needles."

"No other way to do it that I know of, Dora. Didn't you read through your consent form? My doctor went through it all with me."

Harriet, said firmly, "Stand on the scales, now, please Mrs Shane."

There was a creaking noise. Mrs Shane shrieked in dismay. "It can't be that much! Don't you dare look at that dial, Herman!" Then a sigh and an exclamation. "It *can't* be that much! I can't have gained two pounds since I left LA! It must be water retention. Or the robe? That must weight three or four pounds?"

Harriet's voice, resonant with Antipodean vowel sounds: "Only half a kilo, that's about one pound in imperial measurements."

"My earrings and my bracelet? They're heavy! Solid silver, native Indian work, you know? Let me take them off! There!" There was a chinking sound. More creaking.

Another melodramatic sigh. "Your scale can't be very sensitive! It hardly registered any change! They must weigh a pound a piece and I'm still over the 200 mark."

"Ninety-two kilos: 202 pounds."

Mrs Shane squealed theatrically, "Herman! I forgot you were here! You naughty man! Now you know my secret!"

Orloff said wheezily, "We're all here to lose weight, Dora."

Reiss having finished his notes on Orloff, pressed the buzzer and rose politely as Mrs Shane entered. He introduced himself and waved her to a chair. She must once have been an attractive young woman. Aged fifty-six, and near double her ideal weight, her coquettish strut was a grotesque parody.

"You are the company's chief physician?"

He conceded, modestly, "I am the Medical Director, here."

"You personally are the physician in charge of these trials, Dr Reiss?"

"Yes, I am."

"Then I'm flattered you have time to see me." She came closer and he backed away a few paces. "My first husband always used to say, go straight to the top man, Dora ... don't bother with any of the others. Waste of time."

"I wouldn't say that at all. No, not at all."

With Harriet now present, Mrs Shane clambered up on the couch using the steps. She lay back and said, wretchedly, her archness banished, "I weighed one hundred fifteen pounds the day I married my first husband; I've had three, in all." Tears rolled down her plump cheeks. "Jesus, this stuff had better work - I *gotta* reduce. I really hate being the way I am now. You have to help me. Please help me."

Reiss said, kindly, "I'll try, but you mustn't cheat. You must not try and smuggle in food, Mrs Shane and I'm told that some biscuits were found in your room. That won't help at all, you know."

"I forgot they were there. It won't happen again, I promise."

Harriet pulled a face behind her back.

Mrs Shane continued, with a hint of self-mockery: "When I checked in my cases at the airport desk, the clerk said, 'You're overweight ma'am.' I replied, 'That's very rude of you." And she responded, 'Ma'am, I was referring to your cases. There'll be a surcharge.' It sounds funny, but it hurt me like a stab to my heart, Dr Reiss. I don't want the same to happen when I go home."

At precisely nine forty-five, Frank Miller from New York City, came through wearing a red baseball cap as well as his robe. He swept it off theatrically as he sat down opposite Reiss who saw that long strands of dark hair were artfully combed across the bald dome from the back and side. His eyes were dark and a little melancholy, his voice soft and mellifluous."I've been counting the days till I got here. I'm taking a chance as I had to give up my job to do this. They wouldn't give me time out unpaid. I hope I'll find another job when I leave here." He smiled deprecatingly, "Unlike Dora Shane and Herman Orloff, who live on their investment incomes, I need to work to survive. I usually can't take more than two weeks vacation in a year so this is a gamble for me."

Reiss nodded. "You won't have to pay for any medical treatment connected with this trial, Mr Miller and we've negotiated a rate that's cut to the bone for your stay here at Pemberton Manor."

"It's still a lot for a guy like me to find. Don't get me wrong, I'm not asking for a reduction in the price, I'm just explaining that I need to make the best use of my time here. I mean to win that prize you're offering, for the guy who loses the most weight during the trial."

"Good. Go for it."

"You give me a diet plan and an exercise plan and I'll follow them to the letter."

"We'll do all we can to support you."

After another four patients, Reiss buzzed Harriet and told her he needed a ten minute break and slipped out of a side entrance for a breath of air. It was pleasant to be in the gardens, but it was not peaceful: Pemberton was crowded with the trial patients' friends and relatives who would be there until asked to leave at five o'clock that afternoon. Meanwhile they were making the most of a day out and taking advantage of the grounds and facilities in the fine weather.

There were people everywhere he looked. Old and young, fat and thin, strolling, running, jogging, sitting and standing. They were chucking balls, picnicking while sprawled on rugs, or perched on their own folding chairs. Round the far side of the old stable block, the pink and yellow Bouncy Castle (that had been hired for the day) was heaving and thumping to noisy pop music while hoards of children shrieked and leapt and ate expensive organic ice cream, which was selling fast from the booth opposite.

Reiss sat down on an empty bench in the shade of a vast, gnarled oak tree that was concealed by a mass of bushes.

Through the rippling leaves, he heard voices and footsteps. A trio of obese young women, dressed in brightly coloured tops and leggings, walked slowly along the gravel footpath, a little way away. The one closest to him had very short hair dyed a brilliant orange and was puffing on a cigarette as was the girl furthest from him whose brassy hair showed long dark roots. Between them, was a third girl, with dark hair and a sallow complexion. She sounded angry and complaining. Reiss strained his ears to catch the drift of their conversation: the brassy blonde said, "He can't not give you any! I mean, come on, what does he think you came 'ere for?"

The sallow girl in the middle whined, "That's exactly what I told 'im, but 'e just wouldn't, Bella! He says I can stay meantime, but he can't give me this Reduktopan stuff until he's certain I'm not pregnant! It's so not *fair*!"

Reiss frowned. Bill had discussed this matter with him. He had not personally seen any of these women, but he had skimmed their notes again the night before. The artificial red-head, Sharon, (whose file had been given a red sticker marked PP for Problem Patient), had a throaty smoker's voice. She spoke now. "Life isn't fair, Lisa-Jane, my girl! If you 'aven't learned that yet, you 'aven't learned nothing. And if you think I'm going to spend the rest of my life looking after daft, smelly old people, you're wrong. I want something better than that and I mean to get it. That's what I told that first doctor, the thin dark one with a funny name. Something like Davro, wasn't it?"

"E's dead! There's a different one in charge, now, Sharon. You say it like Rice but it's spelt different."

The middle girl who was complaining, Lisa-Jane, had also been given a red sticker by Reiss. Bella, the brassy blonde with navy roots, drew on her cigarette and tossed the butt into the lush grass, earning herself a big black mark from Reiss, watching unseen. Her huge hooped metal earrings were flashing in the sun as Sharon ground her stub into the gravel with the heel of her shoe. "Why did you let him? Was it to spite yer Mum, then?"

"I didn't *let* him! I couldn't *stop* him!" wailed Lisa-Jane. "He came into my room when I was asleep, the pig!"

Bella said, "Shush keep your voices down. Someone might hear you."

They dropped to whispers and moved away before sprawling on the grass by the fishpond, their information packs left unopened beside them.

Reiss's mobile rang on his way back to his examination suite.

"Marcus? I can't talk now, I've got a load of patients to see."

"You need to hear this. I had a letter this morning from a woman called Mrs Penny Wilson, who says she's Jane Lara Bucknell's sister. It was *her phone message o*n David's answering machine. She admits she and her sister had rowed and were out of touch, but shortly before Lara died they buried the hatchet and met up again. In a nutshell, she holds David, and therefore the company, responsible for her sister's illness and death. She's enclosed a copy of the autopsy report: Lara died from an overdose of paracetamol tablets and a bottle of gin on March 5th. She was found nearly two days after she checked into the hotel, who were very keen to get her off the premises before she died a few hours later."

"Horrible way to go. Takes longer than people think. Any secondary findings?"

Pomeroy said hesitantly, "Liver failure."

"That's the paracetamol O.D. Anything else?"

"Ulceration of the bowel, recent onset. Suggested diagnosis is Query early Crohn's disease? What causes Crohn's disease, Raymond?"

Reiss said tersely, pausing outside the Pavilion. "Nobody knows, really, but it fits with the symptoms she described in her note. It's not common in young women, but it happens. David would have picked up on it, I'm sure. I wonder if he sent her to a specialist? But, of course, if he thought..."

Pomeroy said, querulously, "Don't say it. I need your help with writing our response and I'll also taking advice from our solicitors."

"But you *are* a solicitor, aren't you?"

"A solicitor who acts for himself has a fool for a client and this woman sounds like trouble."

CHAPTER NINE

On the following Friday morning, the eighth day of the trial, Reiss, now sufficiently confident of Bill's ability to cope for a short time in his absence, reinstated his trip to see Dr Wengler in Zurich with whose company Forsyte International Pharmaceuticals plc were cooperating on another project. He rang Bill from the airport, keeping one eye on the departures board. "Anything new, today?"

"The pregnancy test just came back from the lab. It's negative. Shall I start Lisa-Jane on R/P today?"

Reiss scratched his chin, reflectively, "She hasn't had a period for five weeks and she admits she had unprotected sex recently. She's an unreliable historian. She's given us two different dates and it could still be too early to show up with an irregular cycle. I think it's too risky. Review her again next week. And next time you do an internal make sure she relaxes first or you send her off to the local District General."

"She started yelling before I got my hand inside her cunt!" Bill snapped, coarse and defensive.

Reiss said, soothingly, "She's had a nasty experience. She might be happier with a woman doctor, but Ayesha and the company medic we used for clerking-in are both too inexperienced and her being obese makes it more difficult."

Bill said, irritably, "You can do it yourself next time, then?"

Reiss said, "Got to go now. They're calling my flight."

"Have a good time in Zurich."

"With Dr Wengler? Have you met him?"

"But I was told you were staying over till Sunday, Chief?"

Reiss ignored this, and instead tried Sally's mobile. She answered, having unusually left it switched on. Their conversation was brief. She was annoyed he would be away for the whole weekend and did not wish him a nice flight.

Reiss went into the men's room and locked himself into a cubicle to re-read Pomeroy's pompous and intimidating letter. It warned Mrs Penny Wilson, Lara's sister, that while very sympathetic to her loss and feelings of bereavement, Forsyte International Pharmaceuticals' lawyers would seek an injunction with damages and costs if she repeated her *false, unfounded, very serious allegations that Dr Devereaux, while acting in the course of his employment, had harmed her sister's physical or mental health.* The letter continued,

Any intimate relationship that may have existed between Dr Devereaux and your sister Jane Lara Bucknell was a purely private matter between two consenting adults and nothing whatever to do with his employment.

She had further claimed that David, had ignored and or failed to treat with due care, her sister's depressive symptoms, which Pomeroy had refuted and added that this was outside his terms of employment with the company. Reiss tore the letter into tiny pieces and flushed them away.

On arrival in Zurich, his business with Dr Wengler was concluded by five o'clock. Reiss bought an expensive bunch of flowers at a stall and hailed a cab to drive him out of the city centre along the misty lake shore to Pension Hebe. Dr Wengler had recommended it saying it was comfortable and there were fine views of the lakes and mountains, but today there was a mist with heavy cloud and drifting rain.

On the way there, Reiss sat back in his seat recalling his first tryst with Beatrice in Prague. It had been a bleak November day and a freezing, sleety rain had been falling. He had followed her out of the conference hall in the middle of a dull afternoon lecture and offered to share his umbrella. Huddled close together they had walked briskly across the cobbles to the Old

City towards the Kafka exhibition.

They walked slowly round the exhibits, reading the captions and discussing Franz Kafka's work and life. Tall and slender, yet satisfactorily endowed, Beatrice's natural blonde hair, dampened by the rain, dried in the warmth to curl around her heart shaped face. She had a sweetness and lack of vanity unusual in such an attractive and intelligent woman. Reiss watched her pink lips moving as she read carefully through the badly printed local guide sheet with its misspelt, clumsy English.

As they exited into the downpour he suggested they share a cup of coffee and cake. Upstairs, in the crowded Milena Cafe, there was a vacant table by the window, facing the famed chiming clock, its figures still and silent in retreat.

Under the menu, lay a battered, damp copy of Baedeker. Beatrice snatched up enthusiastically, "I forgot my guidebook at the hotel. We can read about this clock in this one before they come back for it." She began flicking through the pages.

Reiss peered over her shoulder. "It's in German."

"For me, that is not a problem; I speak German quite well."

He smiled. "Do you. How come?"

Beatrice remonstrated, impatiently, "I learned German in school. We Scandinavians are not like you lazy English who think everyone must speak their language. So, I shall read this out, then I will translate it for you."

Reiss listened attentively as Beatrice read the German text with a heavy accent, then laboriously paraphrased a few sentences into English. "Very good. Go to the top of the class, Dr Svenson."

He grinned and patted her knee affectionately under the table. She pushed away his hand, frowning, "You are laughing at me? Is my English so bad?"

"On the contrary, it's extremely good."

"So? Why then?"

Reiss took the guidebook and read from it fluently and easily and then snapped it closed and smiled at her.

She pouted at him. "Now, I feel really stupid. Your German is much better than mine."

"Just teasing, don't be cross. You weren't to know." He chucked her gently under the chin. She caught his fist and gnawed it with mock anger, "I am cross. I am *very* cross!"

"That's a pity because you're the reason I'm sitting here in this cafe."

She retorted in German, "You are mocking me again?"

He shook his head. "I checked the list to make sure you were coming before I booked my flight." This was a complete fabrication, but it impressed Beatrice.

She squeezed his hand then released it. "Then I forgive you. And, of course *Reiss* (she rolled the R emphatically) is a *German* name, isn't it? It's just I thought of you as so typically English, Raymond?"

He shrugged, "I was born and brought up in London, but my parents were Viennese. They left Austria in a hurry after the *Anschluss* in 1938. My parents spoke German together with me at home; I also studied it at school, then I spent a year in Vienna. I'm bilingual. But since my father died I don't speak it that much, so I'm in danger of getting rusty."

She said firmly, "Me also, I too am in danger of getting 'rusty'. From now on we shall speak in German together. It will be good practice for both of us."

He kissed her hand and clicked his heels in mock deference, *"Jawohl, gnadige Frau Doktor."*

They walked back across the square in the chilly drizzling rain to the conference hotel where they were both staying and conveniently found they had rooms on the same floor.

Reiss followed Beatrice down the corridor into hers and hooked up the "Do not Disturb" sign, chained the door and came towards her. "Alone at last. I should like to kiss you. May I?"

"Can you make love to me in German, as well?"

"Of course, mein schatz, come here." He unbuttoned her blouse and helped her slip out of it. He watched as she removed her skirt, before running his hands lightly over her underwear and pale, smooth thighs whispering in her ear in German, "You are very beautiful, Beatrice ... very beautiful indeed."

She smiled wryly, "I think you have been with many women, Raymond?"

"If I'd met you twenty years ago there would have been no need for them." Reiss had responded, sincere at that moment.

Beatrice had turned on the shower and said reflectively, "Twenty years ago I was a schoolgirl of fifteen. How old were you then Raymond?" He had been twenty-six and married to Sally who had just given birth to Joanne. He kissed Beatrice's neck. "You know, my first experience with a woman was with a Viennese whore and I was seventeen. Imagine that if you can?"

"A whore? In a brothel? That was very risky, Raymond?"

"Well, we both took precautions, and a doctor checked out the place first."

"You asked a *doctor* to recommend *a brothel?*"

"No, it was my father's idea. He said it was part of my education. He must have paid her double rates in advance as she was very conscientious with her tuition." Reiss smiled at Beatrice's disapproval and in recall of the memory." It was thirty years ago, darling and before AIDs and genital herpes, right?"

"And syphilis and gonorrhoea?"

"He warned me always to wear a condom when going with strange women."

Beatrice soaped Reiss's genitals thoughtfully. "You are a Jew?"

"Half. My father was Jewish, my mother was Aryan, if you like. She died of cancer when I was fifteen. I haven't believed in anyone's God since."

They made love first under the shower, then later in the large comfortable bed. Beatrice told Reiss that she loved opera, that she was divorced after a miserable marriage and that she had a twelve year old daughter called Steffie who, together with her work, was the centre of her life, now. But then, Beatrice had gently pinched a fold of flesh around his waist and asked when he last went to a gym? Reiss had taken the hint. Cut back on the calories, worked out more and swam regularly during the week at Pemberton and now with Bill, a willing companion, it was more sociable and agreeable for both of them.

The cab pulled up on the gravel drive outside Pension Hebe. Having paid the driver, Reiss, his heart beating faster, registered at the small reception desk and carried his bags to his room. In case of unwelcome enquiries, he and Beatrice had asked for adjoining rooms. There were locked communicating doors to the left and right. He unlocked the left one and tapped on the door beyond. Beatrice answered, "*Ja*? Who is it?"

"Room service, *mein schatz*. Special delivery."

She opened the second communicating door and smiled.

He said, with genuine emotion, "*Liebe* Beatrice, I have missed you so terribly much."

He swung her in his arms, still holding the bunch of flowers and then they fell together on to the bed.

CHAPTER TEN

Thursday, 21st May 2001

Tim Scott, deputed to meet Sarah Goodwin, gallantly carried her suitcase up the two long flights of stairs to her room in Pemberton Manor House, that was well away from the ugly modern annexes where the trial patients were accommodated. Her face fell, when Tim explained apologetically that there was no ensuite and gestured down the corridor to the bathroom which had "a loo in it". But she would not need to share it as the bedroom on the other side was unoccupied for the next two days. Looking a little relieved, Sarah Goodwin, in her broad New York accent, commented that the room seemed quite warm. Where was the switch for the air conditioning?

Tim had laughed and flung open the two small dormer windows. From these he pointed out the charming view of the terrace and extensive grounds down below.

"Who lives over there?" She was looking at the Dower House that stood to one side and was surrounded by a small fenced garden.

"Lord Pemberton. FIP bought the rest of his estate from the mortgagees and gave him a few hundred shares as a bonus and put him on the board. I wasn't here then but there are photographs of what it looked like then in the library and it was very run down. It's divided up these days into the Health Farm and our R & D compound at Flat Acres - and some buildings on the Industrial Estate that is a couple of miles from Pemberton Village.

"One of us will show you round tomorrow?"

"Thank you, Tim."

"But for now, I'm sure you'll want to rest and freshen up before the cocktail party. It's at six thirty sharp. Out on the terrace."

"Will Lord Pemberton be there?"

"Very much so. He's dying to meet you, Sarah."

"Great. Thanks, Tim. I'll see you downstairs at six thirty."

When he had gone, Sarah looked around the room, feeling a little disappointed. It was a fair size and pleasantly furnished, but it was in the roof and had sloping ceilings and was, in truth, a glorified attic. However, it had a desk and a conveniently placed plug for her computer to charge up. Using her converter, she plugged it in and rapidly typed up her first impressions, before unpacking her case and stowing it tidily away in the cupboard. She was pleased to find her new white suit from Saks, (a steal in the sale at $200), had not become creased during the journey. She had two hours before the party, with time for a few minutes rest on the bed, (a modern divan and not a four poster). She propped herself up on the pillows then removed the thick and formal invitation card from the large square envelope that Tim had given her and read it again, smiling. She was to meet a real live English Earl, even if he was in somewhat reduced circumstances.

Leaving the card on the night table she flicked through FIP's patient information pack and left it with the invitation and focused instead on the New York Globe's Financial Editor's review of the company's current situation:

Forsyte International Pharmaceuticals plc (FIP) is what is known in the industry as an "ethical" company as it invests in and/or carries out its own research and development (R & D) of products before they are licensed. Many products that look promising do not make it all the way to the market place and for this reason the money and effort and time spent in development has to be written off. This is why products are provided with patent protection as an ethical company is entitled to benefit from its investment. But when this patent expires, other companies may produce the same product and then sell it under its generic name but may not use the brand name which remains exclusively with the originator. Sales of the branded product will fall off as the generic product gains ground and is cheaper, sometimes much cheaper.

FIP's problem is that its major products are either patent-expired or are nearing the end of their patent protection period. They have a strong R & D program with some promising new products and in particular, Reduktopan. If this becomes licensed and goes on sale, even if it is only available on prescription, it will be a big earner for FIP but in the meantime FIP is heavily borrowed and is anxiously awaiting the (hopefully successful) outcome of its multi-centre trials on obese patients. There have been small-scale trials already on people designated as healthy human volunteers. If it is even half as effective as FIP would have us believe, they will have a huge potential market extending way beyond UK and Europe generally but also in the USA and Canada and where obesity is a big issue.

FIP is betting its ass on the success of Reduktopan and the word is that it will get a UK license soon and that FDA "IND" approval is not far behind. Several major US companies are known to be courting FIP with the front-runners thought to be Sion and Oribo. FIP's shares are a speculative investment at present but there is serious money to be made.

People:

*CEO : <u>Marcus Pomeroy</u> (57) Lawyer, was formerly a partner in Pomeroy & Nelson in central London, a firm founded by his grandfather. **Warning:** beware: the Britannicus variety of legal rat is reputedly more subtle than its North American cousin. Salary is $425,000 pa. (£300,000.00) + perks and bonus. M P instituted a program of harsh rationalisation. He is considered able and at times has been described as an iron hand in a velvet glove.*

Twelve years ago, on the death of Hugo, the fifth Earl of Pemberton, FIP purchased the bankrupt Pemberton estate from the mortgagees but allowed the sixth earl (Cecil) to retain ownership of the Dower House. He was given a seat on the board where he is viewed largely a figurehead. Title: Lord Cecil Pemberton.

FIP, however, under-estimated the investment needed to make it fit for purpose. Heavy capital investment and high running costs have led to disappointing returns for FIP who also own Pemberton

Manor Health Farm which is reputed to be a very pleasant place to visit. Enjoy your stay there.

Research and Development (R &D) staff.

Dr Raymond Reiss (physician) (47) is FIP's Medical Director with overall charge of R & D. Reiss was head-hunted by FIP and induced to leave his consultant hospital post in Cambridge 18 months/2 years ago. Regarded as a capable physician with good people skills and is generally popular with staff at all levels.

Dr David Devereaux (died 31st March 2001 aged 40). His death must be a blow at such a critical time as he was a key player in Reduktopan's development. He died in a car crash late at night on his way home. No other cars were involved. Nobody has as yet been appointed to replace him so meanwhile RR will have to do more himself and spread DD's work around his team. FIP's press statement says RR will be personally running the residential trial of Reduktopan at Pemberton Manor, so you will certainly see him around during your visit."

Sarah now picked up the Patient Information pack which included a brightly coloured map and checked the layout of Pemberton Manor Health Farm before making her way to the bathroom. It was large with dormer windows similar to those in her bedroom and had a black and white tiled floor. The lavatory, raised throne-like on a dais, had a wooden seat and a high level cistern from which dangled a chain with a china handle. The old fashioned wash basin had separate taps for hot and cold water as did the large and deep tub that stood supported on four clawed iron feet. It filled slowly. The hand shower sent out a feeble spray. Sarah returned it to its rest and lay back in the warm water and turned off the taps with her big toe.

Back in her room, she put on her new white suit over a sky blue fitted top, fastened the catch of her lapis necklace and having brushed her mass of auburn hair stood to admire her reflection in the wardrobe door's long mirror. She then sprayed herself lightly with the new Chanel scent she had bought at the airport.

She would have liked a pair of matching lapis earrings, but tonight her silver clips would look fine. By nature punctual, Sarah descended the wooden stairs slowly in her white leather high heeled shoes as the clock in the hall chimed the half hour. Below, in the dim lobby, Dr Tim Scott PhD, stood waiting for her, polishing his glasses with his handkerchief that he quickly put back in his pocket at her arrival. He too had changed and was wearing a light blue suit.

"I hope I didn't keep you waiting?"

"No, not at all. Perfect timing. Let's go out there shall we?"

Tim, smiling brightly, escorted Sarah through the open doorway where it was a glorious early summer evening and there was a gentle hum of bees and the sound of massed English voices.

Sarah exclaimed, "Oh, it's so beautiful here. And the grass is so *green*, I just *love* it." She had taken the precaution of two antihistamine tablets, however.

"Yes, it is pretty isn't it?" Tim looked around appreciatively, as if seeing it all for the first time and through her eyes. Slung low in the sky, the sun was beaming a golden path across the verdant grass as it warmed the ancient honey coloured stone walls of Pemberton Manor House. Regretting that she had left her Raybans upstairs, Sarah shaded her eyes to survey the crowd of people standing on the paved terrace and gathered on the lawns beyond. More than three quarters of them were overweight. The people taking part in the trial, she supposed.

"Which one is Earl Pemberton?" She made him sound like a jazz musician.

"Lord Pemberton." Tim corrected, pointing him out. "He's the tall thin man with grey hair in the white linen suit."

Sarah was disappointed. The Earl looked to be over sixty and his suit needed a clean and press. He had a curiously skull-like face, with dark bushy eyebrows and a thin wide slit of a mouth into which he was rapidly pouring a glass of white wine. As she watched, he reached out a long languorous arm to replace his empty glass with a full one from a passing tray.

"Mind your step, here, it's quite uneven."

Tim caught Sarah's arm as she tripped on the uneven terrace and turned his head to gauge the reactions of his colleagues, who were standing in a cluster to one side of the gathering. He had told them Sarah Goodwin looked like a Sumo wrestler.

Some of the women looked irritated, but Raymond Reiss was laughing with Pomeroy. Others, including Bill Ryder, whose mouth had dropped open mid-sentence, were staring openly in admiration. Ignoring them all, Sarah Goodwin progressed briskly with Tim across the terrace, moving with a light fluidity, like a dancer crossing a stage, her flaming bush of shoulder length auburn hair haloed by the orange ball of sunlight. Reiss, noting her pale, faintly freckled skin, supposed that her hair colour was natural and speculated that beneath her short, smart, white skirt there would be a smaller second bush of soft curling red hair; it was many years since he had made love to a natural redhead.

Beside him, John Stannard murmured in his ear. "Well, well, well, it seems that Dr Tim Scott has a sense of humour?"

"It seems so, yes. He certainly had me fooled."

They both grinned, as they watched Tim guide Sarah towards Cecil Pemberton, as did Sarah's three compatriots, Dora Shane, Herman Orloff and Frank Miller (in a blue baseball cap), who were now surging forward for a better view.

Reiss said, "Good looking girl, isn't she?"

Bill Ryder mumbled, "Yes, she's lovely. That gorgeous hair and a fantastic figure. Legs to die for."

Ayesha Patel and Molly Owulu pouted disapprovingly as Jessica remarked, her Australian accent, cutting across them. "If you ask me that woman is anorexic. I'll bet you a fiver she's anorexic or bulimic, or both. How else does she keep her weight down that low?"

Ayesha, who was naturally very slim and petite took this

personally. "I'm not anorexic or bulimic and I'm about her size?"

"You're an exception Ayesha. And watch out as you get older. But, I know I'm right on this lady, folks. Just watch her, now. See what she eats and drinks this evening."

Jim Menzies grunted, "She's not wearing a ring. Probably has a boyfriend, back home, though."

Pomeroy, feeling behind the curve, snorted, "Sumo wrestler, is she? Well I'd do a few rounds with her, willingly."

They watched as Sarah Goodwin plucked a splinter of raw carrot and a stick of celery from a proffered dish and then took a glass of fizzing mineral water as Lord Pemberton exchanged his empty glass for another full one as the waitress went by.

Alan Michaels, whose lizard eyes focused on the silent screenplay ahead, murmured, "When do you think we should go and join them?"

Pomeroy responded, ,"Cecil's been promised a few minutes on his own to play the grand host and Lord of the Manor. We'll give him another five minutes, but no more."

Tim Scott, who had been weaving his way back through the throng of people, said, anxiously, "I don't think we should leave them long. Pemberton's drinking like there's no tomorrow. He's already starting to slur his words. I came over to warn you to get over there."

Pomeroy and Reiss exchanged glances. Pomeroy hissed, "We'd better get going. Heavens, they're moving off? Where's that idiot taking her? They're going up the lawns. Perhaps he wants to show her the herb garden? That's up there. Or the rose garden? Tim, get after them. You can be quicker."

Reiss and Pomeroy, followed closely by Bill, John Stannard and then Jessica, Harriet, Ayesha and Molly Owulu a little behind them, were trying to push through the crowd on the terrace, but their progress was continually blocked by the large milling, chattering, throng, who kept reaching out for snacks and fresh drinks from the passing trays and who were eager to chat to the medical and nursing team.

Lord Pemberton and Sarah, who had been standing at the far end of the terrace were together ascending the three slippery stone steps on to the patch of lawn that was separated by a ha-ha from the fields beyond, on which a small flock of sheep were grazing.

Unsteady and garrulous after five or perhaps six glasses of wine, Cecil Pemberton turned not right toward the herb garden or the rose garden but eastward.

Reiss prodded Pomeroy, furiously as they struggled to follow, "Do you see where he's taking her? Is he off his trolley? I just hope Tim is in time to head him off."

Pomeroy snapped, elbowing his way through the crowd, "Unbelievable that he'd do that?"

They were zigzagging slowly around groups of people with their entourage struggling to keep up, and falling by the wayside. Molly Owulu, FIP's nurse monitor and Ayesha Patel both abandoned the chase to stall the three curious Americans who seemed minded to go after Sarah and Cecil Pemberton. All around them, people competitively compared different (failed) diets in raised voices. Tim Scott, at last beyond the milling throng, dashed up the stone steps and across the lawn, leaping athletically over the ha-ha to land in some sheep droppings, barely paused, before racing along the field to leap back across the ha-ha and come up panting behind Pemberton and Sarah Goodwin. But he was too late. They were standing on a raised hillock. From there you could look down over all the land that had once formed part of the Pemberton estate; it was the only spot from which the whole of the Flat Acres complex, which was surrounded by tall electric fencing and security cameras, could be clearly viewed.

Catching his breath, Tim heard Pemberton burbling, his words a little slurred: "All of this land, as far as you can see, belonged to my family for generations. We had a working dairy farm here with some chickens and also arable land when I was a young man. We could hear the cows at milking time even up at the Manor. But it didn't pay well; we had tenants who fell in arrears with the rent and the buildings fell into disrepair and by the time my late father died the place was laden with debts. Then on top of it were the death duties and the bank forced a sale and FIP bought the lot, all except for the Dower House. That's still mine."

Sarah nodded, not sure how to respond. "So you can still enjoy the grounds here?"

"Yes, I can do that. But it's all so different now. FIP kept some of the names for the old buildings, but that's about all. Raymond Reiss and his deputy - well he's dead now poor chap - have their offices in what was the old farmhouse. It looks much the same from without, but they gutted it completely. They knocked down the barn and completely rebuilt it, but kept the name. Odd really. And they keep some very different animals in that barred building over there." He pointed towards it. "Not cows, pigs or chickens; nothing like that. And those sheep are just there to keep the grass down and look pretty."

Tim prodded Lord Pemberton hard in the shoulder.

"Lord Pemberton, Sarah, we really need to get back right now. Sarah, you need to meet Dr Reiss and Mr Pomeroy and all the others. Come with me, now, will you? Please." He knew he was sounding a little desperate.

"In a minute, Tim. I was listening to what Lord Pemberton was telling me. This was all his family home for generations and now it's been completely transformed, like he says. It is just so fascinating. My readers will be so interested. Lucky I always have my camera with me. "I'll take a few shots right now." She stared admiringly at the shimmering complex. The sun's rays gleamed on the windows of the laboratory and farmhouse buildings and the electrified steel fence while a tall thin chimney puffed dreamy streamers of grey smoke into the pale sky.

"No, we can't allow that. We don't allow photographs of Flat Acres for security reasons."

She put the camera away reluctantly. Reiss and Pomeroy, who

had now joined them, hastily introduced themselves. Sarah Goodwin shook hands but then quickly spun round again. "That is Flat Acres? Yeah, well it is quite flat around here, isn't it? Can I see over it sometime?"

Reiss said firmly, "No, our Research and Development park is closed to visitors, I'm afraid."

She stared at it with narrowed eyes. "Looks more secure than Fort Knox. I would really like to see over it."

Reiss shook his head, firmly. "Sorry, no. Not allowed. We should go back to the terrace now. There are two hundred people waiting to meet you."

Pomeroy added, hurriedly, "It's our insurers, they don't allow any visitors. Now, Miss Goodwin, while we're up here, let me show you the rose and herb gardens?"

Sarah tossed her auburn curls. "You can fix it with your insurers for me to go there?"

"No, we can't, they're very difficult people." Pomeroy, glancing at his watch, tugged Sarah's sleeve, urgently. "Come along now, Miss Goodwin, the rest of the team and two hundred patients are here to meet you. We mustn't keep them waiting any longer."

But it was too late.

At seven o'clock the Flat Acres security lights were switched on. Sarah gazed in fascination at the mixed fixed and rotating beams. "Not Fort Knox. It's more like Auschwitz! You've even got an incinerator? What do you burn in that?"

Pomeroy bleated, "Industrial waste, Miss Goodwin; industrial waste. All very dull, I assure you."

"Lord Pemberton says you keep animals in that building. Are they used for experimentation? Is that why you won't let me see in there?" She turned her head for a last look over her shoulder as Reiss and Pomeroy edged her away and steered her down the grassy bank towards the terrace. "What animals do you have there? Rats and mice? Dogs and rabbits?"

Reiss snapped, "Most animal work is done by independent

research organisations not by pharmaceutical companies. A.C.E. does most of ours. You can talk to Dr Stannard here about that?" They went down the steps on to the terrace. Reiss now pushed Stannard forward, "Dr John Stannard is A.C.E.'s chief executive. John, meet Sarah Goodwin of the New York Globe."

"Please, just call me Sarah. Let's not be so formal."

"Sarah, then. John Stannard is the man you should speak to about animal research."

"*I know* you've got animals caged up in that building."

Reiss interjected, "Sarah, you need to understand that the law requires us to test all new drugs on animals before we are allowed to try them on people. It is the same in your country. We're as humane as we can possibly be, I assure you."

"What else do you keep over there, Dr Reiss?"

"Fruit flies."

Sarah laughed contemptuously. "You got more than fruit flies behind that electric fence."

Reiss retorted wearily, "The law compels us to grossly overdose mice and rats with toxic substances until they die, then post mortem them to gauge the effects and extent of the toxicity. It gives me no pleasure to do it." He turned to Tim. "Give Sarah a copy of the regulations, tomorrow."

"Do you use dogs? Do you get them from a dog's home?"

Exasperated, Reiss snapped, "Laboratory animals are specially bred from internationally recognised strains with known traits and responses that can be discounted. They're expensive and we look after them well. A vet inspects them regularly and I personally check the animal houses myself. Satisfied, now?"

Lord Pemberton who was wandering around with yet another full glass of wine, mumbled, "Excuse me, dear Miss Goodwin, I feel I should circulate a little now. I'm leaving you in good hands."

Sarah Goodwin turned to nod and smile at him. She was already being introduced to the hovering entourage. Within minutes, she was deep in conversation with Bill Ryder, her amber eyes smiling at his hazel ones, flirting and charming, her back to Reiss. He heard Bill enthusiastically expounding, "In our healthy volunteer trials, a third of the patients, selected secretly at random, were given dummy pills; we call that placebo. So we could compare weight loss with diet alone and diet with Reduktopan. Neither doctors nor patients knew who was having what, but after only a week it was absolutely obvious and we stopped the placebo. We did the same for a week on the outpatient trials that A.C.E. are running, but again they had to stop the placebo because there was an outcry. Everyone wanted R/P because they lost so much more weight in the same time. We've stopped all the controls: everyone is given R/P, now."

"Can I try some?"

"Sarah, you absolutely don't need it. But you can ask Dr Reiss if you like. He's the boss."

Reiss, on hearing his name, joined them. He shook his head, firmly as he let his eyes travel very obviously over Sarah Goodwin's slight figure. "It's not meant for people like you, Sarah. You don't look to have a spare ounce of flesh. You're very slim as it is."

She retorted, "You call FIP an ethical company? What's ethical about researching an obesity drug when you haven't cured cancer?"

Reiss said shortly, "We have a big R & D programme. R/P is not our only product as I'm sure you know."

Pomeroy said, piously, "Obesity is very unhealthy, Miss Goodwin. It leads to other serious illnesses."

"Obesity can be cured by diet and exercise."

"The people taking part in this trial have all tried a hundred diets and failed. Ask them, yourself. That's why they are here and because R/P really works none of them want to leave."

Sarah changed tack. "Did Dr Devereaux' death cause you problems?"

Pomeroy responded, smoothly, "David Devereaux was a brilliant and dedicated research physician and he led the team that developed R/P. We all of us miss him greatly, but his death will not hold us back or change anything. Dr Reiss has everything well in hand."

Reiss's guarded expression prompted Sarah to say: "I was thinking of writing a feature on him? A brilliant, dedicated doctor aged forty dies in a car crash? What was he like as a person?"

Pomeroy responded quickly, "Oh, Dr Reiss knew him far better than me. They worked together. They had adjoining offices."

Reiss said, slowly. "David was a quiet man. He was very absorbed in his research."

"Wife and children?"

"No, he was divorced for many years. I will get you a copy of his obituary and let you have a group photograph if that helps?"

Sarah, disappointed, jutted her chin and turned back to Bill, "Did *you* know Dr Devereaux?"

"Sorry, I can't help you there. I never met him. He died before I arrived. That's why I am here now, helping Dr Reiss. It's awful to say it, but his death opened up an opportunity for me, Sarah. I've just left hospital practice, you see..."

"Oh, really? Tell me about that?"

Pomeroy and Reiss moved away.

Reiss muttered, "I don't want her poking around in David's private life."

Pomeroy retorted, "If she thinks you're blocking her, she'll start digging. We need to sound cooperative and enthusiastic. You need to turn on that famous charm of yours, Raymond. You're growling at her like a bear with sore head."

"I never wanted her here. Anyway, she seems to like Bill and he's very keen?"

They stared across the grass at Sarah and Bill, chatting and laughing. Pomeroy nodded, approvingly. "Bill needs plenty of free time. Let him keep her amused and occupied off the premises over the weekend. We can give him an entertainment allowance. Shall we say five hundred pounds and anything more he pays himself?"

"You tell him, Marcus."

"Bill is your assistant. It will sound better if it comes from you."

CHAPTER ELEVEN

Friday, May 22nd.

At the start of the fourth week of the trial the weather continued warm with high humidity levels. In the Pavilion medical suites it felt unpleasantly close as the air conditioning system had collapsed and would not be repaired till Monday. As there were no blinds, the frosted windows had to be kept closed during examination sessions. Hot and perspiring in his white coat, Reiss worked through his afternoon clinic and the list of "problem" patients. His interview with Sarah Goodwin was scheduled for five o'clock and he had promised Sally he would not be late for the Blunts' dinner party at Prince Albert College where Dr Geoffrey Blunt was the Master and Sally a senior lecturer in biology. Despite clear discouragement, Dr Blunt still hoped there might be a donation from FIP which would not be forthcoming.

Unfortunately, as the afternoon progressed, Reiss fell behind schedule. Two patients took longer than anticipated, and two extra ones had to be fitted in. Then, Dr Wengler rang up from Zurich for a long, urgent and involved discussion. After that it was Marcus Pomeroy. Reiss was still talking to him when Bill appeared at their communicating door. "Lisa-Jane's here, Chief. Do you want to see her?"

"Okay Bill - I'll come in a minute ... "

Pomeroy asked at the other end of the line: "How's our little romance progressing?"

"I have no idea, Marcus. Bill's a bit busy right now, but later on why don't you ring and ask him yourself?"

Ending the call, Reiss went through to Bill's suite where Lisa Jane did not look happy to see him. He spoke to her in his clipped, authoritative voice.

"Dr Ryder has explained why we can't let you have Reduktopan. We have to be quite sure you are not pregnant. I am really sorry; I know how disappointing this must be for you. It is for us as well."

She interjected, quickly, "But you *can* be sure now. I know I'm not pregnant, doctor. I started my period last night, didn't I? Very heavy. I used up three tampons and me stomach aches, but it's a real relief, I can tell you." She grimaced and clasped her hands over her flabby abdomen, her eyes darting from Bill back to Reiss, whose lips had fused into a thin line. "So now I can start taking the pills, can't I?"

Reiss and Bill exchanged glances. "How much weight have you lost since you've been here?"

"Six pounds. It isn't fair! Sharon and Bella have lost sixteen! You will let me start on Reduktopan today, won't you? Please, doctor; it's why I came, you know that."

Reiss drummed his fingers on the desk as he checked through her records to which he had added a red sticker (PP) then nodded. "Yes, now we can be sure you're not pregnant, Lisa-Jane."

It was after five thirty by the time he was free for his interview with Sarah Goodwin. He flung open the window and splashed his face and neck with cold water then took two small bottles of mineral water from the fridge that was filled with medical supplies. Still wearing his white clinician's coat he told Harriet she could leave after she had showed Sarah through.

She perched on the chair across the desk and set up her tape recorder with deft fingers, pushing back her russet curls as they tumbled forward. In front of her was a page of questions written out in a sloping, loopy script. With her amber eyes fixed on Reiss's face, she asked: "Dr Reiss, can you explain for our readers, how Reduktopan works?"

Reiss relaxed a little. Her acceptance that R/P was effective was encouraging and presumably followed from her informal chats with patients. He had seen Sarah talking to Lisa-Jane, Bella and Sharon that day. They had been hanging around as she approached and were eager to be interviewed.

He explained the basics: "There are three components which combine to reduce appetite and override the body's natural mechanism to resist rapid weight loss after a week of dieting: one is d-fenfluramine which reduces appetite, then there is Vagneuroline which blocks the action of the vagus nerve on the stomach muscle and delays stomach emptying and tri-iodothyronine - T3 -that prevents the drop in the body's metabolic rate which usually accompanies weight loss."

"How about thyroid function?"

Reiss replied, "Excessive use of thyroid drugs to increase metabolic rate destroys lean tissue. That's harmful and longer term it is counterproductive. With Reduktopan the body can't absorb too much T3 because if there's overload the stomach ceases emptying."

They discussed the mechanics and advantages of Reduktopan for a few more minutes, then Sarah changed the subject.

"How much did David Devereaux contribute to the development of Reduktopan?"

"He led the research team which discovered the interaction between Vagneuroline and the other two components and then calculated the minimum effective dose."

"That sounds a very important contribution?"

Reiss nodded. "It was, Sarah, if I may?"

"Sure. I prefer it."

"But David would have been the first to tell you that the compound wasn't his invention: it was developed from brainstorming group discussions and experiments. Don't get me wrong, here: I'm not in any way minimising David's role in all of this. He was a brilliant chap and his death at forty is a tragic waste. We have lost a great physician who had so much more to give the world."

"What was he like as a person? As a colleague?"

Reiss replied, carefully. "He was a quiet rather intense person. Divorced years ago but that's all I know. He kept his work and his private life very separate. I knew the work-side not the private one; we didn't socialise other than at company events. I think he liked classical music and I know he did a lot of running to keep fit. He took part in a few marathons and half marathons that we sponsored for medical charities. He played chess and he liked informatics, but I think his medical research was what really drove him."

"Did he have a girlfriend? Or was he gay?"

"He was straight, I think. But he came to company events on his own and there was no girlfriend at his funeral. The family wanted it to be very private, so Tim and I were the only FIP people to attend. We are planning to hold a memorial service for him here but we will wait until after the R/P trials are over for that."

Sarah nodded and looked down at her handwritten notes. Reiss remained wary, prepared for a barrage of questions on animal experimentation. It did not come, however. Instead she asked him to describe the main health problems associated with obesity. As she seemed genuinely interested, Reiss expanded for longer than he had intended, discussing the problems caused by processed foods that were full of fats and sugar and had no fibre. This was followed by the attitude of major food manufacturers, cheap restaurants, junk food, generally, the petrol engine, exercise.

She switched off the tape recorder and then asked him about the key sights to see over the weekend. Checking his watch as she had packed up her gear, Reiss was dismayed to find it was six thirty. It would take him an hour to get back home and he would need to wash and change. He would be late for the Blunts' dinner party; they had been asked for seven fifteen. Sally would be furious. He left an apologetic message on their home answering machine, then tried her mobile, but it was turned off, as usual. He locked up the suite and rushed out to his car, but his return to Cambridge was slowed by the heavy Friday evening traffic. By the time he had parked in the drive, Sally's little car was gone and it was seven thirty. If he drove straight to the Blunts now he could be there in ten minutes. But he felt desperately in need of a shower and a clean shirt and several glasses of wine to make it through a dull evening with College gossip the main topic of conversation.

Half an hour later, he stood by the front gate waiting for his taxi, mulling over his interview with Sarah Goodwin, who had not been aggressive or argumentative, but pleasant and professional.

By now she and Bill should have arrived at the George & Dragon Inn that was attractively situated in the country and had a Michelin starred restaurant. Reiss had heard Bill asking for a reservation for a deluxe room with a four poster bed.

CHAPTER TWELVE

Reiss was the last guest to arrive. The front door was opened by a college servant wearing a black waistcoat and striped trousers. Geoffrey Blunt, face shiny and perspiring, bustled in from the garden to greet him. "Raymond, hallo. Good to see you."

"Sorry I'm so late but it was unavoidable." Reiss handed over his penance.

"Most kind. Most generous and not necessary but very welcome." The Master grasped the bottle of Teacher's appreciatively before hiding it in the window seat while giving Reiss a conspiratorial wink. "Susan watches me like a hawk."

Reiss followed Blunt into the walled garden and pecked Sally on the cheek. She glanced at her plain every day watch with its shabby black leather strap. "Better late than never - at least you *came.*"

He said defensively, "I left you a message at home and I tried your mobile but it was off. I had to stay late to give an interview to the woman from the New York Globe. Then the taxi was ages coming."

Blunt intervened. "Well, never mind. We're all glad you're here. Have a glass of Merlot and relax."

"Thank you." Reiss took it gratefully and swilled it in his mouth before swallowing.

"From Chile. Rather a find, I think?"

"Yes, it is very pleasant."

Sally now introduced her husband to a balding middle aged man in heavy glasses who was standing beside her on the terrace. John Someone, (he didn't catch the second name) the new college bursar who was wearing a blue spotted bow tie with a matching handkerchief which overflowed from his blazer pocket. After that, John Someone and Sally resumed their conversation in which he had no interest.

Reduced temporarily to the role of onlooker, Reiss saw that the bursar found Sally very attractive. She was a tall, slim woman and she looked elegant in the low cut long straight olive green dress with a single short string of pearls around her neck that was a little tanned. In the dusk of a summer evening she looked once again quite youthful and seemed to be enjoying herself and their lively conversation. But daylight would reveal that her hair, that was now cut too brutally short for his liking and had once been naturally fair, was streaked heavily with grey. She was pushing it back carelessly while she chatted, revealing her bare but pierced earlobes. She had left the pearl studs he had brought her from Hong Kong on the dressing table. He had not taken them with him to give her because he suspected she had decided against wearing them because he was late.

Geoffrey Blunt now propelled Reiss to meet the other guests. His arrival completed the group of ten people, of whom only one was below the age of forty-five, and she was in the final stages of pregnancy, with her anxious looking and much older husband, hovering by her elbow.

Susan Blunt took over from Geoffrey and whispered in Reiss's ear, "Carol's frightfully nervous about the impending birth and Neville's even worse, can you believe? They weren't going to come tonight. They only agreed when I told them you'd be here, Raymond. They feel safer knowing there's a doctor in the house, ha, ha."

At that moment, dinner was announced. Reiss, pushing the bursar to one side, escorted Sally into the dining room which had crimson wallpaper. It was illuminated by five low wattage candle bulbs which were on the minimum setting allowed by the dimmer switch.

Reiss squinted at the handwritten name cards and found

his place between his hostess, Susan Blunt and Carol, the expectant young mother. Her husband, Neville, was a history don at College, who like Geoffrey Blunt was on the College's building committee and Carol had been one of his students. He had evidently taught her more than the Tudors and Stuarts.

She said, plaintively to Reiss, "Now I've finished my thesis, I'd just like to get this over with. It's so uncomfortable. I'm keeping Neville up at night because it's so hard to sleep."

Reiss glanced across at her swollen, distended stomach, twitching through her dress with the prodding of unseen fetal feet and said, comfortingly, "Won't be long, now." Then steered the conversation away from the impending event.

As Reiss had expected, the conversation was concerned mainly with College matters, which was the common link for the guests, apart from him. Gossip, anxiety about student numbers, standards, league tables, political correctness and, of course, money. The College had some generous alumni and benefactors but still it needed more. Beside him, Carol was wriggling on her chair and then she pushed it back, apologising.

"I'm sorry but I'm so uncomfortable. I need to walk about - don't wait for me, please, do just get on with your dinner."

Her husband followed her out of the room.

The guests glanced knowingly from one to another, then to Reiss, who shrugged and smiled and changed the subject, and the conversation resumed, if a little uneasily. Susan Blunt delayed serving the main course for ten minutes, by which time Neville returned to the table alone. "Carol's lying down. She says please carry on. She'll come down a bit later. She's not hungry." His uneasy eyes focused on Reiss who smiled and began a different conversation with his hostess and the single lady opposite who taught geography and extolled the joys of field trips.

Three quarters of an hour later, as Susan Blunt was serving her excellent apple and pear pie with whipped cream, Neville excused himself again. Susan Blunt commented anxiously, "Oh, dear, I hope nothing's wrong." She turned to Reiss. "What do you think, Raymond?"

He replied, "Neville's with her. If there's a problem, the best thing he can do is call an ambulance. It will get here very quickly."

Sally from the other end of the table said, sharply, "Raymond, go upstairs and make sure Carol's all right, will you?"

Reiss snapped, "If she isn't, I won't be much help. I last did obstetrics twenty years ago, and I don't even have my emergency bag here. It's in the car and I took a cab."

Sally glared at him across the table. "It's their first baby. Just go now, will you?"

The Master said, heartily, "You can tell Sally is a doctor's wife."

"*Raymond!* Are you going?"

"Oh, all *right!*" Reiss scraped his chair noisily back.

He met Neville hovering indecisively at the top of the stairs.

"I was just coming to fetch you. I'm worried. I think Carol may be in labour, but she won't let me call an ambulance. You see, she had a false alarm a few days ago and she felt a fool for going then."

"She shouldn't. It often happens with a first baby."

Reiss followed Neville into the Blunts' absent daughter's bedroom. It was an old house. The floor boards creaked loudly under his shoes and he suspected they were over the dining room. Carol lay huddled and groaning in the fetal position on the bed.

Neville announced, annoyingly, "The doctor's here, Carol."

Reiss asked reluctantly, keeping a safe distance, "How do you feel, Carol?"

She mumbled," I keep getting these sharp pains - and I've got an awful backache. Awful, awful backache - oh -"

"Sounds like you've started labour." Reiss turned to Neville, "You'd better ring the hospital. Have you got your car here?"

Carol whispered, "I'm not due for another two weeks. I went

there last week and they said it was wind and they sent me home. I felt such a fool. I'm not going back unless I'm sure I'm really in labour." She groaned again and clutched her stomach and then her back. "Oh-oh ... "

Neville took her by the hand and whispered, "Breathe deeply, darling ... breathe deeply ... "

He looked entreatingly at Reiss, who said, firmly. "Take Carol to the hospital now. The worst they can do is send her home again, but I'm quite sure they won't."

"I'm not going unless I'm sure I am - oh -"

Neville said despairingly, "Darling, please be sensible. Listen to what the doctor here says."

He looked again entreatingly at Reiss. "Could you examine her and make sure?"

Reiss approached the bed and said, reluctantly, "Do you want me to take a look, Carol? Before I call the ambulance - to make sure ... "

"Please - would you?" She nodded, dismally.

Regretting the third glass of Chilean Merlot, Reiss removed his jacket, and rolling up his sleeves went to wash his hands and face in the bathroom down the passage. He returned with a towel for Carol to lie on. "When did these pains start?"

"Just after we left home, they got worse during dinner."

He examined the cervix carefully: "You're certainly in labour. Quite far advanced, actually. Around six centimetres dilated."

"Is that good?"

"Oh, very good, and you're opening up pretty fast." He smiled encouragingly at her. "I'll fetch you another towel. Your waters could go at any minute. I'll ring for an ambulance and warn the hospital you're coming in tonight. I give you my word they won't send you home."

He made the calls seated on the Blunts' matrimonial bed. He could hear Carol sobbing down the passage. He had no analgesia with him so he went into the ensuite bathroom to check the medicine cabinet. There was nothing suitable in there either. But the latest issue of *Private Eye* was on top of the toilet's cistern. Reiss anxiously checked the classifieds: his advertisement was there, under *EYE HELP.* Along with some other very unusual requests. Who, if anyone, would respond to it? And could he trust such a person?

A blackmailing hacker would be worse than leaving the data inaccessible.

Neville's anxious face appeared round the door.

"I've called the ambulance. It'll be here in ten minutes."

Neville said, distractedly, "Please stay with her, Can't you give her something for the pain?"

Reiss dropped the magazine discreetly back behind him. "I haven't anything with me, but don't worry, the ambulance will be fully equipped and they can give her gas and air." He hesitated then said, "Neville, I think I should warn you now that I think Carol will need a Caesarean."

"A Caesarean? Why? What's wrong? Oh, no..."

"Calm down, she'll be absolutely fine. I've spoken to the registrar about it. They'll be ready to deal with it when she arrives."

He saw Carol into the ambulance with considerable relief.

The incident prompted Susan to move her remaining guests into the sitting room for coffee; she did not like having two gaps at her table. "Thank you for reassuring them, Raymond."

"Not a problem."

Later, Sally drove them slowly home. The hall was still and silent. The cat was out hunting. Reiss turned on his mobile but he had no messages and there was nothing on their home answering machine. He bolted the front door and they went upstairs.

"I didn't like to ask before. What was the problem, Raymond?"

"The head was high and she was opening up like Aladdin's cave. But I'm a bit out of practice with obstetrics. It's not my field and I could be wrong."

Sally opened the bedroom door. "No, you won't be. You're a good doctor, Raymond. A bloody good doctor, with all your faults, I'll give you that."

"A good doctor who wickedly gave up his NHS hospital practice for the evil Pharmaceutical Industry?"

Sally sighed and sat down at the dressing table and picked up one of the pearl studs.

"How stupid of me. I forgot to put them on before I left." She looked up and they stared at their reflection rather than at each other. "I know the drug Industry needs doctors, but did it really have to be you?"

He undressed and waited for her in their shared bed. "Sal, come to me, darling. I'm sorry I've not been around that much. It's been a hellish few weeks."

They embraced, made love and then fell asleep. Next morning he telephoned the hospital. His diagnosis of CPD (cephalo-pelvic disproportion) had been correct and the senior registrar had performed an emergency lower Caesarean section within forty minutes of Carol's arrival. She and her baby son, Michael Raymond, were doing well.

Gratified with how things had turned out, and with the baby's second name, Reiss endorsed Sally's card with his own congratulatory message and was rewarded by being let off a trip to the local supermarket. There was a further bonus: he had been at home when both his daughters had telephoned individually from very distant places. Mandy was well and still enjoying herself travelling (in Bengal) and would be coming back for Christmas.

Joanne asked if her father could fetch her along with her luggage and bike from King's Cross Station in London on Wednesday evening? She was coming home to revise for her exams.

On Sunday, Sally announced she would go to Devon in August to spend a week or ten days with her parents who had moved there after her father retired. Reiss was welcome to join them but he told her he probably would not be free to get away then. The dates overlapped with the Bayreuth Festival that Beatrice would be attending and where he had said he might join her for a few days.

With this possibility in mind, as he got in the car to return to Flat Acres on Monday morning, Reiss selected the first tape of "Gotterdammerung" from the sealed boxed set of the Ring of the Nibelungen cycle that Beatrice had encouraged him to buy. He would be seeing her in London before Bayreuth, however. Indeed, very soon. She would be arriving in London this Thursday to speak at a conference at the Royal Society of Medicine where she would stay overnight. He had booked the company flat for himself in anticipation.

He needed to be fit and toned up for Beatrice so he decided to start the day with a swim. At the Pavilion, Joe greeted him cheerily, "You're bright and early, Dr Reiss. First one here, you'll have the pool all to yourself."

"Good." Reiss changed quickly and dived in. A few minutes later, there was a splash in the adjoining lane and he was being overtaken by a slim female slashing quickly and lightly through the water, turning ahead of him so that they were face to face. Sarah Goodwin was almost unrecognisable in her goggles and a white rubber swimming hat.

He sped up and passed her, then scrambled up the steps. She climbed out after him, pulling off her hat and goggles, releasing the mass of auburn curls.

"Hallo - I didn't recognise you at first."

"I know I look a freak wearing this stuff."

"Not at all. Very sensible. They use a lot of chlorine here. Can I get you a coffee from the machine?"

"Thanks. Black. No sugar."

Reiss returned with two small cartons of coffee and gave her one. "Enjoy your weekend?"

She nodded vigorously so that the red curls shivered. "It was really good fun. Bill took me sightseeing, all over."

Reiss smiled. "I'm glad you had a nice time with Bill. Where did you go?"

"Cambridge, Newmarket, Norwich, the Broads. Bill's a really nice guy. I promised him a return tour if he comes to New York!"

"Good." Reiss grunted. He towelled himself vigorously then sipped his coffee. "Have you finished your article yet?"

Sarah dropped her towel over her chair. "Pretty much."

There was no sign of Bill in the gym or the locker room. Sarah was on her own and Reiss wondered whether they had spent Sunday night together? But it was not his concern.

CHAPTER THIRTEEN

From the end of the platform at King's Cross station, Reiss glimpsed Joanne struggling with a trolley loaded with her luggage and boxes and one hand on her bicycle. He gave her an affectionate bear hug. "Darling."

She snuggled against him, "Oh, Daddy, it's so good to see you."

He dropped her back on her Doc Martin boots and pushed the cart out to the car, while she breathlessly updated him with her news. It didn't seem to include much in the way of work; social events took up too much time. He hoped Joanne would get a decent degree at the end of it. He must have written to her about Sarah coming because she asked about the American journalist and how the Reduktopan trials were going.

"All my friends want to try it. You'll make a bomb, Dad."

He said, reprovingly, "It's for people with serious weight problems, not silly girls who don't need it, or people who need to lose five pounds."

"People will take it for that reason, too, Dad."

She switched on the car's player and ejected the disk promptly. "When did you get this? I didn't think you liked opera?" Joanne looked surprised.

"Wagner stops me from forgetting my German, sweetheart."

They both laughed. "Then my next birthday present is a year's subscription to *Der Spiegel.*"

"I'd like that very much."

Joanne selected the Simon and Garfunkel disk they used to sing along to when she and Mandy were small and they hummed along together companionably on the drive back.

After helping his daughter carry in her cases and boxes and had lifted out her bicycle, Reiss checked his post.

There were two hand-written envelopes marked "Private and Confidential". He took them into his study. The first was an untidy scrawl with several simple words misspelt which he put through the shredder. The second letter, dated last Monday, was far more promising. It had been produced on a word processor and the heading had a London address and a telephone number.

Dear Sir,

Your problem sounds intriguing but also challenging. I cannot guarantee you success but I would be willing to try. My background is mathematics and computing and I hold an executive position within a large company. I fully understand and will respect your requirement of absolute confidentiality. Indeed mutual confidentiality and trust must be at the heart of any agreement we may, after careful discussion, eventually conclude. Any fees you pay will be donated to cancer research and I will ask only for reimbursements of expenses for myself and these will be modest.

If you wish to take matters further, please telephone me after office hours or at weekends.

As I live alone you can safely leave a message on my answering machine.

Yours faithfully,

J P Singer.

Reiss hesitated, then dialled. After about six rings, a man's voice answered. An educated pleasant voice. His spirits rose a little. "You replied to my advert in Private Eye under Eye Help for a computer problem. I'd like to arrange a meeting?"

Sally put her head round the door, "Dinner's ready, Raymond. Don't be long."

"I'll come in a minute." He waved her away impatiently, "Sorry about that ... yes? Oh, my name? Dr Raymond Reiss." He spelt it out. "Yes, pronounced like Rice." They agreed to meet the next evening when Sally would be at a College meeting and Joanne, at home to revise, was already making plans to see her local friends.

To celebrate Joanne's return, Sally had laid dinner in the dining room. Reiss kissed his wife and daughter affectionately before they sat down and he opened a bottle of chilled Mouton Cadet. It was nice to eat as a family again even if Mandy was still far away.

Sally asked, "What are you up to, Raymond? What were those letters from Private Eye?"

She was sharp to have noticed that.

Reiss, smiled sweetly. "I'm afraid I can't tell you; I'm sworn to secrecy! All very silly. A nonsense event at the company."

"What sort of nonsense? You mean like a party?"

"Not exactly, no."

"Not like the entertainment you organised for poor David's fortieth?"

"That was a misjudgment on my part, and I regretted it, Sally. I apologised to him."

"I know. He told me, when we met up at the firm's summer do last year."

Sally handed her husband a plate of white fish in a creamy sauce with large chunks of undercooked carrots and too many boiled potatoes.

His wife and daughter, by now losing interest, moved the conversation to other matters.

It occurred to Reiss, as he watched and listened to Sally and Joanne and occasionally contributed, that he had concurrent and compartmentalised lives. His family life here in Cambridge; his working life at Flat Acres and Pemberton and it was better that way; he did not want them to become tangled up in each other. But now, as his women discussed their planned shopping trip in town, his mind wandered.

Was Pomeroy right to discourage him from trying to access David's notes on the firm's computer? He would see how he felt about matters when he met this mysterious Mr J P Singer who had invited Reiss to visit him at his home.

The next morning Reiss left for Flat Acres under a lead coloured and weeping sky. Arriving before Linda he found a fax from Beatrice in the machine letting him know that her daughter Steffie was to spend a few days with a school friend; she would be extending her stay in London until Sunday. Writing in German (with several basic grammatical errors) Beatrice apologised for giving him so little notice; she would understand if he were not free to meet up. He shredded her fax quickly. She should not have communicated with him in this way; a phone call was safer. Anyone could have come in and read this. He would have to warn her to be more discreet in future. Twisting his wedding ring uneasily, Reiss extended his booking for FIP's London flat by two more nights, before ringing Sally to give her notice of his unexpected absence that weekend. Clearing his throat, he prepared to lie.

Sally snapped, "It's the College's Wine and Cheese that weekend, but you never really intended to run the tombola stall on Saturday, did you?"

He said vaguely, "The tombola stall?"

She burst out angrily, "You've *really* forgotten? You agreed to do it when we were at the Blunts only last week!"

"Did I, then I'm sorry, Sal. But I have these guys flying in from Stockholm on company business. I can't get out of it."

"You really don't remember? It was after Neville and Carol had gone to the hospital."

"I'm afraid I was a bit distracted by earlier events, darling. Perhaps Joanne will help you? Or your bursar friend, John Someone? Can't he do it, instead?"

"I don't need you to find me a replacement."

"No, and I'm really sorry, Sal - I'll be back by Sunday lunch time."

"With your case of dirty washing?"

Reiss mumbled, feebly, "Sally, we can go out somewhere..."

But the line was dead.

Sally, understandably, was fed up with him. Perhaps she would take her revenge with John Someone, the Bursar. He looked to Reiss as if he would be content with a kiss and a groping embrace in a dark corner of the cloisters to celebrate the tombola takings. Surely they would not go all the way? But he was divorced and probably lonely.

Reiss paused, his hand still on the receiver. Perhaps he should put Beatrice off and run the tombola stall, himself. He did not want a crisis with Sally. He did not want a divorce. A divorce would create strains and tensions in his relationship with his daughters. It would impose severe financial penalties. It would break up their home: the Cambridge house would have to be sold and their communal goods of over twenty years divided. Reiss would have to buy a flat or a smaller house if that happened. He was not domesticated and had never cooked anything beyond a boiled egg and toast. He would have to employ a daily woman. He would become a serious target for other women, including Beatrice, with her spoilt, disagreeable thirteen year-old daughter (at home for at least five more years).

Beatrice, charming and exciting as a mistress was much less attractive as a full-time partner. Ambitious to advance her own career she would not do his laundry or look after his daily needs but she would ensure he stuck to a healthy low fat diet and reduced his alcohol intake. She would monitor and increase his exercise programme, and in sum, this was not at all appealing. And if they did shack up, where would they live? He would not be moving to Sweden. Either Beatrice would have to come to live in England, with Steffie, her tiresome daughter, or they would have to organise an expensive, tiring and unsatisfactory rota of visiting on alternate weekends. This was not at all what Reiss wanted for the future.

He picked up one of the framed family photographs on his desk. A younger Sally smiled back with his two daughters wearing matching school uniforms. He should not leave Sally too much alone with the new bursar. He should tell Beatrice he could not make it that weekend. He lifted the receiver to dial his home number to let Sally know and then dropped it back on its base. He so rarely saw Beatrice. He would bring Sally flowers and take her out for lunch on Sunday and then after that he would make more effort to overnight in Cambridge during the week.

When the phone rang he was surprised to hear it was Pomeroy who said, irritably, "Mary's got tickets for one of those Lloyd Webber musicals for Saturday night and we were intending to stay in the flat. I see you've booked it for three nights."

"I have meetings in town."

"For three nights on the trot? Are you bringing Sally to town then?"

Reiss snapped, "No, what's that to do with it?"

Pomeroy sniggered, "Meetings? That's a new word for it. Well, you'll have to hold your Saturday night *meeting* somewhere else. Go to a hotel."

"Why can't you and Mary stay in a hotel?"

"Anyone stays in a hotel, it's going to be *you!*"

Reiss conceded sulkily, "All right, you can have the flat on Saturday night."

Pomeroy said quickly, "Don't hang up, yet. Speaking of meetings, do you think Bill got our money's worth? The receipts came through. One double room for two nights."

"Let's hope she didn't spring a headache on him, then."

Marcus said petulantly, "Just as long as she writes something flattering about Pemberton Manor and how wonderful Reduktopan is, I don't care if he slept on the floor."

"She may include a couple of paragraphs about David as well."

"If she does, she does. P R gave her the B M J obituary and a group photo of the team. She's had no time to go digging around and she leaves on Monday morning."

Pomeroy changed tack. "I want you to drop this mad idea of trying to access David's files."

"Don't worry. I won't do anything rash, Marcus. The guy's asked me to his home, so I can see the set up. If I feel I can't trust him completely I won't tell him anything. But to be

101

honest I have the feeling this guy is legit."

Pomeroy shouted, "No, I forbid you from doing this, do you hear? It's much too risky? What David wrote was for his personal use."

Reiss said, soothingly, "I'll just meet the guy. He probably won't be able to help anyway."

"I just hope we don't both live to regret this, Raymond."

CHAPTER FOURTEEN

Camden Hill, where J P Singer lived, looked gentrified and prosperous. Its Victorian red brick terrace houses were well maintained and a number of them, including Singer's, vaunted burglar alarms above their freshly painted front doors. Reiss parked in the next road. Leaving Devereaux' computer locked in the boot, he walked round the corner and stood for a moment on the pavement, glancing uneasily up and down the street. Marcus Pomeroy was right. He was taking a risk even coming here. However, he straightened his tie and ascended the three steps to Singer's front door and pressed the bell.

He was about to ring for a second time when the door opened, cautiously.

"It's Dr Reiss. I put the advert in *Private Eye*. About the computer?"

Singer nodded, "Yes. You'd better come in."

He was in his mid thirties. Of slim build and middle height with dark hair that was cut close to the skull. He wore small gold-framed glasses over his beaky nose and his office shirt was open at the neck and tucked into a pair of clean but faded blue denims. For a putative hacker he looked quite ordinary and respectable.

Reiss followed him into a comfortably furnished sitting room with blue walls and a white ceiling and varnished oak floor boards. Through the open French windows he could see a small patio with budding rose bushes and tubs of lavender where bees were buzzing.

Singer said, brusquely, "You said you'd bring some proof of identification."

Reiss produced his passport. Singer grasped it between a thin white forefinger and thumb with very clean well manicured nails. He turned the pages slowly, checked the photograph looking up and down at Reiss's face, flicked over to look at the stamps on the inside pages and then returned it.

"You're a doctor? Did you train in England?"

"In London. At the Middlesex Hospital. For the last two years I've been working for a pharmaceutical company. We're trying to develop effective new drugs."

Singer said abruptly, his eyes fixed on Reiss. "Okay. If you're really a medical doctor, define pyelitis for me, now."

Reiss asked, puzzled. "Why? Are you ill?"

Singer swallowed, nervously, "That's not the point. I've taken a chance answering your weird advertisement, never mind letting you into my house. I need to be sure you're who you say you are, not some kind of conman or a crook."

Reiss frowned, "I have not come here to play silly games."

"Then define pyelitis for me, then how to treat it."

Reiss shrugged, then watching Singer's stern reaction, spoke slowly and deliberately: "Pyelitis occurs when the pelvis of the kidney becomes inflamed, usually as a result of a bacterial infection. The pelvis is the part of the kidney from which the urine drains out into the ureters and any blockage that prevents the free flow of urine can cause severe pain." He paused. "Is that enough?"

Go on, Dr Reiss."

"Well, all right, as I was saying, a blockage there results in severe pain in the loins, a soaring temperature and rigors - that means uncontrollable shivering and sweating. If the kidney isn't draining and the infection isn't treated properly the kidney will swell and in time it will rot and lose its function for good and have to be surgically removed. If both kidneys are affected, then it's total renal failure. Bad news; dialysis, maybe a kidney transplant if you're lucky."

"How would you treat it?"

"I'd - er -give antibiotics in combination with analgesics, pain killers. You need to maintain a high fluid intake while checking first there are no underlying abnormalities in the urinary system that caused the problem in the first place. Like a PUJ obstruction that's causing reflux. PUJ stands for pelvi-ureteric junction."

"Thank you. Please sit down." Singer pointed to a chair that was facing his and knotted his thin white hands over his knees, his grey eyes staring directly into Reiss's pale blue ones. "Okay, Dr Reiss. I accept you really are a physician. And you strike me as a good one, so what on earth are you doing advertising for a hacker in Private Eye?"

Reiss smiled faintly. "Now, it's my turn to ask you a few questions, Mr Singer. Starting with what you do for a living."

"I'm a systems designer. And for the record it's Dr Singer. I have a PhD in maths and computer sciences."

"*Dr* Singer. Do you work for the pharmaceutical industry?"

"No, I don't. My work is with communications systems." Singer cleared his throat uneasily, "And I am not willing to become involved, if this is some kind of industrial espionage."

Reiss said coldly, "There is no question of that. This computer belongs to my company, Forsyte International Pharmaceuticals Plc. I can produce a receipt for it if you want one. A former senior employee had the use of it at his home by agreement. I need to access what he put on it, but I need expert help to do that."

Singer stared at him. "Isn't it networked into your system?"

"No, and he died suddenly in a car crash a few weeks ago."

Singer said softly, "I see."

"Any information he recorded is highly confidential. It may include research data on one of our new drugs. One drug in particular. David was very clever with computers and a load of warning signs popped up when I turned it on. He probably had some kind of aide-memoir listing the passwords, but I can't find it. And he may have had it on him when he crashed the car and it exploded in flames."

"You have a problem then, Dr Reiss."

"Can you help me solve it?"

"If I do, you must feel able to trust me completely, or we're both wasting our time. I would need to get under this man's skin and into his head. I need to know everything about him you can tell me: his name, his background, where he grew up, what pets he had, his school, his university, his love life, his hobbies, the kind of books he read, the music he listened to and above all, his understanding of computers. I would need the full picture, Dr Reiss, not selected highlights. And even then I might still fail; I probably will, but I'll give it a go."

Reiss responded, cautiously, "I understand, and I would need you to sign a confidentiality agreement with me. But tell me first, what motivates you in all of this? Do you need the money?"

"Not at all. I would regard it as an intellectual challenge."

Reiss registered polite disbelief. "An intellectual challenge? Nothing more? Your brains against David Devereaux'?"

"I like the idea of doing something to further medical research, especially into the treatment of cancer."

Reiss nodded, "Yes, I see."

"Is your drug aiming to cure cancer?"

"Not this particular one, no."

"What then?"

Reiss cleared his throat. "It helps obese people to lose weight."

"Obesity is an illness?" Singer flung himself back down into his chair and began to laugh before exploding into a paroxysm of violent coughing. "Trying to help people to slim is what's driving all this cloak and dagger stuff? Aren't there more important medical problems you should be tackling Dr Reiss? When you've got terminal cancer you don't suffer from obesity. Don't you think you should be looking into that first?" He glared angrily at Reiss. "Well, don't you?" His eyes, behind their lenses, glittered with angry unshed tears.

"We are looking into that as well," Reiss said, half conceding the point. "We have a lot of different products in the development stage, but we're further along the road with this drug than the anti-cancer one, and if it's successful, it will help fund research for the cancer one." His tone was soothing and compassionate. "Forgive me for asking, but are you grieving for someone you cared about who died of cancer?"

Singer nodded and said in a husky voice, "Do you know anything about Kaposi's sarcoma, Dr Reiss?"

So that was it.

Reiss nodded. "A little, yes." His eyes scanned Singer's pale face, his neck and the backs of his hands. He would have liked to check his shins for the tell-tale stigmata of purpling brown and black nodules. Common in Africa, but unknown in the West until the advent of AIDS in the early eighties.

Singer muttered, "A close friend of mine had it. His name was Howard and he left me this house. We lived in it together for ten years before he died. Howard was five feet nine but when he died he weighed barely eight stone. He had surgery. Radical surgery. The wounds wouldn't heal properly. The treatment they gave him made him very sick. His hair dropped out. He wasted away in front of me and I felt totally helpless."

"I am so very sorry. I really am."

"But you're telling me a drug to treat a load of greedy pigs who can't, or won't, stop stuffing themselves on junk food is more important than a drug to cure cancer?"

"I don't say that. Of course not. But you must admit obesity is a problem for today's society. It's very hard to understand by thin people, but it's there just the same."

"When Howard died he looked like a skeleton." Singer brushed a tear fiercely away.

Reiss asked gently, "Are you all right, in yourself?"

Singer shook his head, "No. I'm going the same way as Howard. I have limited time ahead of me. Meanwhile, half the world is starving to death and the other half eats to excess."

"Dr Singer, please listen to me. Our obesity drug is one of a range of compounds my company is trying to develop and bring to the market. It costs a lot to do that. Many compounds that look promising have to be abandoned on the way. We are hopeful that one of our new compounds might help to contain the spread of certain cancers and we will be testing it on mice in the autumn. But we need returns on our investment to do that. Our slimming drug will help a lot of people live happier and healthier lives and generate the revenue to fund other research. Look at it that way."

Singer bit his lip. "Yes, I know that."

Reiss said, tersely. "I need help to access what's on that computer. How much would you charge?"

"It isn't about money. My fees will go to a new cancer charity that I'm setting up. I want one with low admin costs where the donations fund research not a big back office. But for now, bring me your computer and everything else that you have that may help and I'll see what I can do."

CHAPTER FIFTEEN

The session with Singer took two hours. Reiss provided him with David's CV, his personnel file, computer literature and other information he could recall or that he had noticed when at his house. By the time he had parked in the underground bay provided for the company's flat and hailed a cab to take him to Covent Garden, the confidence he had felt in Singer's presence had began to seep away. Pomeroy, at the other end of a crackling line, shouted, "You've handed all this over to a perfect stranger? Did you even take up his references?"

"He's legit, Marcus. He's got an agenda of his own, but he's 100% legit - and he's well qualified. He only wants a donation to charity, nothing for himself except a refund of expenses."

Reiss had decided that Singer was an honest man. And he was clearly knowledgeable from the look of his bookshelves and the battery of equipment in his crowded study. There were some framed certificates on the wall that testified to his interest and expertise. But having ended his call with Marcus, doubts and anxieties swirled over him and his neck and shoulders were aching as he stepped out of the taxi. He felt in need of food and drink. He paid the driver and pushed his way through the painted turquoise double doors of Fellini's Restaurant whose walls were festooned with promotional posters and photographs advertising the great man's films.

Beatrice was sitting at a table for two by the window. Behind her, Anita Ekberg, pictured nearly life sized, cavorted in the Trevi fountain in Rome enjoying "La Dolce Vita". The Sweet Life. It would have been nice to join her there but he made do with the image.

Beatrice was in a powder blue suit that matched her eyes. She fingered her corn coloured hair and smiled at his approach. Her shiny, pink lipstick had left its imprint on the tall glass of sparkling mineral water. Reiss brushed his knuckles gently against her cheek. "Sorry, I'm late. My meeting took a lot longer than I expected. Did you enjoy the ballet?"

Beatrice nodded. "Yes, but it's nicer when you can share it with someone."

"Not with me. I'd ruin it for you. Can't stand men in tights."

He put on his glasses to study the menu for a moment, then turned to the wine list. She would probably choose fish. "A bottle of Sauvignon blanc?"

She said firmly, "Not for me, or for you, Raymond. Your liver needs a rest."

"My liver is fine." He rubbed the side of his neck with his finger tips. "*Liebschen,* I need a drink. I've had a long week and I want a glass of wine with my meal."

Beatrice closed the wine list firmly and poured him a glass of mineral water from her large bottle. "You are tense and your neck is bad again, isn't it?"

He massaged it for a few moments and admitted it was.

She nodded, and continued in German, "Wine will not cure your stress or help your neck. I will give you a massage that will help much more."

"Why can't I have both *liebschen*?"

Beatrice said severely, "Raymond, don't be childish at your age."

"No, *Frau Doktor.*" He clicked his heels, obediently under the table.

She was very serious, now. "As a doctor, I'm warning you to take better care of yourself. Cut back on your drinking and your cholesterol intake, unless you want a heart attack before you're sixty?"

Beatrice moved the butter dish to the empty adjacent table. Reiss snatched it back. "I'm a doctor, too, remember?"

Beatrice jutted her chin. "*Ja.* We say in Sweden, 'The doctor who treats himself has a fool for a patient!'"

A variation of Marcus's comment about lawyers. Reiss conceded defeat. "All right. You order for me, then."

She chose steamed salmon and mixed salads with oil free dressing. No starters.

When the waiter had left them, Reiss, under the cover of the turquoise tablecloth, stroked Beatrice's right thigh.

She snapped, "You think of me as just a sexual object, don't you?"

"You are a sexy and beautiful woman."

"You don't respect my intellect, is that it?"

He ran his hand lightly up to her crotch. "I respect everything about you."

She brushed his hand roughly away. Hissed in German, "Stop it. We are in a public place. It is not appropriate."

Beatrice then took her conference papers from her case. Her talk that morning had been a great success. A lot of questions were followed by a keen discussion that continued throughout lunch. Some man (an epidemiologist from Edinburgh) had then asked her if she was by any chance free for dinner tonight so they could discuss her paper further.

"Yes, I'm sure that was the reason."

"Not every man is like you, Raymond."

The waiter now brought their salads. Beatrice, undeterred, passed her text to Reiss so he could read it for himself.

Reiss, stifling a yawn, read it as he forked in a lettuce leaf and a sliver of cucumber, conscious that Beatrice was watching to make sure he didn't skip a single line. He asked a few pertinent questions then firmly handed back her notes.

"What time did the conference finish?"

Beatrice confessed, "I'm not sure. I left at twelve to do a little shopping before the ballet."

"*You went shopping?*" Reiss frowned, his heavy eyebrows drawn together in apparent disapproval that hid his amusement.

"London is so cheap compared with Stockholm, Raymond. I bought this suit today. Do you like it?" She waited hopefully for his approval.

Reiss shook his head, sternly.

Beatrice sighed, disappointed. "You *don't* like it?"

He grinned wolfishly and pinched her knee fondly under the tablecloth, "Yes, I *do* like it. darling. The blue suits your intellect perfectly, dear, learned, *Frau Doktor*."

Beatrice pushed his hand away. "I hate it when you mock me like this."

"Not mocking you. Admiring you, sweetheart."

"You are impossible. You have a one-track mind."

Their meal over, Beatrice flounced off to the powder room leaving Reiss to pay the bill. It began to rain. Fat droplets of water splattered against the restaurant window and trickled slowly down to form jagged streams and drip on to the pavement below.

Through the open door the scent of a cigar drifted in. The aroma prompted memories of past evenings he had spent with his father in the sitting room of his first floor apartment in Highgate where they had discussed politics, history, medicine and personal relationships in both English and German. Sometimes, their discussions had continued late into the night and over breakfast the next morning. In his head, Reiss heard again the sound of his father's footsteps coming to the door to admit him and felt his warm embrace. They always hugged when they met. His father would lead him to the sitting room and pour a Schnapps or a brandy or perhaps a single malt for them both. Rituals that came before they sat down to talk about anything important.

His late father's papers and books, including the complete set of Remarque novels, in their original German, were on his bookshelf in his study in Cambridge. Other records and tapes and some smaller items were in the Cottage.

Bereavement pierced him anew with a sharp physical pain. He felt a hand on his shoulder and looked up into Beatrice's concerned, blue eyes.

"Raymond, you looked so sad just now. Are you all right? Has something bad happened?"

He jerked back his chair, "No, but let's go. I've had enough of this place."

Outside, the rain was beating down and a chilly wind was whipping and bending the trees. Distant thunder rumbled ominously. Beatrice shivered.

Then, unexpectedly, a cab pulled up and discharged its fare and they climbed gratefully in and Reiss gave the address of the company flat in Queen Anne Street. Beatrice rested her head against his wet shoulder and he kept his arms tightly around her.

When Reiss turned on his mobile there was a message from Marcus. "Ring me back. Up to eleven o'clock tonight or first thing tomorrow morning."

It was after eleven.

Removing his jacket, Reiss leaned against the bedroom wall and watched Beatrice hang away her new blue suit; her black lace underwear emphasised her fair skin. He unclasped her brassiere and turned her round to face him. "Let me look at you, darling."

Beatrice covered her breasts with her hands, self consciously, "l have stretch marks and I know they're too big."

He kissed her neck and removed her hands and cupped a full round breast in each palm as if to weigh them.

"Not for me. I like big boobs on a slim, tall girl, *liebschen*." He squeezed the firm, round rosy nipples gently before releasing them and standing back for a moment as if admiring a statue. "But as for your intellect, that's really superb." He ran his hand from her knee up her thigh and laid it over her crotch. "It matches your pretty, blue eyes"

"Raymond ... " But she was smiling now, not cross. She was still in her high heels and her hand was covering his own and guiding it down under her lace panties. He pulled them off and, knelt down and buried his face in the soft golden fuzz and whispered in German, "Darling *Frau Doktor,* I adore you - I worship you at your altar."

Beatrice trailed her fingers through his neat, greying hair.

"You worship only one thing, Raymond."

"I adore you, I adore everything about you, darling. Everything. You are the complete woman for me."

They lay on the company bed. His sensitive fingers probed and explored the moist, dark welcoming vault while his swollen penis pressed ready against her thighs. He was pleased to find her diaphragm was in place. Beatrice turned her head away, "You were checking up? You don't trust me?"

"I thought you liked a bit of foreplay? Turn over - we'll try something else?"

"Don't insult my intelligence. I put it in before we left the restaurant."

He licked her ear and the insides of her thighs. "Clever sweet girl, thank you ...I prefer not to wear a condom-"

"You will break your thirty year rule for me?"

"Anything to give you pleasure, darling *Doktor Frau* ... "

"So unselfish!"

"That's me. Here to please you. Let me come now." He kissed her on the lips and pushed her willing legs apart. In the hall the house phone rang and the answering machine clicked on. Reiss could hear Pomeroy leaving another message. Reiss called him back when Beatrice was in the bath.

"Sarah Goodwin's article's out in the New York Globe! It's brilliant! She calls Reduktopan a miracle drug. She writes that they need it ASAP in America. It's better than anything P R could have dreamed up."

Reiss asked suspiciously, "Did she say anything about me?"

"The phone didn't stop ringing till after midnight with Yanks making reservations at Pemberton Manor Health Farm. Cecil is over the moon about it even though he's only got a few shares in the place."

"Wonderful. I'm so glad Cecil is happy. What did she say about me?"

Pomeroy rustled the papers at the other end of the line. "Um - ... *Forsyte's Medical Director, Dr Raymond Reiss is of German parentage-*"

Reiss interrupted indignantly, "I'm not. My parents were Viennese."

"*A dominating, large physical presence, Dr Reiss is a strict disciplinarian. He enforces the trial protocol to the letter ...blah-blah... and staff and patients alike respect his authority and judgment.*"

"Thanks a lot. She makes me sound like a Nazi doctor in a concentration camp."

"Rubbish, don't be so vain and sensitive. It's an excellent review. Marlon Strelitz is delighted with it. Good timing as you're flying out to see the FDA next week. You can buy Sarah Goodwin a very nice dinner on expenses."

"Rockville's near Washington, not New York, Marcus."

"'Strelitz will organise a press conference at their offices. She may fly up for it. Then you can take her out to dinner afterwards."

"I don't want to take Sarah out for dinner. She doesn't like eating. She's too scared of putting on weight." Reiss banged down the receiver. The phone rang again immediately. He picked it up as Beatrice came down the corridor her robe gaping open.

"What now?" Reiss growled, gently massaging Beatrice's left nipple.

Pomeroy snapped, "Mary says, don't forget to strip the bed and clean the bathroom before you leave. The cleaner won't be in until Monday. We will bring our own sheets and towels!"

"Don't forget to bring the Flit while you're about it." Reiss banged down the receiver for the second time.

Beatrice said, reprovingly, "You shouldn't speak like that to your wife."

CHAPTER SIXTEEN

Reiss was being overcome by the heat of the flames as he tried to open the car door and pull David out. He knew David was dead but still felt he should to try to give him the kiss of life. Someone though was hindering him, dragging on his arm and telling him to stop. Calling his name. The police searchlight was dazzling and the stench of burning flesh made him want to gag and he threshed about shouting, when Beatrice's voice filtered into his consciousness: "Raymond! Wake up! You must wake up! You are having a terrible dream. Wake up, now, please!"

He opened his eyes, trembling and found himself soaked in sweat. He was with Beatrice in a strange bedroom. Disorientated, he asked in English, "Where am I?"

"The Swan Hotel, Pangbourne."

"Oh, yes - of course, Oh dear, I'm so sorry. What time is it? Did I wake you?"

Beatrice grasped his wrist with firm professional fingers. "You were shouting and crying. Your pulse is over a hundred even now."

Reiss wrenched himself free. "Stop that, I'm all right. It was a bad dream, that's all."

"You have had this dream before?"

Reiss explained about David's accident.

"It might stop if you talked about it with me?"

"I doubt it. I'm going for a pee, now."

"This macho behaviour is very stupid. You should talk this through with me, it might help, you." Beatrice pursued him determinedly into the bathroom. "Tell me what happened."

Reiss explained, briefly.

"Yes, that is terrible. He was your friend?"

Reiss muttered, "More colleague than friend, but that's irrelevant."

"Were you on bad terms?" Beatrice stroked Reiss's ruffled hair.

"No, *mein schatz*. We had quite a good working relationship. I need a shower now."

When he returned to the bedroom. Beatrice was dressed and packing her case. "We have time for a little walk before I leave for the airport?"

They made their way along the tow path beside the lazy green river where ducks were diving and splashing. Above, in the leafy branches of the trees, birds fluttered and cheeped. They sat on a bench facing the water.

Reiss took Beatrice's hand. "There is something I regret."

"What is that?"

"A party I organised for David."

"Wasn't he pleased?"

"I think actually he quite enjoyed it until the Lady Boy from Bangkok turned up. Looked convincing as a girl, but with all the usual gear in his knickers. He'd been very affectionate to David who didn't realise he was a bloke until he'd stripped down to the bare essentials. At that point David totally lost it and he threw up over the carpet. It was gross and horribly embarrassing for everyone."

"Do you dream about this man because you feel guilty about that?"

Reiss shook his head emphatically. "No, *Frau Doktor*. David deliberately misled me into thinking he was gay when he wasn't."

"That is very strange, no?"

Reiss agreed that it was. Later, when he drove Beatrice to drop her off at Heathrow, she commented, "I think that if your father were still alive you would have discussed this man's behaviour with him?"

"Perhaps, yes."

"I think, very probably. Was he a good doctor?"

"I believe so. Meticulous and he had a kind manner. His patients loved him."

"Did he die long ago?"

"Two years, now. I got a call at six in the morning from his mistress. She was hysterical. She'd woken up to find him dead in bed beside her. He must have had a massive coronary in the night. She didn't know Papa was eighty; he looked less and he lied about his age He dyed his hair and was pretty fit, considering."

"Dyed his hair?" Beatrice sounded, shocked. "Will you dye your hair, too?"

Reiss laughed, "No, I won't."

"Is that how *you* want to die? In bed with your mistress?"

"There are worse ways to go. He was a widower for thirty years. My mother died when I was fifteen."

She sniffed, disapprovingly, "I think you are a lot like your father, Raymond."

"We didn't look that much alike, actually."

She hissed, "I was not talking about your appearance. I think you learned from your father to be a meticulous, competent and even a conscientious physician. That is the good part he taught you. What is not so good is that he taught you that women were sex objects for your pleasure."

"He did nothing of the kind. That's complete rubbish."

"He did, Raymond. Why else did he send you to a brothel at the age of seventeen?"

"So I could make women like you happy, Beatrice."

"While you are cheating on your wife with me? How do you think that makes me feel?"

Beatrice burst into tears and pummelled Reiss fiercely with her fists so that the car swerved alarmingly. Luckily he had turned on to the slower airport road. It was definitely time for Beatrice to return to Stockholm.

He snapped back, "You knew from the start that I was married. I wear a wedding ring and I don't take it off."

She sobbed, "I don't want to share you with your wife."

Reiss groaned, "No, please. It's been such a wonderful three nights, can't we leave it like that?"

She sniffed, "You will not leave your wife for me, will you?"

"I never said I would. I love her."

"You love her? And you still sleep with her, too, I suppose?"

"That has nothing to do with you."

"But I am jealous of her, because when you get back, she will be waiting for you and you will make love to her, instead of me, won't you? But I will go back to my empty flat and Steffie will say, "Mummy, you look a bit sad. Why is that?"

"You say, my tears are of joy at seeing you, Steffie." Reiss pulled over to let Beatrice out. "We have children and our careers in different countries. We both have heavy commitments. Your work is in Sweden and mine is here in England. That's how it is. We meet now and then and it's wonderful, but then we go back to our separate lives."

"I think I am getting too fond of you. We have to end it."

Reiss said, rashly, "No, don't be so hasty. Let me think about it. Perhaps I will speak to Sally about us ... "

Beatrice shivered, "When will you do that?"

Reiss prevaricated. "Not now. I'm up to my ears with the R/P trials. Perhaps after they're finished and the results are all in. We can see how we feel, after Bayreuth, can't we? You might be sick of me by then."

Beatrice nodded, appeased.

Reiss came round with her case and with some relief waved her goodbye.

CHAPTER SEVENTEEN

June 2001

A week after Sarah Goodwin's article was published in New York, someone in Flat Acres had pinned up a photocopy of it on the Barn notice board. Her description of Reiss was highlighted in a lurid shade of pink. Underneath, the same person had affixed a typed note with a drawing pin:

"AUTHORITARIAN DOCTOR OF GERMAN PARENTAGE SEEKS NUBILE YOUNG MISTRESS TO BE DISCIPLINED STRICTLY ACCORDING TO TRIAL PROTOCOL."

Reiss pulled them both off and screwed them up before tossing them into the bin.

"Any idea who did this?"

Bill shook his head, smirking. "None at all, Chief. Meant as a compliment, I'd say."

Reiss said, "Not sure about that. Whoever it was, better not do it again."

He strode out to the car park, so that Bill would not see his grin. Bill hurrying to keep up, now asked, "If Sarah flies to Washington to be at the press conference can you give her my photos of our weekend? I'll put a note inside it and address the envelope so if you don't see her you can just post it on?"

"Of course," Reiss said. "No problem. You like her a lot, don't you?"

"I do. I've never met anyone like her. She's so feisty and so different - and such fun to be with."

"Yes, I'm sure..."

Three days later, on a Thursday morning in the second week in June, Reiss was on the plane to Washington. Even travelling club class, he felt cramped and he found himself becoming increasingly irritated as he read through the paper that Tim Scott had prepared for him to present to the FDA. It had arrived minutes before he left for the airport and fell below Tim's usual high standard. Reiss, clucking his tongue, began redrafting it on his laptop, hoping the battery would last long enough to complete the job. Tim's syntax was sloppy and poorly expressed and he did not like the way the data was set out. Fortunately he had time to make most of the changes needed before the battery died and he had to stop work. Ahead lay back-to-back meetings that began with FIP's American lawyers and legal and medical representatives from Oribo and Sion, both of whom were now keen to collaborate with FIP to produce and market Reduktopan in the USA.

Reiss stowed the laptop and reclining his seat leaned back and closed his eyes. He knew that Tim was concerned about Sylvie's pregnancy. Tim, now quite matey with Bill, had confided in him, who had in turn confided in Reiss that Sylvie's blood pressure was high and they had now found protein in her urine. Preeclampsia, now a real possibility, even a probability, was a danger for both mother and baby. It could result in the need for a premature delivery.

After an hour Reiss rose and paced restlessly up and down the aisle for a few minutes, thinking of the two days that lay ahead. He was glad that Dr John Stannard from A.C.E. would be accompanying him and Marlon Strelitz for their meeting with the FDA in Rockville. Stannard was an old hand at this while Reiss was a relative newcomer on the scene. His paper was dependable, if dull.

As they were about to serve a meal, Reiss resumed his seat. When his tray was removed he snoozed, then watched a bad film, then read a book to pass the hours of an endless afternoon as the plane soared westward.

When Reiss at last disembarked it was late at night in Europe so he did not phone Sally and Joanne in Cambridge or Beatrice in Stockholm; they would all be fast asleep by now. Not so Dr

J P Singer of Camden Town, London, who had told Reiss he went to bed late and slept only a few hours each night. Indeed, he might even now be trying to find his way past David's protective passwords and computer codes. He had told Reiss it would "take time."

Carrying his bags and his bottle of duty-free single malt, Reiss emerged through immigration and customs into the crowded, airport concourse. A hefty smiling black man was holding aloft a large sign for a Dr Raymond Rice.

Reiss approached him cautiously. "I think you may be waiting for me?"

"You are Dr Raymond Rice? Flown in from London, England?"

"Yes."

"That's great. I'm Jake, Mr Strelitz' chauffeur. Did you have a good flight?" Jake took Reiss's case from him. "Follow me. The car's right this way."

They stepped out into the shimmering late afternoon heat.

"Wow. It's so hot."

Jake wiped his perspiring forehead. "Yeah, it's something, ain't it?"

They crossed the huge parking lot and halted at a gleaming white Lexus sedan with dark tinted windows. "Don't worry. Be cool as a cucumber in no time. This car's got real good air conditioning, Dr Rice. You can sit back and relax, now."

They set off at a stately speed on the busy highway. Chilled by the blast of icy air, Reiss watched the low rise Washington panorama flashing by as they approached the city centre. They swept along the grand swathe of Pennsylvania Avenue and skirted the White House where multiple sprinklers were sending misty spray down on to the curving green lawns.

In the rear view mirror Jake eyed Reiss's handsome face that wore a rather set expression. He decided not to mention the hotel desk clerk's prowess at finding *"anything you want, man, and I mean anything, man."* Instead, he said, "Tomorrow morning I'll be driving you and Dr Stannard and Mr Strelitz out to Rockville, Maryland. On Saturday, we'll be heading down south for a visit with Senator Rogers, who lives out Virginia way."

Reiss nodded, "Is the hotel near Mr Strelitz' office?"

"Right around the corner, Dr Rice. But if you prefer, I can pick you up tomorrow morning? It's no trouble."

"No, I'll be glad of the walk, thanks all the same."

"Mr Strelitz will meet you in the lobby of the hotel this evening at seven thirty. The restaurant's booked for eight. It's over in Georgetown. It's kind of a swanky place. You'll need a coat and tie, Dr Rice."

"Also a shave." Reiss grunted and rubbed his stubbly chin.

A bellhop carried his bag to the reception desk. The Charter House Hotel was small by American standards, with one hundred and fifty luxurious rooms, recently refurbished with Japanese money. Strelitz, whose firm acted for the Japanese consortium, had arranged an advantageous room rate for his clients. Reiss took the plastic key together with a message that Sarah Goodwin of the New York Globe had called him. She had left her number saying she would be at her desk till seven. There would be a message waiting on the room phone too.

Upstairs in his room on the ninth floor he rang her. Tactfully, he praised her article as incisive and readable. "Will I be seeing you at our press conference tomorrow evening?"

"I can't make it, sorry. I have prior assignment downtown here in New York at four."

"That's a shame. I - er - was hoping to buy you a good dinner." Reiss managed to sound regretful, while hoping she would refuse.

"You *were?*" Sarah sounded genuinely surprised.

"Well, er - I have -er - Bill's photos and his letter to give you, but I can just post them. We can meet up another time, I'm sure."

There was a short pause, then Sarah said: "I *could* make dinner in Washington, if I catch the six o'clock shuttle. I can charge the fare to the paper if I can interview you about the American scene during dinner?"

"Well, yes, but I've only just got here?"

"First impressions are the best ones, Dr Reiss."

"Do - er - call me Raymond, Sarah..."

She laughed. "Thank you, *Raymond*, but I've got used to thinking of you as Dr Reiss. It kind of suits you."

He said, a little amused, "As you wish. Will you be wearing your white suit again?"

She laughed spontaneously. "So you can be sure to recognise me? I'll see."

CHAPTER EIGHTEEN

Even with his blow-dried hair and the lifts in his custom-made shoes, Marlon Strelitz was barely five feet four. He shook hands with Reiss who noted that his chunky gold cuff links bore his initials and his nails were manicured. They had spoken over the phone several times but had never previously met. Reiss, warned by Pomeroy that Marlon was "one sharp cookie", was wary of him. He was a partner in a prominent law firm, and had the reputation of being one of the most effective lobbyists in Washington DC. He had started life as a trial lawyer and learned that to avoid an ambush you needed do your groundwork and be well prepared.

At the "swanky" restaurant in Georgetown, Strelitz explained how he rated FIP's options and how best to proceed with marketing Reduktopan in the States and Canada. Oribo Chemicals Inc had initially offered more generous terms but Strelitz favoured Sion as a better long-term partner and was confident they would raise their offer to match Oribo's in due course. But for this to happen they would need to convince Senator Chuck Rogers and ensure that he backed the deal. He was one of Sion's most influential directors and they would need him on board. Waggling a stubby finger, Marlon Strelitz set out the position in plain language. "You need to watch your step with Chuck Rogers, Ray. Senator Rogers is a 300 lb pro-lifer. He will like the idea of a slimming drug that works, but he's totally opposed to abortion. So if you're in favour of women's choice, don't tell him. Keep your views to yourself. But if he does ask for them, just say you don't approve. Right?"

"Yes, I get it." Reiss poured himself another glass of aromatic Californian chardonnay and yawned as the waiter removed their plates and took a furtive look at his watch. "Am I boring you here, Ray?" "

No, but it's three o'clock in the morning in England."

"You're not in England now, Ray. You're in Washington, DC."

Strelitz leaned forward and added, earnestly. "Ray, as your company's lawyer, it's my duty to warn you straight out that you must never lie to the FDA."

Reiss retorted, irritably, "I have no intention of lying to them, Marlon, and I find the suggestion that I would, rather insulting."

Strelitz brushed Reiss's objections aside."Because if you *do* lie and they find out that you lied, you're dead and buried. They won't treat with you or any company that employs you inside or outside the USA, ever again." Strelitz waggled his finger again, to better emphasise his point. "But, that doesn't mean you have to give them any more information than they've demanded, but what you must not do is lie to them or fabricate, is that quite clear?"

Reiss yawned. "You've made that *very clear*, thank you."

Strelitz' dark, glittery eyes focused on Reiss's face, calculating, evaluating and assessing. "I have a contact inside the FDA. He says they will hammer you over the late Dr Devereaux' ADR and the drug's toxicity potential." He pronounced the name as "Devro."

Reiss snapped, "David had an idiosyncratic adverse reaction. He made a full recovery and the bowel samples that were analyzed after he died prove it beyond a shadow of doubt."

Strelitz said sharply, "I thought his body was badly burned."

"The internal organs were better protected."

Strelitz was undeterred, "If Devereaux hadn't got sick, you wouldn't have known he had tried the drug on himself, would you?"

"No, he didn't tell anyone what he was up to. But he owned up immediately when I found him lying on his office floor." Reiss pursed his lips in recall.

"I guess he told you quickly because he wanted to be sure he got the best treatment?"

"Yes, you could be right."

Strelitz changed tack. "Devro may have had a few shares, but he wasn't on a bonus scheme linked with the drug's success? Was he a fat guy who needed to lose weight?"

"No, not at all. He was quite thin. Did a lot of distance running to keep fit."

"So why take the risk of trying the drug on himself?"

Reiss said shortly, "He regarded himself as a healthy volunteer and he was exceptionally unlucky to get that ADR. A drop more wine?"

Strelitz said wryly. "No, thanks. A little goes a long way when you're vertically challenged like I am. And Ray, as your company's lawyer, I am advising you not to have any more wine tonight. You need to keep a clear head for tomorrow. You'll already be dealing with jet lag and the time difference. Don't add to that."

Reiss nodded and put down the bottle, obediently. Strelitz changed tack, abruptly. "Will John Stannard's figures stand up to scrutiny?"

"Yes. Our in-house statisticians checked them not once but twice."

Strelitz grinned, "FDA likes catching you Brits out." He hesitated, "Your accent, your way of speaking might come across as a little patronising to some people. Can you tone it down a little?"

"No, Marlon, I can't. But Stannard's got a strong, flat Birmingham accent. They can focus on that and feel good about themselves."

Strelitz laughed and motioned to the waiter to bring him the bill.

"Sarah Goodwin did a neat little profile on you, Ray. My FDA mole wondered if there was something going on between the two of you?"

Reiss shook his head, indignantly. "You have to be joking? Absolutely not. She spent the weekend with my young assistant Bill Ryder, not me. And her write-up on me was hardly flattering: she made me sound like a Nazi concentration camp doctor. And I'd like to point out that I'm not of *German parentage.* My parents were refugees from Vienna in 1938."

Marlon smiled. "They speak German in Austria and that's where Hitler was from."

Reiss said, angrily, "My father was Jewish. He had to run for his life after the Anschluss in 1938 like Sigmund Freud, of whom you will no doubt have heard?"

"*I* know all that, believe me, Ray. But you can explain that to Sarah Goodwin yourself when you next meet her." Strelitz smiled showing his white capped teeth. "Obviously, I denied there was anything going on between you. I said, 'Ed, come on, Raymond Reiss is getting on for fifty. He has a nice wife and two grown up daughters. What would he be doing with a woman in her twenties? He's old enough to be her father."

Reiss scowled at him. "I'm not nearly fifty. I'm forty-seven."

"Forty-eight in a couple of months?" Strelitz folded his napkin neatly. "But, that comment made me think. So, acting as the company's lawyer, I took it upon myself to make a few enquiries about both you and Sarah Goodwin, Ray."

"That's outrageous."

Undeterred, Marlon Strelitz continued, "From her photo in the NYG, it's obvious that Ms Sarah Goodwin is a very pretty woman and the word is she's stunning when you meet her in person. Masses of natural red hair and a great figure, was the description that came back. And she has a bit of a reputation with men, Ray. She's had a lot of boyfriends, some of whom have helped her to advance her career. Journalism can be a cut-throat business."

He paused a moment, then looked directly into Reiss's blue eyes. "And you, Ray, I discovered, have earned yourself quite a reputation as a ladies' man. *Quite* a reputation. An *international* reputation, which explains why Ed at the FDA was so suspicious. And if *he* wondered, others will too. Just so you know. So if I were you, I'd step carefully there."

Reiss hissed furiously, "Then it's a pity I didn't know all this a bit earlier."

Defensively, Reiss explained his dinner date with Sarah Goodwin the following evening. "It was Marcus Pomeroy's bright idea that I should wine and dine her, not mine."

Strelitz looked put out. "You both should have consulted me first."

Reiss snapped, "I wish I had, but we can make it a threesome if you like?"

Strelitz replied, seriously, "Unfortunately, I can't make it. I have to attend a law function, but I could send someone from my office."

"No, that would really make it worse."

Strelitz's dark eyes flickered. "Well, just make sure that woman catches the shuttle back to New York after dinner is over. She can't miss the last flight because it goes right through the night, Ray."

Back at the hotel, Reiss was still asleep the next morning when he was woken by Bill's call at eight o'clock New York time, but lunch time in Flat Acres. Bill sounded worried. "I thought you should know: Six people taking part in our trial have come down with 'flu-like symptoms, but so have Marilyn and Susie, who've been helping at the Pavilion, and a couple of other Pemberton staff and Jim Menzies went down with it last night. It's nothing to do with R/P. And Ayesha's rushed off to Bradford. Her father's got a serious heart problem. We're a bit thin on the ground here, now. The nurses are great, though."

"If you need cover, call in one of the company medics, Bill. There are a couple who are quite useful." He named them both. "And Simon lives in the Village like you."

"Yeah, I know. I'll alert them both in case. I haven't stopped anyone taking R/P as I didn't think that was indicated. Do you agree?"

"I agree. Keep it under review. And don't let any of these overweight people lie around in bed for a minute longer than necessary. Get them moving. We need them to stay active. We don't want them developing pulmonary embolisms or DVTs.

If they're not dizzy and in danger of falling get them moving, even if it's exercising in their bedrooms."

Bill said, "Speaking of falls, I'm afraid Dora Shane had a trip going down the terrace steps this morning. I think she's twisted her ankle quite badly. She was most put out when she couldn't see the top man, and it was me not you. I'm sending her to the District General for an x-ray, but I don't think she's broken anything, fortunately."

Reiss sighed, "Is there any good news?"

Bill laughed, "Lisa-Jane's lost a few pounds and found herself a boyfriend this week. He's that West Indian bus driver from South London. He seems a very decent bloke. Too good for her, but I hope he'll keep her on the straight and narrow."

After wishing Reiss good luck with the FDA and the press conference, Bill enquired a little too casually, "Will you be seeing Sarah while you're out there?"

"Yes, She's flying up from New York to join me for dinner tonight in return for my giving her my first impressions of Washington. I'll give her your photos and letter then, don't worry."

CHAPTER NINETEEN

At nine sharp the next morning they set off in Strelitz' Lexus for the FDA meeting in Rockville, Maryland. Strelitz took the front seat beside Jake leaving Reiss and John Stannard to sit in the back, where they occasionally muttered privately. This did not please Strelitz, who would swivel round awkwardly to check on his British charges, who were securely strapped into the car's pale leather seats. They reached the outskirts of the gigantic model compliance city in about forty minutes and were soon passing a series of bland, low rise office blocks set back from the road on smooth irrigated green lawns. The neat pavements were empty of pedestrians. Nobody walked in Rockville. The people on the sidewalk were waiting for the shuttle bus.

Stannard murmured to Reiss, "It's all a bit modest here compared with Nine Elms Lane, don't you think?" They both fell about laughing hilariously.

"Huh? What was that?" Strelitz, was suspicious of jokes he could not share.

"We were comparing Rockville with the MCA's headquarters in London at Market Tower, Marlon."

Strelitz asked in disbelief, "That's not bigger than Rockville, surely?"

Stannard snorted, "No, but it's easier to park there. The first time I came here I had to drive back to the outskirts and take a cab back in again."

Strelitz said, with a superior smile, "That's not a problem this time. Jake will drop us and fetch us later, when we're through. I'll phone him on his mobile to let him know when we're ready to leave."

The three men were deposited outside a large and impersonal building. At the reception, their names were ticked off a list and they were given visitor badges and then left to wait.

Stannard whispered, "We're three, so they'll be five. They won't risk being outgunned."

Strelitz shrugged, "We're haggling about terms. I think they'll grant your IND approval pretty soon now. The real fight comes later when you apply for your product licence to sell the stuff. It'll be easier when you have one of the big local firms with you."

He glanced up, catching the receptionist's eye. She nodded.

Marlon said, "Okay, they're ready for us. Let's go up."

Stannard and Strelitz were right: there were five people on the panel and they did chip away at David Devereaux' serious adverse reaction.

Reiss argued, defensively. "Dr Devereaux' ADR was unlucky and idiosyncratic. We've run the trials for weeks now with well over two thousand people taking part and we've encountered nothing like what happened to David. No serious side effects or anyone dropping out. You will agree that's both very unusual and encouraging."

"You've excluded anyone with diabetes since then, I believe?"

"As a precaution, yes. But I am not convinced it was the trigger in his case; his diabetes was very well controlled at all times."

Stannard commented, supportively, "Our further rat and mice studies that followed that event don't support the diabetes theory and it is not as if David was insulin dependent."

Reiss said, irritably, "He and I had agreed we would give him a minimal dose under close observation in April this year, but unfortunately he died a couple of weeks before we were able to do that. "

Strelitz repeated, "We need this product badly in our country. One in every four people in the US is obese and it's getting worse by the day."

The panel knew of the press conference later that day and disapproved. "We know you're in a big hurry to get it on the market and we don't want to hold it up without good reason, but we feel we need more time to consider your data and we will do that when at least some of your multi-centre trials have ended."

Reiss and Stannard remained silent as did Strelitz. This had been foreseen. The chairman, who might have benefited from a course of Reduktopan himself, glanced round at his colleagues, then concluded. "We'll let you know our decision when we're ready. Meantime, we expect you to inform us if there are any further significant adverse reactions."

"Of course."

Travelling back in the Lexus, Strelitz said, "We can stir up the demand for Reduktopan over here. Put a bomb up their pants. We need to keep the pressure on them."

After a disappointing press conference in Strelitz' law offices, Reiss returned to his hotel with a dull headache. He lay on the bed and fell asleep, waking with a start half an hour before he was to meet Sarah downstairs in the lobby. He was feeling a little disorientated. Knotting his tie before the mirror, Strelitz' words from the previous evening now reverberated, unpleasantly. Sarah's (long list) of boyfriends now included Bill Ryder, whose bill for a two night stay at the George & Dragon and two Michelin starred dinners had been paid for by FIP's slush fund. He picked up the envelope containing Bill's photographs and letter; it would perhaps be as well if the FDA did not learn of this friendship. Dismissing the unwelcome vision of Bill and Sarah entwined under the duvet in the four poster bed that he had enjoyed himself in the past, Reiss instead brought up Singer's number on his mobile.

"You have impeccable timing, Dr Reiss. I have made a little progress; I've breached the first of his passwords." Singer laughed softly, raising the hairs on the back of Reiss's neck. "Give me a call from the airport when you return on Sunday; I may have something more for you by then."

Reiss, feeling a little on edge after this brief conversation, rode the elevator down to the lobby where he saw Sarah was waiting for him. She had on her white suit with her blue lapis necklace strung around her pale neck. The flaming mass of auburn curls quivered over her shoulders as she came forward to shake his hand and then again as they stepped outside. A bell hop whistled for a taxi that slid forward from the nearby rank.

As they sat beside one another on the worn back seat, Reiss pulled down the armrest between them, mindful of Strelitz' warning, and gave the driver the name and address of the restaurant that Strelitz' secretary had booked for them: the New Caprice in Georgetown.

Inside its expensive, dimly lit air-conditioned interior, elegantly dressed and coiffed diners sat at tables that were covered with blue cloths. A suave maitre D, wearing a midnight blue tuxedo and a scarlet bow tie and matching cummerbund, greeted them enthusiastically. "Dr Raymond Reiss? Yes, we have your booking. I understand you're a friend of Mr Marlon Strelitz? Follow me, please, your table is ready for you."

Evidently, Strelitz was a valued client as their table was well placed. The Maitre D promptly produced two large menus framed in fake leather (Sarah's had no prices on it), and an exorbitantly expensive wine list before removing Sarah's jacket to hang it away; She was wearing a blue top that toned with her necklace. Sarah had style, he acknowledged, but Reiss was concerned that anyone seeing them out together would be likely to draw the wrong inferences. He thus took care to keep a distance from her and was awkwardly correct to the point it looked stand-offish as he passed over Bill's sealed and fat envelope that contained at least half dozen photographs.

"Thank you. I'll look at this later." Sarah dropped the envelope into her capacious shoulder bag that bulged with her notebook computer, a dictating machine, a paper pad, pens and a camera.

In the background, in between the musical accompaniments, was the sound of a gently gushing fountain that looked to have been plucked from some nineteenth century chateau in Italy or France. Beyond the fountain there was a long table where eight immaculately suited Japanese business men were eating and chatting, in between episodes of standing and bowing and taking flash photographs and several videos of the room. One stood on a chair to do this, smiling toothily, before sitting down once more.

"They look like they're celebrating something?"

"They probably just bought up General Motors?" Sarah responded with a touch of bitterness. Her attention had switched to a smaller table where a harassed man of about thirty-five was unevenly splitting his time between a very small girl in a primrose yellow frilly dress and a bored blonde wearing a strapless one.

"See that guy? I bet you he's recently split up from his wife and that he has access to the kid this weekend and the baby sitter let him down. He had a date he didn't want to cancel. Oh boy, there's going to be trouble there, if he's not careful."

Reiss turned his head to see the child slide down off her chair and run unsteadily to lean over the basin of the fountain where she trailed her chubby hands in the water, which swirled away to be recycled and spouted out again from the open mouths of the three scantily clad stone nymphs. Grateful that his little daughter had found a peaceful diversion, her father was concentrating his attention on the blonde, who did not augur well as a stepmother.

Reiss frowned disapprovingly. The kid was not much more than two years old. She should have been at home tucked up in bed with her teddy bear. He turned back again to see Sarah was pulling off her chunky blue clip earrings. "They look pretty with the necklace. Why are you taking them off?"

"They pinch." Sarah rubbed her red earlobes and dropped the earrings on the tablecloth between the cruet and bread basket. "Ten dollars down the drain. They're just plastic, not real lapis like the necklace but I was tempted by the colour. I'll give them to a thrift shop, tomorrow."

"Why not get your ears pierced if you like to wear earrings?"

"I'm scared of needles."

Reiss smiled indulgently at this admission as the waiter returned with a dish of savoury nibbles and a bunch of large purple grapes on a dish. He shifted the bread basket and chrome wine bucket aside to make a space for them on the small and now crowded table, before rising to retrieve the small girl who was in the process of wading into the fountain. He led her back to her father who sat her down once again.

"Thank you."

The blonde pouted. "She wasn't doing any harm playing in the water, was she?"

Minutes later the child slid off her chair and came towards their table. Sarah leant forward and switched on a beaming smile, "Hi, what's your name?"

"Kerry. I like candy. Want candy."

"We haven't any candy, Kerry."

The child dropped on her hands and knees and began annoyingly tugging at Reiss's shoe laces. Reiss shuffled his feet and bent down. "Kerry, you must go back to your Daddy, now."

"I want candy."

"I haven't any. How about a grape?" He cut one into two halves and handed them over.

She ate them, and then a few more, before returning to her position under their table and again began pulling at his shoe laces. Reiss, losing patience, carried her firmly back to her father, who said, "I'm sorry if she was bothering you. Sit down honey, so Daddy and Wanda can eat their dinner, now."

Kerry squealed and ran back to the ornamental fountain and dabbled her hands in the water as Reiss returned to his table to continue his analysis of the obesity problem in America, while with his agreement, Sarah recorded him speaking.

A few minutes later he felt his laces being tugged undone again. He bent down to grab Kerry, but before he could do so, she had stuffed something into her mouth and ambled off once more towards the fountain. On the way, she began to cough loudly and violently. Her father left his seat and picked her up and holding her over his shoulder, thumped her on the back, but the coughing continued and she was now scarlet. Reiss watched uneasily as her spluttering became increasingly distressed and her colour was turning dusky and pushing back his chair strode towards them.

"I am a doctor. I'm afraid your little girl has something stuck in her windpipe that's stopping her breathing; her change in colour is due to lack of oxygen. I might be able to help you."

The restaurant, formerly noisy with conversation had fallen silent save for the taped music. The Maitre D now came rushing over, saying anxiously, "I've called an ambulance but they said it won't get here for at least ten minutes more like fifteen."

Reiss said, "It could be too late by then. She could be dead or permanently brain-damaged even if she survives. Do you agree to let me help you?"

"Please, please, doctor. *Do something*. Anything you can to save Kerry!" Her father was sobbing in distress. Reiss took the choking child and started the infant Heimlich manoeuvre, snarling at the hovering maitre D, "Turn off the music and turn up the lights as bright as they go. I need to see what I'm doing, here." He checked her tongue and her throat. "Whatever she swallowed is too far down for me to retrieve it and it's blocking her windpipe and she's suffocating.

"Bring me your emergency medical kit, everything you have. I want some clean cotton wool, heavy duty strong plaster and a couple of clean drinking straws, the strongest biggest ones you have. Now! And a clean glass filled with whisky. If you have a clean, small sharp fruit knife, bring that too! Now! Right now!" He said sharply to the father, "What's your name?"

"Gavin Black."

"Gavin, Kerry's brain is being starved of oxygen and we need her to start breathing again. I need your permission, as her father, to do a tracheotomy. I want you to give me your permission in front of witnesses because I need to make a hole in her windpipe and insert a tube so she can start breathing again. If I don't do this, she will suffocate and die, but if I'm successful, she will live and when the ambulance takes her to hospital the surgeons there can operate to remove the obstruction and close the wound. Doing an operation like this in these conditions is tricky. It's quite dangerous. But I don't see any alternative if we're to save her life. I'm telling you straight: I'm not an ENT surgeon, I'm a physician, but I will do my best to save your child, but it is possible I may fail. Do I have your permission to go ahead, now?"

Gavin spluttering agreed, "Do whatever you need to do. Just don't let her die or be a cabbage for the rest of her life, please try and save her."

Reiss lay the child's limp twitching body on the hastily cleared table and slit the top of her dress open with his penknife "I need two volunteers, one on each side of Kerry, to hold her shoulders and keep her very still. Give me those cushions. I need to raise her back up and then let her head tilt back. I need to get at her neck. I will need to press down on her quite hard to cut a hole into her neck. If I miss the spot we're in big trouble, here."

Two volunteers, now! Nobody squeamish. A middle-aged man and woman came forward, reluctantly. "I'm a dentist and my wife is a nurse, "We can hold her still for you but we can't do more than that. You're brave, sir to take this on."

"What choice is there? What are your names?"

"I'm Sam and my wife is Maisie."

The maitre D rushed forward carrying a first aid box containing plasters and cotton wool and disinfectant a bunch of straws and a full glass of whisky and a small fruit knife. Reiss shook his head. "Not suitable. My penknife has a sharper point; I'll use that." He dropped the blade of his Swiss Army knife into the glass of whisky to the sound of indrawn breath around him and then sliced a straw he placed on a strip of gauze taken from the first aid box and left it there.

Gavin's cheeks were now streaming with tears and he was crying.

"Get back Gavin. I don't want you getting in my way; it will be distressing for you to watch this. Sam and Maisie I need you to keep Kerry like this. Very, very still. Hold her tightly with her shoulders raised on the cushions. Reiss tilted her lolling head back and swabbed her neck with cotton wool soaked in disinfectant and counted down the cricoid cartridges.

Behind him Gavin Black was snivelling. "The baby sitter had a cold. I should have stayed home tonight. It's my fault. I should never have brought Kerry here."

Reiss snarled, "Everyone be quiet, now! There's only one spot I can go in safely. If I miss it I can do Kerry a lot of damage. I could hit an artery, a major nerve or her vocal cords." He glared around him and bellowed, "I *need complete silence.*"

The muttering ceased and there was the sound of breath being drawn in sharply.

Marking the hollow depression with his left forefinger, Reiss pressed the steel tip of the blade into the child's pale, soft flesh so that red blood began spurting out, then manipulated the straw into place, holding it with one hand, pressing her with the other, taping it in while listening for the faint whistle of breathing. He taped the straw more securely and pumped her chest gently; the straw shivered but stayed in place. He cut the straw a little shorter with scissors and pumped her chest until he was sure her shallow breaths were spontaneous. Then her eyelids flickered and she began whimpering.

"Hold her arms down Sam and Maisie. Don't let her move or pull the straw out. She's breathing through it. It's her lifeline." He hauled his leather belt from its loops and trussed Kerry up. "Sorry, I know this looks brutal, but I can't risk her grabbing at the straw and pulling it out. It's sore and it's what she'll try and do. Look, her eyelids are flickering, Gavin, she's starting to come round. I want your face to be the first one she sees now."

"Is she going to be all right?" Gavin was heaving with emotion. "Yes, I think so. Look at her." The child was gasping and grizzling and thumping the heels of her small shoes against the table. "Keep her on her back. Don't pick her up, you have to comfort her lying down like this as best you can. Poor little poppet, I wonder what she swallowed. He stroked the child's chubby cheeks and pinioned arms, then glanced up to see Sarah, tape recorder in hand, and then turned to see the Japanese businessmen who were standing on their chairs, still videoing and snapping as if they were spectators at a circus.

Kerry, her eyes now open, was straining against the restricting belt around her arms and kicking her shoes harder against the table. "Wah! Wah! Daddy!"

Sam and Maisie, smiling with relief, continued to hold on to her.

"Try and fill your lungs and cry, there's a good girl!"

Kerry wailed weakly to a round of applause.

"You were brilliant!" Sarah shouted. She leapt forward and hugged Reiss and kissed him on the lips as the Japanese business men continued videoing and snapping and people shouted and whooped. "Bravo, doctor! Bravo!"

Reiss removed Sarah's arms from around his neck.

"They were filming me? All the time? Glad I didn't mess it up ."

He wiped his brow and took a sip of the whisky, as people clapped.

"I heard one of them calling CNN who are sending a team over here. They'll be here any minute. They'll want to film you climbing into the ambulance with the kid and her father and I will want that photos for my newspaper. You'll be front page news tomorrow morning." She took out her camera and snapped Reiss standing beside Kerry's twisting, furious little body, saying, "I just did what I had to. I'm glad I could help."

"I need to phone in the story to our news desk. I can hear sirens. The ambulance will be here in a minute. As soon as I know where they're taking her, I'll follow you in a cab."

Reiss nodded, then, whispered in her ear, "Check the table

where we were sitting. If you can only find one of your blue earrings hide it and dump it somewhere else."

Sarah looked horrified, but said, "Sure. I'll get our things."

As Gavin ineffectually tried to comfort his little daughter, Wanda was refreshing her hair and lipstick before CNN arrived. "Calm down, Kerry, sweetie, Daddy's here. I know it's sore, but it'll be better soon."

The Japanese businessmen, still standing on their chairs, continued filming as CNN arrived, immediately followed by the ambulance crew, who sent them out again. The uniformed paramedics strapped the moaning Kerry onto a stretcher and loaded her into the ambulance with her father, who begged Reiss to come with them, so he leapt in after them as cameras rolled.

Sarah who had retrieved a single earring discreetly, then made a lightning deal with two of the Japanese businessmen, was now dictating her story over her mobile phone for the News Desk as she looked around for a taxi to follow the ambulance.

The late news desk editor said, "You're telling me this Limey doctor, who has no licence to practise over here and no insurance, operated on that kid using his *penknife*? He's either very brave or very stupid. Didn't he realise that if the kid had died with his penknife in her throat he could have faced a manslaughter charge? And a lawsuit for millions of dollars?"

CHAPTER TWENTY

Back in his room Reiss snapped off the television and poured a second glass of the Charter House Hotel's complimentary champagne. "Everyone's making too much fuss."

Sarah remarked smiling, "Most doctors would have stayed hidden until the ambulance arrived. You're a hero for twenty-four hours, so make the most of it."

"Well, let's hope Senator Rogers will be impressed by all this rubbish."

"Senator Rogers? The pro-life activist? The anti-abortion campaigner? Wait a minute? Isn't he also a director of some big pharmaceutical company? Are you seeing him while you're over here?"

Reiss said, softly, "This is strictly off the record, Sarah, please."

She nodded, "Okay, okay, off the record. On the record, you promised you'd demonstrate the Heimlich manoeuvre to me."

He bit into a smoked salmon sandwich. "Not unless you eat something. Anyway it's a different procedure for children than for adults."

Sarah nibbled at a strawberry.

Reiss grabbed her arm, "If you don't eat some of these sandwiches I'll tell Kerry's creep of a father whose earring got stuck in her throat. And let me tell you, her father is a complete shit. In the ambulance, he told me he would sue the restaurant for a million dollars because they have insurance."

"They can counter sue. This is America, Raymond Reiss. You took one hell of a chance. OMG. If that kid had died, you'd have spent the night in jail."

"I couldn't just stand by and let the child die, Sarah."

"And you saw her mother arriving at the hospital, didn't you?

She's worse than Gavin, so my guess is that Kerry will grow up to be a little monster. But still, you did the right thing as it turned out. Nobody else I know would have dared to try it. You're a big risk-taker, Dr Raymond Reiss."

Sarah ate a sandwich reluctantly.

Reiss stroked the locks of auburn hair with his finger tips and pushed them back. "My, my, what pretty *silver* earrings, you have on tonight my dear." He let the hair fall back. "What have you done with the other one?"

"It's in a city trash can. Thanks for the warning. I pretended I was looking for my pen."

Sarah came round now and leaned against Reiss's chest, "You promised you would show me the Heimlich manoeuvre in case I needed it."

"No, I didn't." He pushed her away. "Ask Bill when you next see him. When you thank him for his love letter and his pictures. Bill will be delighted to demonstrate it with you, I'm sure."

"He can't demonstrate it down the telephone wire, Dr Reiss."

"It's rough. You'll have me up for assault."

"Come *on,* I'm consenting, for Christ's sake."

He twirled her round, "Cough, you're choking, cough a lot."

She coughed, feebly. "I put my arms around you and shove my fists knuckle to knuckle under your rib cage. I press down hard five times like this."

She gasped, "Stop, that really hurt!"

He hauled her round to face him. "Open your mouth wide. I have to check the airways are clear and see if you've sicked up the obstruction and you're not swallowing your tongue." He lifted her chin, flattened her tongue and looked down her throat. "Still got your tonsils. You'll live. If the patient's unconscious you can use the heel of your hand - it's a bit different with kids."

He patted her bottom and pushed her away. "Enough now. I'm tired. I want to go to bed."

"Can't I try it on you?"

"Two minutes, then. If you must." She came behind him and put her arms around his chest, "I can feel your heart beating."

He guided her hands firmly to the correct position and balled them into tight fists.

"Knuckles edge to edge." His large hands covered her small ones. "Push inward and upward five times and check the airways - that will do, now."

She dropped her hands and touched his swollen crotch.

He pushed her hand away, "Always get one when you don't want it."

"*But I do want it*, Doctor Reiss. I want to share this big bed with you. Such a waste for only one person to be in it all alone, don't you think?" She reached out for his trouser zip but he pushed her hand roughly away.

"Sarah, I'm a married man with two grown up daughters. I've got a lot of commitments and I'm in the middle of a very important clinical trial. I've enough on my plate without starting an affair with you. And what about Bill? It's not right. You need to leave. Go back to New York, now." He backed away. "Eat another sandwich and catch your shuttle home. Please Sarah, go now. I don't want to shaft Bill and my life is already complicated enough as it is."

"You needn't worry about Bill. I didn't exactly sleep with him; I had a period and I gave him a hand job instead."

"Must have been a good one, Sarah, Bill seems *very* smitten."

She rubbed herself like a cat against his legs, "Never mind about Bill now."

She slipped out of her skirt and jacket and began unbuttoning his shirt. He caught her fingers and kissed them. "As long as you agree that we're two ships that pass in the night? We go our separate ways after this, as if none of this ever happened. Is that a deal?"

"If that's the way you want it."

"It's the only way it can be."

"Then I agree to your terms, Dr Reiss."

He massaged her small firm breasts and kissed the pert pink nipples as she unzipped his trousers with deft, fingers and caressed his swollen member. With his hands cupped over her round neat buttocks Reiss drew her closer to him and kissed her.

"Dr Reiss, I think you've wanted to fuck me since the first day we met."

"You're a stunning girl, Sarah. What man wouldn't?"

He let go of her and went to bolt the door then took the phone off the hook and turned off his mobile. Then he came across with the complimentary platter of fruit. "Eat something, now. Anorexia is very unattractive and so is bulimia. Are you hearing me?"

"Yes, I hear you."

She ate two grapes and he licked her ear, slid his hand over her stomach and down between her legs, admired her flaming bush, before ardently making love to her. Exhausted, they both lay back and flicked between the different news channels, which included brief interviews with Reiss who kept saying any he was sure any doctor would have done the same in his place.

"Not round here they wouldn't. They'd be terrified. The lawyers have seen to that."

There were interviews with Sam, the dentist, and his wife, Maisie, who were recorded by the Japanese businessman saying they would hold the child still during the operation but were fearful of assisting the doctor in case it went wrong.

As Sarah reluctantly dressed to catch the shuttle back to New York, she told Reiss she felt that the time had come for her to think about settling down and having a family to which Reiss had responded that Bill would make her an ideal husband. He would send Bill to the USA for a visit after they had tied up a collaboration deal. He closed and locked the door behind her and fell asleep.

He awoke the next morning after a strange dream in which

David Devereaux was performing surgery on Kerry with Sarah watching him. Then Sally had walked in, asking what on earth was going on?

A still photo had been extracted from the video footage that showed Sarah kissing Reiss. Unfortunately, her mass of hair hid the look of surprise on his face. It was widely reproduced, reaching the inside pages of some English newspapers by the following day, along with photos of the operation.

Sally, though proud of her husband's brave Samaritan gesture, was understandably suspicious of his relationship with Sarah Goodwin. "You never said she was young and glamorous when she came to Pemberton. Funny, you forgot to mention that?"

Reiss had patiently reassured Sally. "Sarah is dating Bill. The silly woman flung herself at me on the spur of the moment. If today's meeting goes well, there's a good chance FIP will close a deal in the next few days out here."

"Will you be needed for that?"

"I'm afraid so." It would mean flying out to New York. "Could be as soon as Friday. Sorry. It means I'm away another weekend."

"When you can take Sarah Goodwin out to another restaurant?"

Reiss shouted, "No, Sally! If the deal happens, I will be going with Marcus and our London solicitors to meet our American lawyers. And Sion will have their entourage in tow as well. We won't be inviting Sarah Goodwin along. And if she does turn up, I'll leave her to Marcus Pomeroy to entertain."

Sally had snapped, "Whatever. And as for the weekend, I'm accepting the Blunts' invitation to stay in their house for a bridge and walking weekend."

"Don't you need four people for bridge?"

"John will be there as well."

Reiss had then to speak to Beatrice, who had not yet seen the photographs. He said, with some truth, that if she had been there with him they could have operated on Kerry together.

He put down his mobile when the hotel phone rang. It was

Stannard. "Where are you?"

"Sorry, had a few calls to make. I'll be down in five minutes."

"Just so you know, there are reporters and photographers waiting for you in the lobby."

Reiss ate some of the fruit left on the dish and a stale cheese sandwich then took the elevator down to be met by a crowd of curious well-wishers as well as the reporters and photographers with flashing cameras. Reiss had just time to say, "I'm delighted that Kerry is going to be fine. I was just glad I was able to help a little..." as Strelitz and Stannard grabbed an arm each and marched him out. He shouted over his shoulder, "I just did what I'd like to think any doctor would have done in my place."

One reporter shrieked, "I wish! Most doctors would be too scared of being sued to do what you did! Our greedy lawyers have seen to that in our country!"

Reiss smiled for the cameras even as he was being pushed into the back of the Lexus with Jake grinning at the wheel.

"Where are you going, Dr Reiss?"

Reiss, barely visible behind the tinted glass, waved them goodbye and fell back in his seat as Jake accelerated rapidly away.

The drive to Senator Rogers took close to an hour as his ranch-style home was some fifty miles from the capital. He came out to greet them accompanied by Dr Chris Schwartz, who was the Medical Director of Sion and whom Reiss had met once before. He was friendly and agreeable.

Feeling a little up-staged by his British counterpart's hubris, Chris shook Reiss's hand, saying he was a brave guy, but it could have turned out very differently.

But there was no doubt that the publicity arising from the Kerry incident had been highly positive. FIP's PR team were making the most of it and highlighting the fact that it was this same Dr Reiss who was in charge of the Reduktopan trials at Pemberton Manor in Cambridgeshire, England.

However, when Reiss found himself alone with Strelitz, there had been another waggle of the lawyer's stubby finger. "I warned you Ray! I begged you not to get involved with that red haired woman. Now there are photographs of her with her arms wrapped around your neck and her mouth pressed against yours everywhere you look. Ed, my contact at the FDA, was killing himself laughing this morning, when I denied you were having an affair with her."

"I am not having an affair with her," Reiss parried, defensively. "She launched herself at me in the heat of the moment."

"Well, you'd better make sure it doesn't happen again. I mean, it, Ray. If she turns against you for some reason, she'll cut up nasty, you'd better believe it."

"We both agreed it was a one-off. We were ships that passed in the night. She knows that. She agreed."

Strelitz groaned. "What time did she leave?"

"She was aiming for the six o'clock shuttle. She said that way, she'd arrive early in her office."

"I don't like this at all. Very unwise, Ray. Edge away from her, tactfully. Don't upset her, but move her along to Bill if she likes him too. I told you she had a lot of boyfriends and you've just added yourself and him to her list."

Reiss scowled, but said nothing more. Other than this discussion, that took place in the men's toilets, the meetings went smoothly and seemingly well. Sion had, as anticipated, improved the terms of its offer to surpass those of its rival Orion Chemicals. Strelitz said his office would prepare the contract on the basis of the agreed heads of terms. Meantime, FIP's share price was rising, satisfactorily.

CHAPTER TWENTY-ONE

Reiss took an overnight flight from Washington to arrive at Heathrow on Sunday morning; he achieved a reasonable night's sleep as the airline upgraded him from business to first class for his return journey. He was, for a very short time, a celebrity with everyone wanting to shake his hand. But back in England, jet-lag and fatigue came over him as he waited to pull his case off the baggage carousel at Heathrow. And in a few days time he would be flying back across the Atlantic to New York. In between lay a busy few days and after that he would be overseeing the last weeks of the Reduktopan trials.

As he waited for the shuttle bus to take him to the short term car park, he dialled Singer's number,. Singer told him he had seen the news clips and congratulated him before remarking, "I have something for you."

"Lara's notes?" Reiss's heart missed a beat.

"No, sorry, not Lara's notes. Two very different files. I'm at home this afternoon, if you want to come over?"

Reiss drove to Singer's house from the airport. The traffic was heavy round Camden Town on a Sunday afternoon as visitors came in droves to the vast, sprawling street market and it was hard to find a parking space. Eventually, however, he was pressing Singer's bell and waiting impatiently on the doorstep. Nobody came. Reiss rang twice more, this time keeping his finger on the button. He was tapping in Singer's number on his mobile when the front door swung open.

"Sorry, I must have dozed off in the garden. I don't sleep well at night, unfortunately."

"I'm sorry I woke you then."

"No, please come in." Singer's face was pale and drawn and

his clothes looked looser than Reiss remembered from his first visit. He followed Singer up the stairs to his study. "Saw you on TV, performing that operation on that American kid. It was amazing. Lucky for her you were there. I didn't think you were a surgeon?"

"I'm not. Just some basic training twenty years ago."

Singer grunted, then drew down the green roller blinds cutting off the view of his narrow sunlit garden. "I'll show you the graphics first."

Reiss pulled up a chair and sat down beside Singer and watched his nimble white fingers expertly activate the mouse and keyboard. "Your colleague was quite an expert, like you said. Smart guy."

"Have you accessed his menu and the directories yet?"

Singer shook his head, glancing at his notebook, "No, it's rather hit and miss at the moment, but I will get there, given time." He keyed in a stroke and turned to Reiss. "What do you make of this image?"

Reiss exclaimed, "It's a still from a scan of a fetus in *utero*. I'd say it's about thirteen or fourteen weeks gestation. Something's a bit odd about it."

"It's dated November 28th 2000."

Reiss nodded and put on his reading glasses to study the image more closely. He was frowning. "Oh, dear. No, I don't like this at all."

"Because it's sucking its thumb?"

"No, no, that's quite normal. I was referring to the baby's spine. And there's something about the shape of the head that doesn't look right, either. I'm no expert in this field, but still, this is definitely not good. Not good at all." He traced the image lightly over the screen with his forefinger. "Are there any more photos like this?"

"Five more. Shall I run them through?"

"Very slowly, and stop when I tell you, please."

Singer activated the mouse. A different view of the fetus came up on the screen. Reiss commanded, "Stop, go back to the previous one again. Hold it there. Yes ... " He studied the image carefully and then pointed, "On this picture the baby's turned a little. If you look carefully, you can see the spine better; look at the base of it?"

"It's not properly continuous?"

"No and look at the head here. It's taken its thumb out. Next image... stop. Yes, see that? Poor little mite."

"Is it handicapped?"

"Severely. Never seen anything like it. I doubt it would survive more than a few minutes if it went to term and was born. This must have been David's and Lara's baby, or why else would he keep this? She must have had a termination. This is sad. What a shame for them."

"When does life begin, Dr Reiss?" Singer murmured, pedantically.

"Life is a process; it is a continuing process, until we die. Let's not get into that debate now, please, Dr Singer. Can you print these photos out for me? I might show them to a radiologist, rather than hand him the complete disk."

"I've done that for you already."

Singer handed him a sheaf of papers secured with a split pin.

Reiss flicked through them. "I just so wish I could read the notes he made on Lara."

Singer asked, "Are you afraid your new drug caused this deformity? Is that what's worrying you?"

Reiss said brusquely, "We have always assumed the worst outcome and our guidance makes it crystal clear that you do not give R/P to a woman who might become pregnant let alone one you know is pregnant. We have no conclusive evidence that it causes fetal abnormalities but after thalidomide, no manufacturer in his right mind will let a pregnant woman touch a new drug in the first trimester, or even after that." He added musingly, "Most congenital abnormalities like these aren't caused by drugs, Dr Singer. It's more likely they're due to some error in the genetic blueprint or a problem in the gestating mother, but still, it's worrying, yes, of course it is."

Singer persisted, "So David would not have let Lara have your drug if he had thought she was pregnant?"

Reiss said, shortly, "*Absolutely not. He would never have let her near it if he had thought she might be pregnant.*"

Reiss was now wondering privately if the fetus had been analyzed for any impact by Reduktopan, perhaps even by David, himself? He could have asked for the tiny body saying they wished to bury it and, before doing this, he may have performed a basic post mortem himself. Macabre and unpleasant, but not impossible. David had been, first and foremost, a research physician.

Singer said softly, "I wonder if the abortion is linked with her suicide? She must have been very upset by this?"

"It's possible, but there is a four month gap between the two events. But his notes would tell us." Reiss stuffed the photographs into the A4 brown envelope Singer handed to him.

"You said there were two files?"

Singer cleared his throat. "Yes. There is another. David called it *Shadows.*" He pointed to a plain brown A4 envelope on his desk. "I printed everything out for you to read, but my advice is that you should wait until you are alone and somewhere private. You may find the content upsetting?"

Reiss stared at him, unease spreading. "Why? What's in it?"

Singer knotted his thin white hands. "I honestly debated with myself whether I should just destroy this rather than show it to you. But I felt I shouldn't. It concerns er- activities of members of your own family."

Reiss shouted, "What do you mean? What kind of activities?"

Singer snapped, "You'll see. Just don't blame the messenger, Dr Reiss. It's all in the past, anyway -"

He broke off as Reiss snatched the envelope and ripped it open and began reading through the typed pages. He felt physically sick; the colour drained from his face leaving it ashen and he sank down on Singer's desk chair. "The bastard. I just can't believe it; him and Sally in bed? Was it to get back at me? No, it was six months *before* that stupid birthday party."

Singer mumbled, "I should have held this stuff back. He never meant you to find out and he's dead, now. My advice is to try and forget about it if you can."

Reiss covered his face with his hands. "How can I forget about any of this? David and my wife? And then Mandy goes running to him when she's in trouble? He's been intimate with my wife and my daughter, the slimy bastard?"

"Stay calm, Dr Reiss. Don't go straight home. Take a walk, take some time to reflect. You've had a shock, but these notes were never intended for your eyes to see. I'll wipe this file from the hard disk, shall I?"

"Yes, erase it at once. I wish I could erase it from my head as easily."

Reiss rose, and carrying Singer's two brown envelopes filled with unpleasant information, went unsteadily downstairs. Singer paused before opening the front door. "You said David had an answering machine. Did it have a single tape for in and out-going messages or were there two tapes?"

"Two tapes."

"Those old machines don't erase automatically. Messages are erased when you record something new over the old messages. Most people leave the tape running forward till it gets to the end and then they rewind it and the old messages are erased as new ones are recorded over them. It occurred to me that you may find some old messages of interest still on that tape. There might be something that tells you about the abortion? Or what was happening between the two of them before she died, or before he had the car crash?"

Reiss stared, momentarily distracted from his misery. How stupid of him and Marcus Pomeroy not to have realised this earlier. He bit his lip. "You're right, of course, Dr Singer. I will play the tapes through from the start when I get home."

Singer said, quietly, "Dr Reiss, you're tired after your long journey and you've had a shock. Take my advice. Please don't drive home to Cambridge straight away. Take some time to think carefully before you do or say anything to anyone else. Especially to your wife and your daughter. These events are all long in the past and perhaps it's for the best that you leave them there. David didn't expect you'd find out about them and it wasn't his intention that you should."

"I know that. But I have." Reiss said, bitterly.

CHAPTER TWENTY-TWO

Clutching Singer's two brown A4 envelopes Reiss walked on weaving his way through Camden Market's thronging crowds, past busy stalls selling clothes, antiques, jewellery, handicrafts, books and bric-a-brac. Eventually he found himself by the bank of the canal where it was quieter. Further along there was an empty bench daubed with red graffiti. He sat down and with trembling fingers pulled out the typed pages and read through them once again. The last sheet was Singer's invoice. He asked only £25.00 for his disbursements. Singer was an honest man. An honest man whom Reiss felt he could trust. Who knew Reiss's wife had betrayed him with David. The bitter taste of this was compounded by the subsequent behaviour of his darling younger daughter, Mandy, who had turned to David for help and not to her father when she got into trouble.

Staring down into the murky, green canal water, with the envelopes on his knees, Reiss tried to get a grip on his mixed and seething emotions of fury, sadness and bemusement. Singer was right to emphasise that David's brief affair with Sally had ended after Christmas, the previous year, almost eighteen months ago. There had been no passionate desire on either side as was all too evident from David's diary style notes.

Mandy's unwanted pregnancy was more recent. The putative father was a schoolboy of eighteen whom she had not told and she had been desperate to end it without her parents finding out, most especially her "overbearing" father. Like it or not, it was clear from Mandy's behaviour that David was right to conclude that she was terrified he would find out about it and desperate that he should not.

David had been a most reluctant confidant. He had urged her to own up to her parents, but Mandy had begged him to help her and he had done so. He had acted with professional competence, kindness and discretion and paid all Mandy's medical bills at the clinic, noting, ironically, that from their disapproving attitude, some of the nurses thought he was responsible for her wretched situation.

While Reiss hated the intimacy that had been created between David and his daughter, he was, reluctantly, grateful to David for helping her.

The affair with Sally was another matter. It was both disturbing and repugnant. He imagined the two of them in David's bedroom, with the curtains closed, because, Sally, though *a nice woman* was not really his *type*, his note admitting that his taste was for petite girls and *not Amazons with big boobs*. But how could Reiss sit in judgment on Sally? After the way he behaved himself? Indeed, David had noted, somewhat sanctimoniously, after he had comforted Sally and cuckolded Reiss a number of times:

S is aware RR cheats on her quite regularly. Said that the first time she knew of it was actually on their honeymoon in Paris. They had a row over something stupid and he stayed out all night and returned next morning stinking of cheap perfume. They fought and had unprotected sex to make up and Joanne was the result.

Reiss walked back to the car. He set off for Cambridge, keeping to the slow lane. A few miles from home, he pulled up in a lay by and called Sally on his mobile, even then uncertain whether to confront her or to try to put the past aside. She had just returned from the Blunts' cottage in Cromer and was in a more friendly mood than when he phoned from Washington. Had John, the bridge playing college bursar made her feel good about herself? He would not need to make love to her in the dark like David had done. But it would not have happened if Reiss had not neglected Sally the way he had.

At the other end of the line, Sally's voice repeated, "Raymond? Are you still there?"

He said, "What? Sorry?"

"I said, I've asked the Blunts and John round to join us for a drink this evening. To toast your success in America with that little girl."

He snapped, "You might have asked me first. I need an early night. I'm horribly jet-lagged."

She said coolly, "They won't stay long. And if you go to bed too early, you won't sleep."

She had then put Joanne on the line. Joanne, had not escaped mention in David's notes on his family; Mandy had confessed to him that her sister sometimes took recreational drugs at a party. Joanne, happily unaware of this, declared that her father was "brilliant" and she was very proud of him. Her voice drifted to and from him in waves as fatigue threatened to overcome him. He muttered, "Everyone's making too much fuss. I couldn't leave that poor little kid to suffocate to death."

Joanne said, "Daddy, you're famous. Mandy sent us an email from India half an hour ago: she was in a smart hotel coffee shop and your face came on the TV. When she told them she was your daughter, the hotel gave her tea and cakes on the house.

"Oh, and Mum says she's put a bottle of champagne in the fridge and you'll feel better when you've had a nice hot bath?"

He said, "A nice hot bath ... yes that sounds good."

Still parked in the lay by, Reiss thought again now about the photographs of Mandy that he had retrieved from David's sitting room. Was that when she told him she had missed two periods? That she felt sick, bloated and scared? Was it before or after he had unlocked his examination suite in the Pavilion and with his gloved hands performed the bimanual, after which, he had noted:

Enlarged retroverted uterus consistent with stated LMP (4.4.) Refusing to let me speak to Sally or her GP let alone RR. Terrified it will get back to "Daddy". Desperate not to have TOP recorded in her NHS records as he might see them. Has to be done privately. Wants TOP+++ Counselled her. She has no money except what she's saved up for her gap year and was planning to leave on her travels in October. I agreed to "lay it out for her". I won't see it back. We both know that, but never mind. I won't miss it.

In his vintage MG David had driven Mandy to a clinic in London. He had instructed the anaesthetist to avoid the veins in her hands and arms as the marks left there would be more noticeable than on a foot or ankle. He had stayed with Mandy in her room until she went into theatre and then walked along the street for a dismal session of root canal treatment for his troublesome and irregular teeth. When this was over, several hours later, he had sat with Mandy until she was fit to be discharged and driven her slowly back to Cambridge, noting later:

Long chat in car home. Worried re bleeding +. Advised her this should soon lessen. If does not, she should call clinic or me - but from an outside phone. Feels awful. Depressed + Glad she's going away in October with her friends. First stop India.

Reading this again, Reiss recalled vaguely that during an early evening towards the end of last July or it might have been early August, he had come home from Flat Acres to find Mandy in bed. Sally whispered it was a heavy period and he had looked in to see her. Mandy, had looked very pale, humped under the summer duvet. He had kissed her and stroked her cheek and left her to sleep. Now he knew that Mandy, fearful of discovery, could not let David bring her home in the car. He had dropped her at the station so she could take the bus home, with the cover story she had been to London to see a friend there.

Making things worse for Reiss was David's laconic final comment:

M admits she occasionally takes Ecstasy and "other stuff" at parties. Says Joanne does too. "Everyone does." Warned her re drugs. Long chat. Promises not to take them again but I don't believe her. Plans to travel to Far East. Plenty of dope there. Warned +++ re-customs and not to be a stupid mule. Told her what could happen.

Reiss carried his bags into the hall of his rambling Edwardian house. Everything looked remarkably the same, yet it was not. It never could be again.

Notwithstanding, he acted on Sally's suggestion. Had a long hot soak in the bath before dressing in casual clothes and coming down to play the genial hero host and drank more champagne; he would feel hung over tomorrow morning, without doubt.

When the Blunts and John the Bursar had left he went into his study to retrieve the tape he had removed from David's answering machine. He locked it in his briefcase with Singer's two brown envelopes and Sarah's short letter for Bill.

Sally was reading in their shared bed.

Reiss lay back on the pillows until she turned out the light. Then, he made love to Sally as David had done before him. In a darkened room.

CHAPTER TWENTY-THREE

Bill congratulated Reiss on Monday morning.

"I'm sure you'd have done the same in my place?"

Bill hesitated, "To be honest, no, I'm not sure I would have. I've never performed a tracheotomy on my own."

"I'm one up on you, then."

Bill muttered, "Christ, Chief, you're brave."

Reiss handed him Sarah's letter. "Here, this is from Sarah. Don't worry about that stupid kiss. Heat of the moment thing. She misses you quite a lot, I think."

Bill took the letter eagerly, his fingers itching to open it, while Reiss explained about the proposed trip to New York if the deal was concluded with Sion. There might be the chance of a secondment there in September. If all went well.

Bill nodded appreciatively. He read Sarah's short letter eagerly, leaning against the wall while Reiss sorted his post. His in-tray contained two communications in German. A letter from Dr Wengler and a fax from Dr Beatrice Svenson. She had omitted yet again to mark this as "personal" with a cover sheet.

Reiss, recalling that Bill's CV had included GCSE German, asked him irritably, "Did you see these?"

Bill stuffed Sarah's letter back in the envelope. "Linda asked me to check if they were urgent, or if they could wait until you got back."

"You must have realised Dr Svenson's fax was a personal one for me, surely? Or did you need to read to the end using a dictionary to work that out?"

Bill protested too loudly, his cheeks colouring, "I didn't realise, initially, and by then it was too late. Sorry."

"What did you tell Linda?"

"I said you'd deal with both of them when you got back. I didn't tell anyone what was in Dr Svenson's fax, but she needs to be more careful. I can't be the only person in this office who can read a bit of German."

"Thanks for pointing it out," Reiss said, coldly.

Bill muttered, "I met Beatrice Svenson myself a few months ago. I recognised her name, because it's the same as the ice cream parlour chain. We sat next to each other at a meeting about six months ago. She was giving a short paper on endocrine function. She's tall, blonde. Great figure. All the men stayed on to hear her talk and half of them, including me, followed her to the bar and then to the gym. She speaks excellent English, doesn't she? I didn't realise she also spoke German."

"That will do, thank you." Reiss scowled. The incident left him uneasy. He would have to warn Beatrice to be more careful in future and hope Bill would keep his mouth shut, but he guessed he would tell Tim soon. Too good a piece of gossip to keep to oneself. The one bright spot was that Beatrice's fax had put Bill off the scent about Sarah.

As they walked across into Pemberton for the afternoon clinic, Bill told Reiss what he already knew. Sarah had invited Bill to stay at her apartment.

"Will you go?"

"You bet, I will."

Reiss grunted, "You do realise she's borderline anorexic?"

"We spent the weekend together. Of course I noticed. She says she wants kids in the future, but I reckon she could have lost her periods, for now. I warned her about it."

Not just a hand job for Bill, then? No, definitely not just a hand job at the George & Dragon. Reiss wondered what else had been edited out of Sarah's account.

Approaching the Pavilion they met Mrs Shane, hobbling along with her strapped ankle and waving her walking stick.

"Dr Reiss! It's great you're back! We all of us here want you to know how proud we felt seeing your pictures on CNN and in the newspapers."

Reiss thanked her graciously and then shut the door of his examination suite. The constant references to the Kerry incident were becoming tedious. He sat down and looked through the patient notes made while he was away. Everyone who had complained of "flu-like symptoms" was now feeling better. The manipulative Herman Orloff had, (unsuccessfully), tried to talk Bill into raising his steroid dose as soon as Reiss had left for Washington and Lisa-Jane had been found eating a bar of chocolate.

By contrast, Frank Miller, the youngest of the three Americans was turning into a fitness junkie; he had lost thirty-two pounds. More weight than anyone else at Pemberton or anyone taking part in the multi-centre outpatient trials so far. He turned up for his appointment that day wearing his baseball cap and his robe.

"Excellent." Reiss encouraged him. "Well done. I can really see a big difference. Keep it up. I'm really impressed. You're a model patient."

"I'm building on what I've achieved, every day. Each day I do a little bit more, like you said I should, Dr Reiss."

"If you keep this up, you're the front runner for our prize."

Reiss saw him to the door and picked up his bleating mobile.

Pomeroy said, "I'm in London at our solicitors' offices. Sion's contract runs to five hundred flipping pages. Bloody word processors, spewing out reams and reams of unnecessary rubbish. Takes hours just to wade through all the otiose garbage before you can cross it out."

"Got to do something to earn your salary, Marcus."

"Our solicitors are asking if we should wait for the FDA's terms before signing with Sion?"

Reiss said quickly. "No, don't wait. Sign up with Sion. I think the FDA will speed up and offer us better conditions with them on board. It will help us."

Pomeroy added, softly, "Come to me this evening with David's answer-phone tape, will you? Mary will be out tonight."

After a quick meal on his own in the Orangery, Reiss drove to Pomeroy's house which was off the Cambridge road, some seven miles beyond Pemberton Village. An individual, architect-designed, contemporary structure of red brick and triple glazed plate glass windows and solar roof panels, it was set in two acres of well tended, if dull, gardens. In an adjacent field, Marcus rented from a local farmer, two horses were swishing their tails as they moved around slowly cropping the coarse grass.

It was almost dark, and rain was slashing down as the Range Rover's tyres scrunched over the private gravel of the sweep drive. Reiss had previously only visited Pomeroy's house on social occasions with Sally; they invited each other over as couples about twice a year. Through the open window the sound of the nine o'clock news summary drifted towards Reiss as he waited under the cover of the porch for Pomeroy to respond to the bell.

Pomeroy, who had changed from his suit to navy chinos and a freshly pressed grey Ralph Lauren polo shirt, opened the door, commenting, "Your shoes are very wet."

"That's because it is raining, Marcus."

"Mary hates muddy shoe prints on the carpet. Wipe your feet properly - or better still, take your shoes off."

Reiss wiped them on the doormat with excessive vigour before following Marcus across the spotless expanse of creamy velvet pile into the large sitting room. It had a cathedral ceiling and the large windows looked out over the flat lawns and angular flower beds that were bursting with clipped bushes in bloom. The blustery wind had scattered rose petals like confetti over the manicured emerald grass.

Reiss walked past the three overcrowded display cabinets which were filled with simpering china figures (a dusting nightmare) and sat down on one of a pair of contemporary sofas. A side table held a collection of framed family photographs.

Marcus closed the door. "We've got an hour. Mary's never back till after ten and the kids are away at school for another week."

"Just as well. This tape isn't *Listen with Mother*."

Pomeroy nodded and poured out two large measures of Glenlivet and handed one of them to Reiss and raised his glass."Skol. Isn't that what they say in Sweden? Or do you prefer bottoms up?"

Reiss grunted, "Cut out the snide comments, will you. I want you to take a look at these graphics." He produced a text book on obstetrics that he had marked to fall open at an ultra-sound photograph of a fourteen week fetus. "Look at this and then compare it with these pictures." He dabbed at the paper with a fierce forefinger. "The spine doesn't connect fully with the pelvis and the skull is compressed at the top with an abnormal jaw line and not much of a nose."

Marcus asked, gloomily. "You think Reduktopan caused these abnormalities?"

Reiss responded, softly, "I honestly don't know. But the fetus is at its most vulnerable in the first trimester."

Marcus said petulantly, "I can't believe David would have been so irresponsible? He wrote the guidance himself and we've warned everyone till we're blue in the face, that it's absolutely contraindicated for pregnant women."

"I'm sure it was not deliberate if that's what happened." Reiss replaced the scans in their envelope. "But in time we'll know for sure. Singer will crack David's codes eventually, and when I can read his notes we'll know how it happened."

Pomeroy groaned, unhappily, "Raymond, I know you think this hacker chap is trustworthy, but I'd prefer to call it a day and wipe the computer now."

Reiss shook his head, slowly. "No, it's better if we know what's on it, first." He hesitated, "David had some personal information on me. He may have kept something on you, too, is my guess."

Pomeroy rasped, "What kind of personal information?"

"Something that would make you or me reluctant to sack him if he got into trouble?"

Pomeroy moaned, "If Mary finds out about Gina, there'll be blood on the carpet. You need to get that computer back before your hacker works out *he* can hold *us* to ransom."

"Singer's a man of principle, not a blackmailer. He's also ill. I don't think he's got very long. He's gay and his partner died recently of an Aids-related illness. I think the poor guy is going the same way. I reckon he'll be dead in a year or two."

Pomeroy said, wildly, "A year or two? Can't you speed it up?"

Reiss raised his eyebrows. "What did you have in mind? A lethal injection of potassium chloride? A big dose of insulin? It's called murder, so no, I'm afraid not."

Pomeroy ran his fingers agitatedly through his fine silvery hair, "Raymond, as long as this man Singer is alive, he poses a serious security risk to us both, and to the company."

Reiss shook his head. "He's guaranteed me confidentiality and I trust him, completely."

He loaded the cassette from David's answering machine into Pomeroys portable dictating machine to play it back. "We missed a trick first time round; Singer was right and luckily the message Lara's sister left was nearly at the end of the tape so all the earlier messages are still there. We start with David's dentist appointment."

Reiss turned on the machine. A woman's voice said, brightly, "This is a message for Dr Devereaux from Eileen, Mr Porritt's dental nurse. Mr Porritt can fit you in for an emergency appointment at 11.15 this Wednesday morning or alternatively at 4.30 on Thursday afternoon. Please telephone me and let us know when you'll be coming in, Dr Devereaux. I'll repeat, that's either Wednesday 11.15 am 17th November or Thursday 4.30pm 18th November. Thank you."

The machine bleeped. Reiss turned it off.

Pomeroy grumbled nervously, "What's his bloody dentist appointment to do with Lara's suicide?"

Reiss said sharply, "It helps date the messages that follow it. The fetal scan was dated 28th November. Listen carefully, now, this is Lara speaking."

A pleasant female voice said: "Hallo, David ... It's Lara. I'm still at the school. I had to provide cover for Jean today so I won't get away till eight thirty tonight, after all. Be back about nine thirty! Cook something nice for me. Slimming of course." The machine beeped end of message.

Marcus said, "She sounds okay there."

"Now listen to her."

"Hallo. David. The same voice but this time it was tearful and tremulous. "I have to take Jean's class *again*. She's still not well. I'm really tired. I didn't sleep a wink last night but you know that already. I feel so awful and I can't stop thinking about our baby. Promise you will stay with me the whole time and you won't leave me on my own? Come into the operating theatre with me and be there when I wake up. I can't face this on my own... I can't, David and I'm so sorry for you too..." She began to cry, then continued, "I stand waiting for the train sometimes and I think shall I do it? Throw myself under a train? Only thing that stops me is it's cruel to the train driver, isn't it?" She sobbed into the phone.

Marcus groaned, "Bloody hell."

"Wait."

"You said they'll suck the baby out of my womb and incinerate him. Our little boy will be going up in smoke. I know I'm being punished. But it's so cruel to *him*. I can't think about anything else. I want to scream all the time. Scream! Scream! I keep crying. People keep asking me what's wrong. I've told them my favourite aunt's dying of cancer. That I'll have to go and visit her in London and I'm dreading it. Knowing the sex of our baby makes it worse. Every time I pass a woman in the street pushing a pram or a pushchair I want to cry, and I can't talk about it to anyone but you. How I feel - I just want to die with our baby. Our baby, David. Our baby boy..." There was more sobbing.

Pomeroy said, uncomfortably, "This is awful. Awful, Raymond, and it feels intrusive to listen to it like this..."

Reiss retorted, "It gets worse."

"It's their private grief - it's voyeuristic, sitting here listening like we are-"

Reiss waved him to be quiet.

" ... You said it could have happened because I took those tablets I'd stored up. It was only a few, no more than six in all. I honestly didn't think they would matter; I'd started putting on weight and you were angry and told me my thighs were wobbling already. I know you hate it when I'm fat. I do, too. But it's my fault not yours. I was really sick this morning in the bathroom but I didn't wake you, did I?" There was a sob, then: "Why are you always fucking *out when I ring? Or are you just not picking up the phone?* I'm really dreading tomorrow, believe me..." There was a wail then the click of the receiver going down. The machine beeped end of message.

Reiss put it on pause.

"He'd have taken her to the Harley Street area, to some clinic. I wonder who the gynaecologist was?" He thought but did not say, "Surely not the same man who dealt with Mandy last July?"

Pomeroy said, soberly, "I feel sorry for both of them, actually."

Reiss fast forwarded the tape. "This is David's married sister, Anne."

A woman with a dour Yorkshire voice spoke: "David, we need to know soon if you're coming to stay for Christmas next week. If you want to bring her, she'll be made welcome, but she will have to stay in the spare room. Jamie and Ben can double up and you can have Jamie's room. You're both welcome as long as you understand that."

Pomeroy pulled a face. "Sounds a load of fun."

"He didn't go. Anne told me at his funeral. She said David went abroad somewhere warm with his girlfriend last Christmas.

Made it sound like he took a prostitute on a jolly. After the termination, we know from the tape that Lara was severely depressed. And I'd have expected stomach symptoms judging by her note and the autopsy findings."

"You said she rang him on the day she topped herself?"

"Yes, it was a Saturday. He was at home, but he must have turned off his mobile and left the answering machine on. She rang him a few times. Wanted to let him know how she was getting on. Ten, twenty tablets, thirty tablets. She told him she was spacing them out not to make herself sick. Then she started seriously on the gin."

"He didn't believe she meant it, I expect?"

Reiss shook his head. "Oh no, he knew she meant it. Listen to this:"

He fast forwarded the tape: Lara's voice quivered with distress. Words tumbled out incoherently, "David, please, please, answer me. I know you're there, David. This time I mean it. I will really do it. I've bought the tablets. I've taken thirty-five. Only another five to go and that's it. I bought the more expensive ones, the oval shiny capsules as they're easier to swallow." She was slurring her words. "Got some gin ... " a cackle of laughter, "Don't worry, it isn't yours, I bought it at Threshers." She giggled foolishly, "A special offer..."

There was a click and Devereaux' deeper voice cut in, "You're leaving it very late, Lara. You need to dial 999 soon or you'll have permanent liver damage. It's a nasty way to die, darling. I warned you before. You have to stop play acting now."

"You call the ambulance for me. Call it if you love me. I'm at the River Lodge Hotel. Room 16. I didn't want to die alone in the flat..."

"You called me, so you can dial 999 yourself. Do it now, Lara. Straight away, stop being histrionic and stupid."

Lara screamed, "You *want* me to die! You *want* me out of your life! I'm a liability for you, now! Do you think I don't know that? I'm not sure you *ever* loved me! You never said you did,

did you? But now I think you *hate* me! I feel sick but I'm going to drink the gin and when I've done that I'm going to throw my phone with your number on it out of the window. I'm on the third floor, so it will break when it lands ..."

"Dial 999 Lara. Do it, now, please."

"Bye, David. Love you. Always have and always will."

The call ended.

"She did throw the phone out of the window? He should have called an ambulance, he really should." Pomeroy was shaking his head in dismay. "No wonder he'd started drinking by then."

"Because of the guilt? Maybe? But Lara was a liability, like she said. She was threatening to ruin him professionally, this much is clear from her last message. Listen to it: "I'll tell my ... sister, Penny. Saw her yesterday - hadn't - spo -ken to her - for - three - no four - years- but - she - she - came - to see me- after school here and - I- told her my boyfriend is a very - very - ver-r-r-ry clever doc-tor - who - made - people - thin - like - me - she could - - oh - I feel so sick - woozy, David - woooozy -I'm throwing - the - the phone - out --- of the - win - dow - now - bye-bye ... ohh, God I feel terrible ... I'm going to be sick - oh -"

There were crackly sounds, the phone was dropped on the floor, then picked up. Lara's voice said, faintly, "You're there, aren't you? Listening? I wasn't sick. Stopped myself."

There was the sound of a bottle chinking. "I'd better have some more gin, now."

"Turn it off , I don't want hear any more." Pomeroy jabbed off the switch and hissed, "He can't have believed she'd really do it."

Reiss turned the tape on again. Pomeroy shouted, "I've heard enough, thanks!"

Reiss forced Pomeroy's hand away. "He needed to be certain she'd taken enough before he called an ambulance, you see. If he called one, but I don't think he did."

Lara weakly muttered, " ... I've ... had ... forty tablets ... and nearly all .. the ... gin - I feel really strange - have to crawl there

- ow - er "

There was a thudding sound of the phone being bumped around on the floor. "I opened the window - it feels very cold in here - David - very - very - cold - I hope - I don't - shit -myself - very - undigni- digni- fied - to ... be .. found - bye - darling - I'm sorry I let you - down - I did, I know. I - am -- throwing the phone out now - last - chance .... give you ... ten .. seconds ... say ...Goodbye. Won't you even ... say ... Good ... bye?"

There was the sound of sobbing for a few seconds. "Bye, David - feel - awful ... throwing the ... phone ... out now   can't ... speak ... any ... way ... if you want to call .. call ...

an...ambu...lance ... I'm ... in room ... don't ... remem...ber ... sorry ... bye ... "

A thud, then nothing. The tape ran a few more seconds and stopped.

Pomeroy whispered hoarsely, "Raymond, we have to destroy this tape. Don't you understand? David was guilty of manslaughter. He deliberately let her die when a simple phone call could have saved her?" Pomeroy wetted his dry lips.

Reiss ejected the tape and dropped it in his case.

"Raymond, I said, we must get rid of that tape."

"I may need to listen to it again in case I missed some of the nuances."

"Get rid of it. *That's an order, Raymond!*"

Reiss gave his Chief Executive a grim smile. "You can put that in a memo then? Get board approval?"

"If what's on that tape gets out, it'll be a PR disaster for all of us, Raymond."

"I'm not planning on broadcasting it to the nation. But now at least we know for sure that David had a supply of R/P and that he gave some of it to Lara."

CHAPTER TWENTY-FOUR

Carl Oldssohn escorted Reiss downstairs and out into the warm Stockholm sunshine. It was mid-June and the days were long and stretched out until ten o'clock in the evening. "Our research is going well at Uppsala. I am hopeful we will have some success with this new compound and there's always a big market for a good arthritis drug. I think our companies' collaboration has been most useful. But I suppose you are very tied up with your slimming drug trials right now?"

Reiss nodded, "Yes, but I will continue to handle this project personally, if I can; I enjoy my trips to Stockholm, the Venice of the North. Mind, it's better in summer."

Oldssohn smiled and shook his head. "Yes, Raymond. I agree. Our winters are very harsh."

Reiss grimaced wryly. "I was at that Gothenburg meeting in February when they closed down the airport for twenty-four hours. The only things moving in that blizzard were polar bears." Reiss shook Oldssohn's proffered hand. "It was good to see you again, Carl."

"You're sure I can't tempt you to some lunch?"

"Sorry, I've someone else I need to see and my plane for New York leaves at six."

Oldssohn traced a voluptuous female figure in the air. "Give my regards to Beatrice Svenson, then?"

Reiss frowned, "Who told you I was seeing her?"

Oldssohn shook his head, "Stockholm is a village, Raymond. Everyone knows everyone else's business and people talk. Beatrice is a beautiful woman and everyone notices her and where she goes. Johan Berg from Prost Chemicals saw you and Beatrice together at the Prague meeting last year. He had the room next door to hers and he didn't sleep well that night. He recognised your voice. He speaks German and he didn't miss much of your conversation by the sound of it."

"He should have taken a bloody sleeping pill."

"Well, he didn't. He couldn't rest in the afternoon either, when he tried. You need to be more discreet, Raymond, for her sake, as well as your own."

"He should have been in the lecture hall."

Oldssohn shook his head again. "So should you and Beatrice. Stockholm is not London or Paris or New York. There has been talk about you and Beatrice, I thought you should know that."

"People should mind their own business, Carl."

"They should, but they don't. You are a married man. An older married man and Beatrice is still a young woman, who needs a second chance with a new partner. That cannot be you. If she met the right man, who was unattached, she could rebuild her life with her child and perhaps even have another baby?"

Reiss snapped irritably, "She doesn't want to marry again after the first delightful experience."

Oldssohn gesticulated impatiently, "Ach, these independent women, they all say that. Beatrice is scared of failure, that's all. Her first husband was a real swine. A real swine, Raymond. He deceived her with other women, he had a child with another woman and he ran up debts in her name. She needs another chance. There are people interested of course, but while you are around she doesn't see them. You need to let her go now."

Reiss yanked open the door of his waiting taxi and climbed in. "Hotel Diplomaat."

Oldssohn waved as the cab drove off.

Reiss then leaned forward and said curtly to the driver, "I don't actually want to go to the Hotel Diplomaat." He read out Beatrice's address.

"That is in the other direction. I should turn round and go back, it's quicker." He braked in anticipation.

Reiss said hurriedly, "No, keep going. I don't want that

gentleman to know that I'm going that way."

The driver laughed. "*Ja, ja,* I understand."

Reiss let himself in using the key Beatrice had left him under the door mat. He had been there once before when they made love in her wooden-framed hard double bed. The airy, bright, modem flat furnished with angular furniture and geometric contemporary prints was, however, now silent and empty.

Reiss, prowled around restlessly for a few minutes, then went into the kitchen and took an apple and a can of beer from the fridge. Removing his shirt and tie he opened the balcony door and went to sit out in the warm sun. Beatrice would be back soon; she was taking the afternoon off to be with him.

He thought guiltily of Sally as he bit deeper into the crisp apple. She had told him she was sick of the hints and winks about his relationship with Sarah Goodwin and had refused his advances since their brief coupling the previous Sunday night when he had returned from Washington. On Tuesday evening he had driven back to Cambridge to find the house empty; Sally and Joanne were out at the cinema. Only the cat was around to greet him.

In bed that night Reiss had murmured, coaxingly, stroking Sally's thigh, "Come on, Sal? I know I've been away too much lately, but I'm here now darling?"

She had turned her back on him. "I'm not in the mood, Raymond."

"Put you in it, darling?" He had gripped her protesting fists and forced her back struggling.

She hissed, "If this is the only reason you came back tonight, you've wasted your petrol! If you won't leave me alone, I'll move into the spare room, and you can explain the reason to Joanne yourself."

Sulkily, Reiss detached himself. Sally pulled the duvet over her head and rolled to the farthest edge of the bed. He whispered in a hurt voice, "Sally, darling, you're the only woman I'll ever love. Nothing else counts, you know that. I love you."

She said in a miserable voice, "Leave me alone, will you?" Next morning he tried snuggling up behind when she was still half asleep. She quivered responsively then woke and pushed his hands away. "Stop it, Raymond! No, stop it!"

He pressed himself against her. "Sal, please, I'll be away in the States till *Monday*. I *am* your fucking husband, for Christ's sake."

She wrenched herself free. "You can stay away forever, for all I care! Stay with Sarah Goodwin or the next floozy you pick up on your travels."

He snarled unpleasantly, "Don't push your luck. You're not that irresistible these days!"

She shouted furiously, "And you are? Why would I want that thing inside me? I don't know where else it's been! And don't tell me any more lies! I know you fucked that American girl, I just know it! Just for once, couldn't you have kept your hands in your pockets and your flies zipped up?"

He almost blurted out then that he knew about her affair with David, but something stopped him. Instead, he taunted her with the new bursar.

She stared at him furiously.

"You've got a mind like a sewer." She was on her feet, her face screwed up in anger.

He apologised. "I'm sorry. I was jealous. Sal, please come back to bed. Let's kiss and make up?"

She pushed him away again. "No, leave me alone, will you?"

He went to shave in the bathroom. When he emerged, Sally had dressed and gone downstairs. At breakfast in the kitchen, with Joanne present, they were formal and polite.

He kissed Sally goodbye on the cheek. "Enjoy your weekend with the Blunts. Don't play too much bridge."

Sally turned her back to load the dishwasher.

Joanne asked, "Can you play bridge, Dad?"

"Badly. Not my game, sweetheart. Prefer something more active than cards."

"Can you drop me at the station?"

"Sure."

On the way, Reiss spoke casually of the dangers of taking drugs. He hoped Joanne wouldn't be tempted or dared into taking them from peer pressure. He said he was sure she had too much sense. She nodded but didn't respond. And as for Mandy in India?

Reiss swallowed the last of the beer and wiped his mouth with the back of his hand. He and Sally had weathered many storms in their twenty-one turbulent years of marriage. The row with Sally would blow over, but he needed to be careful for the next months.

He took out Oldssohn's report while he waited for Beatrice to return. The collaboration with Zastro Pharmaceuticals was convenient and gave him a legitimate reason to visit Stockholm on company business. But Carl's gentle rebuke was concerning. It bothered him more than he had let on. Perhaps it was time to end his relationship with Beatrice?

At that moment, Reiss felt a firm, affectionate hand on his bared shoulder; he had not heard the front door opening and closing. He looked up at Beatrice and smiled. She smiled back and said in German, "Come with me, my darling."

CHAPTER TWENTY-FIVE

The charming blonde girl at the SAS desk in Stockholm airport upgraded him to first class for the overnight flight. "We are very glad that you travel with us on SAS, Dr Reiss."

After a hearty meal, (there had been little time for eating with Beatrice) Reiss slept. He dreamed that he and Beatrice and his late father were walking together along the Kaerntnerstrasse in Vienna and Beatrice was asking his father whether he had met Freud?

His father told her that he had heard him lecture once.

In truth, Reiss found Beatrice's current interest in Freud rather tedious. She had even suggested Vienna as the place for their next rendezvous so that she could at the same time visit his apartment at Bergasse 19.

Reiss had during his last visit tossed away her new copy of Freud's *"Sexuality"* (in its original German and highlighted by Beatrice with an orange marker pen).

"He only had twelve patients. This is imaginative fiction, not real research."

They squabbled and bickered, then made love.

But by now Beatrice had been shown the photograph of Sarah kissing him and was a little jealous as well as suspicious. Reiss licked her ear.

"Don't be silly, it was a congratulatory gesture! Sarah is dating my handsome young assistant, Bill Ryder."

Nonetheless, Beatrice had sunk in her teeth and the faint tooth marks persisted, hidden under his shirt, when Reiss arrived at Kennedy Airport the next morning. A battered cab drove him jerkily to his hotel where the uniformed desk clerk, who had metal braces on her teeth, welcomed him enthusiastically.

"Hi? The rest of your company's party" (Stannard, Pomeroy and three city lawyers) "checked in an hour earlier. I can upgrade you to one of our super-executive suites on the thirty-second floor if you don't mind being on a different level to them?"

"Sounds good to me. Thank you, I'd like that."

"I recognised you from the news reports showing how you saved that little girl's life last week. It was amazing. You were *amazing*." She smiled, offering him the full vista of her orthodontist's handicraft.

Upstairs, enjoying the splendid view from the plate glass windows of his vast sitting room, Reiss plucked a plump, juicy strawberry from the complimentary fruit dish and checked out the opulent bathroom and bedroom. There was a silver wrapped chocolate on the pillow of the huge bed. He unpacked his case and then checked his mobile which held two messages he had ignored. The first was from Marcus Pomeroy, (room 2034) "We need to talk." The second was from Sarah Goodwin who explained she was a member of the Executive Health Club on the tenth floor of his hotel. She would be there until around 8.30 am and after that at her desk if she was not out on an assignment. Could they meet up?

Reiss meditatively munched a fig. It was two minutes to eight, New York time and barely twelve hours since he had left Beatrice in her Stockholm flat.

The Health Club was a public area and should be a safe place to meet up. He rubbed his neck which was aching as he felt the tension rising. A swim followed by a warm shower might help relieve it and he could hand over Bill's letter at the same time.

He sent Marcus a one line text saying he would see him in an hour, then, wearing his swimming trunks under the hotel's white fluffy towelling robe, Reiss took the Executive Elevator down and exited at the Health Club floor. There were only two people in the small pool and one of them was Sarah Goodwin in her goggles and a white rubber swimming hat. A stout man was paddling gently up and down on his back.

Reiss put on a genial smile and said, cheerily, "Hallo, Sarah. I got your message."

"Hi, Dr Reiss. Did you have a good flight?"

"Yes, thank you. Very good."

He dived in, making a big splash, which unfortunately prompted the stout man to get out immediately, so that they were left on their own. Reiss swam for a few minutes before climbing up the steps. Wrapping his robe around him, he handed over Bill's letter, preparing to depart soon after. "Sarah, forgive me if I don't hang around, but I'm already late for a meeting with Marcus and our lawyers."

She nodded. "I need to be off myself. But I wanted you to see this as soon as possible." Leaving Bill's letter on the plastic table, she dug a different envelope out of her shoulder bag that was on a chair. It had the imprint of New York Globe on its front. I've printed out an email that came to me yesterday at the NYG. It's from England; the writer saw some of my article reproduced in another publication there. I'd like your and Marcus Pomeroy's responses to it before I reply to her. You'll see she's sent me copies of the correspondence she had with Marcus Pomeroy a few weeks back. Her name is Penelope Wilson and she says her sister, Jane Lara Bucknell was Dr David Devereaux' girlfriend. What do you know about that, Dr Reiss?"

Reiss shook his head. "I never met her. I didn't even know of her *existence* until after they were both dead. I heard about this woman's claim via Marcus. You have to understand that David kept his private life to himself."

Trying not to show his dismay, but with a sinking heart, Reiss pulled out the typed sheets and glanced over them before stuffing them back into the envelope. "Like I said, I know nothing about David's relationship, if there was a relationship, with this woman."

"Yeah, I get that. This lady, Penny Wilson, complains that your CEO, Marcus Pomeroy, brushed her off good and hard. Take it and show it to Pomeroy when you see him. I want to talk to both of you while you're over here in New York. Please."

"Yes, I'll make sure that happens."

Reiss held tightly on to the unwanted letter with his damp right hand. One of us will phone you to arrange a meeting, but today is impossible. Tomorrow, perhaps?"

"My phone number and desk extension is on the letter. You already have my cell phone. I'll wait to hear from you?"

CHAPTER TWENTY-SIX

The view from Marcus Pomeroy's suite on the twentieth floor was similar to the one from Reiss's (larger) sitting room, but the people walking and jogging round the paths in Central Park looked like larger ants than from twelve floors higher.

Reiss sank down on the sofa as Pomeroy read Penny Wilson's email before dropping it on the coffee table between them. "What's to stop this bloody woman from writing to every paper and T V station here in the States? This email can be forwarded everywhere and the libel laws in this country are a joke. Plus, of course David's dead, so he can't be libelled anyway. His reputation is up for grabs. But you *can* libel FIP and this needs careful handling. We need Sarah on our side in this, Raymond. You have to keep her sweet and make sure she discourages this bloody Wilson woman. I know Marlon was put out when he found out you'd been to bed with her, but it could come in useful, if you can influence her with pillow talk?"

Reiss looked uneasy, "No, I don't want to repeat that. It was a one-off. And Marlon should have kept his mouth shut."

"With photos of her kissing you everywhere? What is everyone going to think?"

"She took me by surprise."

"You were surprised in bed too, I expect?"

"Marcus, my life is already over-complicated and I don't want to find myself competing with Bill over Sarah. We have no future together and he's genuinely keen on her."

Marcus snapped, "Unfortunately, Bill isn't here to keep Sarah busy and we need to keep her on track in the next few days. And, if you ask me, my guess is that for a woman like Sarah our boy Bill is a bit of a side-show. She probably thinks she can pump him for information about FIP. But you're the big fish not Bill. Never mind Marlon Strelitz, you keep Sarah happy while you're over here."

"It's not that simple, Marcus. The Wilson woman has got her teeth into something here."

Pomeroy exploded, "I know that! I wish she'd take a long run off a short pier!"

"Holding hands with Dr Singer?" Reiss laughed, softly.

"It's not a laughing matter!" Pomeroy stamped his foot and glowered at Reiss. "The Wilson woman is trouble! I'm taking this to show our solicitors right now. I don't want it being forwarded all round the world."

"Even so, we also have to disclose it to Sion's people, Marcus."

"Not today, we don't. Let me sleep on that. "

"I could mention it in passing to Chris Schwartz, kind of casually, later."

"No, let's both of us talk to Sarah, first. You and me. You can ask her to come here to my suite to join us for drinks tomorrow evening. Let's say at six thirty? Where is she now?"

"In her office, I expect."

"Not waiting upstairs for you?"

"No, Marcus, she is not. And I don't want this crap getting back to poor Bill, so no snide comments in front of John Stannard or anyone else about me and Sarah."

"Of course not. What do you take me for?"

"I'd rather not say."

After that, they were in meetings all day. By eight o'clock that evening the English contingent were yawning and had retired to their rooms. After eating a few grapes and the last apple, Reiss had a quick shower, phoned first Sally and then Beatrice, unplugged the hotel phone and switched off his mobile and fell quickly asleep.

The next morning, he awoke and plugged the hotel phone back in as he heard the extension in the sitting room buzzing. Marcus at the other end sounded furious. "Where the Hell are you? You're late. You're supposed to be joining us here in my suite for breakfast?"

"Be with you in ten. Have to shave first, though."

"Get on with it, will you? I've had John Stannard on the phone here because he couldn't get through to you."

"Did he say what he wanted?"

"He's ringing back in fifteen minutes. Get down here, now, will you?"

As Marcus opened the door, his, hotel phone began to ring. Marcus swept up the receiver. "Yes. He's here at last. I'll hand over to him."

"John, sorry, you couldn't raise me. Is something wrong?"

"Three new ADRs in the converted placebo group in three different trial centres. Nothing like as severe as David had, but as a precaution - I repeat as a precaution - they've been detained overnight in hospital for tests and R/P has been stopped, obviously. If David hadn't been so ill, we wouldn't have responded this way. But we can't take chances now."

"No, I see that. Three cases, did you say?"

Pomeroy shrieked, "What is he telling you?"

Reiss covered the receiver and relayed the message.

Stannard said," But we're expecting that all three will be discharged soon."

Pomeroy groaned, "Couldn't they have waited forty-eight hours to be ill? Until after we'd signed up with Sion? The timing is terrible."

Reiss waved him to be quiet and spoke to Stannard again: "I'm going to need all these people's clinical notes and any tests and examination findings sent confidentially to me. Do not, I repeat, not, send them to the hotel business centre here. Send them to Strelitz' firm's New York office but phone them first to make sure we have confidentiality. I don't want this leaking out anywhere. The lawyers can print everything out and courier it here. Send me what you can by email. Let me know when it is coming."

Reiss took out his fat black Mont Blanc Meisterstuck pen and a sheet of hotel notepaper. "I'll make a note of the basics now. Shoot."

Pomeroy squawked, furiously. Reiss waved him to be quiet, once more.

"Two women and a man. Odd, within twenty-four hours and they're all from different centres. Symptoms: acute thirst, then difficulty and pain passing urine. Abdominal cramps and low grade pyrexia, feeling a bit dizzy and faint. Could be something they picked up. Can't be sure it's caused by R/P, but we have to rule it out."

Stannard responded, "May be worth checking if there are any people in your inpatient trial at Pemberton who are experiencing anything like this? Some people may be keeping quiet because they want to keep taking the drug to lose weight?"

Reiss sighed. "Yes, it's possible. Send all this information confidentially to Bill and Tim at Flat Acres. Do it ASAP. It's Friday afternoon, there."

CHAPTER TWENTY-SEVEN

After the business meetings, during which the effects of the three ADRs were minimised as far as legitimately possible, negotiations towards finalising the contract continued between the lawyers.

Dr Chris Schwartz MD had been philosophical. He had given Reiss a gentle punch on the upper arm and said, "It's a new drug, you've got to expect some people will react to it; you've done amazingly well to get so far with nothing much. Let's not get too worried, just yet."

So, the mood generally was positive when they all of them took a break and then met for drinks on Friday evening in Pomeroy's suite. He had ordered a superior Californian Chardonnay and a Merlot along with soft drinks and left his duty free Scotch on show for anyone who preferred this with the nibbles and crisps and fruit platters. Sarah Goodwin, arrived punctually, and accepted a small glass of Chardonnay, which she sipped at delicately, leaving a pink lipstick imprint on the rim before depositing the glass on the coffee table. She was in full professional reporter mode with her recording machine out on show. She said, with a curl of her glossy lips, "So, I now learn that by the time I arrived at Pemberton two weeks ago, you two both knew that Dr Devereaux had a girlfriend called Lara who had committed suicide? You did know that by then?"

Reiss responded, quietly, "We had just found out. I knew nothing about his private life until after he died, Sarah. This was a private matter between the two of them. They were consenting adults and my view is that what happened between them was their business and not ours. And that's how it should stay, dead or not."

"Lara's sister doesn't agree with you, does she?"

Pomeroy interjected, "I gather that this woman and her sister weren't even on speaking terms for years. Lara never introduced her sister to David. They only met when he came to the funeral. I think she has a guilty conscience and is taking it out on us."

Reiss nodded, "She could be suffering from an abnormal bereavement reaction fuelled by her own guilt. Have you asked her why they fell out? It must have been something big if they didn't speak for years. Don't you think it rather strange, that on the day after they meet again after years of quarrelling, that Lara tops herself? If she turned to her sister for help, it looks like she didn't get any. It must have been obvious to her sister that Lara was unhappy and depressed and as it turns out, she was also mentally very unstable. What we do know is that Lara didn't leave a note blaming David for what she did, so I wouldn't give too much weight to this woman's claims if I were you."

Pomeroy added, "It may have been a cry for help that went wrong for Lara?" Pomeroy expansively gestured with his glasses, before replacing them on his nose, "This Penny Wilson, who is now so devastated about what happened to her sister was much less concerned when Lara was alive and needed her. She walked away and left her on her own. It's easy now to blame poor Dr Devereaux. He's dead and he can't defend himself."

Sarah sighed, "Lara sounds a regular person. Why did he keep her under wraps the way he did? Why did she get so depressed? Was Dr Devereaux a depressive personality?"

Reiss shook his head. "Not that I noticed. He could be bit moody and introspective, but no, he was definitely *not* a depressive personality."

Sarah tossed her auburn curls, "I called his sister in Yorkshire.

She said, 'leave my poor brother rest in peace.' Then she slammed the phone down on me."

"She's right, Sarah. Let them both rest in peace, now."

Sarah jutted her chin, the recorder was, Reiss saw uneasily, still running."What do you think could have caused Lara's Crohn's disease?"

"Nobody knows what causes Crohn's, for sure." Reiss paced around for a moment, hands in pockets. "We know it's five times more common than in the 1970's; that may be in part due to better diagnosis, but it doesn't explain it. There is a view that it's triggered by infection. There is some research linking it with people who had measles and mumps in close succession as children? But then again we all know people who had that and didn't develop it, so I can't answer you satisfactorily. But what we do know is Crohn's disease was not the cause of Lara's death. She took an overdose of paracetamol with a bottle of gin."

"Lara's sister claims that her sister told her that her doctor boyfriend gave her slimming pills. He worked for your company and my guess is they were Reduktopan pills."

"Our stock records are complete, we've double checked them." Marcus said, quickly. "And thousands of people develop Crohn's each year without them."

Sarah said, "No, I get that. I have no wish to jeopardize an excellent and effective product that could help a lot of people in my country lose weight." She smiled brightly, "And to prove I have confidence in your drug, I am willing to try it myself."

Reiss shook his head. "No. Sorry. You're not a suitable candidate."

Pomeroy smiled, charmingly. "Sarah, listen to the good doctor here. He's the expert. Now, won't you try one of these nibbles? They're absolutely scrumptious."

CHAPTER TWENTY-EIGHT

Reiss spent Saturday in meetings mainly with Sion's medical representatives, who were headed by the agreeable Chris Schwartz, his opposite number. In the fifteen minutes "comfort break" before lunch, he muttered an excuse, and went somewhere more private to phone Bill. It was after six in the evening at Flat Acres, but Bill was still at work.

"Thanks for your analysis. Very helpful."

"Chief, these latest three people aren't ill like David was. I've been through his medical notes again and compared every aspect of his ADR with these three and they're miles apart. But John Stannard may be right that some people who have mild symptoms are not telling us. We may have some, a few, who have had something a bit odd, but generally they feel okay. They're losing weight and everyone is encouraging them to keep going. The only danger will be if they start accumulating levels of toxicity and then there's a crisis."

"Yes, I agree. I'll raise it with Chris Schwartz."

They batted the idea around for a few more minutes. Then Bill said tentatively, "Do you think Sarah likes the idea of me coming out to New York to work at Sion?"

"It could be a great opportunity for you. Don't let her be the decider on that, Bill. It's your decision not hers. I've raised it with Chris, but so far just tentatively."

Reiss replaced the receiver.

In the light of Pomeroy's pressure, he had slipped Sarah a spare plastic key to his suite, warning her he would be out till late.

"I have my own plans for tonight, but I appreciate your gesture." Sarah flashed him a conspiratorial smile and left the gathering a few minutes later.

After this, Reiss spoke at length with Chris Schwartz, who reminded him that Sion had some years before taken over another company which had its plant and R & D park in California. He was trailing the idea that Reiss should take a trip to see over it as the present Medical Director there was talking about retiring at the end of the year. Great salary and great life out there for someone. You should go and take a look around it. How would your wife feel about living there?"

"Sally likes Cambridge."

"Stanford is excellent as well. Very close by. Talk to her."

"I can try."

Upstairs in his suite, after changing his clothes for the evening, Reiss dialled Singer's number. "I'm in New York. How it's going, Dr Singer?"

"No progress. Been a bit tied up, lately."

Reiss grunted, "Right, of course."

Singer cleared his throat and said huskily, "Dr Reiss, I think I need to be up-front with you. I haven't been able to work on your problem because I've been in hospital for the last few days. Undergoing tests." He paused and waited.

"I'm sorry." Reiss's tone was solicitous. "Which hospital?"

Singer grunted reluctantly. "The Middlesex. Where you trained, I think?"

"Yes, I started out there. Nearly thirty years ago, now."

There was a silence.

Then Reiss said, awkwardly, "I'm sure you're in excellent hands, but if you want to discuss anything, or ask me anything, just say... "

"Thank you. I will."

Reiss, a little embarrassed, said, "Look, it's obviously not a good moment..."

Singer said, "Go on, I can use the distraction."

"I wondered whether David might have kept a personal file on our Chief Executive, Marcus Pomeroy?" Reiss spelled out the name.

Singer laughed throatily, "What are you hoping to find out? And when you do, will you tell him the worst about himself? So he can put his affairs in order?" He cleared his throat again and coughed painfully. It struck Reiss that Singer's voice sounded different. Huskier.

"Did they put tubes down your throat?"

"Yes. I had a biopsy of the larynx. Eating is difficult right now. I won't need to take your slimming drug. And after that I have an array of choices, like radiotherapy, chemotherapy, biopsies, surgery, parenteral feeding and intravenous antibiotics? I went through it all with Howard. I saw what happened to him. I will refuse it all."

Reiss pressed Singer again. "Have all the results come in?"

"A few are outstanding. But I know what's coming my way. Metastases; my body is changing. Not for the better. From normal to abnormal."

Reiss stayed silent. The capacity to form metastases was one of the defining characteristics of malignancy in tumours. Certainly this was bad news, even if it was to be expected.

Singer coughed again, painfully.

Reiss probed, delicately. "Where did they find these metastases?"

"My left lung. And, like I said, there's something new and different growing in my larynx."

"I'm so sorry."

"Howard went through hell trying to stay alive for a few more months, because of me, but I'm not going to do that myself."

The red light on the phone came on. It was Pomeroy calling to whinge that they were waiting for him. Then his mobile bleeped. "Hold on a moment, Dr Singer, please."

Pomeroy snapped, "I need you here. You've been ages."

Reiss said awkwardly, "I have to go. People are waiting for me. I'll ring back later, I promise."

Singer said, suddenly terse. "No, don't do that. When are you coming back?"

I'll be arriving at Heathrow, my flight comes in on Monday morning."

"I may have something more for you by then."

Reiss said, "Of course. You have my mobile."

"And you have mine. I have a new phone but it's the same number."

Reiss went back to Pomeroy's suite. The lawyers had been working on the contract all day; both sides were anxious to get the deal signed off. Sion, in case Oribo put in a higher bid and FIP in case there were more ADRs. The lawyers had been out to lunch together and returned to Strelitz' New York office to conclude matters and everything had been signed off and the tension evaporated into celebrations.

Over dinner, seated next to Chris, Reiss brought up the subject of Bill Ryder, saying that he would welcome some experience of working in the States on a secondment. He's a bit smitten with Sarah Goodwin, the redheaded journalist you met from the NYG, and she's offered to put him up in her apartment."

Chris winked. "Okay. Send Bill over to us for a couple of days. It could be useful as a matter of fact. He can tell us about your set up and we can tell him about ours."

Chris, who was in his mid-fifties and whose stomach was battling to escape from his fitted shirt, gave a mischievous grin, "If you ask me, that redheaded woman is more interested in you than Bill. I mean, I get the emotional heat of the moment thing after you saved the kid, but I'd watch your step with her, Raymond. She looks like she could be a piece of work if things don't go her way?"

"There's nothing between us. I wish people wouldn't talk things up."

"They'll be watching you like hawks from now on, I warn you." Chris topped up their wine glasses."You've been pretty busy with this trial, I gather? Not quite back to walking the wards, but you're seeing a lot of the patients, yourself?"

"Yes, I run the clinics mainly with Bill. Most of the patients are fine, but we've got a few problem ones that David let in before I took over."

"I met him only once at some conference. He struck me as clever, but kind of closed up."

"That pretty much describes him. Not a natural team player, but he led the team that developed Reduktopan and he would have run the trial at Pemberton."

"Shame about the car crash. Poor guy. So that's why you took over?

"Yes, that's why."

"Still you're well fitted to do that. You're not long out of hospital practice and you said young Bill's fresh out of it?"

"How about you, Chris?"

"No, I don't see patients anymore. I joined the Industry twenty years ago. I could never have done what you did. Oh boy, you showed us all up for the cowards we are with your penknife surgery on that kid. You're a scary guy, Raymond. But, here's to our long term collaboration. Talk to your wife about the good life in California, our guy out there will be retiring soon. It could be a great opportunity. Double your current salary and a lot of perks."

They chinked glasses.

After dinner, the party moved on to a "show" and then to a noisy club with dancing.

By the time Reiss arrived back at his super-executive suite, somewhat inebriated and rather weary, he was ready for a hot bath and bed. He opened the door with his plastic key to find the sitting room glowing with soft lighting and Sarah reposing like a Pre-Raphaelite model on one of the pair of cream sofas, her mass of red hair spreading dramatically around her shoulders.

"Hi?"

Reiss spluttered. "Sarah? It's after one o'clock. And you said you had plans for the evening?"

"I was at a party until after midnight, but then I thought, instead of going straight back to my apartment I'd check to see if you were still up. Do you want to tell me how your company's negotiations are coming along?"

"You know I can't discuss that with you."

She had given him a little smile. "How about an off the record chat?"

"No, Sarah. But there is something I *can* share with you. Bill will be over here for a couple of days next week and I want you to be very nice to him."

"I will, Dr Reiss. Bill's a sweet guy. I told him that if he came here he could stay with me in my apartment and I promise I'll do my best to make him happy during his visit. But right now, it's *you* I want to make happy. It's *you*, not Bill, I came to see, tonight. You gave me your key didn't you? So I could let myself in, or did you just forget that?"

Reiss smiled, hoping his unease did not show. He had let Pomeroy persuade him in a moment of weakness and against his better judgment. He bent down and kissed her cheek and stroked her glorious red hair with appreciative fingers. Said with genuine regret in his voice, "Yes, I did, because you are a most beautiful young woman, but I can see now, dearest Sarah, that I should not have done that. It's not fair to either of us. When we spent the night together in Washington, we both agreed that we had to be two ships that passed in the night."

"Well, our two ships are passing a second time, now, aren't they?"

"Briefly. I'm flying home tomorrow. And next week, in just a few days' time, Bill will be coming out here. What happened between us was an interlude. A magical interlude, but we can't repeat it. We have to be sensible."

She whispered, "But I don't *want* to be sensible! I *love* you, don't you understand? I love you not Bill. I wish I did love him, but I *don't*! I love *you*."

Reiss drew back. "No, you don't. You can't. You hardly know me. You have some unrealistic romantic image of me that is nothing like the real me."

Sarah gave a little sob. "I know you're a lousy, unfaithful bastard, Raymond Reiss. I also know I'm being stupid, but I *do* love you. I wish I didn't."

"You don't love me." Reiss pushed Sarah's legs sideways to sit down beside her on the sofa and took her hand in his own. Keeping his voice controlled, measured and calm, he said quietly, "Sarah, I am very flattered. You are a beautiful, intelligent woman. You could have your pick of any number of men, but I'm twenty years older than you and I am married. I love my wife and my daughters and my life is back in England with them. I will be on a plane flying home to them tomorrow morning."

"We can still have tonight, together Raymond?"

"No Sarah, this is a bad idea. I was wrong to give you the key. We mustn't get fond of one another, dear Sarah, because there's no future for us. Let me get you a cab to take you home. I'll pay for it and I'll come down in the lift to see you off?" He was rising to his feet when she pulled him back down.

She replied fiercely, "I want to stay with you tonight. You have a huge empty bed back there. You can pay for my cab tomorrow morning."

"Sarah, no, listen to me." Alarmed, but still in control, Reiss pulled out his wallet and showed her a photograph of himself with Sally and their two girls taken at FIP's last summer party. "That lady is my wife and these are my daughters. I am not free and I'm going home tomorrow to be with them."

Sarah pushed away the photograph. "If your wife satisfies you, why do you cheat on her?"

"It's a defect in my character. You must see that I'm easily tempted. But tonight, I must not be and neither must you, Sarah. We must say goodbye now."

"You have daughters but you don't have a son. I could give you a son. The son I bet you always wanted?"

"I'm happy with my two girls. More than happy. They're wonderful girls."

Sarah stared up at him, her amber eyes gleaming. "I want to have your baby; I can give you a son. We can bring him up together?"

Reiss, his dismay now evident, shook his head firmly. "No Sarah. I don't want any more children; I'm past that stage and I have enough with my two lovely daughters." He launched a side-swipe, "And, you'd need to get your periods back before you can even *think* about having kids of your own?"

She said emphatically, "But I haven't *lost* my periods, *Dr* Reiss."

"Are you sure? Bill told me he thought you probably had."

She shouted, "So, I lied about Bill! God, how you guys *talk*! Did he tell you how many times we had sex in that four poster? So, yes, *doctor,* I do have periods; I admit they're a bit irregular, but I get them, all right."

Reiss, stood up, with an air of finality. "Good. I'm glad to hear it. Now let's get you downstairs and find you a cab."

Sarah stood up too and grabbed his arms. "I love *you* not Bill, don't you understand?"

"You love some romanticised idea of me, Sarah. You don't love the real person. So forget me and focus on Bill, who is a thoroughly decent guy, who would make you a great husband and father. Stick with him, *please.*"

"You sure have an original line in brush-offs, *Dr* Reiss."

"Sarah, come on! I *told* you in Washington that it had to be a one-night stand. We had a wonderful night, but it can't happen again and I'm going back to my wife and my life in England tomorrow morning. You won't see me again."

"I could come and live in England, if I married Bill? That way, we two could go on seeing each other?"

"No, we could not, Sarah. We could not at all. I really think you should go now."

Sarah, now more composed than Reiss who was becoming visibly agitated, gazed up at him with a knowing little smile. "But yes, we *could*. That way, we can *all* get what we want most. Bill gets me and we two get each other and you can stay married to your wife.   My paper's London office has a maternity slot coming up, so how about I apply for that? Then I can have your son and Bill will get up in the night for him if he cries? It's a perfect solution?"

Reiss, pale and in retreat, hissed, "You *cannot* be serious. You *cannot*. No, Sarah. Stop this, right now."

She tightened her grip. "But I *am* serious. I want more than one child, and to be fair to Bill, one at least, should be his, and just so you know, barring twins, three is my maximum."

Reiss removed her arms. "No, Sarah, you're building castles in the sand; I will not be a party to anything like this. It stops right here."

"If we make you our baby's godfather, then you have a reason to stay in touch and see the baby. We can work something out. You just need a little time to adjust to the idea. It's a win-win situation for everyone."

"No, no and *no*. What you suggest is outrageous. Sarah, *listen* to me. You are a nice girl under your feisty veneer and you're also beautiful, intelligent and sexy. You can believe me when I say I'm sorely tempted to make love to you. You look like you stepped out of a Pre-Raphaelite painting and a part of me desperately wants to make love to you, but we must not give in and do it, do you hear? We must not. We say good night and farewell forever, *now*."

"Well, no we don't. Lord Pemberton has sent me a personal invitation to come and stay with him for a few days at Pemberton in the Dower House at the conclusion of your trials there and I will give another boost to the Health Club as well. I've booked my flight already. I'm coming back on 28th June."

"Well, you'll see Bill before that, because he's coming to New York. And if I were you I'd refuse that invitation. The Dower House is very run down and Cecil has a smelly old, dog."

"I will not refuse. I am going to be the guest of a real live Lord. The sixth earl of Pemberton Manor. My readers will be simply fascinated."

She leaned her head against his chest and Reiss put his arms gently around her shoulders. "Oh, Sarah, it's really not a good idea."

"I'll be very, *very* nice to Bill when he comes to New York, if you're very nice to me now. Do we have a deal?"

"Sarah. I'm tired. What I need is a good night's sleep."

"Me, too. Come to bed, now. We can cuddle up together?"

In the morning, when Reiss awoke at seven, Sarah had left, but her scent on the pillow remained along with a long strand of red hair.

CHAPTER TWENTY-NINE

Back at Flat Acres Reiss signed off all the forms for the regulatory authorities on both sides of the Atlantic. Fortunately, the symptoms of the three ADR patients had resolved within four days of stopping the drug and there were no more significant problems, so far. With a few minutes at his disposal, Reiss rang Singer's home number. As it was a weekday, he was expecting to leave a message, but Singer answered after two rings.

"I'm on sick leave; I'm not going into the office for the next few weeks. "I've agreed to a course of radiotherapy, so I'll have more time to wrestle with our little problem. I'm regarding it as a welcome distraction."

"Radiotherapy can make you feel very tired. You should take a rest afterwards."

"I know." Singer cleared his throat painfully, "Dr Reiss, there are some arrangements I'm planning to set up, and I'd like your input, when you have some time. I plan to set up a small medical charity, like I said. I will use the money Howard left me together with my own and the proceeds of the sale of this when I die The charity would fund existing institutions on a year to year basis, after reviewing the quality of their research, and their work. I'd like you to be on the board of selection."

"I would be honoured," Reiss said.

"You asked about your CEO, Marcus Pomeroy? Well my guess is that your colleague didn't find too much of interest."

"No, I expect Marcus is pretty careful to cover his tracks. He's a happy bunny at the moment as our share price has risen with the announcement we've signed up to collaborate with Sion. I'm more concerned about your health than with Marcus's shenanigans."

During his last visit to Singer at his home in Camden Town, Reiss had, at his request, examined him. When he had removed his outer clothes for this purpose, Singer looked very thin and his skin had a dull pallor, there were tell-tale patches on his shins and he was suffering from mouth and throat ulcers. His joints ached and he had loin pains.

Reiss put his instruments in a plastic bag inside his case. They would need to be thoroughly sterilised before they could be re-used. "Your clothes look loose. How much weight have you lost?"

"Fifteen - sixteen pounds. Around seven kilos in the last few months. Eating's becoming an ordeal for me." Singer began to dress again, slowly.

"Are you taking any food supplements?"

"I am, yes."

"If these mouth and throat ulcers get worse you may do better with a stomach tube."

"No. No stomach tube for me."

"You need to keep up your resistance. You can't do that if you're not eating. You'll just get weaker and weaker."

"Eating hurts and I can't taste anything much. I want you to be honest. How long do you think I have left. Years, months or weeks? Tell me the truth. I need to know. I have to make plans, and I need to know how much time is left."

Reiss had responded, evasively, "I'm not a specialist oncologist and there's a chance you might spontaneously go into remission."

"If I don't, will I see another summer?"

Reiss muttered, awkwardly, "You might?"

Singer had actually smiled. He had expected worse. "How about the winter after that? "

Reiss had looked him straight in the eye. "I don't know. Pass."

"Then I'd better make a break through soon with these passwords, hadn't I? I'll redouble my efforts. But in return, there's something I want from you, and it's not money, Dr Reiss. I want you to make sure I don't die a protracted painful death like Howard."

"They'll give you morphine. Ask for a pump that you can operate yourself."

Singer shook his head. "I dream of Howard some nights. Have you ever seen a skeleton screaming with pain? The consultant said he could have more morphine, but the nurses and the young doctors on the ward were scared to hand it out. They said he was becoming addicted. So what? If you're dying, who cares that you're addicted if it dulls the pain? If you won't promise to help me when the time comes I'm stopping work on that computer, now."

Reiss had promised to help in any way he legally could. He told Singer he would help and make sure he was admitted into a good hospice when the time came.

Reiss now dismissed poor Singer from his mind and instead looked through the latest data that Tim Scott had provided. There was a week to go before the end of the Pemberton trial and most of the A.C.E ones but a couple would end a little later. They were now all daring to be optimistic; to believe that FIP had scored a big win with Reduktopan the miracle slimming drug for which the world was waiting.

Reiss glanced across at the two silver plated cups that were on the top of his filing cabinet which had been returned by the engravers which Lord Cecil Pemberton was due to present to the star-weight losers in the "ballroom" of the Manor House. The hot favourite for the men's prize was Frank Miller from the USA. Astonishingly, given their previous problem status, two out of the three East London girls, Bella and Sharon, were neck and neck for maximum female weight loss. It occurred to Reiss that he should procure a third cup for a joint first women's prize so he rang the firm to send another before next Thursday. Putting the desk phone down, Reiss leaned back on his chair thoughtfully. David had wanted to give these young women the chance to change their lives for the better, and, after a very

shaky and unpromising start, it looked as if they might do so.
Bella and Sharon had both tried hard to make the most of their
two months stay at Pemberton. They had given up smoking
and all three girls, including Lisa-Jane, had taken part regularly
in the exercise and activities programmes provided. Not one
of these three girls had been able to swim a length of the pool
when they arrived, but now they were all quite proficient, if
not stylish swimmers.

Then, a retired school teacher, who was also taking part in the
trial, had been persuaded to run English classes on grammar
and literacy and even literature; they had proved to b e very
popular and all three of the girls had attended them regularly.

But for all this, Lisa-Jane's weight loss had been disappointing
when compared with her friends, even when one allowed for
her delayed start. Reiss, who had taken Bill's clinic while he
was away in New York, had chided Lisa-Jane mildly on this
point, concerned she might have been smuggling in extra food
from the Village. She had denied this, vehemently. "No, I never
did. I came here to lose weight and I'm doing everything I can,
doctor."

"I hope so. We won't be running anything like this ever again, I
assure you."

"I know that, doctor."

Lisa-Jane undoubtedly looked better than when she arrived,
but Reiss felt uneasy about her slow progress. He mentioned it
to her boyfriend, Stewart, who promised he would do more to
encourage Lisa-Jane to take regular exercise and make sure she
kept to a sensible diet. And indeed, only yesterday, Reiss had
seen them jogging slowly round the grounds, together. Stewart
was doing well. He had lost twelve kilos and was delighted
and very focused to keep going. He had a sedentary job as a
bus driver and said he wondered if he should switch to home
deliveries which would involve more exercise?

Dora Shane and Herman Orloff were also doing quite well, if
not outstandingly so like Frank, and appeared satisfied with
their progress. Both had hinted broadly that they would like

a supply of R/P tablets to take home with them. "Out of the question, I'm afraid."

Reiss was writing a brief report on the latest trial statistics when Linda came in with the post. "You've had a letter from Dr Devereaux' sister; I'm sorry, but she didn't mark it personal so I opened it. " Pink cheeked, dabbing at her wiry, brown hair, Linda babbled, "It's a renewal form for a post box address. I didn't know Dr Devereaux had one of those? Did you?"

Reiss grunted, "No, but you can leave it with me."

He wondered if perhaps David had forgotten about it as all it contained were two circulars from a tailor in Taiwan. He cancelled the contract. Through the open front window he heard the sound of voices then the thud of feet on the stairs. Bill knocked and entered, apparently in high spirits.

Reiss stood up to greet him. "Hi Bill. You look like you had a good time?"

"I did. Thanks so much for sending me out there. It was great."

"Yes, well, good. You can tell me about it on the way to the Pavilion?"

They began walking across Flat Acres.

"I really found it useful. I've never been to the States before and I saved FIP the hotel bill as I stayed with Sarah. She sends you her best wishes, by the way."

They negotiated the pair of security gates that led from Flat Acres into Pemberton which were monitored 24/7 by CCTV and continued towards the domed roofs of the Pavilion complex.

"How is Sarah?"

"Border-line anorexic like we agreed. And some of the stuff she comes out with?" Bill broke off and looked over his shoulder, but there was nobody nearby. "She asked me if I knew that Casanova gave his women scooped out half lemons or limes to use as primitive Dutch caps? I said I didn't. I have no idea if it's true, but, well, is that weird or not?"

Reiss frowned. He had told Sarah that when they had

performed the lime trick after the Kerry incident. He wondered now if she had tried it out with Bill?

"Sheep's gut for men and oranges and lemons for women - spicy stuff." Bill grinned happily with the memory of his couplings in New York. "Sarah is flying over here next week to write up the end of the trials at Lord Pemberton's invitation and she's thrilled she'll be staying at the Dower House. Of course, I offered her to stay in my flat, but she said, "No, I'm doing this for my readers. I want to tell them what it's like to stay with a real Earl and lord of the manor."

"I said, 'Ex-lord of the manor, Sarah. He doesn't own the manor anymore. The estate was bankrupt and was sold off as you know. All he's got left is the Dower House and I'm told it's not in good repair."

"That's an understatement."

"And her place is as clean as an operating theatre; she's always wiping and cleaning everything. She's says she's owed some vacation and she is going to extend her trip by a few days. I offered her to stay with me, but she says will do that after the trial is finished."

"Well, I hope you both won't be disappointed but until that happens and we've gone through the paperwork, nobody gets much free time. It's annoying that Jim Menzies is on holiday at a key moment, but he booked his week off over a year ago, apparently. I'm calling in the same three company medics to help with the discharge summaries for these two hundred and three people, starting next Monday through till Wednesday.

They were donning their white coats as Bill, added," By the way, I saw Tim in the car park; Sylvie's blood pressure is too high again. I told him he should take her to Addenbrooke's to see a specialist obstetric team, now."

"Sylvie is very obstinate. But I'll add a word, too."

They prepared to split up when Reiss said, "It's looking good if you want to go back to the States to work at Sion for Chris Schwartz's team in the Autumn?"

Bill mumbled, "That might be a little soon. Sarah thinks there is maternity slot coming up at her paper's London office. She'd like the chance to work over here."

Reiss grunted, "Why would she do that?"

"She thinks working in London would broaden her experience."

"Well, you have a great opportunity with Sion. I pushed it because I thought it would work for both of you given Sarah is based in New York."

"I'm not sure how serious she is about London. I'm hoping it doesn't happen. I'd like her to stay in New York and for me to go out there."

Reiss nodded and thought, but did not say, "Me too."

CHAPTER THIRTY

As she would have free accommodation, Sarah had changed her flight to an earlier date and had arrived on Thursday evening a full week before the planned prize-giving ceremony. Anxious to make her feel welcome, Marcus Pomeroy had persuaded his wife Mary to organise an impromptu dinner party on Friday evening. Sarah was invited with Bill and Lord Cecil Pemberton, Alan Michaels and his wife, Leonora and Raymond and Sally Reiss. Unfortunately, Sally had a college dinner that night, so Reiss was going on his own and would stay overnight at the cottage in Flat Acres.

Reiss, showered and changed, with a bunch of flowers in his hand, rang the bell. Mary, smartly casual in a blue Jaeger linen suit and a canary yellow silk blouse, let him in. Her gold necklace brushed against his chin as she bent forward to give him a peck on the cheek. She relieved him of the bouquet. "I've had to reorganise the table at the last minute as that idiot Cecil Pemberton rang to cancel; he gave me some pathetic excuse about having to dash up to London for a business meeting."

Reiss grinned. "He's probably too embarrassed to face Sarah Goodwin over the dinner table, tonight. Bill told me; she's come up in a terrible rash. It turns out she's allergic to the flea spray he used all over the house before she arrived."

Mary looked upset, "She's not going to cancel me too, is she?"

Reiss shook his head. "No, Bill dealt with it this morning. But it means she can't stay at the Dower House another minute and they're trying to find her a room at the Manor. Bill offered her to stay with him in his flat but she says she wants to be in Pemberton until after the trials are finished. Bill is miffed but I think she'll move in with him earlier if her paper won't pay for her room."

"Oh, well, as long as nobody else cancels tonight."

Mary led Reiss across the cream hall carpet into the elegant sitting room.

"I hope yoghurt is not on tonight's menu?"

"No, it isn't. That dairy should be prosecuted." Mary was indignant.

"I'm sure it will be. The health police have been swarming all over it. We had six people down in Pemberton with food poisoning including three of our trial patients. As they went down first, we were scared it was an ADR, so when the poor Spanish maid threw up over the Orangery floor in front of me, I was quite relieved. The worst affected is unfortunately one of our trial people. An elderly man called Herman Orloff, which is a bit worrying."

"Will he be all right?" Pomeroy coming forward grasped Reiss's hand, anxiously.

"Yes, he's a lot better, now. Keeping himself busy planning his leaving party for next Wednesday night."

Reiss sniffed appreciatively at the agreeable aroma of spices, herbs and freshly baked bread. Pomeroy opened the drinks' cabinet. "Whisky?"

"Better make it a tomato juice; I'm driving. I'll have a glass of wine with my dinner instead, if I may?"

Mary Pomeroy said, "Of course, Raymond. You should do the same, Marcus. You'll be running Mrs Mahoney home later, remember?" She turned back to Reiss, "How's Tim Scott's wife?"

"Sylvie is being delivered in Addenbrooke's in Cambridge. She's only thirty-three weeks and there have been some problems; I don't expect we'll see much of Tim in the next few days; he's told his juniors to take over.

"Frankly, I'm feeling a bit jinxed, what with the contaminated yoghurt, Tim's wife and Ayesha's father collapsing all in one week. " And Jim's away fishing in some remote part of Scotland."

Marcus said, "What's wrong with Ayesha's father?"

"He's having an urgent angioplasty tonight and she's gone back to Bradford to be with him. She's not sure it will work in his case and it may mean a bypass later. Meanwhile, Bill and I may have to call in some of the company's in-house medics for back up cover; it's part of the reason I will be staying over at the Cottage tonight ."

Mary pawed the ground with her elegant high-heeled navy and white leather shoe. "We ought to send Tim's wife some flowers, tomorrow?"

Reiss said, shortly. "I would leave that for a day or two."

In the hall, the doorbell rang. "Marcus, it's your turn to answer it."

Pomeroy said, testily, "You go, Mary. I need a private word with Raymond."

Mary tossed her head and said, "Yes, Marcus. All, right, I'll go and then I'll put these flowers in water." She shut the door, ostentatiously.

Pomeroy poured a measure of Glenlivet into his glass and swallowed it quickly then replaced the bottle.

"She'll spot the level's gone down?"

Pomeroy ignored this comment, saying instead. "I've told Mary to sit you and Sarah Goodwin at opposite ends of the table since you made a point of asking."

"The further away the better."

The sound of raised male and female voices preceded Mary Pomeroy showing in Alan Michaels and Leonora, his jolly hockey sticks school teacher wife with Sarah and Bill. Reiss, aware that both Marcus and Alan Michaels were watching him closely, shook hands with Sarah and gave Bill a light comradely pat on the upper arm. Sarah was wearing her white suit but with a lime green short-sleeved top and a jade pendant instead of the lapis necklace. She did not remove her sunglasses. Bill kept his arm loosely around Sarah's shoulder. They made a handsome young couple though Bill's navy blazer had too many brass buttons for Reiss's taste.

"Hi, Dr Reiss." Sarah's tone was bright to the point of brittle.

"Hi Sarah. I hear you came up in a bit of a rash?" Reiss's expression showed kindly concern.

"Bill gave me a big dose of antihistamine this morning, so I'm feeling a lot better. My eyes were so swollen when I woke up I could hardly see out of them. They're red and sore even now and I've bathed them three times. Bill says it's the flea spray not the dog, but I'm not so sure; she's always scratching herself. Lord Pemberton kept apologising to me about it this morning. It was kind of awkward. I had to wait outside until Bill fetched me and drove me straight to the dispensary."

Bill said, reassuringly, "Another day or two and it will all have gone away, don't worry."

Reiss said, with a touch of malice. "So you won't be staying on at the Dower House?"

Sarah shrilled, "Are you *serious*! And one of you two might have warned me?"

"I did, Sarah, when I met you in New York. I said his house was run down and his dog is a bit old and smelly."

Sarah snapped, "She doesn't just smell, she *stinks!* She's deaf and half blind and she messes just everywhere. And when she's not doing that, she's scratching herself."

"Well, you're out of there now?"

"Unfortunately, I have to go back to fetch most of my stuff because I left in such a rush."

They were ushered through to the dining room where the oval table was now set for seven with Reiss placed between Mary Pomeroy and Leonora Michaels who had Bill on her other side. Sarah sat between Bill and Pomeroy who had Alan Michaels on his other side who was in turn next to Mary. Now and then, Sarah rubbed or scratched furtively. Reiss shook his head, responding, automatically. "Try not to do that, Sarah. It aggravates it."

She pulled a face, "I know, but it's so itchy. I'm wondering if I dare go back tonight to fetch my camera and my recording machine and a few other items that I left in the room. I'd prefer to collect my stuff while he's not there. The poor man was so embarrassed and of course he's scared stiff I'll write this up for the paper, but I wouldn't do that..."

Mary ladled out the chilled gazpacho, "You'll have a job making yourself heard if you try ringing the bell later tonight. The dog and the old housekeeper are both deaf as posts and Cecil is away overnight. He told me when he cancelled this morning. We should have been eight this evening."

Sarah pulled a little face. "That's not a problem. I still have the key he gave me."

Bill squeezed Sarah's hand. "I'll take you. We can brave the deaf dog together, darling."

"Thank you Bill. I'm dreading going back there, to be honest."

Mary removed the soup plates and they progressed to the main course.

"Bill says you've been thinking about working in London, Sarah?" Reiss asked.

"It's just a possibility."

Bill, Reiss observed, was eating with considerable appetite while Sarah picked at her food and messed it around her plate. Bill then had a second helping of the chicken and vegetables as Mary beamed on him.

"This sauce is just delicious, Mrs Pomeroy. I must compliment you. Mmm." He mopped up what was left with a piece of bread.

Reiss's mobile was buzzing so he took it out into the hall while Bill stayed at the table chewing his last mouthful before his plate could be removed.

Reiss returned. "That was the lab; they've confirmed the last yoghurt sample was contaminated. It's lucky more people didn't eat it."

Bill nodded. "I was scared they were having ADRs."

"We all were."

As Reiss sat down his mobile vibrated again. He rose to take it outside but stopped halfway. It was Tim, sounding het up, his stammer more evident. "Sylvie's had a b-boy ... he's m-minute and the paeds have taken him to the SCBU. Sylvie had a Caesar and she'll be staying in the labour ward overnight where they can watch her. I'm glad you intervened when you did. We both are. We want you to be Jamie's godfather if he ... well ... you know ...makes it through."

Reiss said quickly, "Congratulations, to both of you, Tim. Well done. Keep me in the loop. If it's okay I'll come with Sally to the hospital to see you all tomorrow afternoon?"

Mary Pomeroy then proposed a toast to mother and baby. Reiss and Bill finished their single glass of wine with sober faces as Reiss's mobile vibrated for the third time. He apologised to Mary and made to get up.

"Take it here, unless it's private."

Reiss listened, then turned to Bill, his hand over the mouthpiece. "It's Jim, one of the guards at the barrier hut. He's stepped on a plank with some rusty nails sticking out of it. They've gone right through his shoe, deep into the sole of his foot. I'm sorry Bill, but you'd better go and deal with it, now."

"But he's registered with a local GP, surely?"

"Closed at this time. Out of hours service have no anti-tetanus apparently. I'd ask Jim Menzies to go, but he's away. We have anti-tetanus at the dispensary at the Pavilion. You can pick some up, give him a shot and clean and tidy him up. And if he feels unwell and he can get someone to replace him you can drop him home? He lives on the edge of the Village."

Reiss spoke back into the phone. "Dr Ryder is leaving now. He'll be with you in about forty minutes, Jim. He'll take care of you."

Bill indignantly rose to his feet. "He could call an ambulance and go to the District General. They have an emergency department for that kind of thing?"

"It will take ages to arrive and then he'll be up half the night waiting to be seen and after that how will he get back home? He only has a push bike. I'm sorry about this Bill, but you'd better get started, now."

Bill sighed and scraped back his chair. "Come on, Sarah, I'll drop you back at Pemberton on my way. You said you were tired?"

Mary Pomeroy said indignantly, "But it's only just after nine o'clock? Sarah can stay here without you, can't she? Raymond is staying overnight at the Cottage, can't he drop her back?"

Bill hovered, irritably. "Sarah? You said you were jet lagged and a bad night with the rash and all that."

Sarah looked at her watch and then up at him. "It is still rather early Bill and if Dr Reiss is going back past Pemberton he can drop me off a bit later. I'd like to stay a little longer."

Reiss frowned. "Oh, never mind. I can go and see to Jim, myself, if that's easier?"

He half rose, but Bill, now pink cheeked and embarrassed, snapped, "No, of course, I'll go." He kissed Sarah on the lips. "I'll see you around lunch time tomorrow, *if* I can be spared for a few minutes?" He glared at Reiss, "Always wanted to know what it was like to be a country doctor, like in those Chekov plays?"

"You might look in on Herman Orloff if he's still up? Phone me if you have a problem. I'll be in my office at the Farmhouse tomorrow morning."

Bill nodded. "Sorry, Mrs Pomeroy. I was looking forward to your pudding. I really enjoyed the first two courses. You're a brilliant cook."

"Thank you, Bill. I'm very sorry you have to leave us."

"So am I."

Through the open windows they heard Bill's car reversing rapidly over the gravelled drive and then accelerate off into the distance. Mary removed Bill's chair and place setting and they closed up so that Reiss found himself opposite Sarah. Mary brought in a lime and lemon tart with a bowl of fresh strawberries.

Sarah smiled, broadly, "Back home we call that Casanova pie, I can't think why."

After coffee, at ten, Bill rang Reiss's mobile. He had dealt with Jim's foot and looked in on Mr Orloff, who said he was feeling much better but a little weak.

Should he come back or was it too late, now?

Alan Michaels looked at his wife, who nodded. "I'm afraid we must be going."

"And I'm actually feeling a bit tired now," Sarah said, rubbing her eyes behind her sunglasses.

Reiss said, apologetically, "I'm sorry Bill, but the party is breaking up. Everyone is leaving. I'll drop Sarah off at Pemberton, so don't worry."

CHAPTER THIRTY-ONE

In the car, Sarah reached out her hand to touch Reiss's knee. "Did you get rid of Bill on purpose?"

"No, I didn't. I would have gone myself, except it would look odd if I did that as he's my junior." Reiss pushed her hand away. "What's this nonsense he told me about you getting a job in London?"

"There may be a maternity slot going in the paper's London office. I've booked a hotel for one night off Tavistock Square. You can come and meet me there?"

"No, Sarah. I'm going home tomorrow for what's left of the weekend. Stick with Bill. I made my situation very clear in New York and it hasn't changed."

Sarah stroked Reiss's left knee, disturbingly. "I really tried with Bill. He's a sweet guy. But I don't love him. I love you, that's the problem."

Reiss said, tightly, "Sarah, you must forget me. There is no future with me."

"Why, when I can feel you still want me? Physically, at least?"

He pushed her hand away again.

"Go back to your job in New York City and stay there, please. And don't blow Bill off course: he has the chance to work for Chris Schwartz at Sion on R/P; it could be a good career move for him."

"Dr Reiss, I will give Bill what he wants if I can also spend time with you?"

Reiss drove through the Pemberton gates and the car rattled over the cattle grid to jerk to a halt in front of the entrance to the Manor House.

"I need to fetch my stuff from the Dower House. Will you come with me, please. I'll be very quick."

Reiss nodded, and drove on there and parked in the empty drive. Apart from a light glowing in an upper floor window, the house looked dark. Reiss escorted Sarah up the steps and tugged the old-fashioned handle. Inside, the bell could be heard clanging, but nobody came forward. Sarah unlocked the front door and pushed it open cautiously. "I don't want to meet his dog - she positively hates me and it's mutual."

"Bessie's harmless, Sarah. She's fourteen and almost toothless." Reiss followed Sarah into the circular bare hall and turned on a pair of low wattage lights. The house was dilapidated and there was a pungent smell of dust, damp, dog and flea powder and anti-moth spray. Sarah began sneezing. "I can't stay here long. I'm so allergic. I can feel my eyes swelling already."

Reiss called out, "Hallo? Hallo?"

There was no reply.

"Mary Pomeroy was right. Both the house keeper and the dog are deaf as posts. Run up and fetch your things and I'll wait for you down here."

"I need the bathroom first. I'm bursting."

She went slowly up the curving bare oak stairs. Reiss turned on another light in the hall and wandered round, idly opening doors and peering inside the different rooms. The house was shabby and neglected with a downstairs lavatory, that like the kitchen, were museum pieces but valiantly still functioning and a tribute to Victorian engineering.

Seeing the door to the sixth Earl's study was open, Reiss wandered inside and switched on the light. There was a pile of papers and letters on the scarred leather top of the mahogany desk. The Inland Revenue and Lord Pemberton's area bank manager looked to be the keenest correspondents though communications were quite one-sided as Lord Pemberton obviously tried to ignore them where possible. Indeed, the bank manager's letter dated last Friday accused Pemberton of deliberately avoiding his calls and not so respectfully reminded him that he had breached the conditions of his overdraft and the mortgages secured on the Dower House and the half acre garden around it.

" *...It has come to our notice that you have applied moneys advanced for the specific purpose of carrying out repairs and refurbishment to the Dower House and specified outbuildings (see schedule attached to our letter of the 14th ult.) for the purchase of further shares in Forsyte International Pharmaceuticals plc.*

We must advise you therefore that we are calling in this loan in accordance with clause 21(i)(c)..."

Cecil Pemberton, had evidently been hoping that as FIP's share price had been rising, the bank might relent. The silence was broken by Sarah's shrieks and a dog's loud yelping and barking upstairs. Reiss switched off the study light in a hurry and bounded up the stairs two at a time to find Sarah on the landing, wailing and clutching her ankles.

"She bit me! Both my ankles are bleeding. She bit me and I'm coming up in the most terrible rash as well!" Sarah burst into tears.

Reiss put his arm around her. "She wouldn't just bite you, not without provocation."

"I didn't see her. I think maybe I trod on her paw or her tail."

Reiss snorted and strode into the guest room where, under a sagging bed, Cecil Pemberton's aged and smelly water spaniel was crouching and growling, with a pair of black frilly knickers hanging out of her mouth.

"Good doggie, good doggie."

He grabbed Sarah's camera and a carrier with her recording machine in it and pulled some stuff out of a drawer then came back out again. "Honestly, it's probably better if we leave the rest of your stuff till tomorrow morning. I'm afraid she's now eating your knickers, so you won't want them back."

She wailed, "That's right, laugh, go on! You don't care that horrible dog bit both my ankles and that I'm bleeding. You won't even look at them and I can feel the blood trickling down into my shoes. I'll have the most hideous scars. I don't want scars! that dog's chewed up my new pantyhose as well and my skirt is filthy from where she jumped and pawed at me."

Reiss comforted her like a small child. "You hurt her when you trod on her paw and you gave her a fright. She's deaf and blind so she couldn't see or hear you coming, could she?"

He bent down to inspect Sarah's ankles.

Sarah sobbed, "Is it my fault she's deaf and blind? I didn't see her because she was hiding under the bed. And those panties were new ones from Saks."

"Do you want me to try and get them off her?"

"Shut up and stop sniggering, will you?" Sarah tugged at Reiss's Liberty print tie. "For Christ's sake get me out of this fucking, awful place. I'm itching all over. I can feel that rash breaking out again all over my body and my eyes are swelling, I can feel it. That old moron did a double spray round my room and it's worse in there than anywhere else."

Reiss started to laugh.

She shouted, "That's right, go on, laugh! That dog's got halitosis! She's probably got gum disease! She's bitten me to pieces and you're falling down laughing! I hate you! You son of a bitch!"

"Stop making such a fuss, it's not that bad. She's given you a couple of little nips."

"It is, bad, look at me!"

Reiss squatted down to inspect her ankles, again. "You're right. It's an amputation job. I'll get my saw out of the car."

She sniffed noisily and limped to the top of the stairs. "I'm not sure I can walk down, now."

"I'm not carrying you, so will you be staying the night here after all then?"

"You're so *unsympathetic!*"

"Poor little Sarah, come on, let's get you out of here." He took her arm and guided her descent. "She's broken the skin, so we need to get you cleaned up. Then, I'm afraid you're going to need an anti-tetanus shot. We'll go straight to the Pavilion and I'll open the dispensary. Better hope Bill hasn't taken all of it away to give to Jim."

Sarah sniffed, "I hate needles."

Reiss patted her bottom. "I'm very good. You'll hardly feel a thing. Only be sore for a month or two."

She sniffed again, "It's *not* funny. I hate you."

He drove her back towards the deserted Pavilion and opened up his examination suite and first washed and then disinfected her ankles and put a neat plaster over them. "Stay sitting on the couch, I won't be long." He opened up the dispensary to fetch antibiotics, anti-tetanus and antihistamine and some disposable syringes.

She said, woefully, "I feel sick when I see a needle coming at me."

"Turn over and shut your eyes and you won't see it. Just three little pricks."

"Three? I'm not having three."

"Over in a minute." He filled the first syringe from the ampoule on the trolley, approached the examination couch, pulled down her pants and swabbed the right upper quadrant briskly. "Ready?"

"No- ow!"

"That's the anti-tetanus. Turn the other cheek, now, there's a good girl?" He squirted off a minute droplet of fluid and prodded her bare thigh. "Come on, roll over. You need a dose of antibiotics, that dog's got nasty sores. I need to give you a quick shot and then you can have a course of pills."

"You're really enjoying this, aren't you?"

"Naturally, I'm a doctor. I like inflicting pain."

"Asshole."

"Don't tempt me, sweetheart, I'm the one with the needle, remember?" He waved the syringe around, threateningly. Reluctantly Sarah shifted position and moaned, as he swabbed the exposed upper quadrant of white flesh. "Why can't I have *pills?*"

"This'll work much more quickly, ready now?"

She nodded, shut her eyes and gripped the end of the examination couch. "Get it over with, will you?"

He stroked the back of her neck with his free hand. "Try and relax. If you tense your muscles it just hurts more."

She mumbled into the crook of her elbow. "How can I relax while you're standing over me with that needle?"

"Let yourself go limp. Let your arms drop down by your side. Come on, sweetheart. Please. I'm very tired. I've been up since six this morning and I've a long day ahead of me. I want to go to bed."

She let her arms droop over the sides of the couch with an exaggerated gesture. "That's better, good girl." He pinched a fold of skin within his gloved fingers, angled the needle and jabbed it in neatly.

"Ouch- that hurt. "

"Stop whingeing. I'm brilliant. You hardly felt it."

He pressed a piece of cotton wool hard down on the puncture site. "Hold it there for a moment, please."

"My ass hurts *both* sides now."

"One more. There. All done." He threw the syringes into the sharps box and disposed of the used swabs and medication wrappers and checked the injection sites. "Good. That looks fine." He covered them with tiny plasters. "You can take those off tomorrow." He sat her up briskly. "Get dressed, now, there's a good girl."

She said unsteadily, "I feel faint. I feel sick."

"No you don't!" He pushed her head between her knees. "Stay like that for a few minutes, it'll pass off." He made a further note then brushed off her skirt and wiped over her nip-marked white leather shoes with moistened cotton wool. "Feeling better, now?"

She grimaced, "A bit."

"That's the spirit."

He locked up and she climbed back into the car. "Let me stay with you tonight, please. I just want to be next to you. I know I look awful, but you can turn out the light and not see me. I don't feel well."

Reiss patted her arm. "Sarah, I can't take you back to the Cottage, it's inside Flat Acres and we don't let journalists in there. I'll drop you back at the Manor House. You'll be fine from now on."

"Nobody will know I've been there. I can crouch down in the back of your car in the dark. I really don't feel well, please."

"I'll take you to Bill's flat then. It's not far. Just up in the Village."

"If you let me stay with you tonight, I give you my word, I'll go back to New York and Bill can come out in September as planned? I won't look for a job in London. That one is too junior anyway, I wouldn't take it, don't worry. Just one night, Dr Reiss?"

"No, Sarah, I can't. Flat Acres is floodlit and there are security cameras everywhere. And how can I trust you not to boast about doing it?"

"No, I give you my word. I feel traumatised by that dog and the rash and everything. You have my word. I would never write about that anymore than I would betray my sources. Journalist's honour."

Reiss hesitated, reluctantly considering the practicalities. There were in fact no security cameras pointing at the front door of the Cottage to take a tell-tale video and Jim, the barrier guard could not see them on his screens, either. He prevaricated feebly, "The antihistamine will make you drowsy. You'll be asleep in half an hour, this is silly, Sarah. Let me take you back to Pemberton Manor." He regretted now not slipping her a sleeping pill in the Pavilion.

"Please let me stay with you, *I promise* I won't make any trouble."

At the barrier to enter Flat Acres, Jim, was loyally still at his post, but conveniently disabled from taking a midnight prowl. He was sitting with his bandaged foot raised up on a stool. "How're you feeling, now?"

"Bless you, sir, Dr Ryder came and fixed it up beautiful. He was very kind. Even made me a cup of tea."

"Good. Any problem, you can call me. "

Reiss, who had locked Sarah's camera and recording machine in the car boot before leaving the Dower House drive, drove close to the Cottage's front door. He switched off the alarm and then the porch lights and hustled Sarah inside with a tartan rug covering her head. She pulled it off as he bolted and then locked the front door from the inside and pocketed the key. "Can't risk you running round the complex frightening the guard dogs, darling."

She said nervously, "Jesus, this place is scary."

A fox barked hoarsely beyond the perimeter fence. Sarah, rather pale, asked, "Is that one of the poor dogs in your laboratories?"

"That was a fox, silly. We don't have dogs in our labs here." He embraced her firmly. There was a frantic high pitched squealing, then silence. Sarah mumbled, nervously, "What was that?"

"Foxes mating. Mrs fox makes a lot of fuss. Or they could be out killing rabbits."

She shivered. He pushed her up the stairs. "This was one of a terrace of farm workers' cottages. It was done up for me when I took over as Medical Director. The others were demolished."

"It's a cute little house." Sarah put her head into the crowded box room and followed him into the chintzy main bedroom. "The bathroom's the next door. There's a second loo downstairs by the kitchen."

Sarah peeped through the drawn curtains.

He pulled her back so that she sprawled on the bed. "Stay away from that window. And I find you anywhere outside the Cottage, I'll say you broke into the compound and you'll be thrown out and on the first plane home, understand?"

"You play rough. You're the kind of man who should have a son. I can give you a son."

"Don't start that again." He started to undress. "Get into bed and go to sleep."

He showered, cleaned his teeth and came back wearing pyjamas, but she had stripped off and was lying naked with her hair spread over the pillows like an artist's model. She whispered, "Make love to me this one last time? Then I go back to New York, if that's what you want?"

"Is that a promise?"

"Yes."

"On little Kerry's life, Sarah?"

She hesitated. "Yes. On Kerry's life."

He felt around in the drawer of the night table. "Shit. I'm out of condoms."

"I'd rather you didn't use one."

"So I gather. I'm going downstairs. Feel a bit peckish."

She responded angrily, "Can't you just *withdraw* for once?"

"Don't enjoy it much and the Bible and Freud are against it. I may have another solution. Stay there."

Indignantly, Sarah ran after him down the stairs and watched him from the doorway to the kitchen where Reiss took two apples from the fridge and bit into one of them as he began rummaging through the drawers in the dresser.

"What are you looking for, you crazy Brit?"

"Found it!" He came towards her, clutching a roll of Clingfilm.

"You crazy Brit! You want to wrap fruit at this time of night?"

He laughed uproariously. "Not fruit, you idiot. Come back to bed, now."

The next morning, when the alarm beeped at five Reiss turned it off instantly. Beside him, Sarah slept on. Taking the mobile into the bathroom, Reiss called Beatrice; it was an hour later in Sweden and they would be up. Unfortunately, her disagreeable daughter Steffie answered. He had not intended to use her land line. Steffie left him hanging on for several minutes, after asking his name in Swedish, then in laboured English, even though she knew perfectly well who he was. Steffie was a definite minus in this equation.

Reiss peered round the bathroom door to check on Sarah while he waited for Beatrice. Still fast asleep, apparently.

"Beatrice *Schatzie*," Reiss switched to German. "Sorry, I couldn't call you back last night. It got too late."

"Raymond, I can't speak now. I have to take Steffie to the dentist before school; she has toothache."

He said, shortly, "I spoke to Carl Oldssohn yesterday.   Our meeting is fixed for July 10th. I can stay in a hotel overnight?"

"You can't just fit me round your appointments with Carl Oldssohn. I'm busy that evening. I'm taking Steffie and her friend to the ballet; I already bought the tickets."

Annoyed, Reiss raised his voice, "Change the tickets. You can go another night. That's the only one I can do."

"They want to see Swan Lake. That's the night it's on here, It's a touring company."

He pleaded, "Beatrice, *liebschen*, you can take Steffie and her friend to the ballet another night, surely?"

Beatrice snapped, "I have to go, now. You can change your meeting." She hung up abruptly.

Irritated, Reiss pursed his lips and then wet shaved and had a shower.

Beatrice was losing her charm, rapidly.

He had reserved but not paid for the Bayreuth tickets and he was having serious second thoughts.

Why not, instead, take Sally for a week to the Italian lakes and mountains in the summer where they could go hiking which they both enjoyed? Reiss splashed his face thoughtfully and opened the bedroom door to see Sarah lying still naked in bed. She was quite blotchy in the bright morning light and her eyes were a little swollen. He tossed over her grubby skirt and the lime green top. "Time to get up now. I need to get you out of here. We leave in five minutes. No later. Understand?"

"Who are Steffie and Beatrice?"

"My cousins in Vienna. My mother's family still live there." She had not been asleep after all. Reiss regretted telephoning Beatrice. Fortunately, however, his explanation seemed to satisfy Sarah, who did not understand German. He was sure of that at least. He had tested her out by whispering abuse in a loving tone.

He went downstairs so did not see Sarah searching for something in the waste bin before she followed him. Checking a little furtively first that there was nobody around, Reiss pushed Sarah on to the floor of the back of the car under a rug and drove out past the barrier round the Village war memorial and turned into Pemberton Manor, rattling over the cattle grid. He headed straight for the Dower House, where, happily, there were no security cameras and the deaf housekeeper was still in bed.

Sarah climbed out and he handed her back her camera and the carrier with her recorder and other items in it. He said, softly, "Goodbye Sarah. It was fun knowing you. Look after yourself, won't you?"

CHAPTER THIRTY-TWO

Reiss, having parked his car conveniently by the Pavilion, went for a swim in the pool. He followed this with a hearty breakfast in the Orangery then drove back once again into Flat Acres to catch up on some paperwork in his Farmhouse office. It had been a long and tiring week, but the end of the trial was round the corner, just a few days away. It would be a relief when it was successfully concluded. But he would miss the hustle and bustle and the patients, with many of whom he had forged a strong rapport.

Leaning back and glancing through his smaller side window, he saw Tim's three white-coated clones, moving around, busying themselves. They were being paid overtime to come in that morning to sort out the data from all the A.C.E. trials as well as the one in Pemberton so that Tim was free to be with his sick wife and child in hospital in Cambridge.

Then Bill rang, sounding cheerful. "I've fixed us up on-call cover, Chief, but Simon can't do Monday night when I'm at the lecture in Cambridge. Are you still okay to do that if Ayesha's not back by then?"

Bill had persuaded the most capable of the three company medics to help him out. Simon, like Bill, rented a flat above a shop in the Village. He was studying for a pharmacology exam. "Simon's got our mobiles, and our landlines if we're at home? Any chance you can look in Orloff today before you go, chief?"

"Yes, I'll do that. Then I'm off home to Cambridge."

It was approaching midday when Reiss drove back into Pemberton and carrying his medical bag went to see Herman Orloff. He was resting in his bedroom which was on the ground floor of the nearer of the two modern annexes to the Manor

House.

His diarrhoea had ceased; he was still experiencing occasional stomach cramps but these were far less severe than two days ago. His stridor was evident and he admitted he was feeling anxious about his end of trial party on Wednesday night. "There's still so much to do and I feel so frustrated just sitting around here, making calls."

"Have a light lunch in the Orangery and then take a slow walk around the grounds and sit down when you feel you need to. Take a bottle of water with you, we don't want you to get dehydrated. It's quite warm out there, today."

Orloff smiled. "Yeah, it's warm for England. Not hot, like it is this time of year in New York or Miami. I'm glad, as you have no air-con in these rooms."

"We don't need it most of the time."

"I know that. It's different where I come from. Thanks for coming by to see me, Dr Reiss. I really appreciate your visit. Go home now and see your family."

Walking back to his car, Reiss tried both of Singer's numbers, but there was no reply. He left a brief message. He hoped there had not been a health crisis that had put Singer back in hospital.

It was one fifteen by the time he had carried his case, filled with five days of used clothes, up the uneven path and opened the front door of his rambling red brick Edwardian house. Inside, a pleasant aroma grew stronger as he opened the kitchen door.

"This smells good. Is all this baking for me, darling?"

Sally wiped a floury hand over her apron and then pushed back a lock of hair, which Reiss was pleased to see, had been allowed to grow a little longer.

"No, you idiot; I suppose you've forgotten? We're hosting a fund-raising party for the Friends of the Earth tomorrow night. Let me just put this next batch in the oven, then we can have lunch."

When she had done this, she removed her apron and Reiss

kissed her floury cheek and whispered in her ear. "I like your top. That colour blue suits you. It is new, isn't it?"

"Yes, well noticed. Joanne helped me choose it, yesterday."

"Get yourself a few more pretty things - you can put them on my card. Where is Joanne, now?"

"She's out with her friends."

Sally, finally persuaded that Sarah was Bill's girlfriend, allowed her husband to kiss her neck and massage her full breasts before she held him close to kiss him on the lips. "You are going to be here for the party tomorrow night, aren't you, Raymond?"

"Yes, unless there's some new crisis. It's infuriating because we're so thin on the ground. Ayesha's still in Bradford because of her sick father and that selfish bastard, Jim Menzies, is away on holiday till Wednesday."

"He couldn't know in advance that Ayesha's father would be ill, Raymond?"

"Don't be so reasonable." Reiss removed his hands from under her top and wiped his finger around the basin to lick off the last fragments of the mixture left behind. "Mmm. It's really nice." He put his hand over hers, observing that her finger nails were painted bright pink; usually she wore a colourless varnish. "I like the pink polish."

"Joanne did them for me."

"Good for her."

She said you would like it."

"She's right. I do. I like you to look glamorous and pretty."

"Oh, Raymond...I'm glad you're back. You've been away so much, these last few weeks."

"I know and I'm sorry, it's all come together. But the trial will be over on Wednesday. Will you come and watch that stupid idiot, Cecil Pemberton, hand out the prizes on Thursday morning?

"I can't, Raymond. It's really annoying but there's an all day college brainstorming meeting. I can't get out of it even though there's just the usual stuff on the agenda."

Reiss nodded. He knew about the meeting and was not surprised. Stroking Sally's hair, he said, "The night before that one of our three Americans is organising a "Bad Dress Party" and I'm going to have to go. Have you any ideas what I could wear?"

Sally laughed, "That horrible Hawaiian shirt with the matching shorts? It's in the bag waiting to go into the college jumble sale in a couple of weeks."

"No, Sally, I'll look ridiculous. Really ridiculous if I wear those."

"But that's the whole idea, isn't it? To look silly and outrageous and let your hair down? Have some fun? End of term entertainment? Don't be so pompous. Your dignity can stand it."

Reiss kissed her again. "I suppose so. Okay, dig them out, for me. It's forecast to be hot this week so I suppose that at least I'll be comfortable. Can you iron them first at least?"

"Yes, Raymond, I can do that for you."

He took a chilled can of beer from the fridge and sat in the garden under the shade of the copper beech tree with his briefcase from which he took out his laptop to read the latest schedule of figures that Tim's three clones had e-mailed since he left his office. But there would be no more coming through until Monday; they too were signing off now. Flat Acres would be deserted save for the security guards and the animal welfare people who visited twice a day over the weekend.

The latest information from Tim's department included an updated spreadsheet that showed the actual and then relative weight losses in percentages related to individual body weights at the start of the trial. Of the two hundred and six who had enrolled only three had dropped out which was remarkably few, given they had to remain resident at Pemberton Manor throughout, although they could take a day's leave here and there by arrangement. But there again, Pemberton Manor Health Farm was a very pleasant place and there had been a variety of activities run by the staff and by many of the trial "patients" themselves.

Many of them had told Reiss that they had enjoyed the most wonderful holiday of their lifetime with most expenses paid by FIP; only the foreign contingent were paying "hotel charges". It had been an expensive gamble for FIP which looked to be paying off well with the prospects of a market winner that would soon recoup FIP's investment and enable it to repay its loans.

The media had been invited to the prize-giving ceremony. Those present would include Sarah Goodwin, whose readers could take pride in the achievement of Frank Miller, from the USA. He had lost two kilos more than his closest male rival at Pemberton and also in the multicentre trials run by A.C.E. Frank's name was already engraved on the cup.

Sharon, whose hair was now dyed a more natural colour and smartly styled, was just ahead of her nearest rival, her friend Bella. Reiss was glad he had ordered a third cup to be handed out, given there was only a half a kilo between them. However, the progress of the third girl of the original trio, Lisa-Jane, continued to be disappointing, even though she had been trying harder than before, with the encouragement of her boyfriend Stewart, (who had made good progress himself). Reiss had seen them out together only yesterday, jogging slowly round one of the fields dodging the grazing sheep and a curious goat.

Even better than the very low drop-out rate from the trial was the fact that every single person had lost a significant amount of weight, with even Lisa-Jane six kilos lighter than on her arrival. The big issue now was whether they would keep the weight off when they left Pemberton and stopped taking Reduktopan.

Reiss, sitting on a chair and waiting for Sally to call him in for lunch, knew all the trial patients were anxious about the challenges that lay ahead of them. Every member of the medical and nursing team had been pestered with requests to provide them with "a few extra tablets" to take home after they left.

Mrs Shane was a case in point; she had been lurking in wait for "the top man" when Reiss left Orloff's room that morning and had pounced on him as he came out. She had done well, having lost forty- three pounds, and though not svelte, she certainly looked far trimmer in her lemon trousers and cream silk shirt than when she arrived eight weeks earlier.

"My ankle injury stopped me from exercising properly for over two weeks, Dr Reiss. If you could give me a few extra tablets to take away it would really help. I might even lose fifty pounds."

Reiss smiled wearily. "No, Mrs Shane, you know I can't do that. You have to change your way of life and not rely on tablets to keep your weight down in future."

Strongly perfumed, Mrs Shane tried another favoured tack among those who could afford it: "I can pay to stay on here at Pemberton and so can Herman. And we could help cover Frank's bill if we all knew we could have some more tablets?"

Reiss had smiled and shaken his head.

Then Frank had ambushed him as he was opening his car door. Reiss pretending this was a chance encounter, hailed him cheerily. "Congratulations Frank. You're in the lead for our prize. You've done fantastically well."

"Yeah, if I could just have a few more of those darn pills, I could finish the job. Can't you let me have another week's supply?"

"No, I can't. And please don't ask me that again."

"People would steal for those pills, you know that? You need to keep that dispensary properly locked up."

"I do and I will in future, but we don't keep our stocks in there, so don't bother trying to pick the lock."

Reiss closed his laptop and left it on the grass and sat back on his chair. Seeing his empty lap, Simba leapt up and purred contentedly as he stroked her soft fur. He closed his eyes and allowed himself to doze and then fell fast asleep. He woke with a start, causing the cat to leap off his lap after it had dug its claws into his knees.

Sally was calling him in to lunch from the kitchen window, but in his dream it was a scream for help from inside the burning wreck of David's car. He had run forward to try to help but his medical bag felt different; it was clumsy and heavy and it bumped against his thighs as he ran. When he looked down he saw it was not his own but his father's original leather case which he had used when Reiss was a little boy. Inside it was a metal syringe like the one his father had used on his dying mother.

CHAPTER THIRTY-THREE

Reiss and Sally set off for Addenbrooke's to visit Sylvie at six o'clock. The last patient they had visited there together had been David Devereaux when he was hospitalised following his ADR. He had asked Reiss to keep Pomeroy and Alan Michaels away, but indicated that Sally was welcome and indeed he would be pleased to see her. She had walked with David up and down the corridor. He had not benefited from losing a lot of weight and being subjected to unpleasant, invasive investigations (to which he had willingly submitted).

Given the intimacy that had at one time existed between Sally and his late colleague, Reiss imagined that, like him, Sally would be thinking about David, now. But neither of them mentioned his name as they made their way to the maternity ward, with Sally holding their present, wrapped tastefully in blue tissue paper.

They found Sylvie pale, puffy and hypertensive. Tim, stammering greetings, then escorted them to the special care baby unit, pointing through the glass case to a tiny infant connected to a mass of complex equipment. "That's Jamie."

Sally said, "Oh, Tim, he's a beautiful baby. He's even smaller than Joanne was ... " Sally's tone was gentle, her face softened with kindly concern. "But of course, she weighed nearly 5 lbs..."

Reiss said, pedantically, "2.013 kilos."

Tim shifted his eyes briefly from his small son to Reiss's troubled face. "Was Joanne premature, then?"

"Sally went into labour when she was eight months. There were some problems. She had an emergency Caesar."

Tim stared through the glass. "I wish we could cuddle Jamie, but we can't even touch him."

Sally squeezed Tim's hand, "You will soon."

Reiss rested his hand on Tim's shoulder. "Think of this as an advanced viewing; Jamie's seven weeks premature, and if he were still in *utero,* you couldn't see him never mind touch him, could you?"

Tim sighed, "Sylvie feels cheated. She's separated from him and she can't do anything for him. She wanted to breast feed. She hasn't any milk yet, but when it does come she'll have to express it into a bottle."

Sally said softly, "I couldn't breast feed Joanne, Tim."

They paused in the corridor near the entrance to the labour ward. Tim mumbled, "Thanks for coming. Thanks for everything you did, Chief." He yawned and rubbed his eyes. "I couldn't sleep a wink last night." His hands were trembling and he had developed a nervous tic.

Reiss said, quietly, "You can stay over at our house tonight, if it would help. We're only a ten-minute drive from here. We have plenty of room."

"I have to go home to fetch some stuff for Sylvie. I can have a bath and change my clothes there, then I need to get back here. Sylvie's not out of the w-w- woods and neither is Jamie. Don't pretend you don't see it."

"They need you fit and well, not a gibbering wreck, Tim."

"But I *have* to be here. Suppose there's a crisis? If I take a pill to sleep at home I might not hear the phone or be fit to drive back."

Reiss said firmly, "Tim, as a doctor and as your boss, I'm *ordering* you to go home and have a rest, before you come back." He dropped four pills into Tim's pocket. "You need a night's sleep. Take two of these tonight, but don't drive for four hours after that. You can ring for a cab if you need one."

Reiss left him to catch up with Sally, who had been tactfully edging away down the passage and together they went out to his car. He opened the passenger door for her and then drove them to the smart restaurant where he had reserved a table.

She said, softly, "You remembered Joanne's exact birth

weight?"

He said, "Yes, Sally. I remember it all. She's turned out perfectly, but I'm sorry it was so traumatic for you and now for Sylvie. A baby's birth should be a joyful time."

"Joyful like our honeymoon was?"

He said fiercely, "There was joy on our honeymoon in between the stupid rows. Joanne was conceived on our honeymoon, and she was conceived in love."

"Physical love. Your kind of love, Raymond."

"It is the only kind that makes babies, Sally."

She gave him a little smile and he took her hand. After that their conversation turned back to Tim and Sylvie and then moved on to more general issues.

It was ten thirty when they returned to the house. As Reiss turned the key in the lock, his mobile vibrated. He glanced down at the number. "Sorry, Sal, it's work. I need to take this. I'll be up in a few minutes."

Singer must have overheard him. "Was that your wife you were speaking to?"

"Yes. Do you have some news for me?" Reiss went into the dining room and sat down at the table in the darkness. Overhead, he could hear Sally's footsteps moving across the landing and then the sound of water gushing through the pipes as she ran a bath.

Singer said, "I've had a bit of a break through. I have retrieved David's file on Lara; I have put it on a disk for you to collect. It's a big file and you won't want it circulating."

Reiss gripped the phone tightly his palm a little clammy. "I can drive over tomorrow and fetch it?"

"No, it cannot be tomorrow. It's the first anniversary of Howard's death. I'm visiting his grave with some friends and we'll spend the rest of the day and the evening together. You can come on Monday, though?"

Reiss said, tightly, "Did you read his notes?"

"I glanced through them." Singer paused, then added, "It didn't end well. But you know that, already."

"Did he give her a lot of Reduktopan?"

"Yes, he did. Several courses, I'm afraid."

"*Several* courses?"

"He didn't want to but she threatened to ruin him. Said she'd tell RR if he didn't do what she wanted. RR would be you, I suppose, Dr Reiss?"

Reiss groaned. "Yes, that would be me. Can I come very early on Monday morning? Otherwise, I can't get to you until late on Tuesday night."

Singer said, "Then come early on Monday."

Reiss mounted the stairs slowly.

Upstairs, Sally was soaking in the bath. Seeing his anxious expression, she asked, "Is something wrong, Raymond?"

"No, but I will need to leave here very early on Monday morning. I'll try not to wake you." He held up the bath towel for her as she emerged. He wrapped it round her and kissed her gently and held her close. "Come to bed, now."

CHAPTER THIRTY-FOUR

On Sunday morning, leaving Sally in the kitchen baking a further assortment of quiches and cheese scones for the Friends of the Earth party that evening, Reiss walked down to the bottom of the garden to update Pomeroy.

Pomeroy snapped: "What do you mean you're afraid it could cause people to develop dependence? I thought that was impossible?"

"I'm talking about a *psychological* dependence, not a morphine-type addiction. You like the effect it has on your appearance and you want more? Imagine you're overweight and you take Reduktopan and the weight falls off, but when, you stop taking it, if you're not careful, the weight comes back, so why not take some more? Then still more? I'm guessing that's what happened with Lara, but I haven't read David's notes yet and Singer's not a doctor."

Marcus shrilled, "Your hacker can blow us sky high with these revelations, you do realise that, don't you? If he tells the world that our deputy medical director went rogue? That he kept a secret supply and gave too many pills to his girlfriend? Who then kills herself?"

Reiss replied calmly, "Singer won't do that. He's guaranteed me confidentiality and I trust him, completely. He's a decent man."

Pomeroy raged, "Why did we need to know all this? I told you to wipe that computer! To destroy everything David had written on it unread, but no, you have to find us a hacker? A loose cannon: boom, boom and we're dead! And you'll be the first casualty, Raymond! David was *your* deputy. *Your* responsibility! *You* knew he'd breached our guidelines once before. You should have kept a closer eye on him. We know he met Lara in the healthy volunteer trial that he was running? Did you *really* have no idea of this woman's existence?"

Reiss snapped, acidly, "No more than you did. Not till after his death."

"I wasn't working in the next room though, was I? Raymond, you must destroy that disk once you've read what's on it. Then you take our computer back from your hacker and destroy the hard drive, do you hear? You take out the hard disk and then you drive your car over it and then you set fire to it in a tin can till it's beyond retrieval. David and Lara are both dead so you can bury their notes with them. And when you've done that, you can make sure of your hacker as well."

"What do you mean, make sure of him?" Reiss pulled off some rose petals and pricked his thumb on a thorn.

Marcus hissed, "He's terminally ill. You can do him a big favour and save him a lingering and painful death."

"Goodbye, Marcus."

The Friends of the Earth party ended at ten. As half a dozen of the guests helped them clear up, Reiss and Sally were upstairs by eleven. During the night he awoke moaning and sweating with the nightmare of the car crash yet again, but fortunately Sally slept on. After a restless night, Reiss was on the road as the sun began lighting the sky. He had parked in Singer's crowded narrow street and was pressing his bell a few minutes before six.

Singer opened the door wearing striped pyjamas that looked too large on him; with his razored head he looked like a Belsen inmate.

"I would have printed the notes out for you but I've run out of paper." He handed Reiss the disk. "You will see that his early entries are short; the later ones are much longer - more of a personal diary."

"Did he keep a running total of all the R/P he gave her?"

"Not that I could see. Shall I delete the file on the hard drive?"

"Is it password protected against any occasional thief who

might break in?"

"Absolutely."

"Then keep it on there for now. I'm tied up all day and I'll have to wait till late tonight to read this. It's very frustrating, and yet a part of me doesn't want to read it at all."

"I can understand that." Singer cleared his throat, painfully, "Should I keep looking or do you want to call it a day?"

Reiss said, "Please keep looking, if you can."

In the car, he slipped Singer's disk between the pages of a National Trust Guide book and pushed it under the passenger seat. He drove through the gates of Pemberton Manor to eat breakfast in the Orangery where he shared a table with Jessica and Mollie Owulu. After this, the three of them strolled companionably to the Pavilion where all but one of the six treatment rooms had been requisitioned by FIP's medical team until Wednesday when the trial was officially over.

There was some encouraging news at least: Sylvie was off the danger list and Baby Jamie's condition had stabilised. Tim expected to be back at work at Flat Acres tomorrow.

Harriet, her hair a little damp from a shower after a session in the gym, approached them. She looked bronzed and energetic in her freshly laundered nurse's uniform..

"Hi guys. Hi doc. Did you have a good weekend?"

"Yes, I did, thanks. How about you?"

"Very good, thanks."

The others split off from them and Reiss followed her into his temporary consulting room and glanced down the long list of names. "How many *are* there on here? Looks like I've got more than my fair share?"

"Like Dora Shane says: Dr Reiss is the top man, so why see anyone else?"

"Thank you for that, Harriet."

It would be a long day. And after that he had agreed to do that evening's on-call shift while Bill took Sarah to Cambridge for a lecture followed by dinner in college. During this time, unless there was some kind of emergency, Reiss should have ample time to read carefully through David's notes before Bill returned and took over. But his brief discussion with Singer about what the notes contained had left him increasingly troubled. If Lara had found it difficult to come off R/P it was likely there would be others like her as he had told Pomeroy.

On the spur of the moment he sent an email to the medical and nursing team asking them all to attend an urgent impromptu lunchtime meeting in the Barn. This would not be popular as it required everyone working in Pemberton to go to and from Flat Acres during their lunch break. But he needed to alert them to the potential for psychological dependence on Reduktopan. He sent a message to this effect to John Stannard at A.C.E. who responded, promptly.

"There's no budget to cover anything other than physical illness caused by an ADR. We have advised people on the changes they need to make to their lifestyle. If they lapse – as some are sure to when they stop taking the drug - then that's their responsibility not ours."

Reiss emailed back: "Could we encourage them to form self-help groups? We could run a basic help-line for those who want some support? Can A.C.E. assist in this?"

"I'll cost it out for you."

Harriet buzzed him. "Mr Orloff is waiting. Shall I send him in?"

At that moment, the communicating door flew open and Bill came in, running his fingers distractedly through his hair.

"Give us two minutes, Harriet."

Bill said, "Please tell Chris Schwartz that I definitely want to come to New York in September, if it's still on offer?"

Reiss grunted, "Is this about Sarah? You can't mess Chris about. Leave her out of it."

Bill muttered, "No, I want to do it for myself. But I warn you that Sarah's been in a strange mood since she met Lara's sister, Penny Wilson, yesterday."

Reiss exploded: "She met Lara's sister? Why?"

Bill flushed, uncomfortable with his divided loyalties. "She's a journalist, Chief. And I'm afraid this woman convinced Sarah that Lara and David were lovers. That he was responsible for her sister's depression and her suicide. She says, he must have known the state she was in. I quote: 'He was a bloody doctor, after all.'

"And I know she's made an appointment to meet the principal of the school where Lara taught foreigners English. She's obsessed with this story. She knows I never even met David Devereaux, but she still keeps asking me about him. Keeps asking what I've heard on the grapevine? And she says she wants to talk to you again about him."

Harriet opened his door. "Are you two docs going to see *any* patients this morning? We're running out of chairs in the waiting room!"

"Sorry, yes, of course. We're both ready now."

Bill slipped away through the communicating door into his own suite as Reiss stood to greet Herman Orloff, who sat down heavily opposite and leaned across the desk. "Did you know that I came to England last summer? That I spent a few weeks at Pemberton's Health Centre under the care of Dr Devereaux?"

"No, I didn't. Why didn't you mention this earlier?"

"I asked him then if I could try a few Reduktopan tablets?"

"He would have said 'No.'" Reiss' tone was firm. He kept his expression neutral.

"He told me to enrol in this trial instead. He warned me that my medical history might disqualify me, but he said would do his best to include me; he said he liked a challenge."

"Yes, and here we both are?"

"Thing is, Devereaux hedged his bets a little, Dr Reiss. He allowed me to take the same dose for three weeks as the healthy volunteers had taken so he could see how it went with me."

"No, he didn't. He couldn't have done that." Reiss blustered. "We keep a very close eye on our stocks of pills and if any were unaccounted for it would show up on our records. There aren't any missing." His face displayed righteous indignation."Even if he had access to some extra pills, why would he give them to you?"

Orloff rubbed his fleshy nose, pensively. "He felt sorry for me, I guess. I was desperate and I was stuck on close to 300lbs then and I'm only five foot six, Dr Reiss. I lost weight with his help. Even before I came on your trial I had lost over 100 lbs under him. And I've lost another forty here during these last two months. Your drug is nothing short of a miracle; if I could only keep taking it for a few more weeks I could achieve my target weight.

"But even now, I'm able to wear smart clothes and I don't mind looking at myself in a mirror. I'm very grateful for this, but I still have a little way to go and I'm worried that my weight will start to creep back when I go back home. What it comes down to is that I need you to give me some extra pills to take away with me when I leave here."

Reiss shook his head. "No, I can't do that. It's a new compound and we have to be very cautious. Once we get our general licence so that it can be obtained on prescription from your doctor, then it will be a matter for her. But, if you keep to small portions and off fatty foods, you'll be fine. But we can see how it looks after Christmas or even next summer, if you want to come back here."

"I don't want to wait another six months, I'm sixty-seven. I want to finish the job now - I have no more time to waste."

Reiss snapped a pencil and chewed the end of one half, irritably. "No, Mr Orloff. I'm sorry to disappoint you, but what you're asking for is out of the question. I can't give them to you and that's final. Don't ask me again."

Orloff sighed, "I'm sure Dr Devereaux would have let me have some extra. Like I said, he let me try your pills for three weeks last summer. He explained the risks and I accepted them. Gladly accepted them and I still do."

Reiss scowling, said coldly, "If what you claim is true, which I find hard to believe, then I am shocked. It would have been a flagrant breach of our company's rules. But David is not here to defend himself so you leave me with no option but to investigate this matter, fully. You will need to make a full and detailed statement in writing, but as I have thirty patients waiting to see me it will have to wait a day or two. Right now, I need to check everybody out of this trial before I can discharge them, including you.

"However, with regard to this investigation over Dr Devereaux' alleged misconduct, I will have to inform our solicitors forthwith."

Reiss began slowly to enter this unwelcome information into the computer. *Alleges for the first time today that DD gave him R/P last summer for 3 weeks. Now asking for more tablets. REFUSED. His claim about DD will need careful further investigation … "*

Orloff leaned forward and pulled Reiss' fingers off the keyboard, "No, stop! Stop typing. Delete what you just wrote! I'm not getting involved in any enquiry and I take back everything that I said earlier. I deny that I said it. I deny Dr Devereaux gave me any tablets. I begged him to give them to me but he refused. He said I wasn't a suitable candidate for a healthy volunteer trial and the drug was too new for a sick old guy like me with my complex medical history.

"Look, I'll come clean with you. I was just trying to persuade you to let me have some more of your miracle pills so I could keep on taking them after I leave here. I'm a wealthy man, Dr Reiss and I am prepared to pay for them. I'll pay whatever you think is the right price for a few more tablets?" He took out his wallet which was over-flowing with large bank notes.

Reiss stood up, snapping, angrily. "First you say David gave you pills and now you say he didn't? And put that money away. I've a good mind to call the police right now!"

Orloff, his stridor, sounding like a saw on wood, shoved his wallet hastily back into his robe pocket and spluttered breathlessly, "No, Dr Reiss, no, please don't do that. Please don't get so angry. I'm truly sorry. What I did just now was terrible, I can see that and I apologise to you. But you just don't understand how it feels to be me and stuck in my situation. I have spent the last thirty years trying failed diets. And now at last, I am getting close to owning a decent body shape? You and your company's medical team have succeeded where everyone else has failed in the past. Forget the stupid lies I told you. It was a try-on for more tablets. Dr Devereaux never gave me Reduktopan! I begged him for some but he refused point blank."

"You're telling me now that Dr Devereaux definitely *did not* give you any Reduktopan last summer?" Reiss, his fingers hovering over the keyboard, glared at Orloff.

"He *did not* give me any, no, sir, he didn't. The only time I took Reduktopan has been this summer here at Pemberton in *your* trial under *your* supervision, Dr Reiss."

Reiss sat heavily down again and swore under his breath in German, a superior language for such occasions. His fingers hovered uncertainly over the keyboard.

"You must delete what you just wrote. I lied about poor Dr Devereaux. That was terrible of me. But I won't be involved in any enquiry! There's no need for one. None at all. And anything like will harm the product and your company. It might delay you getting a product licence to sell it and I don't want that to happen. It's a great product and we need it out there."

Reiss glowered at him. "If it weren't so close to the end of the trial, I'd ask you to leave."

"You're an honest man, Dr Reiss, and I respect that. I'm afraid that in business I found very few people were truly honest. Most people have their price, and it isn't always money, though it usually is. But you *must* delete what you just wrote. I *lied*, pure and simple and I was wrong to do it."

Sighing, Reiss deleted what he had written. As Orloff was leaving, he turned back and pleaded:"You will come to my leaving party though, won't you, doctor? I'm having real French champagne and it'll be a whole lot of fun and I really want you to be there. It wouldn't be the same without you."

Reiss nodded. "Yes, Mr Orloff, I'll come. I promise."

CHAPTER THIRTY-FIVE

By the afternoon, tension pains were spreading down Reiss's neck and across both his shoulders. But for the hastily convened lunch time meeting he would have gone swimming in the lunch break, but there had been no time. Then, after seeing off his last patient, he found the pool closed for "essential maintenance".

He ate dinner alone in the Orangery and drove back into Flat Acres. The floodlit complex was quiet with few people around though some were at work in their offices in the laboratory block as windows were lit and he could see white figures flitting around silently before he pulled down the window blinds and sat down at his desk. He signed off the half dozen letters Linda had left on his desk and dealt with a few pressing emails, including one in German from Dr Otto Wengler in Zurich, delaying the moment when he would insert Singer's disk with its big file of David's private notes.

The earliest records were copies of what he had seen recorded in the system when he searched for her name. Lara had lost 7 kilos during the three week trial. She had stuck to the dietary advice, for the most part, with one or two lapses. She was recorded as *delighted*, but had then been *Lost to follow up*.

This was followed by a contemporaneous note prompted by a chance meeting in Cambridge: *Told her she should have kept in touch. V. apologetic. Says she dropped her pay-as-you-go mobile down the toilet the same week she moved to a different rented flat. Chaotic. Pretty face, but still overweight+. Pleasant companion, but no more at this stage. Would like me to help her slim down. Admit I am tempted."*

They had a few casual dates. Then she came to stay for a

weekend and it had begun. David had noted her weight and height and other key measurements before starting Lara on a six week course of Reduktopan.

On June 12th 2000 David had jubilantly recorded:

"Wt. 49.5 Kgs. Target wt. achieved in 38 days!! Best 40th present I could have. L looks fantastic. Wanted to continue for another week as achieve target 4 days early! Refused. Explained risks to her underline. No more R/P. Meantime, L has changed what she calls her "look" completely. New hairstyle and new clothes. She looks gorgeous. Adores me. Feels a different person. Thrilled to be able to wear a bikini or go topless on holiday with me in Crete next week."

They had left the weekend after his fortieth birthday a few days after the disastrous office party and Reiss recalled David had returned from his holiday looking tanned, fit and in good spirits. But soon, Lara was putting weight back on. As David insisted she stand on the scales in front of him every Saturday morning this was quickly discovered.

In July he recorded sourly:

Wt. 53 Kgs. Hates herself. Admits to comfort eating during the week. Asking for more R/P. Refused. Told her to eat less and more sensibly and the weight will come off. Needs to leave the car at home and walk more.

His entry a week later noted Lara was edging up to 54 Kgs and was *very upset*. Then, on Sunday morning: *Woke to find the bed empty. L in the kitchen at 3am eating toast and jam. When I remonstrated she said she had "such a craving she could not help herself," then burst into tears saying she is miserable because her new jeans are now too tight. Told her to buy a larger size or reduce her calorie intake. Advised her again re diet. No more R/P. Tears + +*

By the end of July, Lara had regained still more of the weight she had lost.

Didn't want to stand on the scales today. Not surprised as Wt. 57 Kgs. Burst into tears. Agreed she can have 2 wks R/P to kick start new diet plan. Will stay here with me and commute to Cambridge for work. Then STOP!

His entry five days later. *"Wt. down to 55 Kgs. Came jogging but gave up half-way moaning her ankle hurts.* Her weight dropped down to 54 Kgs and then 53 Kgs.

Now 53.5Kgs. Tears + + + Asking for more R/P. Will do 'anything I want' but at the same time issuing veiled threats if I don't ! Will give her R/P till wt back down to 50Kgs. Then STOP!"

By August Lara's weight was hovering a little above 50 Kgs and R/P was stopped and Lara had been living in her flat during the week. The following Saturday David had noted: *Bulimia? Admits to this in the past but promises she won't do it again. Not convinced.*

A week later he recorded: *Caught L with her finger down her throat in the bathroom when she thought I was asleep. <u>Warned about impact of doing this on teeth and her insides.</u> I suggested we train for a marathon together. Too much for her. Suggested a half marathon. Agreed but not enthusiastic! Her legs ache after standing and teaching all day!!! Explained to L for nth time about need to balance calorie intake with energy expenditure. Agreed she will count calories. Promises, promises. Heard it all before. Disappointing me and herself.*

A week later, Devereaux, noticed an empty box of Belgian chocolates in his dustbin:

L says it was a present from a student and she offered them round but then she finished the box herself in an evening.

On Sunday night, Devereaux noted a disturbing new phase:.

I woke to hear a noise which I thought was a burglar. Bed empty next to me and I found L trying to force the door to my study where she thinks I keep R/P in my desk. (I don't). Pleading with me to give her more R/P so she can be slim and beautiful for me when we go on holiday to Corsica in September. Have agreed she can have 2 weeks R/P if she stays with me and I oversee it. Agreed. Kissed me. All smiles.

However 2 weeks later:

Wt. 51 Kgs. L much happier as clothes all fit properly now. Says she would like a few pills to keep so that she can take them when she feels she needs to. Says my controlling what she is allowed increases her "craving" for them and I need to trust her. Refused: explained she has already had more than she should and she needs to get a grip. L threw a tantrum and said if I didn't do what she wanted she'd tell RR. I said that would certainly end it with me and R/P for good. She apologised and was contrite. Wanted to make up for it and was very sweet and loving saying she only wanted to look good for me. She wants to be slim for herself but also for me but she struggles to keep the weight off. When she does, she is beautiful, sexy and I admit I'm very attracted by her. She wants me to feel that way for her and so we're in a cycle of mutual dependence I suppose. But the flip side is that L is also highly volatile and can be frightening. She screams so that I have to keep the windows shut or the neighbours will think I'm murdering her. For example, this morning, when I said she needed to stop R/P now she picked up the bathroom scales and hurled them at me. Missed me but they smashed on the floor. I lost my temper and whacked her hard on her backside after which we made up in bed and then cleared up the mess together. I keep the other set of scales locked in a cupboard in my study and I've told her she can't go into it without me being there. I keep the door locked at all times. This is what it has come to...

The following Saturday, a week before they were due to go on holiday, he recorded:

Says she wants to try a low "maintenance dose" to stop her seesawing up and down. Says she would be very careful and sensible and I should trust her. She finds the commute from here to the language school in Cambridge too much for her to do every day. She also knows I'm finding her being here all the time is too much for me. So I said for the next week she should go back to her flat in Cambridge and I gave her 3 days of pills.

Reiss skimmed the entries about the holiday to the one two weeks later.

Saturday 25 Sept. 50Kgs. L looking great and says she has been really good about regular exercise since we came home. Busy all day at the school as start of new term. I suggested we now try stopping the maintenance dose for a week and she flew into a rage. NO, this is what keeps her stable and happy and the way she likes it and I like it. She needs to feel in control and this helps her. Her response was like a drug addict when you threaten to reduce their permitted fix. She may even be hoarding a few at her flat? R/P doesn't work on the brain receptors so any dependence on it is purely psychological so I'm planning to substitute some placebo tablets; I can take a few from our stockroom; nobody will look for them as we don't use them anymore

Ten days later, Devereaux noted:

Wt. 50.5 Kgs and still looking good. I praised her for staying close to her base, but she says she would feel safer if she could go below 50Kgs. She'll come running with me next week. Then, she wants to try for a baby. Very fixated on this. Two of the college teachers are now pregnant and this has made her feel "broody". She wants my child and for us to be a proper family. Talking about getting married? I said I was in no rush to repeat the experiment and our relationship is v. up and down and we haven't known each other that long. She assured me she would be a model wife and mother if she could feel secure in our relationship. Re: pregnancy I explained at length (again) that I need to be sure that all traces of R/P had left her body before we could consider this.

A long weekend away in Paris was apparently successful. Two weeks after their return Lara's weight had begun to creep up.

Wt. 52.5 Kgs. Wants to go back on "maintenance "dose. Told NO. Must learn to manage without. Tears and tantrums + + + Tonight I will 'forget to lock' study door and leave placebo tabs where she can find them in an unlocked drawer of my desk where I keep bits of stationery.

The next entry noted:

All 6 placebo tablets taken.

A week later on Saturday, there was another entry.

Wt up. 54 Kgs. L denied taking tablets from my study then became furious when I told her the pills were dummies and I had to see whether I could trust her. I could not. Tears and tantrums + + +

Shouting I had played a base trick on her! She can't trust me!!! I am trying to punish and cheat her! Says if she had known they were only placebos she would have taken more care to stick to her diet and what I had done had was the reason she had put on more wt. Told her she has to have more self-discipline. She burst into tears saying it's so hard and she knows I don't find her attractive the way she is. I do not when she's in a rage and her jeans do not do up and she won't buy a bigger size on principle.

The next week Lara was caught searching through his pockets to find his keys while she thought he was asleep. *Caught her red handed trying to get one of the cabinets open. Row+ + Hysterical. Exhausting for both of us. Wt up again. 55.7 Kgs. Says she feels bloated, nervy and restless. Not sleeping more than 3 hrs at a time. Disturbed dreams + Miserable at wt. rise. Craves chocolate and biscuits. Still saying she wants a baby. I said not until she can control her weight without tablets. 5mg diazepam nocte so we can both get a night's sleep. She has started phoning me to the office but nobody noticed as it was to my direct line. Warned not to phone unless real emergency or it's over between us."*

A week later, after struggling with Lara's increasing outbursts and failure to lose weight Devereaux recorded that he had reluctantly restarted her on R/P.

I have warned her about the potential effect on her stomach lining. Gave her antacid. Tears + Obsessed with thoughts of food all day. Behind with her marking. Problems concentrating in lessons. Labile mood. Tearful. Students are asking if something is wrong? Called into office by the principal. Clothes are all too tight. Wt still 55 Kgs. May have to try her on another course of R/P for 2 weeks but only if she stays here in the house with me. Two days later: *L hysterical again. Beating her fists on my study door. Says she knows I have R/P here and I am torturing her by not giving it to her when she desperately needs it. Don't I want her to look good? Tears +++ Tantrums. Says she can't go on and will top*

herself. *Not serious. A ploy to force me to give her R/P. As is her threatening to telephone RR. Told her RR certainly wouldn't give her any R/P and might dismiss me. If that happened it would be worse for both of us. Is that what she wants? NO, NO!!I love you David!*

Tears + + + Says sorry +++. Wouldn't do that, really. But <u>please</u> can she have more R/P. Warned that if she <u>ever </u>approaches RR we're finished for good. She says won't ever do that. She can't live without me. (I can live without her and increasingly I would like to). She will stay with me all this week and commute to and from Cambridge. Wants me to monitor her calorie intake and exercise... continuing with diazepam 5mg.

In early October, David recorded:

Wt. now stable for 1 week at 50Kgs. Will stop R/P completely for now. L looks fantastic and says she feels very well and happy.

A week later: *Still taking diazepam 5mg. nocte. Wants a "maintenance dose" of R/P. Gave her 3 to last the whole week. Hope she is not hoarding any. Warned her about this. Desperate for a baby now that "will bind us together forever". Long talk about future. Told her I cannot take the tantrums and rages. Admits she has been 'difficult' at times, but only because she wants to look her best for me. Told her I am not ready to make the commitment to have a child with her until completely off R/P. Tears + + Advised <u>again she must not get pregnant</u> while taking any R/P. We have made a 'deal': if wt. stays below 51 Kgs for a calendar month <u>without any R/P</u> I will let her try for a baby ... L now v. motivated.*
Exercising + + + Jogging.

Looks good. Libido up too. To reduce then stop diazepam over next week.

Then came the bombshell.

Being sick every morning. Did a bimanual; I can't believe it. L is six weeks. Sent off a urine sample but it is a formality. I know when it happened. My carelessness as I never relied on her. L is thrilled and making plans but I told her to keep her flat on in Cambridge for now. I'll give her the rent money for the next few weeks. I've a series of lectures in New York next week and I'm closing up the house while I'm away.

There was an obscure reference to Mandy's abortion a few months earlier that year.

We agreed L will have baby privately in London. Different consultant at different clinic from the one where M went.

Two weeks later, Lara was gaining weight again.

Warned by me and gynae. Not to eat for two. Wt up to 54Kgs. Must stick to low calorie diet. Says feels faint if doesn't eat 3-4 times daily. I said eat a carrot not a chocolate or a biscuit. Arranging for a scan to be done in London at fourteen weeks. All well so far. FL (presumably the gynaecologist) warned L she was gaining too much weight too quickly. L in a sulk on the journey back. Not sure how I feel about becoming a father with L as baby's mother, but too late now. Make the best of it.

Reiss read the depressing entry dated 28th November three times: David had taken Lara to a clinic in London for the 14 week scan.

L was devastated +++ we both are. The fetus has major abnormalities of the spinal column and skull. Baby would not survive at birth. Unusual combination and am wondering if L took any R/P during the first trimester? L crying agreed to TOP ASAP: L feeling shattered and depressed+++ as I am too. I am surprised how upset I feel about all of this. So stupid and if she'd only been honest with me and herself."

The gynaecologist had prescribed Lara antidepressants and suggested she saw her GP about this as well.

When he said this FL gave me a bit of a look but did not actually say, you shouldn't be trying to deal with all of this yourself, David. It's not a good idea for you to act as her treating doctor in this instance. I asked him to send me a disk with the scan photos on it. Lara cried all the way home and I had to give her a sedative; had it prescribed in London. I feel stunned by these events myself. Am wondering if I should have the fetus autopsied? But what if they find traces of R/P? Maybe better if I do this myself and send samples to an independent lab? Grim prospect. Not sure yet.

The next note was made the following morning.

29th November 6.30am

L admitted she had "kept back" a few R/P tablets to take when weight seemed to be rising and still has two at her flat in Cambridge. Had to phone in to work saying she was unwell and I left her in bed to go to work zonked out in drugged haze. Whisky will do for me tonight but where do we go from here?

After the termination in London on 1st December, Devereaux had requested the fetal remains for a private 'burial' ceremony. As Reiss had suspected, his research curiosity had overcome his repulsion. Traces of the three compounds which made up Reduktopan were found in minute quantities.

The circumstances of the termination and its sordid aftermath took their toll on Devereaux who admitted in his diary-style notes that he was drinking more than usual. He refused his sister Anne's invitation to spend Christmas at Merrivale Farm:

The only thing that's merry about that place is its name. Instead, he took Lara away for a week of winter sunshine in Morocco. On their return he recorded:

L ill with ? "holiday tummy"? Wt 51.5 Kgs on return. Able to wear bikini and looks good in swimming costume but mood still very low. Me too.

A week later:

Wt 50.5 Kg No energy. Can't face new term. Went to bed and left me to unpack and load the washing in machine. TAT. Depressed and anxious. Worried about the future.

Refusing to persevere with antidepressants. Says they give her "a dry mouth". Willing to take diazepam. Becoming addicted to them? I have suggested she see a psychiatrist about her depression. Offended. Says it is a normal bereavement reaction. All R/P stopped since termination. <u>No More.</u>

Several weeks later:

"L remains depressed. Desperate to try for another baby. Assures me she will never take R/P again during pregnancy. I believe her this time. But awful punishment.

Her depression did not remit. In late January 2001 Devereaux recorded:

"L's mood still low. Tearful. Has guilt feelings +++ about causing injury to "our baby". Suffering severe pain before her periods. Cried when she had her period today. Not pregnant (I took care of that). Is she developing IBS? Phoned A B in Oxford. Explained briefly about TOP and asked if L's behaviour in line with expected bereavement symptoms? L sleeping badly as am I. TAT. So am I. AB says bring Lara to see him. She is exhausting both of us. Had 3 hours sleep last night. Concentrating at work now difficult and RR giving me concerned looks. L agreed to sleep in guest room tonight. (Not that I encourage guests).

The following week Devereaux rang AB again. Reiss looked up psychiatrists in Oxford and concluded it must be Albert Berns, whom he now vaguely remembered David referring to as his mentor when he was at Oxford. He had asked AB for advice on how best to manage Lara's depression and what looked like her growing dependence on benzodiazepines:

Explained to AB that I fear L is developing tolerance to diazepam. She has to take more than before to achieve the same benefit.

He noted two days later that he had been at a conference at the Royal Society of Medicine where he had spent some time in the library:

Is addiction a disease that medicine can and should treat, or is it a voluntary state?

Etymologically, the word addiction is from the Latin, originally denoting a process in Roman law, whereby one individual was given over to another by judicial pronouncement, often for non-payment of debts. Ergo, addiction equals a species of slavery. Is Lara my slave because I have supplied her with R/P that she wants (albeit I now do this reluctantly) or am I her slave because I feel unable to refuse to give her what she wants?

The truth is that we continue in our cycle of mutual captivity and interdependence to achieve our own goals which coincide, namely, to keep her weight at circa 50 Kgs. There are also sub-aims to be achieved. Namely, she satisfies her wish to please me and I to please her. But at what cost? She is not ill. With more effort and resolution she could maintain her weight without R/P. Am I now the primary source of her problems? *Lara is manipulative ++++++++ and I am being manipulated. But I must be willing to be manipulated or this would not happen?*

Massaging his aching neck, Reiss read gloomily on.

David had scanned in the gynaecologist's last letter, addressed to him which provided a name (Francis Lepton) and his address in Harley Street in London. It repeated the advice that Lara should take antidepressants with specialist psychiatric referral if she did not start to improve. It also noted:

The irritable bowel symptoms she told me about are almost certainly worsened by her anxiety and depression prompted by her termination.

Matters went further downhill. There were more frequent rows and Devereaux himself was becoming depressed to a near clinical level:

Neither of us able to sleep. Last night we had another awful row. I can't take much more. I feel exhausted. We both called in sick today and RR rang me offering to come over. I told him not to. I know he's scared I'm suffering from a recurrence of ADR symptoms but I assured him it definitely <u>wasn't</u> that and I would be in tomorrow. Will work from home. Agreed to have my check up at Addenbrooke's brought forward to reassure him. L will stay in her flat in Cambridge for those 3 days. I wish it was permanent but she'll be back.

In early February, following his discharge from Addenbrooke's, David, at the end of his tether, telephoned Professor Albert Berns for professional help and advice: *"Explained to AB that L is refusing to take prescribed antidepressants and getting hooked on diazepam. She admits she has some "IBS" symptoms, worsened by stress. Says had these for last month but didn't tell me she had these before because she was afraid I would stop R/P if she needed it. Low mood combined with low pain threshold. Sight of a baby in a pram makes her upset and tearful. Desperate we try again for a baby. Advised her she is not well enough at the moment...*

Professor Berns suggested a different antidepressant. This did not suit Lara either. *Complains makes her mouth dry, face itchy and she put on 1Kg in 5 days.*

David increased Lara's diazepam to 10 mg three times daily. By the third week of February, new and ominous symptoms had manifested:

... Losing wt .Now 49 Kgs. Denies has taken R/P for months and urine and blood tests confirm this. Looks unwell and for first time in her life she is below her ideal weight for height. Pale and tired. Says her IBS flares and then goes and she is fine. Advised to drink more water. Must not get dehydrated. Advised L she needs specialist gastro investigation. Promised her to arrange this privately in London. She is not keen but has agreed.

Differential diagnosis:

1.IBS

2.Diverticulitis

3. Ulcerative colitis

4. Crohn's disease*

5. Tumour (unlikely but possible?

On February 26th Devereaux once again consulted Professor Berns by telephone.

AB has agreed to assess L informally. We are invited to lunch this Sunday.

Three days later, Devereaux noted: *Wt down again. 48.5 Kgs. TAT. No energy. Suggested she try a higher calorie diet. Not tempted by chocolates (says they make her feel sick) rejecting full cream yoghurts, custards, steam puddings, cake, potatoes, etc. Says she is eating and denies anorexic behaviour. Stood her in front of a mirror as anorexics view their body shape as larger than life but L said: "I look thin, don't I? First time in my life. It's amazing!" Reason? Hope it doesn't come to bowel surgery and a stoma bag. Staying with me all week and driving herself to and from work. Very tired. Asleep before 10pm.*

The last entry before the visit to Berns was a Saturday morning. Reiss noted it on his pad and ringed it twice as coincided with Lara's note that he had found in David's night table drawer.

Wt 47.4 Kgs. Looks pale and unwell. Diarrhoea and vomiting. Bowel cramps + + Sudden desire for spicy foods! Denies she has been taking purgatives. Says sorry she refused my offer of a jab of Pethidine last night. While I was asleep she took 3 temazepam from bottle because she was sure she had sicked everything I gave her earlier. Drowsy a.m. Locked away the bottle of temazepam. Told L she needs urgent specialist gastro investigations next week. Will make appointment with CM (whom I knew in Oxford). Hope she's not developing a stricture. Warned L she must not cancel this again behind my back. I think she fears she has cancer despite my reassurance this is v. unlikely. She cannot recall any close family members with bowel problems. Cannot be sure if she had measles as well as mumps as a small child. Parents are dead so can't ask them and doesn't speak to her sister Penny, who is a year older. Said they haven't spoken for 3 + years. Fell out over boyfriend or something stupid. L's early GP records were lost when she moved from London to Cambridge. Will take temazepam instead of diazepam nocte to help her (and me) sleep before we go to Oxford for lunch on Sunday.

The trip to Professor Berns' house in Oxford was described in some detail:.

"... L saw psychiatry books on AB's shelf and was suspicious. Became very upset when he asked her questions she didn't like. Left the table after the soup course and ran out of his house, crying. When I cornered her and grabbed her arm in the street she wouldn't stop screaming and people opposite were staring at us. I put my arms around her and calmed her down and persuaded her to go back inside and talk to AB privately in his study without me present. Mrs AB and I sat on our own in the dining room and she told me AB was now worried about me! "Let him help you, David. Listen to him, this is his field. It's what he does every day. You're out of your depth with this girl, we can both see that."

Journey home was a nightmare. Had to stop three times at different garages for the loo because of L's diarrhoea and painful stomach cramps. Stress and not eating aggravates matters. Looks ill and moaning a lot. People filling their cars on forecourt stared at us in a hostile fashion. A woman approached me and asked if L didn't need a doctor? I said, "I am a doctor. I am taking her back to hospital after a day out." Must make sure L attends appt to ensure urgent gastro investigation. 9.15 pm L in bed and asleep (doped to the eyeballs).

Reiss noted an important postscript to the day's record.

10 pm. AB rang landline. Said to check first L really asleep and will not be listening in. Long chat. AB thinks L is severely depressed with ?suicidal ideation. Labile and volatile. Anything might push her over the edge. L needs specialist psychiatric treatment and AB advises immediate admission. He will deal with it if I allow this? She can be seen by a gastroenterologist from Oxford while hospitalised there. Thinks L might benefit from ECT but in her current state will not cooperate voluntarily. I must consider getting L sectioned to admit her and treat her without her consent. AB offered to arrange this at his unit in Oxford. I said I need to think this over. Not comfortable with making L a compulsory psychiatric patient. Would have to explain to school about absence but school concerned at her state anyway. Should I agree for her to have ECT under section? I have no standing. Not her nearest relative. Not married. AB said "Don't leave it too long, David, she may try and do something stupid and attention seeking." Said I will try my best to persuade L to cooperate with AB.

Two days later there was another long diary-style entry:

Tuesday morning 10 a.m. Big row last night and another this morning. I feel shattered and we both called in sick. Lucky the house is detached and I have double glazing and the windows were closed. L hysterical at suggestion of psychiatric admission and refusing to consider ECT. She's not "mad" and she will run away if I try and put her in a 'psychiatric ward with mad people. I offered to pay for a private room though v expensive. Screaming and shouting. Accused me of wanting to lock her away to get rid of her. It's my fault she's depressed. <u>I'm cruel as all she wants is the chance to have a baby with me and I am not cooperating.</u> AB *advised strongly against when we discussed it. Said she needs to get well first. L says she has moments when she's tempted to snatch a baby from its pushchair in a supermarket.*

I have been through this loads of times; get yourself well first and then we can try again. Tears + + last night and this morning. I'm just looking for excuses not to let her get pregnant. I don't love her and I never did love her and it was just the sex for me. Now that's not so good she's becoming a "millstone". Feels insecure. It would be different if we were married. Even if we were engaged. She wants to marry me and have our children. I don't want to marry her but I couldn't tell her that now. I told her we can talk again about it and another pregnancy after she's seen a gastroenterologist. He may need to give her treatment that wouldn't be compatible with pregnancy. Ditto with psychiatric medication. L went berserk at second mention of psychiatric treatment. Will have to be done under section. AB is right and I know that. No viable alternative. Will ask AB to arrange if I can somehow get L to Oxford again on some pretext.

Tried to follow AB's advice. Kept my voice quiet and reasonable and stayed calm. Did not shout back when she screamed at me. Told her if she cooperated with treatment and improved then we could think about trying for a baby. Reminded her she deceived me and took R/P that she had hoarded after she knew she was pregnant and that may have caused the abnormalities. She was in floods of tears. No she didn't take any after she knew she was pregnant. I'd given her the pills. She didn't buy it over the counter! It was my fault! She couldn't have know even a few tablets would harm the baby like this. I should have warned her! At that point I snapped. Told her I had warned her till I was blue in the face. That I was sick of her tantrums and moods. No, I didn't love her. She is vain and lazy and she has no self discipline and so right now I didn't feel like giving her another baby as what kind of a mother would she be? Even if she were fit in mind and body which she isn't! She'd make a lousy mother. She never once asks how I feel!

I locked myself in my study. She yelled through the door that she was leaving me and that she wouldn't ever come back. I didn't answer her even though she banged on the door like crazy. She kept yelling and crying I didn't love her, that I wanted her dead! It was a relief when I heard her car driving off. I went into the bedroom and checked. She's left most of her clothes here. She'll be back by tomorrow. She still loves her pretty clothes, even though she's depressed.

Reiss scanned the remaining entries quickly. There was no reference to Lara's desperate messages left on his answering machine the next day.

The next entry was dated 8th March recording the news of Lara's suicide in an ingenuous note.

Lara is <u>dead:</u> O/D on paracetamol and gin. Principal of Lara's language school rang me. He was very shocked. I said I was too. He told me my home number was the one Lara had left with the school office in case of emergencies. She had booked herself into a cheap hotel on Friday night then put a "Do Not Disturb" sign on the door. By the time the chamber maid found her in a coma two days later and called an ambulance she was beyond help. She didn't leave a note. Didn't blame anyone. I feel bereft. Never thought with all her histrionics that she would go through with it but I was wrong and she did. Principal rang me a second time to tell me he had been contacted by L's estranged married sister (Penny Wilson). I said, L had told me she was meeting her sister for the first time in more than 3 years. Apparently, Penny had expected Lara (or Jane as she called her) to be in touch and her phone did not answer. Glad to leave it to her sister to make arrangements for the funeral which will be in London; the principal will let me have the details when he has them if L's sister does not contact me and I would prefer she doesn't.

The coroner has ordered a P M which is routine in the circumstances. I doubt there'll be an inquest. Hope not. I don't want to be called as a witness. Lara described me to the Principal as a good friend (but not her boyfriend thankfully).

A long diary style entry described Lara's funeral.

16th March: Golders Green Crematorium. Gloomy red, brick buildings but lovely gardens at the back at least ... Chapel was very full. The principal had laid on a bus so all L's students and her friends among the staff could attend it. Nice man. Seeing Lara's sister gave me a bit of a turn. Lumpish and suspicious. She looked a little like L did before she lost weight and acquired what she called her "new look" and became slim and sexy and beautiful. Those early months were glorious. Poor L. I don't like to think of her as she is now, starting to decay inside her coffin having been tidied up after the P M and then wrapped in a shroud. Don't like to think about her like that, but it is the reality.

I sat in the back row. I shut my eyes and tried to block everyone out and remember our good times, when we delighted in each other's company and enjoyed our time together and had holidays abroad and in the sun. The Minister was making some generalised speech cobbled together from what L's sister and the principal had told him. He had never met Lara and didn't know her from Eve and mostly referred to her as Jane and then Jane Lara. I knew Lara very well though. In the Biblical sense and every sense. I tried to keep the image of her in my head as she was when we went away for my fortieth birthday last summer. When she was beautiful and joyful and happy and we made love all the time and kept laughing and being silly. When we delighted in each other's bodies. Before it all began to go sour and wrong. No more love for Lara where she's going. No more love for me left behind.

LOVE. Did I love Lara? I think now she has gone that I must have done. I never told her so and it hurt her, I know that. All she wanted was to hear me to say those three little words, but I didn't say them to her. Too late now. But, just in case her spirit was lingering near me, I whispered, 'Lara, I love you, darling' when the box slid away from view. Not into the flames then, as I expect they save all the coffins up till the end of the day and then whoosh, up they all go in a great pillar of smoke. So I told L I loved her and I missed her terribly, just in case somehow she could hear me. Also, I admit, I needed to say it. To be at last honest with myself about what I'd lost with her death.

We sang, Onward Christian Soldiers to help her on her way and then exited to Lara's theme from Dr Zhivago that the school principal had suggested, telling the sister that they only knew her there as "Lara".

There was a pile of wreaths outside on the back steps including one from me. I was getting too emotional so I went to the bottom of the crematorium gardens and walked around for twenty minutes pretending to study the flowers on my own. Misty, cold and raining. A lot of people had gone by then and the bus was filling up to return to Cambridge. L's sister grabbed me suddenly by the sleeve from behind the colonnade and manoeuvred me into a corner, hissing from under her headscarf, "Jane said you gave her an experimental slimming drug? Something your company has developed?"

I told her that her sister had taken it when she had been a healthy volunteer eighteen months ago. That was what she was referring to. But yes, I had helped her sister lose weight with diet and exercise over the last nine months. We sang in the same choir in Cambridge which was where we had bumped into each other as I expect Lara told you? I was her friend but no more than that. She didn't believe me of course. Became threatening and unpleasant. Said she <u>knew</u> I'd been her sister's lover and L had boasted about how clever I was and told her I had a lovely house out in the sticks somewhere. Why was I denying it? She'd met J/L on the afternoon before she took an overdose. J/L had asked her to come and see her in Cambridge and she had taken the train from London and done so.

She had been surprised but glad to get this call from J/L. Admitted they were not on good terms for nearly four years. L had said they were not on <u>speaking terms</u> during that time. L's sister told me she was stunned by her sister's appearance. How did she get so <u>thin</u>? J had been overweight since her teens. When pressed she had said that her brilliant doctor boyfriend "that's you, Dr Devereaux, there's nobody else it can be", had let her try a new miracle slimming drug his company had developed.

I said, "I'm afraid L was trying to impress you. We don't hand out experimental drugs like sweeties." But then I added that we hoped our product would soon be licensed to take on prescription and her doctor could prescribe for her if it was appropriate.

At this point, sister P became v. unpleasant. Said whatever the basis of our relationship, L obviously regarded me as a very close friend. I must surely have realised L was seriously depressed? She was trying to shove her own guilt on to me. I said, if it came to that, L had told me that you and she quarrelled over a boyfriend that L had dated first but you had no qualms about stealing him apparently and marrying him? Wasn't that the basis of their quarrel? Hadn't Lara refused to go to the wedding?

"Well yes, but that was all years ago."

In fact L said these days she wouldn't have looked twice at the man who was now her brother-in-law. He was at the funeral looking glum. He was certainly not a young girl's dream. I said "I'm afraid that L exaggerated our relationship We were good friends, that's all.

"Just good friends. Perhaps she wanted it to be more." I repeated that I'd only tried to help Lara as a friend. Then, in a stupid moment, I asked if I might see a copy of the P M report. Sister P became instantly even more suspicious. Why did I want to see it? Said, not important, but as Lara complained of "IBS" symptoms before she died I had just wondered etc. L's sister harangued me. Were they due to my miracle drug? L had explained it worked on the gut.

I repeated Lara was just a healthy volunteer. Took it for 3 weeks over a year ago and let's face it IBS is a very common disorder. Ask her GP if she doesn't believe me. Told her on second thoughts not to bother with the P M report. Doesn't matter now. I was about to walk off when she caught my arm. I'll send it to you if you give me your address. Or would you prefer me to send it to your place of work? I gave her my home address.

The final entry dated ten days before Devereaux' death noted, simply:

Large intestine showed recent signs of ulceration. Query Crohn's disease. No obvious cause.

CHAPTER THIRTY-SIX

Experiencing a turmoil of mixed emotions and dread Reiss stared dismally at the final entry. He was poised to scroll back up to the beginning to start totting up the total quantity of R/P David had given Lara when he felt his mobile vibrating in his breast pocket. A man with a midlands accent, sounding agitated, demanded, "Is this the 24 hour emergency medical help line?"

"Yes, Dr Raymond Reiss speaking. Who is this?"

"It's Stewart Black. I'm Lisa-Jane's friend here at Pemberton. Oh, Dr Reiss, something's terribly wrong with Lisa. She needs a doctor badly. Can you send someone quickly, please. It's really urgent!" He was panting as if he had been running.

"Where are you phoning from?"

"The payphone outside the clubhouse on the golf course. I had to leave Lisa to come here to phone for help. I'll go back to stay with her until a doctor comes. I phoned 999 but they say it will take ages for an ambulance to get here. Can you send someone quickly, *please*?"

"What's wrong with her?"

"She collapsed while we were out jogging, tonight. She said a bit before that she didn't feel well and she had cramps in her tummy and then she said she was bleeding. Like really fast and she had to pull off her leggings as they were soaked in blood and I left her lying bleeding on the grass! Please send somebody out here! Quickly, she's really bad!"

"It will be me coming. Don't hang up. It will save time if I know roughly where she is. The golf course is a big place and it's getting dark, now. Did you notice a flag with the number of the nearest hole?"

"She's near the bunker where the flag had a nine on it. I'll go back to her now."

"It sounds like a major vaginal bleed. If Lisa is haemorrhaging the way you describe it she could go into shock. Go back to her as fast as you can and try and keep her warm. If you have a jacket or a sweater put it on her. It's going to take me at least ten or fifteen minutes to reach you. I will have to go first to the dispensary at the Pavilion to pick up some equipment and then I'll drive my car on to the golf course. I'll have the headlights on. When you see my car, stand up and wave at me!"

"Yes, okay, but come as quick as you can. She's really bad!"

Reiss distractedly switched off the computer then ran down the stairs and rushed out of the farmhouse slamming the front door without stopping to set the alarm in his haste. At the barrier he hooted impatiently, as he waited for the guard to let him out and then raced round the War Memorial to turn into the delivery entrance of Pemberton and park on the terrace outside the Pavilion where the examination suites and dispensary were locked up for the night. Inside, he fumbled with the two keys to the different padlocks and then rolled back the dispensary's metal grill and switching on the lights hurriedly took out anything he thought he might need along with some items he hoped he would not. He grabbed some ergometrine, a pack of syringes, an extra bag for the portable drip, additional ampoules of pethidine and then slammed the grill closed and re-padlocked it securely. Back in the car he drove rapidly across the smooth and undulating sward of the golf course towards the ninth hole. It was some way downhill and at the furthest point from the clubhouse. He could see nobody waiting anywhere near it, not by the tee or the bunker, nor on the green itself.

Reiss cursed. People always exaggerated. Lisa-Jane must have felt better and started walking back while Stewart was away telephoning him. He swung the car round and then he saw them both caught in the beam of the headlights. Stewart was fortunately wearing a bright yellow tee shirt and was standing, but Lisa-Jane was lying down and moaning. Leaving the car lights blazing Reiss, carrying his medical bag, ran towards them.

Stewart, squat and square, waved, unnecessarily, shouting: "She's over here, Dr Reiss, this way."

Lisa-Jane lay, shivering and groaning, on the damp grass, covering her face with her hands.

"This the tenth hole not the ninth, Stewart."

"She crawled over here on her hands and knees while I was away phoning you."

"All right, never mind." Reiss squatted down and took Lisa-Jane's pulse. "You never thought you'd ever be pleased to see me, did you?"

She muttered, with an attempt at her old defiance, "Hello, Dr Reiss - oh - oh..." She grimaced and groaned,"I've got these awful pains in my stomach and I'm bleeding and bleeding. I feel cold, very cold..." Her teeth began to chatter. "My legs feel like rubber."

He released her wrist, noting the bloody patches on her clothing and bared legs and rolled her on to a disposable paper sheet, motioning Stewart to move back. She whispered, "That awful bright light is in my eyes. Please turn it off."

Reiss said shortly, "I will soon, but I need it to examine you first. Have you been passing clots of blood?"

He tugged on a pair of rubber gloves.

"Yeah. I have and I feel faint." He took her blood pressure and then did a quick bimanual, conscious of Stewart pacing uneasily a few yards away. He pulled off the his bloodstained gloves and hissed in her ear, "You lied to us about having a period, didn't you? You're miscarrying, aren't you?"

She mumbled "I'd have had a termination, only there wasn't time before the trial."

He said, bitterly, "You won't need one now." He bared a buttock and injected the ergometrine to slow the bleeding.

"Which of your friends provided the fake urine sample for

you? Was it Sharon or Bella?"

She sobbed, "I stole a little from their sample to put in my container. I wanted to stay in the trial. Dr Ryder said you wouldn't let me back even if I had an abortion."

"Was it Sharon or Bella who gave it to you?"

Lisa-Jane whimpered but didn't answer.

Reiss cursed. He should have demanded a blood sample, not accepted her explanation that she had started a period. No court would find him negligent, but he was angry with himself as well as with this poor, silly young woman, whose blood pressure was dangerously low and dropping further. He said more kindly, "Lisa-Jane, we need to get you to hospital now. You've lost a lot of blood and you may need a blood transfusion ... and we can't do that here. He dialled 999 and said, we requested an ambulance fifteen minutes ago. He gave the location. It hasn't left yet? When will it be with us? I'm a doctor and it's urgent!"

The controller responded, laconically, "Between forty-five minutes and an hour, sorry. You'd do better to drive her there yourself, doctor."

Reiss disconnected in disgust and rang the local general hospital to warn them of his imminent arrival only to be immediately discouraged. The obstetric registrar said flatly, "We've no free beds and three people waiting on trolleys in A & E. Go straight to Addenbrooke's if you can get there."

Reiss hissed, "It's over forty miles away."

"Budget shortfall, ward closures, staff shortages? Do us a favour and complain about it to your MP the press or anyone else you know. Why not try the so-called Minister for Health?"

Swearing, Reiss punched in the Addenbrooke's'number to warn them of his arrival.

Lisa-Jane wept, "Am I going to die?"

"No, of course not. I will drive you to hospital in Cambridge, now."

Even with Stewart's help it was a struggle lifting Lisa-Jane on to the high back seat where Reiss set up the drip and told Stewart to hold it in place as he spread the plaid rug from the boot over her shoulders and legs. As the car bounced slowly back over the golf course towards the house, he glanced back at her reflection in the rear view mirror. She looked ill and feverish and he felt a deep concern that this would not end well.

As they left the golf course Reiss heard Stewart reminding Lisa-Jane that she had to get better because they were going to live together in his flat in Leicester when they left Pemberton this Thursday. Together, they would carry on with their diet and exercise programme. Reiss thought Stewart was a decent bloke. And an optimist.

He was anxious about being responsible for Lisa who was slumping in the seat and asked Reiss if they could not change places?

"Let me drive, Dr Reiss. I'd rather you stayed with Lisa in the back. I have no points on my licence and I drive a bus for a living."

They swapped places at the Village war memorial.

The car chugged along cautiously at thirty miles an hour.

Reiss said tersely, "Put your foot down or I'll have to change back with you. You need to go much faster than this. This is an emergency! Put on the hazard lights and get going or I'm taking over, right now!"

The car jerked forward and Lisa Jane lolled heavily and uncomfortably against his left shoulder. Reiss prodded her. "Wake up, Lisa. I don't want you going to sleep now. Tell me your name? What's your name?"

She mumbled incoherently. Beyond talking, she leaned heavily against him moaning and muttering.

She had surely lost the fetus earlier on the golf course which would be consumed during the night by rats, foxes or crows. There would be nothing to find in the morning, which was perhaps just as well for the ground staff who would not be pleased with his car's tyre tracks on the manicured greens.

The journey took fifty-five minutes. Relieved to have made it, Reiss accompanied Lisa-Jane to doors of the operating theatre and then returned to stay with Stewart in the waiting area. His red rimmed eyes were brimming with tears. "She will be all right, won't she?"

"Now she's here, yes." I'll wait with you until she's out of theatre, but I can't stay after that. I can give you a lift back to Pemberton with me? They wanted her next of kin and we've provided her mother's name."

Stewart looked gloomily back at him. "Her mother is a horrible woman. It was her disgusting boyfriend that raped poor Lisa when she was lying in bed in her own room and she's still with him even after that. I'll stay here till I'm allowed to see her. I know she's lied to you and been very stupid, but she so wanted to make a better future for herself. She's never had any luck in life, Dr Reiss." Stewart wiped his cheek with a shaky hand.

"Don't be too angry with Lisa. She was very stupid to lie to you the way she did and to me as well, but she didn't mean no harm … she's only nineteen. Not much more than a kid really, and with her dreadful mother and those men coming and going, she hasn't had what you might call a good start. But thank you for looking after her tonight. I dread to think what would have happened if you hadn't come out quickly like you did. You saved her life just now. I know that. Thank you."

Stewart was eight years older and protective of Lisa-Jane. He said he had a new job starting next Monday in his home town of Leicester and that Lisa was going to move in with him there and look for a job in the area.

Reiss excused himself to take a look at Tim and Sylvie's baby boy Jamie in the SCBU, who still looked small with tubes everywhere. By the time he returned, Lisa-Jane was being wheeled out of theatre. He spoke to a member of staff and was advised: "She should make a full recovery."

Reiss relayed this encouraging news to Stewart.

"I have to go now. I suggested they let you sit with her for a bit. It might help her recovery."

Then he walked rapidly away, his footsteps echoing along the corridor.

CHAPTER THIRTY-SEVEN

Driving back to Flat Acres, as the adrenalin drained away, Reiss was left feeling weary and dispirited. He would need to write up notes on his treatment of Lisa-Jane along with a report for Alan Michaels, FIP's compliance officer, explaining the reason for this evening's emergency.

Then, there was the issue of what he should do with David's records which made it clear he had given Lara far more than the recommended dose of R/P, albeit intermittently and over a period of some eight months. Was this the reason for her bowel symptoms and the ulceration of her large intestine? It was certainly a possibility and not something he could ignore and Pomeroy needed to be informed. Reiss rang him from the car.

Putting the best gloss that he could on the incident, Reiss told him Lisa-Jane was expected to make a full recovery. She would be removed from the trial along with her statistics. But it would get out.

Pomeroy, grumbling, and keen to get back to his television programme, said he would ring FIP's head of P R first thing tomorrow and tell them to have a bulletin ready to run past Reiss. They would keep it simple for the Board as well.

"Sarah Goodwin will notice Lisa is not with her friends; she often chats to those three girls. She has moved into Bill's flat with him so she's bound to pick up on the gossip. I wish she hadn't come back. I'll remind you that I never wanted her here."

Pomeroy ignored this and countered: "Why did you have to go yourself? Why not Bill?"

Reiss explained then mentioned rather too casually that he

been reading through David's notes on Lara when he was called out.

Marcus yelled, "You want the whole world to know what he did? Get rid of them, will you? ASAP. Tonight, do you hear?"

"Marcus, I need to go through them again, properly. What I can tell you is he gave Lara too much. Far too much. It may have caused her bowel symptoms. When I've looked into it properly we can decide what to do."

"No, this is not FIP business, I tell you! He was acting outside his employment. You've insisted on reading them but now you can destroy them! I'm ordering you to destroy them. He stole our product and used it for his own purposes in his own time! This is not company business and I don't want to know about it!"

"We will speak about it again in the morning. When I've had a chance to read them again."

Pomeroy shouted, "No, Raymond! No, I don't want to hear any more!"

After this unsatisfactory conversation, Reiss tried ringing Bill again, but his phone was still off. He left a terse message on his landline answering machine. "Ring me when you get this."

Parking the car in the deserted Flat Acres compound, Reiss wondered how far Lisa-Jane's two friends had been complicit in her deception? Sharon and Bella had both done much better than expected during their two month stay at Pemberton. He would see how they responded tomorrow when he told them what had happened, but perhaps they already knew by now. Stewart might have phoned them from the hospital payphone. He walked rapidly to the Farmhouse, feeling in his jacket pocket for Singer's disk, but it was not there; he must have had left it in the computer when he rushed out and failed to set the alarm. But he told himself that at this hour there would be nobody with any reason to go into the Farmhouse.

Still, it was a relief to find his room looking exactly as he had left it and the disk was sticking out of the machine. Reiss sank gratefully on to his chair, noting absently that the leather seat felt slightly warm, but it was a warm evening. He had turned on the computer and entered the password when Bill appeared suddenly in the doorway. "Hi Chief?"

Reiss started. "Where did you come from? I didn't see your car?"

"I left it in front of the Cottage; I thought you'd be in there at this time of night. I tried phoning you but you were engaged on another call so I walked over here."

"Didn't you pick up my earlier messages? I left you two."

"No, I forgot to turn my phone back on till just now. Sorry."

Reiss, exasperated, explained briefly what had happened.

Bill's hazel eyes anxiously met his blue ones. He said defensively: "She lied deliberately. She told both of us she was having a period. It's not normal practice to do a blood test and the urine test we did earlier was clear ... "

"I take full responsibility for what happened. You consulted me. Don't worry. But you must not discuss this with Sarah. It is absolutely confidential."

"Of course. Absolutely."

"And now I have to write it up for the record. You can go now but any more emergency calls are for you not me."

He logged into Lisa-Jane's file and began typing.

However, Bill lingered, then sat down on the visitor's chair. Reiss asked, irritably, "Was there something else you wanted to talk to me about? It's very late. Can't it wait till the morning?"

Bill toyed with a crystal paperweight. "I came in here to find you. I assumed you must have been checking the discharge data for the trial when I turned on the computer. But you weren't. You'd been reading David Devereaux' notes about Lara, hadn't you? How long have you had them?"

"Got the disk at six o'clock this morning. This evening was the first opportunity I had to read them and then I was called out to deal with Lisa-Jane's miscarriage. Not that it's any business of yours, Bill. Those were David's private confidential records. They were not made in company time or for company business as must have been quite obvious to you. How much have you read?"

Bill snapped, "I skimmed them to the end." He replaced the paperweight on the desk. "Did you really not know about all this stuff before now?"

Reiss responded, furiously, "No, not till tonight. His files were password protected: I had to employ an expert to break through them and it took him a long time."

"But David died three months ago? You must have been suspicious he was hiding something if these notes were so hard to access?"

Reiss snapped. "David was obsessive about security and his privacy and he was brilliant with computers. How long have you been here snooping around behind my back?"

Bill shuffled his feet. It was not the moment to admit he had made a copy of the disk to read again later. "I wasn't snooping. I just found them on screen when I turned the computer on so I read them." He moved to the offensive. "You told Lara's sister that all our stocks were complete, but from these notes it's obvious he had his own supply. You must have missed something?"

Reiss shook his head. "No, I didn't. And Alan Michaels double checked everything twice as well. And before you ask me again, the answer is no. No, I didn't know about Lara's existence or that he even had a girlfriend until after he was dead. And his notes confirm it."

Bill mumbled, "What about her suspected Crohn's? Is there a link with R/P? Have you totted up how much he gave her in all?"

"No, I was about to do that when I was called out. And as for whether there is a causative link, honestly, who knows? It may just as well be malign chance. But it doesn't look good, that's the trouble."

"It can be difficult to prove a negative."

"I know that, Bill. It could reduce confidence in the product for no good reason."

There was a silence. Then Bill said: "If Penny Wilson learns what's in these notes she will make one hell of a fuss. Do you plan to inform the authorities about this?"

Reiss said, harshly, "I need a few days to digest this, then I'll decided how to deal with it. Meanwhile, it remains confidential as if poor Lara were still alive. I will discuss the notes with our CEO and inform my opposite number, Dr Chris Schwartz at Sion in the next day or two when I get a moment."

"I see."

"What does all of this really tell us? That the drug is strongly contraindicated for pregnant women? We knew that already. That he gave her too much and it was a bad idea? That somehow he stole some R/P without leaving a trace? That he ignored his own advice to give R/P only for short term use?

"If I'd known what he was up to I'd have stopped it and he knew that, but I didn't know. David was my most senior colleague and I trusted him - we all trusted him - and he let us down. Now he's dead and it's too late to discipline him."

Bill muttered, "You need to keep in mind that Sarah is fascinated by the David and Lara secret love story. She told me she went to meet Lara's old principal at the language school before the lecture this afternoon and she made me drive past his house so she could photograph it. She told me that the principal said Lara wasn't at all well before Christmas and was never really her old self even afterwards. The timing fits with her TOP for the abnormal fetus."

"Yes. It does."

Reiss stared back at his assistant while he massaged his aching neck with the tips of his fingers. "I need a couple of days to digest all of this before I decide how best to deal with it."

Bill got up and paced around, "They might both still be alive if they'd never met?"

"I agree. But right now spare me the violins."

"Will you show these notes to Tim and Alan Michaels?"

Reiss responded, guardedly, "Not yet. Not immediately. But as you've seen them and you're here, you can help me tot up how much he gave her in total."

It was midnight by the time they had done this and then discussed their findings. They walked back to the Cottage where Bill's car was parked.

From the cottage doorway Reiss watched the tail lights vanish as Bill headed for his flat above an antique shop in the Village where Sarah was waiting for him. He would tell her he had been delayed by a second call out on the medical help line.

CHAPTER THIRTY-EIGHT

30th June.

Wednesday marked the end of the Pemberton trial. The last pill had been consumed and the two hundred and two trial patients remaining had all been checked out as fit and well with their respective weight loss duly recorded by five o'clock. The frenzied activity of the last three days had ended and a blanketing stillness had fallen over much of Pemberton Manor. However, in the Orangery and its kitchen, staff were very busy preparing for Herman Orloff's much publicised "Bad Dress Leaving Party". Everyone was invited from both Flat Acres and the Health Farm, but right now most patients were packing up in preparation for their departure after the prize-giving ceremony the next day.

Reiss, who had elected for a brief swim at the end of the working day, stood in his wet bathing trunks looking out through the open sliding doors, enjoying the flower-scented air that mingled with chlorine emanating from the pool. On the horizon, some clouds were gathering that threatened to obscure the orange evening sun that was shedding long shadows over the grass. A light breeze riffled his hair and rustled the leaves of the mature arching oak trees. From a distance there were the first sounds of cheerful voices and strains of music that heralded the end of this era at Pemberton. From Friday, Pemberton Manor would be filled with clients paying the full fees and it was booked up for weeks ahead.

While the successful conclusion of the trial would be a

relief, Reiss knew he would miss being once again involved in the clinical care of patients. He had been circumspect in his dealings with Bella and Sharon, whom he suspected had known of Lisa-Jane's foolish deception. But he had decided on reflection not to probe further given Lisa-Jane had left a message for him with Harriet saying that her two friends were not to be blamed for what she had done. She was still weak but feeling much better.

So, he said simply that their friend would make a full recovery but would not be returning. Stewart would take her suitcase as she was to live with him in future.

He added, a little awkwardly, "But you two have both done well. Very well indeed. I'm proud of you. You've done brilliantly."

Indeed, Bella, in addition to being the runner up to Sharon for the greatest proportional female weight loss, had won a prize for dress making for beginners and a special mention in an embroidery competition. She was applying to fashion houses for an apprenticeship and had an interview next week.

However, the afternoon had also brought annoyances. While he was trawling through the trial data, an email from Carl Oldssohn popped up on his screen advising him that their planned meeting in Stockholm was being postponed; he needed surgery on his big toe. Reiss groaning, sent an apologetic email to Beatrice who would be furious. After a lot of cajoling on his part, and fuss on Steffie's, she had exchanged their ballet tickets for a different night when Swan Lake was not being performed. Beatrice did not respond. And this was even before he broke the news that he would not after all be joining her at the Bayreuth Festival in August.

He went back inside and showered. Then reluctantly donned the luridly patterned Hawaiian shirt and matching floppy shorts that Sally had retrieved from her jumble bag and tramped off in the direction of the Orangery. Half-way there, he looked down and realised he was wearing his formal black leather shoes and navy ankle socks instead of his intended trainers. He must look ridiculous, there was no other word for it, and he was tired and cross; in no mood for a party, let alone one like this. Yet, as he drew closer, the bright lights of the Orangery and the sound of laughter and cheerful voices interposed by music lifted his spirits, causing him to smile in response. From the terrace, where multi-coloured bulbs twinkled from bushes and overhanging tree branches, came the eager babble of voices, the sound of chinking glasses and the wafting refrain of "She loves me, yeah, yeah, yeah!"

People greeted him and told him he was a good sport and as he glanced around him at their flamboyant and bizarre outfits he laughed and was glad he had listened to Sally and dressed up. Inside, the Orangery's functional long white tables had been covered with bright patterned plastic cloths and balloons floated and scented candles glowed inside closed containers. Reiss accepted a glass of chilled dry Monopole champagne and was soon engaging in jovial exchanges with everyone around him. There was an end of term atmosphere of anticipation and regret. People who had barely spoken to one another in two months were animatedly conversing while others were exchanging addresses and phone numbers and their plans for the future.

Reiss looked around for his host when he felt a hand resting on his shoulder. He turned round spilling a few drops of his drink. It was Herman Orloff, strikingly attired in a mustard and orange striped shirt that he had tucked into his red and blue tartan trousers that were supported by a pair of startling green braces.

"Welcome, Dr Reiss! I'm delighted you made it, tonight. And so badly dressed as well."

Reiss laughed. "These were my wife's idea." He added with genuine enthusiasm: "You've done an amazing job here with all of this and I love the Beatles music. Thank you for asking me to come along. It's time we all had a bit of fun..."

Orloff waved a deprecating hand. "It's not bad, but I would really have preferred the ballroom. They told me that wasn't possible as it was set up for tomorrow morning's prize giving. Still, it looks pretty good and we can spill out into the gardens which is nice as it's a fine, warm evening." He emptied his glass with obvious relish. "This is my second glass of champagne and my first alcoholic drink since Christmas. I want to celebrate in style tonight, so, it's to hell with carrot and cucumber juice, Dr Reiss, I'm taking the night off. Tomorrow I start again with the diet, because I mean to finish the job this time." He mopped his shiny forehead and glanced around happily. "I wanted our last evening here to be special. I have enjoyed taking part in your amazing trial these last two months and I'm delighted with the way I look and feel tonight. And when I compare how I look and feel now compared with when I first came to Pemberton a year ago, it's like I'm a different person.

"I'm grateful to Pemberton. To Dr Devereaux, bless his poor soul and also to you, Dr Reiss. All these people here are, believe me. You've done good here. Tomorrow, this group here breaks up and people will go their separate ways and I guess I will never see most of them ever again. Yet tonight I feel like they're my best friends because we bonded here in our common purpose of losing our excess weight." Orloff waved his arms around, expansively. "And you have the satisfaction of knowing that your miracle drug really works! It's truly amazing and I have such confidence in the company I bought shares in it. My only regret is that poor Dr Devereaux didn't live to see it, too. That is sad. How about you set up a prize or award in his name so it's not forgotten?"

Reiss nodded, "We're discussing it. And a memorial service, don't worry. He's not been forgotten."

"Good, good, I'm so glad to hear that. You must miss him?"

Reiss muttered, "Yes I do, of course."

Orloff, now hissed in Reiss's ear, "I spoke to Sarah Goodwin earlier today. I told her to give Reduktopan another publicity boost in the NYG. He leaned closer, "She seems very close with Dr Bill Ryder; they make a good looking young couple and it's kind of romantic? Do you think they'll meet up after she goes back to New York?"

"Your guess is as good as mine, Mr Orloff." Adeptly, changing the subject, Reiss pointed to his host's checked pants. "Is this your family's historic tartan?"

"Sure it is." Orloff grinned and plucked at the green braces with his plump white fingers. "You think I look terrible, huh? Tell me, I look terrible."

"Terrible, yes, but I look even worse!"

"Oh, no, don't say that. It's just you're out of context. In Hawaii, you'd look part of the scenery. But as bad taste goes I'm envious of Frank's shirt."

Reiss assessed it in awe. It was a shiny black material festooned with broad silver, purple and red stripes. It hung over his blue trousers and clashed with his red baseball cap.

Frank approaching said, "I'll take your word for it, Herman. I'm colour blind as you know, and I took pot luck."

Orloff, feigning mock distress, wailed, "Frank's no fun tonight. He is refusing to drink a drop of my real French champagne!"

Frank shook his head. "It's how the rot starts, Herman. For me, at least, if not for you. I can't risk it." He pirouetted around lightly on his trainers, looking less than his forty-five years and took a sip from his glass of iced herb and lemon juice. "I want to lose another pound before we leave for Scotland tomorrow, Herman! I'll finish what I've started here. I'm not going to slip back to the way I was ever again. It starts with a little of this and a little of that which, added together, makes a whole lot of fat. A few more months and I'll be as slim and fit as you, Dr Reiss. I'll send you a photograph so you can see for yourself."

"Please do. I mean it."

Reiss smiled, then turned as Frank waved and shouted, "Hi girls! Wowee! I love those tops! And you look just great in them, both of you!"

Sharon and Bella, in multi-coloured tee shirts and orange

leggings, looking a little embarrassed, hurried past Reiss.

Frank touched his arm, his dark eyes were moist and sentimental, "Dr Reiss, those two silly girls didn't understand what they were doing, that is, if they did try to help their friend Lisa stay on this trial. Don't be too angry with them. They've done great since they came here. And poor Lisa-Jane's paid a heavy price so I heard. She will be all right now, though, won't she?"

"I hope so, yes."

"Be a bit generous with those two young women. They need to be praised for what they've achieved here. It's not been easy for any of us, believe me. Even with all your support it's taken a lot of willpower to stay the course at times."

Reiss nodded. "I know that. You've done brilliantly, Frank. I admire you all, actually, for what you've achieved. And Sharon and Bella will get their prizes tomorrow. Their names are already engraved on the cups like yours is."

Reiss noting Cecil Pemberton chatting to Dora Shane at a quiet table muttered, "Well, well, well, who'd have thought...?"

Frank whispered, "I heard the vet put his poor old dog down this afternoon. She had a stroke and couldn't move her back legs and he is very upset about it. But I'm guessing Sarah Goodwin won't cry too many tears over her. But the poor old guy was very attached to her and Dora is trying to console him." He gave Reiss a conspiratorial poke in the ribs. "She's looking for husband number four. I think she fancies being Lady Pemberton and she has enough money for both of them."

Dora Shane, exuding a heavy scent and looking not unattractive in a rather strange multi-coloured mismatched outfit, could be heard making soothing, sympathetic comments: "Lord Pemberton, I'm really so very sorry. We always used to see you out with your dog walking around the grounds."

The slit in the Pemberton's skull-like face mouthed, "I buried her this afternoon. I dug her a grave near her favourite spot by the hydrangeas. I'll put up a little plaque later on to mark the spot. She was a loyal companion to me for fourteen years."

"Will you get another?"

"Not right away. Need time to mourn her."

Reiss wondered if Pemberton had sold his shares under pressure from the bank. Or had he had convinced his mortgagees to hold off for a few more days in the hope the price would rise after the prize giving tomorrow when the press would be present?

Most of the medical and scientific team had gathered and were standing at the far side of the terrace. Alan Michaels' sharp eyes were darting about but he did not attempt to mingle. He had not bothered to dress up and was probably feeling awkward for this reason. He stepped back into the shadows after he had unsuccessfully tried to chat up Dr Ayesha Patel. She was swathed in a purple and gold sari and looked like a princess from the Arabian nights. She was gratefully rescued by Tim Scott and his posse of three young acolytes who were wearing an assortment of zany and bright shirts and psychedelic ties over their work trousers. They were now being joined by Bill and Sarah. Bill had on a 1970's orange and green flowered shirt with a huge pointed collar and mauve tie and flared trousers and Sarah, Reiss admitted, looked charming in a 1960's lime green mini-dress she must have found in the Village's charity shop.

Relaxed and a little merry on a second glass of champagne, Reiss waved at all of them. They waved back and Sarah wriggled slightly in acknowledgement, causing, Reiss noticed, her small and unsupported breasts to bounce; her pert nipples made little points in the thin fabric. A shoestring strap slithered wantonly off her pale shoulder which Bill hoisted up then massaged her slender upper arm. Reiss had not seen or spoken to Sarah since he had dropped her outside the Dower House very early last Saturday morning.

Sarah giggled now at Reiss's appearance, causing the other

shoe string strap to slide off. Without thinking, Reiss stretched out his hand to raise it. She gave him a crooked little smile at this gesture as he hastily apologised.

"Sorry. Forgive me. Force of habit. I always do it for my wife and two daughters."

"Well, I'll take care of it from now on." Bill kissed Sarah's neck and rested a large hand with very clean, trimmed nails on Sarah's slender hip. "I'm taking Sarah to Bristol to meet my folks on Sunday. They're all dying to meet you darling."

"And me them." But her amber eyes were trained on Reiss. He kept his face blandly smiling as Bill ran his fingers through her massed auburn curls, saying, "I just can't wait to show you off to everyone at home, darling."

Reiss stepped away to speak to Tim Scott. "How's Sylvie doing? And the baby?"

"She's a lot better, but Jamie will be in there for weeks."

Reiss nodded, "I know. Difficult for you both."

Bill, tugging Sarah away from the chattering group, shouted, "Let's dance, darling? We've never danced together, so let's do it now?"

She gave a responsive sexy wiggle in Reiss's direction. "Sure, why not? Let's enjoy ourselves while we're still young?"

Bill propelled Sarah towards the dance floor where she draped her arms around Bill's neck and he pulled her close to him keeping one hand on her buttocks as they gyrated to the beat.

Tim murmured to Reiss, "Bill's crazy about that woman, but I'm sure she's just using him. She's like a bitch on heat, but he's serious about her. I told him, earlier, 'Bill, you need to slow down, here', but he won't listen to me. Just got annoyed." Tim pushed his spectacles up his nose and said, uneasily, "I'm worried that she's playing with him, while she's here."

"Well if she is, he's enjoying the process."

"Yes, I'm sure the sex is good. You might try to warn him off?"

"No, I'm not interfering, Tim. They're both adults."

Jessica, tall, blonde and scantily clad in her fake tiger-striped leotard came up and took Tim's arm. "Come on, Tim, you need to relax now. Let's dance?"

He smiled, shyly, "I'd love to, Jessica. Let's go for it?"

They swirled around the dance floor to the vigorous beat of the music for a few bars when Reiss felt Harriet take his glass from his hand. "You don't need that." Her long dark hair was spread over her strong, tanned shoulders, with the mock leopard-spotted leotard revealing her fit, bronzed body with its rounded firm breasts and her long, muscular, yet shapely slim legs. "Come on, Doc? You're not the wallflower type and neither am I, so how about we show them how it's done?"

"Great idea."

They whirled energetically around the floor cutting across Sarah and Bill for several dances, before going over to the bar for a fresh glass of chilled champagne and a dainty salmon and celery nibble. Seeing Sarah make for the ladies' room Reiss slipped away to wait in the shadows for her to emerge. He put his arms around her and kissed her on the lips.

She pushed him off fiercely. "Leave me alone. You want some fun, go take a vacation in Sweden with Beatrice. Your cousin from Vienna? Only, she's not your cousin from Vienna, is she? She's a hot number from Stockholm and your mistress!"

Reiss hissed furiously, "Who told you that?"

"Bill told me. I have never been so insulted! You called her on the phone to whisper sweet nothings in German while I was waiting for you naked in your bed? I hate you and I never want to talk to you again, do you hear?"

He steered her away to a quiet spot. "I thought you were asleep."

"You think that makes it better?"

"Well, what difference did it make? I told you I wasn't free and I was married."

"She pummelled him on the chest with her angry small fists. "Were you thinking about Beatrice while you were in bed with me?"

"No, I wasn't. It's just that I owed her a call."

She sobbed, "I loved you. I'd have even been willing to marry Bill and had your child with him and when you were ready to divorce your wife, I'd have left him for you. I'd have done all that for you, but all the time you were deceiving me with Beatrice?" She stamped her foot like a petulant child. "Beatrice, who Bill says has big bouncing boobs?"

"Bill should keep his mouth shut." He would be having a word with Bill, later.

Sarah hissed, "I hate you. I feel betrayed by you! You set me up with Bill. You paid him five hundred pounds to take me out that first weekend? You think someone needs to be paid to take me out? How insulting is that?"

"It was er - a kind of - er - fatherly gesture. I knew he was a bit short of cash."

"Did you pay him overtime for working nights with me? Did he send you *a report*?"

"Of course not. Don't be so *ridiculous*, Sarah."

She switched tactics, suddenly, sounding colder and calmer. "You lie easily, Dr Reiss. You have a lot of practice, I guess. You deceive your wife and Beatrice and me and also Bill. You know, when I went to meet Lara's sister, she said she was sure you and Marcus Pomeroy were lying when you denied knowing anything about David Devereaux' affair with Lara?"

"We weren't lying. We knew nothing about their affair until after they were both dead."

Sarah snapped, "I asked Bill to drive me to see his house. I spoke to some of his neighbours. When I showed them your photograph, two of them recognised you. They said they'd seen you go in there the day after he died. That you took a lot of his stuff and put it in the trunk of your car."

"That is correct. I had to take back our company's equipment that he kept there."

She glowered at him. "I think you know a lot more than you pretend. I think Devereaux gave Lara extra Reduktopan pills.

The neighbours said she was quite fat when they first saw her but she became very thin. You know that too, I'm sure. You know he gave her Reduktopan even if you really don't know how he got hold of it; he sounds clever enough to beat your systems to me. What we do know for sure is poor Lara's bowel showed signs of ulceration when she died and my guess is that it's linked to him giving her too much Reduktopan?"

Reiss now thoroughly alarmed did his best to sound calm and reassuring. "We know nothing of the kind. Look, Sarah, I *am* doing all I can to investigate what David did, but it was in his own house in his own time and his notes were password protected. But now that these trials are completed I'll have more time to spend on this problem."

"Well, you'd better do that, very soon, *Dr* Reiss. Just remember, like you wanted, it's over between us, and as far as I'm concerned the gloves are off."

CHAPTER THIRTY-NINE

Sarah, switching on a bright smile, flounced off to chat animatedly to all and sundry on the terrace while Reiss watched from the shadows where he saw Bill, temporarily side-lined, pouring beer from a bottle down his throat. Reiss grabbed his muscular arm. "Come with me. I want a word with you. Now." He steered Bill to a quiet shadowy spot. "How dare you gossip about me and Beatrice to Sarah? How dare you?" The words came out in a hiss as if from a boiling kettle.

Bill looked uncomfortable. "I didn't mean to. It was when she said Beatrice was your cousin from Vienna and I corrected her. It kind of slipped out."

"Slipped out? How does that make me look? You've given her a juicy bit of gossip that she can trade for something else or hint at in her next charming article so my wife and the rest of the world can read about it?"

"Look, I'm sorry, it was a mistake."

"But not satisfied with one gaffe, you then tell her I *paid* you to take her away that first weekend? Are you completely insane?"

"It - look - it came out when I said I couldn't afford to go somewhere expensive last night... not without an entertainment allowance like before. And she's being ridiculous to be upset over that. She claims on expenses with her paper all the time. I told her that I had wanted to take her out but without FIP's help I couldn't have afforded the George & Dragon that first time."

Reiss snarled, "Well done, Romeo. Top marks for that as well.

Now, you listen to me. You go and find Sarah and you stay glued to her side for the rest of the evening. You monitor what she says and does here. Then, after that you take her back to your flat and you keep her amused and out of mischief, do you hear? I'm making you responsible for her until she gets back on that plane to New York."

They separated and from a distance, Reiss watched as Bill joined Sarah, who had put on her sunglasses and was standing with Frank Miller on the terrace in front of the open doors of the Orangery. He heard Bill exclaiming irritably, "It's almost dark. Why are you wearing those, now?"

She whimpered, "Because my eyes are *streaming* right now. I'm so *allergic!* And I'm still taking the pills you gave me. And I'm cold, come and warm me up."

Bill put his arm around Sarah and pulled her close to him. "My poor darling. You're covered in goose bumps. He rubbed her bare arms and kissed her on the lips and guided her indoors.

Reiss already inside was standing with Harriet when Orloff tinkled a glass, and using the DJ's microphone, asked for silence. "Just a few words, ladies and gentlemen - friends all of you - from the UK and from my great country, the United States of America. I feel that here in Pemberton Manor we forged a new and stronger Anglo-American alliance and for two people it is a romantic alliance? They look good together, don't they?"

There was laughter. Bill, with his arm around Sarah, held her tightly to him and smiled fondly down at her and she looked up at him smiling.

"Yeah, they do. But bonding need not be about love and romance. In Pemberton, during these last two months, all of us have bonded because we have a common goal. To lose weight. To be less is more!" There was spontaneous laughter and applause. Orloff, continued, "So now, I want to propose a toast to Dr Raymond Reiss and his wonderful team who have looked after us all so well here. Please raise your glasses.

Cheers."

Orloff, waved a hand, "I'm not finished yet. I believe Reduktopan is nothing short of a miracle pill that brought us together. Like everyone here I have made some wonderful new friends here." Orloff, paused, wheezing a little breathlessly now, "But I want us to drink a toast to us, we, the people, who in partnership with these wonderful doctors and nurses and scientists who made this trial happen, played an important role as well by taking the drug here. From tomorrow, we will be going our separate ways which makes tonight a bitter sweet occasion. But, if any of you plan to come to Miami or New York in future, do please let me know and we can meet up again. Let's drink a toast to that now, shall we?"

They all drank deeply. Then there was a chorus of "For he's a jolly good fellow and so say all of us." Followed by clapping.

Orloff nodded, smiling broadly and happily, "Thank you so much. This evening has given me great pleasure."

Frank Miller, his cap now on back to front, shouted, "I vote we drink a toast to you, sir! A toast to Herman Orloff, the worst dressed man at his own party!"

Orloff beamed. "Frank, coming from you, that's real praise."

His stridor increased, noticeably, magnified over the loudspeaker system. "But on a serious note. I hope Sarah, that you and other journalists, will tell the world and most importantly, the folks back home, about Reduktopan. Tell them it's not a gimmick - that it *really works!* With more than one in four people obese in our country, we badly need it there, and we need it now!"

He pointed a finger at Reiss, "We'd all like to take your magic pills for longer, Dr Reiss. After we leave here. There are people here who would beg, borrow or steal to get their hands on a few more of them so I advise you to keep your stock securely locked up and out of the way of temptation."

There was enthusiastic clapping and cheering. Reiss nodded, smiling.

"Only kidding, Dr Reiss! Only kidding! Don't get mad at me!"

Dora Shane yelled, "Herman's not kidding. He means it!"

"Have fun now, all of you. That's why we're all here. To have fun."

Orloff waved his glass around, splashing a few drops of champagne which foamed on the floor at his feet. "Let's all of us have a real good party, now!" He tipped up his glass and drained off the contents, then spluttered and coughed, swaying unsteadily on his feet.

Reiss thought, "Blast, he's had too much to drink."

Then to his dismay, he saw Orloff groan and stagger before he clawed at his chest and dropped his glass with crash on the floor.

Frank, beside him, looking horrified, grabbed Orloff's arm while Dora Shane shrieked, "Help! Herman's having an attack! Don't let him fall!"

Sweat was now prickling out over Orloff's forehead and he tore with fumbling, clumsy fingers at his shirt collar and then clutched his chest, gasping and moaning, "I have such pain."

His jaw was clenched in spasm, as Reiss and Bill ran forward to grab hold of him and tried to stop Orloff dragging Frank down on the floor with him to a chorus of horrified gasps.

Reiss shouted, "Clear the room. Everyone get out except the medical staff. I want everyone out of here! Now! Move, please!"

But even as they retreated, most of the guests were looking over their shoulders trying to see what was happening. Reiss grabbed the microphone, "Everyone get out! Now please! Ayesha, Tim and Jessica fetch the defibrillator and the rest of the gear from the Pavilion and grab an oxygen cylinder. Quick! Run! I'll stay here with Bill to keep his heart going with CPR."

As he spoke, Bill was ripping open Orloff's shirt and Harriet had placed a chair cushion under his head. Bill then felt urgently for the neck pulse and looking grim, he shook his head minimally at Reiss and raised Orloff's chin to check his mouth. He had not swallowed his tongue. Taking a deep breath, Bill blew down his throat and then began a cycle of compressions.

Reiss said, "Harriet, call an ambulance. Tell them it's a cardiac arrest and it's very urgent!"

He turned back to the room. "Alan and Molly, get everyone out of here; they can go up to the Manor House. Get them away from here. Now!"

Molly Owulu, who had on a bright candy pink striped skirt with a blue top, was already firmly pushing people out through the open doors.

Bending down, Reiss could feel no pulse. He feared the unfortunate man had breathed his last whistling breath. If he had only waited another twenty-four hours he would have been off the premises.

Frank and Dora wailed as they were being shooed out.

"Poor Herman! Please save him!"

Reiss snapped, "We're doing all we can. We'll have all the equipment here in a minute."

Alan Michaels moved them through the door trying to reassure them. Indeed they could now all hear the trolley wheels racing and rattling down over the concrete path before it was pushed through the doors into the Orangery. This was a well rehearsed procedure, yet the team were nervous under pressure and Ayesha dropped something with a clatter. Bill, energetically, continued with his efforts at manual resuscitation pumping Orloff's chest even as the last few onlookers were hustled out, their heads twisted round for a final view, so that they bumped into some stray chairs.

"Anything?"

Bill panted, "No. No pulse and no breath sounds. Not looking good, is it? We need the de-fib, urgently."

"Have a rest. I'll take over from you." Reiss knelt down beside Orloff, who lay like a beached whale on the Orangery's cold, tiled floor.

Harriet, in her skimpy leotard, squatted down beside Reiss:

"Ambulance will take about thirty minutes to get here, doc. But they've diverted one to us and it's on its way, now."

Reiss nodded and continued his compressions. It was hard work trying to inflate a man like Orloff with his constricted lungs and a layer of fat on his chest. Within minutes there were dark patches of sweat growing over his back and under his arms. Ayesha was setting up the de-fib with Jessica, while Bill oversaw them, still panting a little from his exertions.

Hovering outside, Frank stood with one arm around Dora Shane's shoulder, mumbling, "Someone should call Herman's son, Ronnie. He should know his father's very sick. Not that they were that close. Herman always said Ronnie was really just after his money, but even so, they were in touch a lot, lately, I know that. Poor Herman. He was looking forward so much to our trip to Scotland. He'll never get there now. And when we do go, it won't be the same without him, will it, Dora?"

Inside the Orangery, Ayesha and Bill had readied the resuscitation equipment, connected the defibrillator and the oxygen cylinder and Jessica had set up the venflon.

Reiss ceased his cycle of compressions. "Bag him, now Bill. Quick as you can."

Bill placed the oxygen mask over Orloff's grey motionless face, felt his neck again and shook his head. "Nothing. You'd hear him breathing a mile off with that stridor."

"Have to shock him. Better be quick about it. It's not looking good ... "

Reiss now stood up to watch his team wire Orloff up. Bill adjusted the paddles.

He checked his watch. "It's five minutes since he collapsed. There's still a chance we can pull him back across the Styx?" But his tone lacked conviction and the monitor trace was zigzagging erratically across the screen.

"V.F. Looks like a massive infarct... "

Ayesha shouted, "He's had adrenaline, I'm flushing through

with saline."

"Oxygen, Bill."

Bill pressed the oxygen bag.

Reiss said, sharply, "Get back all of you, I'm shocking him now."

The medical team, grotesque in their odd and lurid clothes, hastily retreated. Supine on the floor, Orloff's body jolted and lay still. There was a faint smell of burning. The electrode pads weren't on properly.

Reiss bent down to adjust them as Bill felt for a pulse in the neck. "Nothing, Chief."

They retreated rapidly again.

"I'm giving him 360 joules."

The body lifted and flopped back with a dull thud.

Bill felt for a pulse and shook his head again. "Nothing. Try again?"

Reiss nodded, "Yes. Get back Bill. Unless you want to fry with him?"

They watched the body jump and then lie motionless. On the screen the ECG trace was deteriorating.

Bill said, wearily, "I think he's had it, but I can try another cycle of compressions?"

Tim said, "No, let me do that. You must be tired."

He knelt down and began, text book precise.

Reiss said curtly to Ayesha, "We'll have to intubate him. Your anaesthetic experience is more recent than mine or Bill's, isn't it? Check first he hasn't got dentures. We don't want them rammed down his throat."

Ayesha said resentfully, removing the oxygen mask, "Bill did a year in anaesthetics and he's got a diploma; I only did six months basic stuff."

"That was *yonks* ago!"

Tim shouted, breathlessly, "I'm geting no response."

Reiss snapped, "Get on with it, my girl. Intubate him, *now!* "

Ayesha fumbled inexpertly with the tube trying to force it

down poor Orloff's windpipe while he lay inert, his eyes staring grotesquely up at the ceiling, his bloated tongue protruding from his mouth. "I'm not sure it went through the cords. I'm afraid it went into his stomach. It looks distended?" Reiss snapped, "Bill, for Christ's sake blow down the tube and listen to his chest - we're running out of time, here."

Bill listened and snapped, "Oh, for fuck's sake, she's put it down his oesophagus. All right, I'll do it, then." He tugged the line out and reinserted it correctly past the cords and down the trachea and squeezed the oxygen bag. The chest inflated unevenly. He looked up at Reiss. "It's not feeding into his left lung. I can try again if you like?"

"Leave it in, we've no more time. It's better than the mask on its own."

The ECG signal was flattening out. The team glanced uneasily at one another. They all of them knew it would make no difference. That Herman Orloff was dead and beyond revival.

"Chief, how long do we go on doing this?" Bill squatted back on his haunches and wiped his forehead with the back of his hand.

Reiss took up the switch again. "I'll give him one more shock. If there's no response, we call it a day." They knew he was only doing it for the record. In case there was an inquiry.

Ayesha injected a shot of adrenaline and flushed through with saline. Reiss activated the current. The body leapt and flopped back inert. Bill checked for a pulse. "Nothing."

"Sorry Herman. We really tried to bring you back. Thanks everyone." Reiss pulled out the tube and closed Orloff's mouth and his surprised staring blue eyes.

Bill scrawled a note. *Pupils fixed and dilated, no breath sounds, no signs of life.".*

Reiss muttered, "RIP where ever you are now, Herman. We really tried. I'm so sorry."

CHAPTER FORTY

Ayesha slowly removed the venflon and crossed Herman's hands over his chest and closed his staring eyes. The ECG signal was a flat line. Reiss turned off the machine and checked the time. "Ten sixteen. I'm officially certifying Herman Orloff dead. We need to pack up all this gear and then inform his family in the U.S."

Ayesha, humiliated by her failure to intubate correctly, looked upset. Reiss patted her shoulder. "Never mind. It wouldn't have made any difference in this case, but I'll see you go on a refresher course. I will join you there. It's important."

Tim said, "I'll check if Dora and Frank have been able to make contact with Orloff's son, Ronnie. They said they would try ringing him. I've given them Herman's phone and his number is on it. We'll have all his emergency contact details on file as well."

"When you've tracked his son down, tell him I'll speak to him later." Reiss turned to Bill, who looked tired and deflated, with perspiration patches soaking his shirt.

"We'd better wash and change now. We can't announce Herman's death looking like a couple of sweaty circus clowns."

Bill said bitterly, "On Thursday afternoon he'd have been on his way to Edinburgh. Sod's law, he has to die on us now? Do you think the excitement of the party did for him? It's such a shame it happened on everyone's last night here. It was all going so well, too."

Reiss sighed, "I know. The timing is terrible. Jessica, can you cancel the ambulance and tell the mortuary to send a van. As soon as they can, please. We'll have to move Herman out of here. We can't leave him lying on the Orangery floor. Is there a cold room somewhere he could go?"

"I'll deal with it, doc. But I'm going to need some guys to help me lift him." Harriet came towards him, tossing her long dark hair, inappropriately sexy in her skimpy leotard.

"Tim round up some men to move Herman somewhere cool and for heaven's sake cover him up and keep people away from here."

Reiss now looked around him at the gloomy faces. "The party's over, folks. No more alcohol for anyone. Those of you who can, please clean yourselves up and change into your normal clothes. If your clothes aren't accessible then put on white coats."

Harriet said, "But they're all still dressed up, doc? Won't it make them feel awkward if we change now and they don't?"

"We're the professionals, not them. We've had a death here. Death never goes down well, even when it's expected, and this one wasn't. They'll be very upset by it."

Reiss now turned to Ayesha. "Ayesha, write up a full report, now will you? But mark it draft and don't network it yet, I want to check it before it goes out.

"Bill, with me, now." He and Bill, their earlier altercation put aside, cut across the grass to the Pavilion, talking in quiet subdued voices.

"I suppose Herman's son will fly over? We'll need his permission for a P M."

"Do you think his stomach bug was a factor?"

Reiss responded, "I doubt it. He wasn't that ill. More likely it was all the excitement of the party. And I know he was worried about leaving here and stopping R/P? But there again, he was looking forward to his trip to Scotland with Frank and Dora. He wasn't in good health as was obvious and he should never have been in this trial - but David had already accepted him and he wouldn't budge when I asked him to think again."

Bill nodded and replied, quietly, "I know."

At the Pavilion they had a very quick shower. Reiss dressed in the clothes he had left in his locker. Bill, who had come in party gear straight from his flat put on his navy track suit.

In a toilet cubicle, Reiss dialled Singer's number. He needed to know if David had given Orloff R/P in the past and if so, how much. Orloff's admission, which he had then promptly retracted had been deleted by Reiss from his notes that had since been networked into FIP's system. He could not alter them at this stage. But he needed to know the truth now.

Singer answered on the second ring. "Can you search for any notes David may have made on Herman T. Orloff. He died this evening from what I'm guessing was a heart attack. Something he said makes me think that David gave him R/P before he came into our trial. He's from the USA. Florida and New York..."

Singer croaked, "If it's really urgent, I can skip my radiotherapy session tomorrow. It is useless as we both know and it leaves me feeling tired and sick and reduces the hours I can work."

"No, you mustn't miss it. It's not useless. It's important you go. You *must* go. Do *not* miss your treatment on my account, *please.*"

Singer coughed again, fatigued and discouraged. "It's not going to change anything. They gave me some copy x-rays that I can show you when you next come. It's not looking good and I want the truth, not fairy stories, Dr Reiss."

Reiss said, "I'm not a radiologist or an oncologist. It's not my field. And you could still go into remission."

"No fairy stories, please, Dr Reiss."

Bill tapped on the door. "Chief? Are you okay?"

Reiss flushed the loo. "Coming now."

In the great hall of the Manor House two hundred and one patients and some members of staff had clustered in uneasy whispering groups. At the sight of Reiss and Bill, sombre faced and changed out of their party clothes, the crowd fell silent before surging forward. Reiss caught a glimpse of green fabric as Sarah pushed herself towards the front with her camera held aloft and it flashed several times. She then exchanged it for her portable dictating machine to record his announcement.

Reiss spoke slowly and gloomily: "Ladies and gentlemen. I am sorry to inform you, that despite all our best efforts to save him, Herman Orloff died tonight." There were some groans and moans. "We cannot yet be sure yet of the cause but we think it most likely that he suffered a massive heart attack. He was, as most of you will by now have realised, a man with several serious and long-standing health issues that he bore bravely. They limited what he could do but they did not stop him from having fun and wanting others to do the same. It is some consolation that Herman told us all, barely an hour ago, how much he had enjoyed his two months stay here and how he felt he was among friends. So we must look at this way. He died among friends. He did not die alone somewhere in a hotel bedroom as might have happened even twenty-four hours later."

There was some nodding along with the sound of snivelling and noses being blown.

Bill, standing beside his boss, shuffled his feet and glanced at Sarah, who ignored him; her eyes were fixed on Reiss, who continued in his deep, slow, grave voice, a touch guttural with his contained emotion.

"We are still trying to contact Herman's son, Ronnie, who lives in New York. When I have the opportunity to speak to him personally, I will convey your sympathy and good wishes. If you send us your condolences we will forward them in due course. That is all I can say at this point. We may know more tomorrow."

Sarah asked, sharply as he was about to turn away, "Will there be an autopsy, Dr Reiss?"

"I can't do it without his son's permission. Given Herman's state of health it looked to be a perfectly natural death and most likely resulted from his longstanding heart condition and as you could all hear he also had respiratory problems. He had been seriously overweight for too many years and he was not young."

"If there is an autopsy you would know for sure. And you could check that your drug didn't cause him any harm?"

"There is nothing to suggest it caused him anything but good, Sarah. Herman told us all only minutes before he collapsed that he considered Reduktopan to be a miracle pill. He believed in the product to the point that he said he had bought shares in the company. And as for what an autopsy would show, it has to be remembered he was taking a cocktail of medication, and that he had taken much of his medication for many years."

"I still think there should be an autopsy, Dr Reiss."

"Yes, and I want one, but, as I've just explained, I will need his son's permission for that."

Bill fidgeted at his side.

Reiss, snapped, annoyed that Sarah was deliberately stirring the anxiety pot: "Sarah, you're pushing at an open door. I will do my best to persuade his son to agree."

Beside him, Bill muttered under his breath. "Sarah, what's got into you?"

Sarah exclaimed, loudly, "I don't think it should rest with Herman Orloff's son. The people who have been trying your new drug are entitled to know what the autopsy shows. Ask the people here in this hall how they feel about that."

There was a murmured consensus of support.

Frank Miller took off his baseball cap and wiped his forehead and said, "Sarah's right. It shouldn't be left to Herman's son. Suppose he won't agree? Can't the coroner order it? Can't he overrule the family?"

Reiss said, carefully, "A coroner can override family objections and insist on an autopsy, but the coroner won't be involved here. It's not a case for the coroner. It's not a suspicious death. As I've already explained, Herman Orloff died a perfectly natural death."

Frank persisted, "If Herman's son won't consent I feel the coroner should be invited to overrule him." He replaced his cap, peak forward. "We here would feel a whole lot

happier if you will report this death to the coroner should Herman's son not agree. We're all of us here trying your new drug. I want the reassurance that an autopsy can give us." He turned round, "How about the rest of you folks?"

There was a murmur of stalwart approval.

"I understand how you feel. I will do my best to persuade Herman's son to agree, but-"

Frank interrupted, "We all of us are a little worried here. We don't talk about it, but it's there, lurking away at the back of our minds. That we're trying something new in our bodies. A new substance that changes something about the way our bodies work. And your literature makes it very clear that you recognise there are risks involved. But we're the ones taking them not you, Dr Reiss."

Reiss declared."I will do my utmost to persuade Herman's son to agree to an autopsy."

Sharon yelled, *"We're* taking it! He just hands it out! There's *got* to be an autopsy!"

Sarah turned round to gauge the response and smiled her cat's smile at Reiss and then Bill. "Bill, you're very quiet. Don't you have a view?"

Bill glanced sideways at Reiss, and said, "Ten to one Herman's son *will* agree - we'll persuade him."

Sarah turned back to the crowd of anxious faces. "Hands up everyone who thinks there *must* be an autopsy?"

A forest of hands shot up.

"Anyone against?"

There were no hands raised against. Sarah

looked triumphantly at Reiss.

Reiss said, coldly, "In that case, if Herman Orloff's son refuses permission for an autopsy I will report this death to the coroner and then it will be up to her."

He went to the back office where Tim was still trying the number at Ronald J. J. Orloff's apartment. It rang unanswered. His work phone rang unanswered. His mobile was out of service. There was an email address and they sent a message to that. No response. They agreed to keep trying.

Tim put down the phone in frustration. "He might be away on holiday or on business. How long will you leave Herman in the fridge before you ask the coroner to intervene?"

"There's no big rush. Let's see if his son consents first."

Meantime, hopefully, Singer would find David's file on Orloff. Reiss was now sure there was one.

CHAPTER FORTY-ONE

By breakfast time on Thursday, Pemberton's staff, who came in early, had cleared away the detritus left from Herman Orloff's ill-fated end of trial party. His corpse had already been transported to the mortuary in Cambridge. The Orangery floor had been mopped clean and the disposable coloured tablecloths, balloons, streamers and empty cans and bottles bagged up and thrown into the giant dumpsters in the yard at the back. In the warm July sunshine, the traumatic events of last night seemed distant and unreal.

The patients, attired in their smartest and most flattering clothes, queued at the breakfast counter with their trays and then sat chattering quietly at the tables. Herman Orloff's death was not discussed. Addresses and telephone numbers were exchanged along with future plans. They took photographs of one another and walked around the grounds or went to finish last minute packing in the last hours before the prize giving ceremony in Pemberton Manor's ballroom.

A professional photographer and his assistant, who had come up from Cambridge were taking pictures of FIP's medical and scientific team by the Pavilion. Reiss, as FIP's Medical Director, featured in most of them. Ayesha, looking slender and elegant as well as professional, was wearing a new black linen suit with a red silk blouse and matching very high heeled shoes. She sat in the front row beside Bill as when she stood she was a head shorter than Jessica and Harriet who were put with some of the men to stand at the back. Molly Owulu, in high wedges, sported a jaunty little hat with a waving feather to give herself extra height.

Tim Scott, his Adam's apple bobbing nervously, stood between Reiss and Bill and blinked at the flash through his glasses. The whole team was present including the three company medics from Head Office, John Stannard from A.C.E. was allowed in as a token member with Jim Menzies who was now just back from his fishing holiday.

The photographer adjusted the lights: "Blink now, not later! Ready, everyone? On the count of three..."

The session concluded, the photographers hurriedly picked up their gear and hastened across to Pemberton Manor. They were hopeful of attracting some additional private commissions.

While they set up, Reiss, seeing he had twenty minutes to spare, slipped into the pair of rooms that had for the last two months served as his examination suite. Tomorrow, it would resume its normal function as a "therapy" and massage room. He unlocked the door quickly. The computer he had used while there, was boxed up with any paper medical files and notes, awaiting their removal to the Farmhouse's small spare office.

Dialling Singer's number, Reiss glanced around him with a faint pang of nostalgia. He had expected the answering machine as he knew Singer had a treatment session that day at the hospital, but Singer answered on the third ring. When Reiss asked him why he was at homem he replied hoarsely, "I called in sick. They told me it would be better to rest today and they'll add on another session next week."

"*Are* you resting?"

Singer coughed. "I am lying on my bed, but my mind is busy. I've thought of something I want to try on the computer, so I'll get up in a minute."

"Have a proper rest first, please."

"The last idea I had didn't work out, but I'll keep trying. It will come to me."

Reiss made his way towards the Manor House, his shiny black

leather shoes crunching slowly along the gravelled path. The notes for his short speech safely in his pocket. He approached the entrance a little warily in the light of last night's unpleasantness but people greeted him in a friendly manner. The retired school teacher, who had run two English study groups, reached out to shake his hand, smiling apologetically.

"It was the shock, Dr Reiss. Death makes us feel vulnerable, but we all have complete confidence in you. It was perfectly obvious to everyone that poor, old Mr Orloff had a number of medical problems. We think he probably had a massive heart attack. It was just such a shame it happened the way it did and at his own party, too."

Then Dora Shane, wearing a tight pink dress and too much scent, made a public fuss of him and he felt grateful in that moment. She held his hand in her own and with tears in her eyes thanked him and his team for trying to save Herman last night and for helping her as much as they had. She declared loudly that she was recommending a stay at Pemberton Manor to all her friends back home. Frank, standing at her side, looking trim in a checked jacket, also shook Reiss vigorously by the hand. "I feel real bad about how I behaved last night. I don't know what came over me. If Herman's son doesn't want an autopsy, I don't think he should be forced into it by a coroner."

Reiss grunted, "We've not managed to contact him yet. He's a hard guy to reach."

Dora Shane said, tartly, "He won't care either way. Herman says - said - he thought Ronnie was more interested in his money than him. But all the same, Frank and I will delay leaving for Scotland for a few days until he gets here. We feel we should meet him and try and go to Herman's funeral."

"That's so kind of you."

Reiss left them for a word with Marcus Pomeroy, whose wife Mary, was dutifully at his side. Sir Morris's wife was there too making Sally's absence more noticeable.

Sir Morris, who was short and balding with a toothbrush moustache and a loud booming voice, was most cordial. As was Cecil Pemberton, whose thin face was creased into a wide smile. His linen suit had been cleaned and pressed. He and Sir Morris were discussing how they would spend the profit on their shares when they sold them.

Cecil Pemberton fluted, "My bank was so impressed with what they'd read in the press, they extended my loan and okayed the share purchase. I was thinking of selling my shares today, or tomorrow, after we've announced the results in front of the media here. Or would I do better to hold on till after the weekend?"

"The financial journals and the Saturday FT will have more time to write up our results if you wait till after the weekend. It could add a bit to our share price."

"Architect feller is meeting me and the builder at the Dower House this afternoon. I'm glad I'll be in a position to do the place up at last."

Reiss, recalling the bank's letters, commented, "You'll make a tidy sum even if you do sell this afternoon and you'll pay tax on the difference, anyway."

Cowperthwaite said, "If Cecil can hold on for another few days it could make a difference of fifty pence per share or even a bit more. Thanks to your efforts, there'll be some pretty glowing reports, coming out, Raymond."

Pemberton said, smugly, "I'll take Sir Morris's advice over yours, then, Raymond. I'm sure you are an excellent doctor, but shares prices are a different matter."

Pink cheeked and tense, Marcus Pomeroy shepherded the VIPs on to the platform of the crowded rectangular ballroom, that was packed with people seated in tight rows on hired gilt chairs with red plush seats.

Sir Morris, beaming, praised the company's chief executive. "Remarkable achievement, Marcus. You've earned your bonus and more. You've trebled our share price in the last two years.

And unless our Medical Director knows something that I don't, I'm holding on to my shares and so are the rest of the Board. How about you, Marcus?"

Pomeroy spluttered, "Yes, absolutely. We've everything to go for now with Sion on board and the American market opening up for us."

They took their places behind the long oak table facing the audience with Reiss a few seats to the right of centre, one along from Pomeroy who was flanked by Sir Morris with Cecil Pemberton on his left. John Stannard from A.C.E. was at the end of the row.

Behind, them in a second line, on uncomfortable, creaking wooden chairs taken from the store room, sat the more junior members of the medical and science staff with Alan Michaels who was indignant at being relegated this way.

In the audience, interspersed at intervals in between the trial patients, sat members of FIP's marketing and public relations team who cheered and clapped enthusiastically whenever they could, encouraging others to do the same.

In the row reserved for the press, Sarah had set up her recorder at her feet and had her camera on her lap. In a smart navy and white dress she was chatting brightly with the man sitting next to her.

Reiss twisting his head, murmured to Bill, "I hope she's not looking for trouble today, as well?"

Bill said, "No, she said she was sorry about stirring things last night."

But was she, though? Reiss was not convinced. Sarah had made it clear he would get no special treatment and worse, she now saw herself as insulted and bore him a grudge. Last night had been a show of power on her part.

He shifted his gaze to the front row where Frank sat beside Sharon and Bella and other prize winners. Sharon, her hair today dyed a rich chestnut brown, with gold streaks, looked smart in a scarlet top and a black trousers. When she caught him looking, she raised her fist in a clenched salute to him and he returned the gesture, but they both grinned in an amiable fashion. Bella had been less than a kilo behind her friend, but Frank had lost two kilos more than his closest rival.

He sat, blowing his nose and wiping his eyes, turning back now and then to whisper to Dora Shane that this was the first prize he had ever won in his whole life.

Sir Morris opened the proceedings then invited Marcus Pomeroy to give a brief report. Smooth talking, silver haired and silver suited, Marcus Pomeroy, briefly mentioned the sad fact of Herman Orloff's passing, before extolling the recent, remarkable and excellent achievements of the company's medical and scientific team. A very bright future lay ahead.

"We are hoping that trials of Reduktopan will begin in many other countries later this year with the support of our newly associated company, Sion Chemicals Inc. who are based in the USA."

From the audience Frank shouted, "Bravo, sir!"

Behind Reiss, Bill's chair was creaking as he fidgeted while Pomeroy burbled on. Looking downward, Reiss saw that Sarah was wearing the white leather shoes that Cecil's late dog Bessie had scarred with her few remaining teeth a few days before. Unlike her shoes her slender ankles had fully healed.

Sarah intercepted his glance and tossed her head and looked away as Pomeroy sat down to lukewarm applause. "Great speech, Marcus."

Pomeroy preened himself, "Went down rather well, I thought."

Reiss spoke next for ten minutes and received a standing ovation.

Lord Pemberton then presented the prizes, and ignoring the typed order, called Frank up first, saying this was only fair as he had achieved the greatest weight loss of everyone taking part in the trials all round the United Kingdom, a total of over two thousand people. "In a period of eight weeks Frank Miller has lost an amazing sixty-five pounds or 29.54 kilos. Well done, sir! What an achievement. We wish you every success in the future."

Photographers stood to take photos of the new slim-line Frank, who swivelled round holding his cup high as he faced the audience and the cameras, his eyes moist with tears.

"Thank you! Thank you everybody for sharing this wonderful moment with me. And I know that our dear friend, Herman Orloff, is here with us in spirit as well. God bless all of you!"

Next, it was Sharon's turn. She raised the cup above her head with an exuberant shriek. "Yes! It's been very hard, but it's been worth it! My life is going to be different from now on!"

Then Bella, wearing a dress she had made herself and for which she had been given the beginner's prize, held her cup aloft.

They were followed by a stream of people accepting smaller prizes or certificates for achievements in arts, crafts, sports and games competitions and healthy cooking and devising new recipes.

Finally, after a few concluding words by Sir Morris, it was over. Chairs were shoved roughly aside and people rushed out on to the terrace where some soft drinks and healthy nibbles were on offer while others went to fetch their suitcases from their rooms in preparation for departure. Everyone, except for Frank and Dora, was leaving that day. On the terrace, Reiss was waylaid by people saying goodbye, then had to spend time talking with Sir Morris and his wife, after which, John Stannard wanted a "word". Mary Pomeroy pecked him on the cheek and said he must come over again soon with Sally.

By twelve thirty the crowd was dispersing and there was nobody other than Alan Michaels left of the medical and scientific attendees. A pretty young woman from the P R department whispered to Reiss, smiling: "They've sloped off to the Pemberton Arms, Dr Reiss."

He, like Alan Michaels, had not been asked to join them. It was not relaxing to have the boss present sometimes but he felt, nonetheless, a little hurt by his exclusion. He made his way through the security gates to return to Flat Acres and his office in the Farmhouse.

CHAPTER FORTY-TWO

Ronald J.J. Orloff made contact mid-morning on Friday. He had been "out of town on business" and he had to abandon his old mobile number, but could provide a new one now. He asked if someone would call him right back as his phone had no credit on it. When they did, he said it was good to know his Dad's stuff was safely locked in his old bedroom in Pemberton. He planned to buy a standby ticket to come to England within the next twenty-four hours. He travelled light. Unfortunately, due to a temporary cash flow problem, he would need to charge the costs of his stay onto his father's account at Pemberton, which would in due course, be settled by his father's estate. He would phone his father's lawyer to let him know and hopefully be provided with the cash to pay for his flight.

Reiss, who had been given this message by Linda, phoned Ronnie to let him know that his father's close friends, Dora and Frank, were staying on at Pemberton until he arrived, so they could spend a little time with him.

"That's very kind of them. Er - where is my father right now, Dr Reiss?"

"I'm afraid he is in the mortuary in Cambridge. I am sorry to have to ask you at this time, but we would like your permission to do an autopsy."

"Why do you need one? You told me he died from a heart attack?"

"I think he did. But as he was taking part in a trial of a new compound it would help us with our data if there was an autopsy."

"I'm not sure...I don't like the idea of Dad's body being, well - you know - cut up?"

Reiss responded quickly, "Your father had food poisoning a few days before he died and the dairy who supplied the yoghurt is being prosecuted. There may be a claim for compensation and it is just possible the autopsy might help with that."

Ronnie sighed."Okay, then I agree. But I don't want to delay the funeral, too long. I feel my father should be buried in England where he died. He loved it over there. And it is very expensive as well as a big hassle, to move a dead body from one country to another. Would you be able to help me arrange a local funeral?"

"My secretary and the Pemberton Manor staff will provide you with a list of recommended undertakers when you get here. Thank you for giving me permission to have your father the late Herman Theodore Orloff to be autopsied. I will arrange for this to take place as soon as possible. Any costs associated with that will be borne by my company, but we retain the right to use any data that is retrieved, anonymously. Is that agreed?"

"I agree, Dr Reiss. You can go ahead with the autopsy."

Reiss immediately contacted Dr Jerry Evans who said he had would have a slot around lunch time. He rang Reiss with his preliminary findings at one forty-five.

"It was a massive infarct. His arteries were occluded and his lungs were in poor condition; you couldn't have saved him. His bowel wasn't in great shape either, but all those steroids he was taking probably masked the symptoms."

Reiss, his heart diving, said, "What? What do you mean, Jerry?"

"There was some ulceration in the large intestine. It had nothing whatever to do with his death. Look, I'll send off some samples to our lab; I suppose you want some for your lab as well?"

"Yes, please."

"We'll send them out today. You'll get my written report later this afternoon electronically. I'll be dictating it as soon as I put the phone down and my secretary will send it straight to your office?"

"Thank you. I can't wait."

The call ended. Reiss sat gloomily at his desk. In Lara's case there was clear evidence that she had ingested much more than the recommended dose. He regretted allowing Orloff to persuade him to delete his record of their conversation. If they could not prove Orloff had ingested more than the recommended dose, the autopsy findings might be regarded as potentially concerning, particularly when taken together with Lara's. The MCA would have to be informed and FIP's share price would dip when word got out that Reduktopan was associated, however loosely, with potential ulceration of the large intestine. It would raise levels of anxiety among the two thousand plus people who had been trialling it and two of the A.C.E. trials were still on-going.

The prospect of offering colonic investigation to a selection of the worried well was beyond appalling. A colonoscopy was not only unpleasant but carried with it a small risk of morbidity. But they were a long way off from anything like that.

Reiss's mobile rang and he snatched it up to hear Singer, huskily triumphant, announce: "I have something for you. It's a file on an American man with the initials, H.T.O."

"Go on - please."

"He's in his late sixties? Born in New York? Gives two addresses, an apartment in New York city and another in Miami. Does that sound about right?"

"Yes, yes, that's definitely him! Thank you, I'm very grateful. Is it a big file?"

"Not too big. I'll send it over to you now. You can take the floppy disk away tomorrow morning when you come here. Can you be here by nine o'clock tomorrow morning? I'll leave you my key. Same place as before."

Reiss went into Linda's small office. "I'm sorry Linda, but something urgent has come up and I need you to stay a bit later than usual. I will be dictating a basic letter which needs to be sent out but addressed personally to a lot of different people and I'll give you a list - you'll have their details on file. I'll dictate that first so you can get started. Then I'll need you to type a long report to go with each of the letters tonight. This is all highly confidential until Monday morning when I will tell everyone else. So shtum for now, understand?"

"Of course, Dr Reiss. Oh look, there's a fax coming through for you right now?"

Reiss grabbed each page sent by Singer as it came through and returned with the complete document to his office. While he cursed David for embarking on a succession of illicit courses of Reduktopan with a man as manipulative as Herman T. Orloff, he took some relief from the fact that Orloff had ingested far more than Lara. But he had been double her weight at the outset and had far more to lose overall. Notwithstanding, it did not augur well for FIP , indeed for himself.

He left Linda typing his standard letter while he composed a carefully worded report, to which he attached key sections from David's notes on Lara and also now on Orloff. He omitted David's description of his attendance at Lara's funeral as they were not relevant. But the findings in the autopsy report most definitely were. He was still drafting when Linda brought him Jerry Evan's faxed post mortem report on Orloff.

He told Linda to make eight copies of each document that would be sent out both electronically and by post.   At last, with everything despatched (and keeping back copies for his own use) he personally emailed the medical and scientific team to warn them to attend an urgent meeting on Monday morning in the Barn at nine o'clock.

Reiss sighed. There would be unpleasant repercussions. He had no liking for Cecil Pemberton but he felt a qualm of sympathy for him as FIP's shares would dip as a consequence, at least temporarily, and the bank was running out of patience.

The other board members, too (most of whom had invested heavily in FIP's ordinary shares), would be dismayed when they learned of these developments. But they could wait out the storm, after which the shares would recover.

The MCA offices would be closed now until Monday morning, but, as it was five hours earlier in New York and Washington, there was a good chance his report would be noticed before they shut up shop for the weekend.

Reiss tried to phone Chris Schwartz but he was out and his mobile was off. He left him a message: "Check your emails ASAP. Talk to me first before you advise your CEO."

He checked his watch again on the way out to his car. The New York stock market, like London's would have closed for the weekend.

He arrived home a few minutes to eight. Seeing his set face, Sally touched his cheek with her fingers. "Is something wrong, Raymond? You look upset?"

"There have been a few problems that I need to deal with Sal. I have to go to London first thing tomorrow, but I will be back before lunch. I'll tell you about it, then."

"Very mysterious?" But Sally did not press him further.

The next morning, after a restless night, Reiss drove to Camden Town, arriving before nine. He retrieved the front door key from under the heavy terracotta pot and let himself in as Singer had requested, ringing the bell as to warn Singer of his arrival. The July morning was already warm, but inside the narrow hall was cool. Reiss stuffed the large brown envelope containing the disk with David's notes on Orloff into his briefcase as Singer came slowly down the stairs looking thin and pale.

"We can walk to my solicitor's office, it's not far."

"I hope she knows what she's doing; there's a lot riding on this?
"

"She does. She's an efficient and sensible woman."

Reiss followed Singer out into the street.

Singer said, "I know I shouldn't be, but when I read his notes on Orloff, I felt sorry for your late colleague. He never intended for things to get out of hand the way they did."

Reiss snapped, "You felt *sorry* for *him*? He's left me and the company in deep shit."

Singer led the way slowly. "I know, but that wasn't his intention and he wasn't motivated by greed. He wanted to help people and he had a real thirst for knowledge."

"That's a kind way of describing it, Dr Singer."

The solicitor's office was in Camden High Street.

A plain, brisk, young woman in her late thirties, noted their suggestions and amendments.

Singer coughed, "Frances, Dr Reiss will need to satisfy any enquiry that may follow, that he genuinely had no access to any of this information until I was able to retrieve it and hand it over to him and I do assure you that is the case. He did not see the content of any of this material until I made it available to him."

"Yes, I've got that. I've made that very clear."

The document she had drafted provided a time-line setting out the dates when David's notes were first accessed, in case, as Reiss feared, Singer might become too ill to testify in person at any enquiry.

It omitted mention of the personal files David had kept on Reiss's wife and daughters, which Singer had explained to the solicitor, (Frances) were not relevant to this matter.

Neither he nor Reiss disclosed the existence of the messages found later on David's answering machine tape. There was no attempt to explain the means by which David had obtained his illicit supply of Reduktopan capsules. The affidavits exhibited "true copies" of David's notes on Lara and Orloff along with the original advertisement Reiss had placed in Private Eye and Singer's reply.

When everything was ready, they had to take the documents a few doors down to "swear" to their veracity before a different and independent solicitor, who pocketed the fee cheerfully. For a further fee he made five further certified copies of both affidavits which were signed before him one at a time by

Singer and Reiss. The original document, with its exhibits, was sealed down in an envelope by the second solicitor, who told them to return it to Frances to keep in her office safe until it was needed.

Reiss paid both solicitors' accounts.

They walked slowly back to Singer's house. It was a pleasant day and a short distance but he became breathless and collapsed on the second of the three steps leading up to his front door. Reiss grabbed his bony arms and helped him inside where he sank into an armchair in his small living room.

Singer apologised, pathetically. "I'll be okay if I have a rest, now."

Reiss made him a cup of tea then drove rapidly to Flat Acres. Disabling the burglar alarm, he let himself into the empty Farmhouse building and went into Linda's office to fax off certified copies of his affidavit to the key people, concerned. Sir Morris's would go to his home so it was likely he would see it over the weekend. John Stannard at A.C.E. and Alan Michaels would need to be tipped off to look for it. He would give Pomeroy his copy personally.

He rang Pomeroy at his home.

"Something's come up. It's important and it can't wait till Monday. I'll be at your house in twenty minutes."

He parked on the drive and followed Marcus into the sitting room where he shut the door behind them. Through the windows he could see the two horses careering over jumps with Pomeroy's teenage children on their backs.

Marcus said, impatiently, "I hope this isn't going to take long? We're expecting some friends for lunch with their kids in half an hour."

"You need to read these documents, now, Marcus." Reiss pushed the bundle into Pomeroy's hand. "Start with the letter and report I sent off yesterday evening to your office. You'll find a list of recipients on it, some of whom will I'm sure be getting touch with you quite soon. Then keep a hold of these two copy affidavits. Mine and Singer's. It's not good news, I'm afraid."

Pomeroy spluttered. "What are you talking about? What letter? What report? What affidavits?"

"Read them and you'll know. When you've done that you need to contact our PR people. they need to prepare a release for Monday before this gets out officially. I've sent copies of all this stuff to Sir Morris and the others on the Board so I expect you'll be getting some calls pretty soon."

Marcus, glancing over the letter and report, looked shocked and upset.

"This will blow the bloody lid off! And if there's a link isn't it because David let them have too much R/P? If there *is* a link?"

Reiss, voice calm, responded, "Yes, I agree with you. But I am under a duty to inform the regulators here and also in the USA as we've applied for an IND licence. We can argue that it's an unlucky coincidence or due to excessive ingestion or interaction with other drugs in Orloff's case. But it's not good news, no."

Marcus exploded. "I *told* you to leave David's computer alone, didn't I? Have you any idea what this will do to our shares?"

"Might send the price down a bit for a few days? "

"A bit? A bit?" Marcus, incandescent with rage, hissed like a snake. "You bastard, Raymond. I see Orloff's P M was done at lunchtime yesterday. You've known about this finding for twenty-four hours, haven't you? You didn't think to tell me sooner?"

Reiss shrugged. "What difference would it have made?"

"And as for his notes on Lara, you say you saw them *five days ago*? You didn't think to discuss the implications with *me* before going public?"

Pomeroy flung the documents down on the coffee table. "I think you've been most underhand."

Mary Pomeroy put her head round the door. "Raymond, I'm just making us some coffee? Would you like one?"

Reiss shook his head. "No, thank you, Mary."

Pomeroy glowered at his wife, "No he doesn't want one, because he's just leaving. I told you we weren't to be disturbed, Mary!"

She shut the door, indignantly.

Pomeroy, snarled, "You're fired, you treacherous bastard. I told you not to poke about in David's private notes, but you went ahead and did it anyway. You just had to know what was in them, didn't you? You've opened Pandora's box and all hell is flying out of it."

Reiss made for the door. "Be careful with that affidavit. It's a certified copy and it's important for both of us. It cost an arm and a leg to prepare. I'll be sending the bill to accounts to refund me next week. It's in case there's an enquiry, later on."

Pomeroy glowered at Reiss from behind his steel rimmed glasses, his colour rising. *"In case there's an enquiry later on*? Of course there will be an enquiry! You pious two-faced hypocrite. The Board will slaughter us. Me as well as you, only I'm going to tell them I knew nothing of any of this from day one."

Reiss responded, coolly: "No, you're not, Marcus. You're going to be backing me up, every step of the way. And as for warning you on Friday afternoon? It was too late for that and it wouldn't look good. You could be prosecuted for insider trading if you'd sold off stock. If I'm sorry for anyone it's poor old Cecil who's up to his ears in debt. Sir Morris told him not to sell before the weekend."

Marcus shouted, "I'm *not* backing you, Raymond! And *you*, not *me*, will held responsible for what David did. He was *your* fucking deputy, after all! He worked in the next office! You should have known what he was up to?"

"You *are* backing me, Marcus. We're in this together. Always were. Oh, and by the way, I'm taping this meeting, like I have all our previous ones."

Marcus gasped, faintly, "What do you mean, you taped

318

all our meetings?"

"And some of our phone calls. People's memories can be so unreliable, can't they? I'm leaving you now, because you're going to be very busy and I have to drive home to Cambridge. I'm taking Sally and Joanne for a nice dinner this evening. I've booked our favourite restaurant."

Pomeroy lunged for the small recorder which Reiss snatched away out of his reach. He ejected the cassette and dropped it into his inside jacket pocket. "The other cassettes are at home, quite safe, if I need them."

As Pomeroy, purple with rage, drew breath, Reiss pointed to the party wall with the dining room. "Mary may be in there and your friends are arriving very soon. You need to calm down and get a grip, Marcus. I *mean* it."

Pomeroy hissed, "You total shit, Raymond! Taping our meetings."

"It's my insurance policy. I would much prefer not to use them."

Pomeroy snapped sharply, "And what about Bill? Sarah will try and pump him. Can we trust him to keep his mouth shut? Perhaps you should speak to Sarah, yourself? Give her a few edited nuggets to keep her onside?"

"No, leave her to Bill. She's - er - turned a bit hostile to me." Reiss made for the door. "Oh, and by the way, Bill says she's been digging around into the Lara and David tragic love story."

"Shit, shit, shit."

"I've told him to keep her occupied and stay glued to her side until she is in the cab heading for the airport. He says he's taking her to meet his Mum and Dad tomorrow in Bristol?"

Marcus shook his head. "She'll duck out at the last minute. I'm quite sure she's just using him."

Reiss sighed. "Unfortunately, I agree."

The phone rang in the hall.

Pomeroy said, wearily, "That will be Sir Morris demanding that I organise a crisis meeting with the Board and our financial

319

advisers in London. What fun. Our bankers, lawyers, brokers, accountants, the lot. You'll have to be there, Raymond. You've a lot of explaining to do."

Mary put her head around the door."Marcus? It's Sir Morris. He wants to speak to you. He says it's very urgent."

Reiss said, soberly, "I'm really sorry, Marcus, but I was left with no choice. Patient safety comes first. Don't tell him I'm here or give him my mobile number."

"I Chris Schwartz is on this list?"

Reiss nodded. "Yes, and I phoned him yesterday to warn him what was coming. He's seen it all. He will inform his CEO, I'm sure, but it will look better coming from you."

Marcus scowled, "I'll deal with that later."

Mary raised her voice: "Marcus? Sir Morris says he needs to speak to you, *now*!"

Pomeroy paused at the door. "But you do still think R/P is safe for short term use, don't you?"

Reiss responded, slowly, "Safety's a relative concept, Marcus. If a drug is effective it causes changes in the body's mechanism. It's a trade-off between benefit and risks, you know that. On the evidence we have so far, I believe R/P is reasonably safe for most people used in the short term."

Mary shrilled from the hall. "*Marcus!* Sir Morris says he *really wants to speak to you! Now!*"

"Good luck Marcus."

CHAPTER FORTY-THREE

Reiss had returned home to Cambridge when the receptionist at Pemberton Manor rang to say that Ronnie Orloff had arrived in a cab.

"Did you leave the envelope with his father's autopsy report in his bedroom?"

"Yes, Dr Reiss. I made sure of that, like you asked me."

"How does he seem?"

"He's okay. He's with Dora and Frank now in the lobby."

Relieved he did not have to deal with Ronnie that day, Reiss rang off.

Ronnie was still chatting to Dora and Frank when Sarah Goodwin, alerted by a different desk clerk, rushed over from Bill's flat in the Village. Within minutes, she had invited Ronnie (but not Dora and Frank, so sorry) to join her for dinner as her guest that same evening. She explained she planned to write a little feature on his late father and wanted a son's perspective. "If you're not too tired after your journey? Shall we say seven thirty?"

Ronnie, temporarily revived at this prospect, agreed, eagerly. Sarah was an attractive young woman and she was also offering to pay for his meal. An unusual combination in his experience.

He hurried away to his father's old room in the annexe to shower and change into fresh clothes and at seven thirty, as agreed, he followed Sarah into the back seat of the cab she had called.

Even a little spruced up, Ronnie was unappealing. Of middle height and in his mid-thirties he had sloping shoulders and a beer gut that bulged over his belted beige polyester pants. His small dark eyes were set deep on either side of his prominent nose and his thinning hair needed cutting. Sarah hoped that anything useful he had to tell her, would not take long, and that he would want an early night. She had booked a table at one of the expensive restaurants Bill had taken her to on FIP's expense account during her first visit to Pemberton.

Beside her, Ronnie stared out through the car's windows commenting in a whiny voice on how green the grass was and that it was nice to get away from New York where it was hot and humid right now.

On arrival at the Mill Stream Gastro Pub, Ronnie expressed himself enchanted by the oak beamed interior and the scent of wood smoke that lingered from winter fires. Seated at a quiet corner table, Ronnie scanned the menu and selected the most expensive starter and main course and then suggested a fine vintage French Merlot from the wine list. Sarah ordered half a bottle of something cheaper, explaining apologetically, that she did not drink wine, herself.

Ronnie's conversation, thereafter, unless firmly checked by Sarah, centred on himself. He complained bitterly about the stops on his credit cards, told her that his late father's lawyer in New York was not helpful and had been a bad influence will-wise. Worse, the lawyer had refused to disclose the will's content without proof of his father's death which would now have to wait until Monday as his office was closed for the weekend.

"I hoped Dad might have taken a copy of his will with him? But it wasn't in his safe deposit box, so I think he probably didn't. I'd just like to know that he left me *something*? Like one or even both of his apartments? A little cash and some shares? I hope it won't all be going to that old age home across the street that he talked about..."

Sarah cut in hastily, "Tell me, Ronnie, how did your father make his money?"

Leaving half his caviar on the plate, saying it was too salty, Ronnie told Sarah that his father had built up a chain of dry goods stores. A few years ago, he had sold them out for a large sum, which he had invested prudently. Unfortunately, Ronnie's business had not done so well. Although he was sad about his father's death, he was glad to have the chance to stay at Pemberton Manor for a few days while his father's estate was paying the bill. He would try to string it out to a full week or more. Pemberton Manor looked to be a nice place and he would feel closer to Dad by being there right now.

"I need a little time to adjust to Dad's passing. I was his only child and my Mom died nearly ten years ago. We fell out from time to time, but at heart, we were real close."

"What will you do about his funeral?"

"Dad liked it here in England, Sarah. He'll be staying here. They did the autopsy yesterday, so there won't be a delay releasing his body, but I'll need a little time to organise his funeral. It's Sunday tomorrow, so I guess I'll speak to some local firms on Monday. Meanwhile, I can take some time to go through Dad's things and take a walk round the grounds and feel Dad's spirit here with me. Dad said there was a good golf pro here, so I might arrange a few lessons. I can use Dad's clubs and be thinking of him that way."

"Do you have a copy of the autopsy report, Ronnie?"

"I may have. They left an envelope for me that's marked Private and Confidential. I won't read it tonight, Sarah. I mean, I know poor old Dad is lying in the mortuary like a chilled salmon, but do I need to read about it before I go to sleep? It can wait till tomorrow as far as I'm concerned."

Sarah squeezed Ronnie's hand sympathetically. "Tell you what, Ronnie? My paper will pay you, let's say, five hundred English pounds? If you can talk me through your father's life story and I can take a peek at the papers in his room tonight. While you're present, of course. But it has to be tonight, not tomorrow morning as I'll be flying home then."

"You'll pay me five hundred pounds? In cash?"

"Yes. I can get dollars but it will take much longer."

Ronnie nodded. "Pounds will be be fine. You ask me some

questions and I'll answer them if I can."

"What was it about Pemberton Manor that your father liked so much?"

Ronnie chewed thoughtfully on a piece of his fillet steak. Remarking that the portions were smaller here than back home, he replied: "Well, Dad liked the place itself but it was more than just that. He had confidence in the doctor here; the guy who used to be in charge of the slimming clinic last year. He died a few months ago in a car crash. Dad was very upset when he heard about that; his name was Dr Davro? Or Devro? Something like that. My father said that Dr Davro helped him and it's a fact that Dad lost more weight with this doctor than he ever did with anyone else. By spring last year, Dad's weight had ballooned to around three hundred pounds and he wasn't tall; he was a couple inches shorter than me, as you know. But with this Dr Davro's help, Dad lost a whole lot of weight. He said he wasn't starving himself; he ate less and better. Dr Davro told him to use smaller plates and cut out the obvious fattening stuff and it worked really well."

"May I record our conversation please, Ronnie?"

"Sure. Go ahead."

Sarah placed her small recorder on the table, which she had in fact been running for the last ten minutes. "Did you ever meet with Dr Devereaux yourself?"

"Not to have a conversation with, but I did see him once. It was in January this year. I was visiting Dad in his apartment while he was in New York and I arrived a few minutes early. I was about to ring the bell when this guy came out. A thin guy, a bit taller than me. He looked around forty. A regular looking guy in a suit and a top coat. He smiled politely and we said, "Hi" as he went past me.

"When I asked Dad who he was, Dad told me he was this Dr Davro. He had been giving some lectures in the city and he'd dropped by to see Dad. Dad was real pleased he came by. Like I say, he liked him a lot."

"He came specially to your Dad's apartment just to say, "Hi"?

"Well, that's what Dad said, Sarah. I think they'd become quite friendly when Dad was staying in Pemberton last year. It looked like a social call, but I wasn't in the apartment with them. It's just how it looked to me."

Sarah nodded thoughtfully. She produced the copy of David Devereaux' obituary which included a small photograph. "Is this the man you saw coming out of your father's apartment?"

Ronnie nodded, emphatically. "Yeah, that's *definitely* him. Dad told me, before he came on this trial, that he was really sad the poor guy had died. He really liked him because he helped Dad lose so much weight during the last year. He lost over one hundred pounds with Dr Davro, so he was very disappointed that he wasn't going to be in charge of the residential trial at Pemberton. He told me before he left for England that he'd made enquiries and he'd heard that the doctor who was taking over from Davro was a very different character. He sounded just fine to me, when we spoke on the phone after Dad died. Dad said he thought the new guy would be less flexible than Davro. Tougher I guess. He made Dad cut down on his steroid medication which his doctor here never managed, so he was right on that point.

"But then after a few weeks, when we emailed or we spoke over the phone, Dad said it was all going fine." He fiddled with his wine glass for a moment.

"Look, Sarah, I have a bit of a cash flow problem at the moment until Dad's estate pays out. It would help me to have the five hundred pounds before you leave for the States? Is that okay?"

"Sure." Sarah drew out the cash from her purse and a receipt for Ronnie to sign.

"Thanks. Yeah, so it all turned out okay as you know. Well, until he had his heart attack that is. Dad was very happy with his progress before he died. He went shopping and he bought some new clothes in smaller sizes and he said he felt more energetic and he could do much more in the day than when he arrived. He had great plans for the future. He should have been travelling in Scotland now with Dora and Frank." Ronnie looked mournful. "I'm wondering whether I should join them and go along too. I've never been to Scotland and Dad paid in advance for the hotels and Dora said they were delaying their trip until after the funeral. They're so kind, staying on to help me and so I'm not alone here. I think I might travel to Scotland with them after the funeral."

"Yes, why don't you?"

Sarah signalled to waiter to bring the bill which she paid promptly. She stored the receipt to charge to the paper. Smiling gently, she said softly, "Let's go back to Pemberton Manor now, Ronnie. I'll take a quick look at your father's papers and leave you in peace. You look very tired?"

"I am. It's starting to catch up with me. It's been stressful travelling here in a rush and there were a few problems with my business in the days before I left. That's why I was out of town and incommunicado for a couple of days."

Sarah stood up and turned off the recorder and hustled Ronnie out to the cab she had ordered to take them back. Her mobile rang.

"Excuse me, I must take this."

It was Bill. " Are you sure you won't come with us?"

"Honey, I can't. I have to work on my article. Can I use your desk at the flat? I have the key you gave me."

"Yes, of course, you can do that. I'll be back quite late. Not before midnight. We're having an end of trial celebration and I'd have loved you to be there."

"I'm sorry, Bill."

"I'll try not to wake you if you're asleep when I come in. Bye, sweetheart. Kiss, kiss."

"Kiss, kiss, Bill."

On the way back, Ronnie babbled on about his father, telling Sarah much that she already knew, repeating that Dad had thought Reduktopan was nothing short of a miracle product. By the time they alighted Ronnie was yawning widely and she had to propel him back to his room in the annexe.

"Can't this really wait till tomorrow?"

Sarah persisted, "No, and it will only take a few minutes, I promise."

"Okay." Ronnie sighed, feeling the pound notes in his pocket. "The room is a bit of a mess. I wasn't expecting visitors..."

As they walked in, he began picking up his discarded travelling clothes and throwing them on a chair. The two doors of the fitted cupboard had been left open with his father's brightly coloured clothes on view. Ronnie gave a sob, and said, "Poor old guy, I can't believe he's gone, forever."

He unlocked the safe and said, "There's just his passport and a few letters as I took the cash out already. Excuse me, Sarah, but I need a few minutes to lie down on the bed right now."

He lay back with his head on the pillows and closed his eyes and was soon snoring.

Sarah opened the envelope which contained the autopsy report, read it quickly, took photographs of it and then replaced it then decided she would "borrow" it for the evening. She checked the thin bundle which was the print out of an email string that included the notification of Dr Devereaux' sudden and tragic death. Reiss, having explained that he would be taking over charge of the trial suggested that Orloff might wish to withdraw? He did realise it would require him to be resident at Pemberton Manor from 29th April until the first week in July at his own expense? Only medical services connected directly with the trial itself were included.

Orloff's prompt response confirmed he would definitely be coming. He fully understood and accepted the risks and the costs involved as per the completed forms. He had already paid for his flight and a deposit for his stay at Pemberton Manor.

Sarah checked Orloff's passport. The stamps in it showed he had visited England three times during the previous year, flying in from both Miami and New York. She photographed all the relevant entries with the dates of entry and departure listed.

What did the term "flexible" imply? Had the flexible Dr

Devereaux given Herman Orloff Reduktopan when he stayed at Pemberton last year? Had he brought Orloff some Reduktopan tablets when he saw him in New York? She felt increasingly sure that somehow the wily Devereaux had circumvented FIP's control systems and kept a supply of Reduktopan for his own purposes.

What did Reiss and Pomeroy know or guess about this? Surely Reiss must be concerned by the findings at autopsy which recorded that Oroloff's large intestine showed signs of ulceration of recent onset similar to those found on Lara?

In fairness, (but who wanted to be fair here) Sarah supposed Reiss could reasonably argue that Orloff had a complex medical history and had taken other medications concurrently. The autopsy report did not link either his death or his bowel condition to his ingestion of Reduktopan. But it did not rule it out, either and Sarah, was not satisfied that it should be ruled out.

If she could prove that both Lara and Orloff had been given excessive doses of Reduktopan, it could suggest a stronger link. As Devereaux, Lara and Orloff were now all dead, she could say what she liked about them without fear of a libel claim. But criticising FIP plc and its current employees was a different ball game. She would need to work around this.

She began to plan her article: she would state the facts she could prove and then ask pertinent questions that invited her readers to draw their own inferences and demand answers:

Fact 1: Orloff had reduced his weight from around three hundred pounds (or one hundred and thirty-six kilos) to 79 kilos on the autopsy report, which, using her calculator, Sarah translated back to one hundred and seventy-four pounds. He had been grateful and had not had to "starve" himself to do it.

Fact 2: He had stayed in Pemberton four times if you counted the trial. Why was he so keen to return there?

Fact 3: He had described Devereaux as "flexible". Why?

Fact 4: Why was Orloff afraid that the new doctor, Dr Reiss, would be too strict? Because he stuck closely to the rules?

<u>Fact 5:</u> FIP's stock records for Reduktopan were in order. But the wily Dr Devereaux could have found a way to cheat FIP's system. What did Reiss and Pomeroy know about this?

Taking the envelope with the autopsy report, Sarah left Ronnie sleeping fully clothed on the bed and walked the half mile back to Pemberton Village where Bill's flat was situated above an antique shop. On the way, she reflected yet again on her brief affair with Reiss. He had been right when he told her she was in love with an illusion and not the real him. Reiss was a middle-aged philandering doctor who serially cheated not only on his wife but also on his mistresses. Sarah recognised now that she had been foolishly infatuated with him. She had behaved like a teenager with a crush, but that was over now for good. And yet, as she opened Bill's front door, she allowed herself a little smile at the memory of those three nights that had been such fun. Making love with Bill was like performing with the star's understudy. The understudy whom they had both betrayed.

And Bill, who hero-worshipped his charismatic boss, had leapt to his defence after revealing that Beatrice was Reiss's mistress and not his cousin. "So what?" Bill had pointed out that Reiss was supportive of their relationship and had himself proposed Bill for a secondment to Sion's R & D compound in New York State when it was inconvenient from his perspective.

Sarah went into the bedroom to change out of her smart clothes into a pair of light trousers and a sloppy tee shirt. Bending down to retrieve a dropped tissue she noticed Bill's document case that he had pushed far under the bed. It had a combination lock that she had watched him open a few times; she had an idea that it was his birthday. She tried this out now, but it stayed firmly closed. Then it occurred to her that the Brits wrote their dates with the day *before* the month and year. With the case now open on the bed Sarah rummaged through the contents. There was not much of interest: several bundles of rather boring trial statistics. She was closing the lid when she noticed an unmarked disk lying at the bottom of the inside flap.

She took it next door where her laptop was plugged in and loaded it and then gave a shriek. "Yes!"

In a frenzy of excitement, Sarah quickly downloaded the entire content on to her laptop then replaced the disk in Bill's case, relocked and pushed it back under the bed. She skimmed rapidly. Here was the proof that Devereaux had his own private supply of tablets and that he had indeed given some secretly to Jane Lara Bucknell.

And she had proof that Bill knew about it. And if Bill knew about it so did his bosses, Raymond Reiss and Marcus Pomeroy. But never mind about that now. She needed to transmit the file to her desk terminal at the New York Globe and then to telephone the Editor of the News Desk who reminded her that it was July 4th.

"It's not for today, Matt."

"I guess they don't celebrate that date in England?"

"No, they don't talk about it."

They both laughed.

"Okay, I wanted to give the powers that be notice that I'm going to need a page or more on Monday. It's going to be explosive."

"Then you'd better book the lawyers as well."

"Don't worry, I will."

The Globe's lawyers would need to read and clear this article for libel before it was published.

Splitting her screen so that she could display Devereaux' notes on one side and write her own text on the other, Sarah began typing. It was clear that Devereaux had been weak when put under pressure by Lara and she had taken too much Reduktopan. Far more than the trial patients were allowed.

Had this also been the case with Herman Orloff? Had Orloff blackmailed Devereaux with the threat of exposure during his repeated visits to Pemberton's slimming clinic? Is that why he had visited Orloff when he went to New York last January? Having met Herman Orloff, Sarah thought it more than probable.

And both had suffered ulceration of the large intestine of "recent onset". "Was this due to their ingestion of Reduktopan?" She then asked: "Is Reduktopan safe for short term use?"

She asked other questions: who knew what and when? When did Bill get that unlabelled disk and where did it come from? Why was it unlabelled? Did Reiss know Bill had it? What about Marcus Pomeroy? What did he know and when? Why had Reiss not informed the regulatory authorities on both sides of the Atlantic about any of this? Should he not have done so? Had there been a deliberate cover-up of potential adverse side effects from Reduktopan?

Sarah had finished her first draft and emailed it to her own terminal as well as to the News Desk with a note to send it straight to the paper's lawyers, when she heard the front door slamming. Hurriedly shutting down the computer, she turned to smile at Bill as he came into the room. He looked and felt a little drunk after his revels with his mates in town. Sarah flashed him a welcoming smile.

"Hi - did you have a good time, Bill?"

"I did, thanks. You're not *still* working?"

"No, I've finished for tonight."

"Good." Bill tilted her face up to his and kissed her. He tasted of beer and garlic. "How did it go with Herman's son, Ronnie? What's he like?"

"Boring, broke and hoping for a legacy." She stood up and stretched. "I'm stiff from sitting. Look, Bill, I'm sorry to let you down, but I will have to work tomorrow morning so I can't go with you to Bristol. I'll need a few more hours to finish and you said it's a long drive. Can we leave Bristol for another time?"

"I suppose so. They'll be disappointed after the build-up I gave you. I wish you weren't leaving on Monday." Bill kissed her neck affectionately.

Aroused by the Lara and David love story, Sarah responded and encouraged Bill to make love to her. But with her eyes tight shut, she imagined herself instead with the lean flawed genius of David Devereaux, whose notes admitted he was attracted to slender women with small breasts. He would have surely been attracted to her. Perhaps if she had met him they would have had an affair and he would not have crashed his car?

After Bill fell quickly and deeply asleep, Sarah lay wakeful, thinking about Lara and David and then how she would make Raymond Reiss pay for concealing David's misconduct and for his perfidy to women.

CHAPTER FORTY-FOUR

Sunday, July 5th.

Sarah, waking to see Bill's eager, pleasant face beside her on the pillow, marvelled again at his duplicity and his loyalty to his boss. Then, as she felt in the mood, she allowed him a final act of love. After which, she offered him another chance: was there really nothing more that he knew or had heard on the grapevine about Devereaux and Lara? Bill looked a little uneasy, but denied knowing anything. Unlike Reiss and Pomeroy, Bill was not a man who lied frequently and well. He mumbled, turning his head away, "Sarah, I never met either of them; I know no more about them than you do." This, however, was truer than he realised.

"Are you quite sure about that?"

"Sarah, like I said, I never met either of them."

She dressed and became unexpectedly businesslike. "You need to tell your folks we're not coming today?"

"They'll be disappointed. I'm disappointed."

"Look, why don't you go to Pemberton and have a swim or play a round of golf or something this morning while I'm here working?"

Bill grumbled that he was sick to death of the place, but having phoned his parents, he was finally persuaded to depart with his golf bag in his car. Sarah kissed him goodbye on the lips and waved affectionately from the living room window as she watched him drive off.

Returning at lunch time, Bill opened the door and called, "Sarah!" His good humour was restored; he had spent a pleasant few hours on Pemberton's golf course followed by a coffee and chat in the clubhouse. Calling her name again, he walked into his empty living room as the phone started to ring. Sarah's voice said, "Bill? Hi, it's Sarah."

He responded, surprised. "Sarah? Where are you?"

He glanced about him uneasily. All her things were gone. A deep gnawing pit opened in his stomach. He asked, more urgently, "Sarah, where *are* you?"

"I'm at Heathrow Airport. I'm taking an earlier flight home. I rang to say goodbye."

Bill gripped the receiver with trembling fingers, "Why? Is something wrong? Is someone ill?"

"No, Bill. Nobody's ill. Bill, it is over between us. I didn't know how to tell you, but it wouldn't have worked out, you and me. I'm sorry, and I didn't want to just leave you a note."

He yelled in bewilderment, "Why are you doing this? It would have worked! This morning you seemed happy and the same last night. We made love, didn't we? You can't just run out on me like this?"

Sarah shrieked, battling to make herself heard over the ambient noise and the loudspeaker announcements, "I didn't want a row. It's easier this way."

He said, dazedly, "I don't understand? You knew I was asking to be transferred to work for Sion in New York State in September so we could be together?"

Sarah responded, sharply, "Don't come to New York if it's to be with me. We're finished, Bill. It's over."

"Sarah, no, don't say that, *please!* I love you."

"I'm sorry, but I don't love *you*, Bill. And by Monday afternoon your time, you won't want to even know me - not after my article comes out!"

He exploded in anger. "You coward! Running away and ringing me from the airport!"

"I opened your case and I found the disk with Devereaux' notes and I made a copy! You're a lying sneaky bastard, saying you didn't know anything about David and Lara!"

"You broke into my case? You read confidential notes? You lousy bitch! I trusted you and I left you alone in my flat!"

"I'm a journalist, Bill and that's the reason I came to Pemberton, remember? I copied the disk and I now have proof that Devereaux treated Lara with Reduktopan for months so she could stay thin the way he liked her? He had a big stock of tablets - he's not worried about running out of them, is he? And you knew that and I'm sure your wonderful boss knew that too! How long have you both known about this?"

Bill bawled, as if in pain, "I first saw those notes late on Monday night! I came across them by accident!"

Sarah shouted, "I gave you another chance this morning to tell me, but you lied! You said you didn't know anything! You lied to me and now the content of that whole file is in New York along with my draft article that exposes your company's shitty cover-up!"

Bill yelled, desperately, "There's not been any cover-up, Sarah! Devereaux' notes weren't accessible until a few days ago. They were all password protected. Reiss only got access to them on Monday night. He was going through them when he got the emergency call out to deal with Lisa-Jane. It happened you may recall while we were away in Cambridge together. He was still on the road when I got back and I found the file was in the computer and I saw it then for the first time..."

"Reiss knows you took a copy, does he?"

"I was going to tell him-"

"Oh, boy, this gets better and better. You were spying on Reiss and now both of you are lying? To cover up what David Devereaux did?"

"There's been no cover-up. What Devereaux did was a private matter, it wasn't in company time or on company business, Sarah!"

"So neither of you were going to tell the FDA and your own licensing authority about it?"

"These were David's personal notes, not our company's

records, Sarah. There's a big difference!"

"And I'm betting a hundred dollars to one that David Devereaux gave Herman Orloff some extra courses of Reduktopan pills just like he did with Lara. Have you seen Herman Orloff's autopsy report yet?"

Bill shouted, distractedly, "No, I haven't! What are you talking about?"

"I've seen it. I borrowed it from Ronnie last night and I've left it on your kitchen table for you. Did you know Herman stayed at Pemberton *three times* last year where he lost of a lot of weight under David Devereaux. I think he took Reduktopan that came from the same secret stash!"

"You don't know that, Sarah! Where's your proof?"

Sarah shouted back, "I think Reiss was suspicious even if he wasn't complicit at the time. He became suspicious later. He's a good liar, Bill. You think you can trust him? Well, you can't! We had an affair the same time I was seeing you, did you know that? The first time was after he saved little Kerry's life in his hotel room - the next was in New York."

"Shut up!"

"The last time was after the Pomeroys' dinner party. We went back to his little house in Flat Acres."

"He'd never risk taking you back to the Cottage, I don't believe you!"

"We're both risk-takers Bill! It adds to the fun for him and for me!"

"You hateful deceitful bitch!" Bill picked up an ugly china vase and hurled it against the opposite wall where it smashed into a dozen pieces. "You disgusting ginger headed slut!"

Sarah sobbed furiously, "I thought I loved him then, but he can't even be faithful to his bloody mistress, never mind his poor wife!"

Bill said, faintly, "You led me on you deceitful, lying bitch. I was going to introduce you to my parents today, but you never had any intention of coming, did you? Not ever?"

Sarah screeched, "Never mind us! What matters is I think Reiss is suppressing important evidence. If you don't report this to the authorities within forty minutes I'm naming you as complicit in my article!"

Bill moaned, "I can't do that unilaterally. They'll sack me when they find out."

"So, go back to treating patients in hospital like you did before!"

Bill wailed desperately down the line, "Sarah, *nobody* likes whistle blowers! Nobody trusts them! I need a reference from Reiss to get a decent job when I leave here . He'll be furious if I do something like this behind his back. That's even if I can convince him I didn't show you those notes and that you stole them from me!"

Sarah hissed, "Your choice, Bill. Which is it?"

"You bitch! This isn't about you and me, is it? It's about you and Reiss, isn't it? You're using me to get at him?"

"You have until I turn off my computer in the plane to report what Devereaux did to the authorities. You copy me in - blind copy me is okay - but I want proof you've sent those emails, understand?"

"Sarah, this is stupid. Two thousand trial patients have taken R/P. Okay, we now know David gave Lara far too much of the stuff, but he was acting alone! It had nothing to do with Reiss or FIP. We're an *ethical* company. Years of research and a ton of money have gone into developing Reduktopan. Just because an arrogant and stupid research doctor secretly gave one - or even two people too much of it and their bowel was affected, doesn't mean it's not safe given in smaller doses under supervision."

"That's for the regulators to decide, Bill, not you and Reiss. You have forty minutes before I board my plane. And if I find you tipped Reiss off before this article comes out in New York on Monday morning your ass is in a sling and your medical licence along with it!"

CHAPTER FORTY-FIVE

Bill sent off his first emails with a blind copy to Sarah. Then, taking her off the list of recipients, he immediately followed this with another email, explaining this was an interim notice as Dr Raymond Reiss, FIP's Medical Director, was in the process of compiling a full report, that would be sent to them within the next few days. After this, Bill went for a run to try to work off his anger and misery, finishing up in the small sunny garden of the Pemberton Arms where he spent the rest of the day, becoming increasingly drunk and maudlin.

Meanwhile, at his home in Cambridge, and unaware of these unexpected and unwelcome developments, Reiss had approved the revised draft press release prepared by FIP's PR team. This was to be sent out at nine o'clock that evening embargoed until 9 am on Monday. It was disappointing to have to issue this so soon after the enthusiastic and positive publicity generated last week and with the last two of A.C.E.'s multi-centre trials due to end in two weeks.

On Friday afternoon, FIP's shares had closed at their highest price ever recorded in the expectation that Reduktopan would soon be licensed in the UK and Sion's shares had risen similarly in New York.

However, consumer confidence was all important. Concerns about Reduktopan's safety would dent this and send the share price down. It would factor in the likelihood of a delay in obtaining a product licence or a reduction of the maximum recommended dose.

Pomeroy, sounding irritable but resigned to the situation, had rung Reiss twice that Sunday, to share first his disagreeable conversation with Sir Morris Cowperthwaite and then to let him know that Cecil Pemberton had rung him as well. He had sounded drunk and been angry and abusive. Reiss blocked his number on his mobile and told Sally to leave the answering machine on at home for the weekend so they could delete his messages. There were two, both furious and slurred.

An emergency Board meeting had been arranged for 6pm on Monday afternoon at FIP's investment bankers' offices in London. Pomeroy told Reiss to be prepared for fierce questioning from all and sundry. He should realise what was at stake. The previous week, FIP had issued an optimistic half yearly report. With this latest announcement, if the shares fell and did not quickly recover, FIP might have to issue a profits warning and this would depress the shares yet further. The company would be at risk of a hostile take-over.

Reiss's next call was from Elizabeth Coleman, the company's new finance director, who sounded harassed and cross. She told Reiss she had been working over the weekend to recalculate the projected figures in the event of possible different scenarios. She reeled off a series of questions to which Reiss could not provide satisfactory answers. He did not know whether there would be delay in issuing a product licence or what prescribing limits might be imposed or whether they might have to put forward a lower-dose pill that would be less effective. They might even have to run more patient trials with that one.

"How will it affect us in the USA?"

"Not well, obviously. I've spoken to my opposite number, Chris Schwartz about this. We both feel we need more time to consider the implications. David's private notes have only just been made available to me. Orloff's autopsy was done just two days ago on Friday afternoon. I didn't create this situation, I inherited it, and I'm dealing with it as best I can. It's only thanks to me all this has come to light."

Elizabeth retorted, "Don't expect to be thanked for it!"

It was a relief that Ronnie Orloff had gone out for the day with

Dora Shane and Frank Miller.

The cat rubbed herself round his ankles and leapt on his lap, purring and he petted her, glad of her quiet affection as he stroked her soft fur. Sally padded barefoot towards him with a mug of steaming brown tea in each hand. Sitting down on the chair beside him, she said, "I still find it hard to believe that David did all this and it's taken so long for it to surface? He's been dead three months."

"It's been very difficult to retrieve his notes and poor Dr Singer is very ill, now. He's terminal, unfortunately."

Sally, uninterested in poor Singer's health responded, "I can understand in a way why David might have given Reduktopan to Lara, but why on earth did he give it to that old American man as well? Did he pay him a lot to do it or what?"

Reiss shrugged, then massaged his aching neck. "No, I really don't think this was about money. He wasn't short and he didn't have an extravagant life style. I think he wanted to try out his miracle drug on a seriously obese man and Herman Orloff was keen to take it. He was grateful. He made that pretty clear in the minutes before he dropped dead."

Sally asked, uncertainly, "Are you saying David lost his way because he was so dedicated to his work?"

Reiss retorted angrily, "No, I'm not. Not at all. I know you were fond of him once Sally, but don't try and excuse what he did to me." He glared at her fiercely. "He kept notes on all that as well. I wish I hadn't seen them."

Sally whispered, "It was only for a few weeks and ages ago. I think we both regretted it."

"I regret it too."

She said with a flash of anger, "Don't you *dare* lecture me. It was only the once in our marriage, but you must have lost count years ago?"

Reiss snapped back, "You weren't his type. He liked petite girls with small breasts. You don't qualify on either count."

"I knew I wasn't his type and he wasn't mine. He'd been very ill and I helped him recover and it just happened."

"I know that, too. He kept full notes on everything. I've destroyed those."

Reiss stood up angrily, causing the cat to leap off and stalk away with her tail in the air. He dusted her hairs off his trousers, then said, bitterly, "He traded on the fact that we all trusted him. Even after his ADR, when we knew he had broken the company's rules and I got flack from it, we all continued to trust him. But he betrayed us all, the arrogant bastard."

In the kitchen, the phone by the open window started ringing. Sally put down her mug and ran to answer it. Reiss shouted after her, "See who it is first. If it's for me, tell them I'm out."

Through the window Reiss watched Sally wait for the answering machine message to click on before she lifted the receiver. She began talking animatedly, running her fingers girlishly through her hair. Was it John the bursar? A man who found his wife attractive.

Reiss sat down again. Sipping his cooling tea, he regretted his altercation with Sally. He should have kept quiet. There had also been a scene with Beatrice the day before when he told her he was not coming to Bayreuth in August. Was it only a few weeks since Carl Oldssohn had pleaded with Reiss to give Beatrice space to start new relationship with a man free of commitments?

Reiss checked his watch: it would be morning now in New York. He would need a further conversation with Chris Schwartz, but after Chris had time to read FIP's announcement that had been sent both to him and Sion's CEO a few minutes ago.

Putting down his empty mug, Reiss leaned back in his chair, closing his eyes to the summer sky. Into his head, unbidden, came not the image of Beatrice's tanned and full figure, but Sarah Goodwin's pale, slight body with its light sprinkling of freckles and mass of flaming red hair that flowed over her shoulders. Unaware that she was now boarding her flight to return home, Reiss imagined her in Bristol with Bill, being introduced to his family. Soon, he supposed, they would all be sitting down to lunch. Afterwards, they would suggest a quick tour of the city, to show Sarah the SS Great Britain and the Suspension Bridge and then take her for a walk along the charming and quaint hilly streets of Clifton.

This charming vision was shattered when Reiss's mobile shrilled plaintively. Reiss groaned, as he checked the number but the caller was unknown. He snatched up the phone and barked disagreeably, "Hallo, who is this?"

"Dr Reiss? It's Stewart, Lisa-Jane's boyfriend." He was sobbing, down the line.

"What's the matter, Stewart?"

"There's been a terrible accident! Lisa's dead! It's so *awful*! *Awful* and it's my fault it happened!"

"When? What accident? Where?"

Stewart broke down into loud sobs. "It happened on Friday night when she ran across the road and was knocked down by a lorry. She was crushed under the wheels. It's so terrible."

Reiss asked, dazedly, "How did it happen?"

"I live near a busy road ... "

The reception was poor. Reiss stood up, accidentally kicking over Sally's tea mug and moved to another part of the garden, shouting, "Speak up, will you? Tell me what happened?"

Stewart gabbled, "I caught Lisa eating a bag of crisps. I'd specially made a salad for the both of us and I was angry with her! We -we - had a bit of a row! I was angry that she was eating crisps and I shouted at her. She threw the packet in my face and ran out of the flat! I live near a busy road! I ran after her to stop her but I was too late. I was just in time to see it all. She ran straight out into the road and the next minute she was under the wheels of a great big truck! " He began to sob wretchedly, "The poor driver stopped as fast as he could, but she just ran out in front of him. It wasn't his fault. There was a pile up and lots of cars were jammed up on top of each other and the truck couldn't even reverse off of her at first, because the car behind was so close and the one behind that too. She was lying squashed under them great wheels! It was terrible! I'll never forget it as long as I live!"

Reiss groaned, "Did she survive, Stewart?"

"When she got to the hospital they put her on a ventilator. The doctor rang her mother after he told me and I heard her mother yelling at the doctor that this wouldn't never have happened if Lisa had gone home to her and not come to live with me! And it's true! I feel like I'm to blame!"

"No, you mustn't blame yourself. She did something stupid and you couldn't have known she would. It's *not* your fault, Stewart, you mustn't think like that."

"It *is* my fault! Lisa died because I shouted at her for eating a packet of crisps!" Stewart sobbed, loudly down the phone.

Reiss shouted, "Where are you?"

"I'm at the Leicester General! They wanted to use her organs. I told them Lisa had been in a drugs trial with me, but she'd stopped taking anything since Monday! The doctor wants to talk to you, before they donate her organs. He's called Dr Fitz Johnson. I've given him your number, but I wanted to let you know first."

Having further unsuccessfully attempted to comfort Stewart and telling him not to blame himself for the accident, Reiss looked up the number for Leicester General Hospital and asked to speak to Dr Fitz Johnson.

CHAPTER FORTY-SIX

Monday, 6th July.

From his front office window Reiss looked down at the car park again, but Bill's blue Ford was not there. It was eight forty-five and he was normally in by eight. There was no reply from Bill's home number and his mobile was off. Had he overslept? Or was he saying a long goodbye to Sarah? Whatever the reason, Bill had picked a bad morning to be late.

Down the corridor, Linda was printing out copies of his letter and the reports for team meeting. Reiss snatched them up and hurried over to the Barn's conference room where Tim and his three closest assistants were waiting with Alan Michaels, Ayesha Patel, Molly Owulu and Jim Menzies. The in-house medics had not been invited and they and everyone else would receive the copy documents through the internal post later that day.

Tim, chewing on his ballpoint pen, looked tired as well as gloomy. He and Sylvie visited the hospital most days to see their premature baby who was slowly making progress. It was an eighty mile round trip. Reiss hoped that Tim would feel grateful, rather than aggrieved, that he had not been contacted (like Alan Michaels) over the weekend with these troubling developments.

Ayesha, too, looked weary and anxious; she had been back to Bradford. Her father was still unwell and would require bypass surgery in the next few days. Only Jim Menzies, back from his fishing trip, looked fit and tanned as he sat frowning in disbelief and dismay.

Tim muttered, "It's hard to believe that David did this. And with this woman, Jane Lara Bucknell? A healthy volunteer who was his patient? Then he gives a load of R/P to Herman Orloff, of all the people to choose?"

Jim Menzies, removed his glasses, rubbed his eyes and then replaced them. "I knew he was drinking more in the last months and that something was bothering him. I did try talking to him but he just brushed me aside. Pretty much told me to mind my own business. Said if he needed advice he'd ask for it."

Jim glanced from Reiss to Alan Michaels, who responded sharply. "I had no contact with the healthy volunteers; I never once met Lara. Did you ever meet her, Tim?"

Tim shook his head. "No. I had no direct contact with the volunteers, either. David sent me the paper work but he handled all of the clinical side himself. He was the doctor and there were only a handful of them at any time. Anyway, he had Ramesh assisting him. Ramesh went back to Pakistan nearly a year ago. He would have met Lara, I'm sure, but so what if he did?"

Reiss looked across at Alan Michaels, who sat grimly stroking his gingery moustache, his heavy lidded eyes glancing around from face to face. "Where is Bill, Raymond?"

"I don't know. He's not usually late."

Tim said, defensively, "No, he's not. There must be a good reason, but I don't know what it is."

Reiss nodded. "I'm sorry I had to act unilaterally, but I couldn't be seen to be delaying. I've obviously had a little more time to digest this, but I want it minuted and on the record, that like all of you here, I was very shocked when I found out what David had done. We trusted him and he betrayed our trust."

Alan Michaels said, "We knew he broke the rules when he had the ADR, but I thought he'd learned his lesson. I was wrong, obviously. Tim, you worked closely with David for a long time on R/P. Did you really never suspect anything was amiss?"

"No, I didn't." Tim glared at Michaels. "If I had, I'd have done something about it."

Reiss asserted himself, "Alan, let's stop the blame game now. David did all of this off company premises and it was way outside his employment. These notes, you could even argue, are not even the company's property?"

Jim Menzies, shifted his burly frame so that his chair creaked. "Raymond, he used the company's product and the company's equipment and he met Orloff and his girlfriend Lara as an employee of FIP. He gave them pills that he took from FIP's stocks. The same pills we've been providing for over two thousand people?"

Reiss said, glumly, "I'm afraid, I have some more bad news. Lisa-Jane, the woman who lied about being pregnant, whom we dropped from the trial last week, died on Friday."

Alan Michaels, who had been told the previous evening, pursed his lips and shook his head reprovingly. "Shocking news, Raymond. Unbelievable bad luck as well."

Tim gasped, "What do you mean she's dead? You said she was making a good recovery?"

Ayesha groaned, "I heard from her friends that she was doing okay. She'd been discharged home from the hospital? Did she haemorrhage or something?"

"No." Reiss explained about the road accident. "They're doing a routine P M this morning, given she was in our trial. There shouldn't be anything untoward to find there ... "

Ayesha mumbled, "Poor Lisa-Jane. She had a horrible childhood. I think, with all his faults, David just wanted to help her? To give her a new chance in life? And it worked for her friends; they've both done really well..."

Tim switched the subject, aggrieved that Reiss had not previously confided in him about accessing David's records and Dr Singer's involvement.

"Marcus Pomeroy wouldn't allow me to share this until this morning, Tim." This was half-true.

"How do you know it was just Lara and Orloff?"

"I don't. Singer's still looking. Unfortunately, he's very ill. Terminal cancer."

Tim shook his head, "Why did you let Bill see Lara's notes last week? A bit risky with that nympho journalist hanging around his neck, wasn't it?"

Reiss snapped, "I didn't. He came into my office when I was out dealing with Lisa-Jane. He switched on my computer and saw them: I was not pleased."

Ayesha muttered, "I'm just gobsmacked..."

Tim shifted uneasily on his seat. "The real issue here is whether R/P is safe even in short term use, isn't it?"

Michaels interjected, sharply, "Tim, are you sure looking back you didn't pick up on *something*?"

Tim snapped, "No, I didn't. You're the compliance officer, not me, Alan. How come *you* didn't notice anything, yourself?"

Reiss intervened, hurriedly. "David's notes are the best evidence we have that none of us knew what he was up to. He doesn't say where he got his stash but my guess is he used that substandard batch he signed off for the burners."

They all nodded sagely in agreement. Tim said, "That was a couple of weeks before his ADR as I recall."

"I've had endless calls from our finance and PR people. I'd welcome your responses before I face the inquisition later today?"

Tim nodded: "Well, let's get this in perspective. Over two thousand patients have taken R/P for eight weeks with no major problems reported. The only blip lasted a few days and the handful of patients involved all recovered completely. There are a couple of weeks to go with the last of the A.C.E. trials and I think we leave them to run to the end."

There was a murmur of agreement. "Absolutely. Let them run. No reason to stop them. None at all."

Ayesha mumbled, "Should we consider offering random investigations of some patients' bowel function? Give a few of them barium enemas and sigmoidoscopies? That way we'd know if they were on the way to developing a stricture?"

"Any benefits would be outweighed by the anxiety this would arouse, not to speak of morbidity from what is probably an unnecessary investigation."

Reiss broke off as they heard footsteps on the stairs and Bill came in.

"Sorry I'm late. I overslept." He sat down on an empty chair. He looked tired and tense and there was a flicker visible in his right eyelid.

Reiss snapped, "You're very late." He recapped briefly. "Everything is set out here in my letter and report that I had sent out on Friday evening to everyone you can see listed on the basic letter. In a nutshell, it turns out that David secretly gave Orloff several courses of R/P before he arrived to take part in the trial. Unfortunately, the autopsy shows some ulceration of his large bowel like in Lara's case."

"And we just heard poor Lisa-Jane died in a traffic accident on Friday." Molly Owulu added quickly. "It's so sad. She was only nineteen poor girl."

Bill glancing over the reports and affidavits stood up with his cheeks flushing scarlet. "Why didn't you tell me about this before? Why didn't you?"

He walked out slamming the door behind him so that the windows rattled.

Reiss said, quickly, "Alan, take over here for a minute. Something's up with Bill. I need to find what's going on with him."

Tim hissed, "I'll tell you what's wrong. That nympho journalist squeezed all the information she could out of him and then she dumped him before she flew back to New York."

CHAPTER FORTY-SEVEN

Bill must have run all the way back to the Farmhouse as by the time Reiss arrived panting he was already on the telephone. Reiss standing in the doorway, snarled, "What's going on with you?"

Bill waved him away holding the receiver tight to his ear, muttering, pleadingly. "Go away, please, this is a private call."

Reiss ignored him and strode up to the desk. "I *demand* to know what's going on."

Bill gestured for him to keep quiet, speaking urgently into the mouthpiece. "Yes, sorry ... my emails were sent in error. Yes, I am aware that Dr Reiss has already sent you a full report so you can shred mine. There was a muddle over the timing: it was my error entirely, not his."

Reiss grabbed Bill's shoulder in a vice like grip, "What have you done? Who are you talking to?"

"Yes, I am Dr William Ryder ... yes, I'm employed by Forsyte International Pharmaceuticals as Dr Reiss's personal assistant..."

Reiss hissed, "You won't be for much longer!"

Bill, now scarlet, said, "Like I said, it was my error, yes. Goodbye."

Reiss thumped the desk angrily. "That was the MCA, wasn't it? What email did you send them? Why wasn't I copied in?"

Bill sat for a moment, clenching and unclenching his fists, then said tightly, "I need to email the FDA now. It's better I do that before they open their offices."

Reiss slammed his fist down on the desk.

"You lousy little shit, how dare you behave like this behind my back?"

Bill stood up and shouted back, "If anyone's a lousy shit, it's *you*! You paid me to take Sarah out and then you went and fucked her yourself!"

"Do I take it Sarah has dumped you? Was this stupid attempt at whistle-blowing your revenge on me?"

Bill sobbed, despairingly, "*No*. Sarah broke into my locked case; she found my disk with David's notes about Lara . She threatened to name me as complicit in suppressing evidence if I didn't-"

Reiss, furious and paling visibly, interrupted: "You made a copy of David's notes? And she's got them? We need to get an injunction to stop her using them. I must phone Marcus now - I'll come back to deal with you later!"

Bill mumbled miserably, "I'm so sorry. At least let me fix things with the FDA now."

"You can do that. Then you stay in this room and you speak to *nobody* unless I say so. We have to stop her before that article comes out."

He pulled his ringing mobile from his pocket.

"Marcus? I was about to ring you. "We're going to need an injunction to stop that woman -"

"Too late-"

"What? No, wait - I can't talk here."

Glaring at Bill, Reiss slammed the door behind him and retreated to his own office while Pomeroy babbled furiously at the other end.

"Too late for that. It's out. Vile and defamatory about both of us. Marlon Strelitz has just phoned me. He's seen a copy - it's being distributed everywhere as we speak. Too late to stop it, he says."

Reiss sat down heavily.

"She's accused us of deliberately suppressing evidence that indicates R/P may cause serious bowel injury. This is bad, Raymond. It'll smash confidence in the product and it's very damaging to both of us professionally, even though we can prove her allegations are false."

Reiss snapped, "Yes, I realise that."

"Strelitz says Sarah's made it plain she's seen all David's notes on Lara! This is your fault! I told you to destroy that hard drive, didn't I? To get rid of it, but oh, no, you just had to see what was on it and now she has too."

"Marcus, listen -"

"No, you listen. I'm going to play you the highlights that Strelitz read out over the phone before he left for his law office to deal with the fall out. He'll be sending us the complete text in a few minutes." There was a click, then Strelitz' shrill voice:

We ask when Dr Raymond Reiss, FIP's medical director, first knew of his late colleague, Dr David Devereaux' affair with Jane Lara Bucknell, who was also his patient? As the two doctors worked in adjoining offices and knew each other well it seems surprising that Reiss did not know or even guess? Or had he become suspicious? He was certainly in a hurry to visit Devereaux' empty house. He was there within 24 hours of his death! Was this only to collect the company's loaned computer and documentation - or was Reiss secretly concerned that Devereaux had gone off track in some way? Did he find out then that Devereaux had procured a secret stash of Reduktopan for his own purposes?

From Devereaux' own records it is clear that he continued to provide Reduktopan to Lara for months on end after the first course was finished. She struggled to keep her weight down with diet and exercise and he liked her very slim. Devereaux was fully aware that long term use could put her health at risk in the longer term and when Lara unexpectedly became pregnant the deformed fetus had to be aborted. After this episode Lara became seriously depressed and she eventually took her own life. Her autopsy revealed ulceration of the bowel "of recent onset. Query Crohn's disease?"

Was this due to her excessive ingestion of Reduktopan? This needs further investigation by both FIP and the regulators on both sides of the Atlantic.

What also needs to be further investigated is the date when Dr

Reiss first read Devereaux' notes. We know he had possession of the computer immediately after his colleague's death. It is now July and still he has not informed the regulatory authorities of what happened to Lara? Why not?

When I interviewed them, both Dr Reiss and Marcus Pomeroy (FIP's CEO) denied knowing anything about the Lara and Devereaux affair, let alone that they had seen his notes yet they had possession of his computer from April 1st; Dr Reiss had collected it within twenty-four hours of Devereaux' death! What else did he find there to take home? Were there clues suggesting he had not lived alone?

Yet, when Lara's sister, Mrs Penny Wilson wrote to Marcus Pomeroy with her concerns enclosing a copy of the autopsy report, they both denied knowledge of the affair adding, that what two consenting adults did in their own time in their own home was not FIP's business.

Had they run Jane Lara Bucknell's name through their system they would have discovered her connection to Devereaux. We can assume they did run a check and from this point onward they would have known that Lara had been Devereaux' patient in the first healthy volunteer trial FIP ran last year. Why was FIP so reluctant to admit they knew about this for weeks afterward?

We ask when Dr Raymond Reiss first knew about Devereaux' secret treatment of the late Herman T. Orloff from the USA who had apartments in Miami and New York City? Herman Orloff came to Pemberton Manor on no less than three previous occasions last year because he lost more weight there than anywhere else. Why was that?

Unfortunately, while celebrating his remarkable weight loss at the end of the trial last Wednesday, Mr Orloff died from a heart attack. This was in no way connected with his taking Reduktopan, but what may have been connected was that his autopsy noted recent ulceration of his large intestine. Given that Lara had similar ulceration of the bowel we ask if this is an unlucky coincidence? Or is there a causative link with taking too much Reduktopan?

Pomeroy turned off the tape and shouted down the line.

"Strelitz says there's a double page spread peppered with direct quotes from David's private notes! I take it you didn't give them to her?"

Reiss snarled, "I was about to phone you! Bill told me five minutes ago that he'd copied them on to a disk from my computer! He says she opened his locked case while he was out of the flat and found them."

Pomeroy shrieked: "I don't believe it! First you and then him leaving sensitive stuff like that lying around? Where is he now?"

Reiss snarled, "In his room. I've not finished with him , don't worry! And after this, he'll be lucky to get a job in a war zone! I'll have to sack him - I can't keep him on."

Pomeroy snapped, "No, Raymond, you need to calm down. You keep him in post, do you hear? We'll need Bill's testimony for part of our claim against that woman and her bloody newspaper. We need his evidence to prove that she stole our confidential information from a locked case. That's a breach of our contract with her paper. Not content with that she uses this confidential material in support of her libellous allegations? We can prove these are false and unfounded and we'll sue the bastards till the pips squeak. So you do not sack Bill. You keep him on. You think of the bigger picture."

"But Marcus, I can't trust him. He's behaved appallingly - he's gone behind my back - stuff you don't know about-"

Pomeroy shouted, "Raymond, listen to me! We are where we are!" He lowered his voice and said, icily: "This is what you do next. You interview Bill formally for the record and put it on tape so he can explain what happened. This could finish up in court both here and in the USA and there are millions of dollars at stake! Tell him not to touch that briefcase; her finger prints will be all over it and on the disk.

"Keep in mind that Sarah wrote the article, not Bill. He's just a pawn in her game. He was a sideshow for her. A diversion, nothing more. We were the real targets. She's a great actress mind - she had me fooled: I had her down as genuinely keen on you. Obviously, I was wrong and so were you."

Reiss, his vanity pricked, retorted: "She was keen at first but she's a crazy bitch and I wish I'd never set eyes on her."

"So do I, Raymond."

"Bill could have warned me about this article on Sunday, you do realise that?"

"Yes, but we are where we are -"

"But he waited till this morning when it was too late to stop it going out. I could kill him ..."

Pomeroy interrupted. He spoke firmly and slowly, as if counselling a particularly foolish client: "Raymond, you must listen to me. Bill has been more than stupid, but he has owned up to what he did and we *need* him on side now. He will be a key witness. We need him to explain where and when he got that disk; when he first saw what was on it. She has admitted she stole the content from him?"

"That's what he says."

His testimony adds strength to yours and Singer's that we did not knowingly suppress evidence of adverse effects. You must stay calm. Try and act pleasant with Bill."

"*Pleasant*? After what he's done?"

"Yes, Raymond. You act pleasant for the sake of the bigger picture and the future court case. Get it?"

Reiss in a sulky tone, responded."All right."

In the next door office he found Bill leaning disconsolately against the desk.

"I've copied you into the email I just sent to the FDA. I'm so sorry, Chief about what happened. Sarah played me for a fool, I can see that now. "

Reiss's anger subsided a little. "She played both of us. She had her own agenda, I'm afraid. Come with me to my room. I'm going to interview you about what happened for the record."

With Bill seated opposite, Reiss was reaching forward to turn on the recorder when his desk phone rang.

"Linda, I said, I don't want to be disturbed."

She said, "I know, Dr Reiss, but I have a Dr Simon Singh on the line. He's a consultant pathologist at Leicester General Hospital and he says he must speak to you."

"All right. Put him through."

It was a brief conversation.

Reiss repeated gloomily, "You found ulceration of the large intestine? You're absolutely *sure*? No, well, of course I accept what you say - but it's so unexpected in a girl of nineteen. Yes, I'll want a copy of the PM as soon as you can let me have it ... Yes, I will be sending a yellow card out, obviously ..."

Bill, like Reiss, looked shocked.

"Well, yes, I did. I knew Lisa-Jane quite well. I know all about the miscarriage as I was the doctor who got the call out. I drove her to hospital myself.

"It's dreadfully sad, but at least you could use her kidneys and liver and her corneas to help others."

Reiss hung up, and said unnecessarily, "This beggars belief. They found early signs of ulceration of her large intestine."

Bill whispered, "*Lisa-Jane? But she took R/P for less than six weeks? I can't believe it. That's awful*"

Reiss groaned, "Yes, it is. I'm going to have to ring John Stannard and tell him to pause the last two A.C.E. trials at once."

Bill mumbled, "But she *can't* be typical, surely?"

Reiss groaned "Probably not, I hope not... but how can we take the risk that she isn't? Not after Orloff and Lara as well." He went over to the window and pulled at the security bars as if he were in a prison. "She was only nineteen, Bill. She smoked and she was obese and, alas as we discovered a bit late, also pregnant. But her pregnancy aside, Lisa-Jane was a low risk patient."

He turned back to face Bill. His voice, when he spoke, sounded more guttural and constricted. "When this news gets out - and it is *when* not *if* - it could lead to widespread panic. We could have two thousand worried-well patients jamming our switchboard. Our shares will plummet and as FIP's Medical Director, I'll be in the firing line. Not that I could possibly ever have foreseen this outcome for Lisa-Jane or any of the others in the trial."

Bill muttered, "But even if she isn't typical, how can we prove a negative? Not without carrying out a load of random bowel investigations?"

Reiss paced around restlessly, "That carries its own morbidity. It's not on for now. This is dire. And if Lisa *is* typical, God forbid, we could have up to two thousand people claiming their bowels have been damaged by taking Reduktopan."

"But Chief, Lara and Orloff took it for *months and months. They had about three or four times the recommended dose. Lisa-Jane took it for barely six weeks!* Do you think it could be linked to pregnancy? Lara was pregnant too, wasn't she?"

"Orloff wasn't and I can't see the mechanism, can you?"

"No."

Reiss speed dialled John Stannard's number as Bill muttered, awkwardly, "I'm so sorry, Chief. Is there anything I can do?"

Reiss glowered at Bill, "Haven't you done enough?"

Bill gnawed his fingers. "Do you want me to resign?"

Reiss shook his head. "No, Bill. I want you to stay and make yourself useful."

CHAPTER FORTY-EIGHT

"What do you mean, you've halted the last A.C.E. trials?"

"I felt I had no choice, Marcus."

"Couldn't you have given them placebos?"

"It would have leaked out and made it look worse."

"How can it look worse than this?"

"It would look underhand, Marcus. That's worse."

Pomeroy moaned, "A phone call from you and it's millions of pounds gone up the spout! The company's up the spout! We're all up the spout! And why? Because a stupid pregnant woman lied her way on to the trial and you missed it, didn't you?"

"She faked the test results and lied. Neither Bill nor I are to blame for this. But the real problem is she took R/P for such a short time and still ..."

"You stopped these trials for one bad outcome?"

"No, there's also Lara and Orloff ."

"But they took R/P for months on end. And you said their bowel trouble could be coincidental?"

"It's a possibility - but as R/P works on the gut, three out of three is discouraging. I *hope* it is coincidental -"

Pomeroy screeched, "*Hope! Hope*! I like *hope*! But *hope* doesn't pay bank interest, Raymond! Hope doesn't pay salaries, but still, it's good to have hope."

Reiss retorted, **"As the company's medical director with responsibility for these trials I have to take all reasonable measures to protect patient safety. I'm truly sorry about this but we can't carry on in the knowledge we could cause serious injury to five hundred more people."**

"We've beggared ourselves borrowing from the banks. If we don't get Reduktopan on the market how are we going to repay

our loans? Now, thanks to you, I'm going to have to instruct our brokers to suspend dealing before this news gets out and there's a selling frenzy and our price goes through the floor."

"That's your problem, Marcus, not mine."

"Yes, *my problem*." Pomeroy's voice was shrill. "Worse, we've just issued a statement that *you* approved which says Reduktopan is safe for short term use. A few hours later and we'll be issuing a second statement saying, sorry folks, but we're not sure now that it is. We're so not sure we're stopping the last two trials today."

"Our statement will also say we are acting promptly as a result of evidence we only received just hours ago because we are a responsible company."

Marcus yelled: "The timing couldn't be worse! All this on the same day as the Globe's article comes out vilifying us? They will think her article is the reason you pulled the plug."

"I've acted throughout *on the evidence available to me* to protect patients and I can prove it."

Pomeroy yelled down the phone, "Don't kid yourself, that you'll come out of this smelling of roses! As Medical Director, you'll get the blame! And for the avoidance of doubt, it is not a question of whether FIP is taken over in future, it is when and by whom."

Reiss snarled, "I will not be made a scapegoat by you or the Board, Marcus. None of this is my fault; I inherited David's poisonous legacy in good faith."

"David was your deputy and you'll be held responsible for everything he did! The Board will be looking for a head, I can promise you that!"

"And it's not going to be mine! Don't think you can jump into a lifeboat without me, Marcus. I'm counting on your full support, remember? Any jumping, we do together. I hope you understand what I'm saying?"

Pomeroy howled, "It's not just a matter for me and the Board. You'll be the major target for the media and two thousand frightened patients and their families. By tomorrow there'll be a pressure group out for your hide and some group legal action will be gathering to get compensation from FIP's insurers. You'd better believe it."

Reiss snarled, "Oh, I do believe it, but we're in this together, matey."

Minutes later the company's insurers rang about the earlier press release. Reiss advised them briefly of the latest developments even as he typed a personal email to Chris Schwartz. Marcus was meanwhile having to update the company's insurers which would not make for an easy or pleasant discussion.

Indeed, Pomeroy rang Reiss back half an hour later to say that the insurers were demanding an urgent meeting at which they must both be present. They were demanding copies of all the reports and relevant correspondence, the two affidavits but Julie would deal with that.

Reiss had no time to return Ronnie Orloff's call from Pemberton Manor before Ms Elizabeth Coleman came on the line. She was agitated and upset.

"I spent my whole weekend working on these bloody figures and the different scenarios you gave me. I just had a call from Marcus Pomeroy who says I have to tear them all up and start over again after talking to you! Why didn't you factor in this problem *before?*"

Reiss yelled, "Because the post mortem was two hours ago and I've just heard about it myself!"

"You could have anticipated it, surely?"

"No, I couldn't."

A woman from the company's insurers then called Reiss to ask if he had contacted his medical defence society? He would be well advised to do this as there could be a conflict of interest between Reiss personally and in his role of Medical Director of FIP.

Reiss retorted that there should be no conflict of interest; his contractual duty to the company required him to have regard for the safety of patients as well to have regard for the interests of the company. They were not at odds, were they?

But he would contact his defence organisation forthwith. Lara's sister would probably lodge a formal complaint about him to the General Medical Council and she might not be alone in that. He would need their expert advice and support to defend his professional reputation.

He dialled the number and spoke to a doctor on the secretariat who said commercial insurers had "deeper pockets". If there was to be a libel action that arose from his conduct while employed by FIP they would be better placed to deal with it. But if there was a complaint to the General Medical Council they would help him with that.

As soon as Reiss put down the phone it rang again.

The day was taking on a nightmare quality.

It was FIP's senior press officer. Would he read and approve the company's latest statement? They were emailing him it to him right now? Reiss amended it slightly and returned it.

On his desk the office phone rang again.

Pomeroy, sounding anxious and flustered, told Reiss he had formally instructed the company's solicitors who were "taking urgent steps". He had also spoken to the company's accountants, stockbrokers and financial advisers.

The Chairman, Sir Morris Cowperthwaite, was "fuming" but agreed to contact the other board members as Marcus was busy dealing with the company's lawyers. "I told Julie not to put Cecil through again. He had left a hysterical and angry message with Julie, saying he was going out to look for Dr Raymond Reiss with his shotgun. She thought he sounded drunk.

"You'd better keep away from Pemberton until Cecil calms down. The barrier guards have been warned not to let him anywhere near Flat Acres. He's flat broke and he's blaming you for it, Raymond."

The brokers had issued a notice to the stock exchange to suspend all dealing in FIP's shares before the news got out that the two A.C.E. trials had been "paused."

Reiss groaned and put the desk phone down again. It rang instantly. It was Dr Wengler from Zurich, determined to discuss a problem in German that arose from their shared project. He was a difficult man to cut short and was still in full flow when Linda came in, looking anxious, gesturing she needed to talk to him.

"What is it, Linda?"

"It's the BBC. It's a man from The World at One, I didn't catch his name. I told him you were a wonderful doctor...I've left him on hold..."

"Linda, *please*, I asked you *not* to speak to reporters. Not even if they're from the BBC."

"I told him you were the brave doctor who saved that little girl in America from choking to death by performing a tracheotomy with your penknife. That you had saved another woman's life only last week and driven her yourself during the night to get her to hospital. I told him you were an honourable man, Dr Reiss..."

"I can't speak to him. Put him through to the P R people."

"He wants to talk to *you*. He asked me about Dr Devereaux as well. When I said I was your shared secretary he got really excited; he kept asking me what Dr Devereaux was like? Did I think he was a good doctor? Was I surprised at all these revelations? Did I know he had a girlfriend called Lara? I said none of us knew about Lara. He always came on his own to company events. None of us had ever met her. But I said, Dr Devereaux had always been polite and pleasant to me as his secretary..."

Reiss spoke in German to Dr Wengler, "I'm so sorry, Otto. We have a little problem here that I must deal with. Forgive me, but I have to put you on hold for a minute."

He kept his hand over the receiver just in case Wengler could hear them. "Linda, transfer this man to our P R department. The company's lawyers have issued strict instructions that we do not speak to the media and you can tell them that. Blame our lawyers if you like. They have forbidden me to speak to the press or anyone else."

"He wants you to explain about ulceration of the intestine and the cause of Crohn's' disease."

"The BBC can find another doctor to do that; they don't need to hear it from me."

"I know, Dr Reiss. I told him that nothing that had happened, or that might happen in future, was your fault. It *wasn't* Dr Reiss, and I don't want them trying to pin it all on you. It's not fair."

Reiss sighed. "Thank you, Linda, and I appreciate your loyalty, but you must not talk to reporters from now on."

"There's a rumour going round that the company's going bust and we're all going to lose our jobs?"

He groaned, the rumour mill was as usual working overtime. "We're not going bust. Don't listen to stupid rumours."

Linda, looking tearful, went back to transfer the BBC man to the harassed P R department, then went outside to smoke a cigarette.

Glancing through his side window Reiss could see that several white-coated people from the science block had already gathered for the same reason and were at the same time exchanging gloomy forecasts of what would happen to the company.

At the end of the line Dr Wengler was protesting indignantly about being kept hanging on. It was almost a relief to deal with his query. It seemed so trivial compared with everything else.

As he replaced the receiver, Pomeroy rang to let him know that P R were being bombarded with questions about the company's announcement that the A.C.E. trials were being suspended. How long for? Were they expecting Reduktopan to get a product licence this autumn? Why, if there was only a *possibility* that the drug might cause ulceration of the bowel, were the trials being paused after only six weeks ingestion?

When Pomeroy rang off, Linda, now back at her desk, put through first one and then a second hospital physician who had been involved with the A.C.E. trials. They complained they were being pestered by the media and would tell all their patients to contact FIP so if there wasn't a help-line there needed to be one set up and the sooner the better.

On the intercom he called Bill to come into his office.

"I need you to set up a help-line. Do it right away. You and Ayesha are personally to handle all the calls for people complaining of symptoms. If there are too many, then ask Molly to help and then, if you're getting overwhelmed we draft in the three in-house medics. These are my orders, you can tell them that from me. Every single call must be logged in and all the conversations recorded. Set up designated phone lines and a new email address. Can I rely on you to organise this?"

"Yes, sir, you can. I'll get on to it right away."

Bill scarlet-cheeked and penitent, said he would inform the P R department and John Stannard who would alert all the key doctors involved with A.C.E.'s trials.

"Some reporters may pose as patients, so be wary and check out their case number and details before you say too much. What you feel you can't deal with yourselves you can refer to me but not today, I have no time today."

Bill left the room looking purposeful.

Reiss told Linda not to put through any more calls unless it was his wife, his daughters, Marcus Pomeroy. Or Chris Schwartz from Sion, with whom he would need to speak at some length if possible before he left for London for the emergency board meeting.

After his protracted conversation with Chris, Reiss tried Sally yet again but her mobile was off and the answering machine was on at their house. He warned her on this that he would be home late.

The happy spirit that day was Ronnie who left a cheery message for Reiss. He had spoken to his father's lawyer in New York; his father's will left almost everything to him with a few small legacies to charity.

After lunch, Linda told him she had heard a news bulletin that featured an interview with Penny Wilson. Unsurprisingly, Sarah had evidently sent her a copy of her article. She said she had always suspected Devereaux had given her sister a slimming drug. Why did he deny they were lovers at the funeral? Why did FIP not want to look into it earlier?

She was followed by an emeritus professor of gastroenterology who pontificated on the origins and effects of ulceration of the large (and small) intestine and on the possible causes of Crohn's disease. When asked if Reduktopan could cause this, he admitted he knew little about this drug as it was not yet on the market. The presenter noted that Dr Raymond Reiss, the Medical Director of Forsyte International Pharmaceuticals plc, had declined to be interviewed for the programme.

Reiss complained to Pomeroy that he was being made to look evasive which was damaging to his reputation. Pomeroy had replied firmly,

"We stay *shtum*, Raymond. We clear everything we say with our lawyers. Our insurers will look for reasons to weasel out of covering us so we keep our mouths shut for now."

"But I need to refute these shocking and false allegations, Marcus. Mud sticks."

"You refer them to the documentation. You say nothing more, however much they try to bait you - and they will."

"Will that lunatic Cecil be coming to the meeting?"

"Oh, don't worry, he can't bring his shotgun there."

Now that they were en route to London in separate cars. Pomeroy, who had called again, was shouting into his phone's loudspeaker which was at the same time relaying the traffic noise on the M11.

"Cecil left me another message asking if I could give him a lift.

Julie told him I'd already left. He'll have to take the train."

Arriving a few minutes early, they spoke briefly in the waiting room. Reiss told Pomeroy of the rumours circulating round Flat Acres.

"It's the same at Head Office."

"Do you think the banks will let us go under?"

"No, they'd much prefer us to be taken over. When that happens, our shares will recover a bit. Too late for Cecil, I'm afraid. The Dower House will have to be sold to pay off the loans. Won't be much over, I'm afraid."

Reiss said, "I suppose you've lost out as well?"

Pomeroy gave a brief smile. "No, I'm a little up overall."

"How's that?"

Marcus shrugged. "I believe in taking a profit when it's there. At the start of the trial I bought a load of FIP shares for Mary and the kids and I instructed my broker to sell them last Thursday afternoon. I have to keep the ones that came with the job..." He looked directly at Reiss. "Be straight with me, Raymond. Do you think we'll ever get R/P on the market now?"

Reiss prevaricated. "Chris Schwartz asked me the same question earlier today: could I tell him "off the record", whether I think we could rescue R/P. The answer is I don't know. What I do know is that Sion have got their eye on us. I know because he told me today. I emphasised our excellent R & D programme and it's true that we have some promising new compounds in the pipeline that have gone through the first hoops but still a long way off human trials. We've some good people in our R & D team that they will want to take over."

"Like you, by any chance?"

"Possibly, if I can hose off the mud fast enough. As you know, Chris is flying over from New York tomorrow with a couple of side-kicks to take a look around Flat Acres. The vultures are already circling, Marcus. They'll be more of them sniffing round our carcase."

Pomeroy nodded, "I'm expecting that. Sion wants a UK base that will provide them with a foothold in Europe and we'd be a good fit for them. But what about your other contacts? Like Otto Wengler in Zurich? Or Carl Oldssohn in Stockholm? We've joint projects going with both their companies. Small beer, by comparison with Sion, but still?"

Reiss shook his head. "No future with either of them; Wengler's a pedantic old ditherer and they've had a recent merger they're not too happy about. It's not the right time for them. And Oldssohn is on holiday this week, but Zastro is too small to take us on." He looked down at his shoes. "I'm dreading this meeting, actually. Have you any advice for me?"

"Yes, speak slowly and clearly. You must distance yourself as best you can from Devereaux; you make it clear that he had his own fiefdom with charge of R/P that was set up long before you arrived on the scene."

"It's true."

"I know that, but as you were his boss and you worked in the next door office, they'll try and pin stuff on you. That aside, there's the issue of your and Bill's relationship with Sarah. I'll be frank - I know about Beatrice, obviously - but so do a lot of other people."

"Thanks to Bill, I think."

"No, it's been an open secret for ages. It's even reached Head Office and Strelitz found out about it in no time. If I were you I'd present yourself as a susceptible middle-aged man who was targeted by Sarah Goodwin along with your young assistant and both of you were taken in by her. At the same time you must make it clear that this never affected your clinical judgment or any of the decisions you had to take."

Reiss snapped, "It didn't. A susceptible middle-aged man? Is that how you see me?"

"Do you prefer an ageing wolf?"

"I am *not* an ageing wolf."

"Take a good look in the mirror. And it's bye-bye Beatrice and Sally, please forgive me from now on."

Reiss glowered at him. "You wouldn't believe it from her

behaviour now, but a couple of weeks ago Sarah tried to persuade me to leave Sally and have a second family with her? She offered to marry Bill and have my child, with me as its godfather? I said no, and she's not forgiven me. She's a fantasist and a nymphomaniac and I wish I'd never set eyes on her. I *hate* her. I loathe her."

"The feeling is mutual, that's for sure, Raymond."

CHAPTER FORTY-NINE

The emergency meeting was held in the investment bank's large and starkly modern boardroom. Nineteen men and women, power-dressed in smart dark suits, sat on either side of a long table of pale varnished wood. Reiss took a seat next to Marcus Pomeroy, whose cheeks were flushed pinker than usual.

Sir Morris opened the proceedings then invited Pomeroy to give his report. Pomeroy read from the printed page, concluding: "My actions with regard to Reduktopan reflected the advice of our medical team led by Dr Reiss who will provide us with a clear time line for some of the key events that are the subject of the article in the New York Globe today. After that he will explain his reasons for pausing the last of the A.C.E. trials. Please wait with your questions until he has finished speaking."

Reiss looked around him. The expressions that confronted him ranged from quizzical to challenging and outrightly hostile. They had in front of them copies of his reports sent a few days before to the regulatory authorities with the further one that dealt with the tragic death of Lisa-Jane and its unexpected aftermath which had been sent separately. They had also his own and Singer's affidavits with all their attachments, which they were glancing through as he spoke.

He was halfway through his address when Cecil Pemberton arrived and looked around him for a seat. His skull face was tighter and paler than usual and his dark suit was both creased and grubby. His red spotted bow tie was lopsided.

Interrupting Reiss in full flow as he bumped into a chair, he explained, slurring his words, that his train was late. Having been persuaded to sit down, he was rebuked by Sir Morris on four occasions for banging his fist on the table when he disagreed with something that Reiss was saying.

Though more restrained, the rest of the Board made it plain that they too were angry. Someone had to be held to account for what had happened and the men in the frame were right there in front of them.

But Reiss and Pomeroy had prepared their defences well.

Steely-eyed and grim faced, Reiss ploughed on. He deliberately invoked medical jargon where possible. Like a politician, he stated his position and repeated the key important points irrespective of any query raised. He repeated that he had acted at all times in what he had reasonably believed to be the patients' and the company's best interests. Were these two not synonymous? If not, please would somebody explain where they diverged?

After an hour of this, as he looked up and down the faces sitting at the long table, Reiss felt a surge of contempt for his accusers. Was it to be only about money for these people? Mourning, as they were, their lost chance of a quick profit? Who needed someone to blame for something they should have anticipated might happen: namely, the risk of side effects emerging when a new drug was tested on human patients. He refused to offer them reassurances he felt unable to justify.

Sir Morris's wife (who had no legitimate right to be present, but whom nobody dared ask to leave) persisted in asking why Reiss had been so determined to read the notes on Devereaux' computer if he had *not been suspicious about something.*

Reiss replied, coldly and calmly, "Once and for all, I was not suspicious of David. I had no reason to be. He was my trusted colleague. We respected each other's operating territory and his territory was Reduktopan and he guarded it very closely. It was only after his death that I needed to know much more about what he'd been doing. So I thought I should be able to read what was on his computer. And as it turned out, I was right, wasn't I? But I suspect there may be some people who would have preferred what he wrote to have remained hidden."

"No, of course not." interjected Sir Morris. "Nobody is saying that."

"Not out loud, no."

Marcus stood up and snapped, "This discussion should not be minuted."

It was at this point that Pemberton rose unsteadily to his feet and bawled, "You bloody well knew there were problems bubbling up, didn't you? You could have tipped me off when I told you after the prize-giving that I was thinking of selling my shares."

"Cecil, he couldn't tip you off, this is most unfair."

"He could! If he had, I'd have sold them! But *you,* Morris, *you,* told me *not* to sell then because if I waited a few days they might go higher still? But they won't go up now, will they? And as a result I shall be both bankrupt and homeless tomorrow! Well done! Well done, both of you!"

Sir Morris looked shocked. "Cecil, please. Members of the board must not profit from inside information as you very well know!"

"I'd like to blow both your heads off and I've a good mind to do it!"

"Lord Pemberton, any more comments like that and you will be escorted from the building, immediately."

Lady Cowperthwaite whispered loudly, "Morris, the man's deranged as well as drunk. Should we call the police?"

Sir Morris bellowed now: "Sit down, Lord Pemberton. Dr Reiss? Last words, please?"

"I will sum up. Until poor Lisa-Jane's death and the post mortem that followed it, we had no reason at all to suppose that Reduktopan was not safe for short term use. This has been a game-changer. We must hope she proves to be a very unlucky one-off, but I fear, having regard for Orloff and Lara, it may not be. On the upside, even if Reduktopan never gets a product licence there are other new compounds in development. We are collaborating with Zastro in Sweden to develop a better NSAID and we are working on a new antidepressant with Dr Leo Wengler's company, in Switzerland. These are just two examples. Our existing patented products are still selling well. "If our short term financial problems are resolved FIP can still have a good future even without R/P on the market. That's all I have to say."

Elisabeth, the finance director, hissed audibly, "What planet is he living on?"

Somebody else then commented, unpleasantly, "A few days ago you were happy for the press to describe Reduktopan as a miracle drug?"

"It is very effective, but it may not be safe. That is why I felt it necessary to pause these last trials."

One of the lawyers present spoke now: "You do realise that FIP and its insurers may face claims from the two thousand people who took Reduktopan under your supervision Dr Reiss? Does this not bother you?"

Reiss retorted, "We have the development risk defence in this country. We complied with due processes and monitored all our patients rigorously. But that said, of course I'm not happy about it. Of course it bothers me."

A senior banker volunteered. "There are rumours that there may be a personal element in this woman's attack on you, particularly, Dr Reiss? I've heard she's a very attractive woman. Was there something going on between you two?"

Reiss pursed his lips. "No comment."

"That is not a denial, is it? But I also heard she was going around with your assistant?"

Sir Morris jumped in here: "No doubt about that. I personally saw them holding hands together after the prize-giving last

Thursday. Will you enlighten us on these points please, Dr Reiss?"

Marcus Pomeroy jabbed him in the thigh. "Now."

Reiss frowning, nodded. "All right. You may be right about a personal element here. Sarah Goodwin is clever and she can be charming on occasion. But, as we have since discovered, she can be ruthless and unscrupulous about how she obtains her copy. She is a strikingly beautiful young woman who could have modelled for a Pre-Raphaelite painting."

"Go on, Dr Reiss."

"She flirted with my assistant physician, Dr Bill Ryder, and then er - turned her attentions on to me and I admit I was flattered; I am a little older than her."

"Indeed?"

"Yes." Reiss raised his voice irritably. "But when Sarah found she would get no information from me she turned her attentions back to Bill, presumably in the hope of getting hold of some confidential information. She led him to believe she was serious in a long term relationship, so he probably dropped his guard a bit."

Some wag shouted: "Along with his trousers I'm guessing?"

There were some titters at this.

Lady Cowperthwaite boomed, loudly. "This is shocking Morris! Quite shocking. What did these men think they were doing with this woman?"

Loud laughter erupted around the table.

Reiss interjected quickly, "My assistant Bill was, as I say, serious about this woman and she took advantage of his trust. After she had secretly opened his locked briefcase and stolen confidential information she dumped him by phone from the airport. Before that, she persuaded Herman Orloff's son to show her his father's passport and other papers including the autopsy report. She breached our trust and confidentiality agreement and much else."

He broke off as Cecil Pemberton shouted, waving his fist,

"You're a disgrace to your profession, you lecherous old goat! She was twenty years younger than you. But you still think you're irresistible, don't you? Well, you're not!"

There were more sniggers and giggles.

Reiss retorted sharply, "Oh, but you fancied her too, didn't you, Cecil? She'd not have been here for the second time if you hadn't invited her back to stay for free with you in the Dower House. Only problem was she was so allergic to your flea-bitten old dog that she had to move out after only one night. And that is how she ended up staying with Bill in his flat. *You* are the reason she was here and caused all this trouble!"

"Me? That's rich!"

One of the senior bankers, shouted, "Dr Reiss? You admitted just now that you were, like Bill, susceptible to the charms of this American Mata Hari? Were you having an affair with her?

"It was not an affair."

"But you spent time alone with her?"

"A little."

"And you never let slip even a little bit of information when you were murmuring sweet nothings in her ear?"

"No. And she did not distract me from my work for FIP or influence any of the medical decisions I took."

"So you were not distracted by Sarah Goodwin even when you were curled up in bed with her?"

There were howls of ribald laughter.

"Did Bill know you were sharing this woman with him? That you too were having an affair with her."

"It was *not* an affair. It was a weak moment, that's all."

"But Bill was serious about her?"

"I didn't know that then. And she obviously wasn't serious about him."

"Did anyone else know of Sarah Goodwin's relationship with Bill?"

"Everyone knew about it. They didn't hide it. On the contrary, they were very public."

Marcus squawked, "This discussion is not to be minuted."

There were more loud sniggers.

Reiss continued, very coolly: "We laid on a welcome cocktail party for Sarah the evening she arrived and it was soon obvious that she and Bill were attracted to one another. Marcus suggested I give Bill an entertainment allowance to take her away for the weekend, so I did."

Pomeroy hissed, "Shut up, Raymond."

Sir Morris, sounding disapproving, responded: "Are you telling us that you and Marcus Pomeroy agreed that Bill should be paid to take this young woman away for a romantic weekend?"

"We didn't want her hanging around Pemberton unsupervised. It was for the good of the company."

There was a burst of laughter from one of the male bankers at the end of the table. "And also for Bill, obviously? Win-win?"

"Well, yes. But he paid for himself after that."

Marcus groaned. "Too much information. Be quiet, will you."

There were snorts and peals of laughter and several loud giggles. Even Sir Morris was grinning until Lady Cowperthwaite snapped, "Yes, I'm sure our shareholders would agree this money was well spent."

Reiss turned to her: "But it was, Lady Cowperthwaite. Sarah Goodwin gave Pemberton Manor and FIP and Reduktopan an excellent write up when she returned to New York. Our shares rose and the Health Farm bookings boomed as a result. Unfortunately, her attitude changed after Lara's sister contacted her and she became increasingly obsessed with the David and Lara affair. She tried to pump Bill but, as he had arrived after David died, it didn't get her far. That is probably why she turned her charms on me, albeit not for long."

Pomeroy prodded Reiss to sit down again and took over.

"Dr Reiss made it clear to me that he opposed this woman coming to Pemberton even once, let alone twice. Yet, without first consulting him or me, Cecil, you asked her to stay with you but she was so allergic to your dog she finished up in Bill's flat."

"I couldn't foresee that." Cecil Pemberton, retorted, sulkily. "And I didn't know that Reiss and his assistant would take turns to jump in and of bed with the woman."

More ribald laughter.

Sir Morris stood, decisively.

"The time has come for an independent enquiry. We will need to convince others beyond these four walls and in anticipation of this, I phoned an old friend of mine, this morning, Sir Robert Millington, who recently retired from sitting as a High Court judge. He said he would be willing to chair such an enquiry. Our solicitors have already prepared the terms of reference which they will now circulate. Hands up all of you who are in favour?"

There was a unanimous show of hands.

"Carried. He will start next Monday."

After the presentation of a depressing financial report Sir Morris closed the meeting and people began to disperse. However, Reiss and Pomeroy found themselves being ushered into a small side room by Elizabeth Coleman, who said she needed more information from them to prepare her revised figures. As they were concluding, Reiss turned on his mobile. He was about to retrieve his messages when it rang.

Beatrice, at the other end, shrieked in English, "I know for sure that you deceived me with that red haired woman journalist because she telephoned me to the hospital to tell me so, herself!"

She was screaming so loudly that he had to hold the phone away from his ear. He responded hastily in German, "Schatzie, I am not alone. I am with other people... "

But Beatrice's German was inadequate to express her strong feelings: "I don't care who hears me, Raymond! It's not enough that you deceive your poor wife, but you must deceive me as well? With this horrible journalist woman who says you deceived *her* with *me*?"

"Beatrice, please calm down -"

"I never want to see you again! I never want to hear from you again! *Not ever!*"

Reiss now backed into a corner, tried again in German, his tone soothing: "Beatrice, please calm down. I can explain everything - but not now. I'm in a small room with two other people. We will talk later."

She yelled in English, "Let them hear me! You can tell them I'm your cousin from Vienna for all I care! Oh, yes, this horrible Sarah told me about that as well! That she was naked in your bed when you telephoned me in Stockholm!"

Reiss opened the door to the landing, in the hope of escaping his curious audience, but Sir Morris was outside arguing with Cecil Pemberton. He shoved the door closed again as Beatrice, still at full volume, screamed, "She says you told her that she was more beautiful than any other woman you had ever been with? That you loved her *sweet* little breasts. That some women had breasts so big and heavy they were like ripe melons hanging down? Did you mean me?"

He replied in German, "No, no, of course not! She was trying to make you jealous. Schatzie, you are far more beautiful than Sarah and I adore your beautiful big breasts. I told you so every time we were together."

"I don't understand everything in German, Raymond. Speak to me in English."

"You understand me perfectly well."

Marcus was staring at him, his mouth a little open and his eyes popping, while Elisabeth looking embarrassed, stared discreetly out of the window.

Reiss turning his back on them, lowered his voice and spoke slowly and reluctantly to Beatrice in English. "I never said anything like that to her. Why would I? She's a mad, jealous woman and she hates me like poison. She's doing her best to ruin me professionally as well as socially, Beatrice. Can't you see that? Why else would she contact *you?* I'm going to sue that woman and her newspaper the New York Globe for libel. You must not believe anything she tells you."

Beatrice, speaking more calmly now in slow accented English, replied, "But some things she told me I know *are* true, Raymond. Do you deny that you took her into your bed?"

He stayed silent.

"*Ja,* that is true, isn't it? She told me some of the little tricks you played together; the same little tricks you played with me that were just for us two, but now it is for three or maybe four?"

"Speak in German, *please* Beatrice."

But Beatrice, responded in English. "She said she has evidence that you are a crooked doctor as well as a crooked lover. You are a liar, Raymond. You have lied to your wife and also to me and I am sure you lied also to her. But there is more. She said she has spoken to your wife. She rang her first. So beware of what happens there!"

He responded in German: "She rang *Sally*? That's outrageous. That's terrible." Reiss now truly alarmed and appalled fell silent for a moment.

Elizabeth Coleman whispered to Pomeroy, "Raymond speaks German very well doesn't he?"

"He's bilingual."

"Really? I didn't know. Who is he speaking to? She sounds very upset about something?"

"It's his cousin Beatrice from Vienna. She's a charming lady, but very excitable. I think she's upset about the nasty article in the New York Globe. It sounds like someone sent it to her."

Beatrice was now sobbing. "You deceived me with this hateful woman, Raymond."

"I'm sorry. I wish I'd never set eyes on her. I *hate* her."

"Ja, I am sure you do now. She says you hid evidence about your colleague, the one who died in the car crash. That you knew for three months he had given his girlfriend too many of your wonderful slimming pills?"

"No, I *didn't*! I *really didn't* know. I knew nothing about his private life or even that he had a girlfriend. He led me to think he was gay, remember. Meanwhile, as I found out much later, he had been sleeping with my wife? That was before he met Lara of course."

Beatrice screamed, hysterically, "He slept with *your wife* Raymond? And you thought all the time he was gay? Now I find that *really* funny! Ha ha! I see now, why he wanted you to think that, of course. He had a sense of humour. *Ja, ja. Ha ha.*

"But, I also know you are a good doctor, Raymond. I know you care about your patients. You would not put them at risk or give them a drug if you believed it wasn't safe. And I told that horrible woman she was wrong to accuse you of that. You would never put patients at risk intentionally. But she didn't listen to me! She didn't want to hear that, but I told her anyway."

"Thank you Beatrice."

"You are a good physician, Raymond, I know that. But I never want to see you or hear from you again, so don't try and get in touch because I won't take your calls or read your emails or letters. It is over between us. Over. Finished. Ended. Understand?"

"Oh, Beatrice, I'm so sorry."

But Beatrice had hung up.

Finally able to escape to his car, Reiss drove back to Cambridge. On the way, he tried repeatedly to contact Sally, but her phone was still switched off and the answering machine at their home came on with his own voice asking him to leave a message. He and Sally had not spoken since that morning and since then he feared Sarah had injected her fatal poison into their shaky marriage.

It was eight o'clock and the sun was sinking when Reiss reached his house to find the drive empty. Anxiously, he locked the car and went towards the front door fumbling for his key when there were sudden flashes of light. A posse of reporters and photographers appeared suddenly from behind the front hedge.

"Dr Reiss?"

"Who are you? What are you doing here?"

"Dr Raymond Reiss?"

"What do you want?"

"Have you seen the article in the New York Globe? Have you any comments on it?"

"I've instructed my solicitors to deal with the load of false accusations and lies in that article. They have advised me to say nothing at this time, but I will just say this, and you can write it down: I have always and at all times done my best to act in the best interests of all my patients on the basis of the information available to me. Every decision I have taken is based on this principle. I cannot comment any further because the matter is now in the hands of my lawyers and my company's lawyers. We will be suing the New York Globe for a vicious and false libel. Now, please leave me alone and get off my drive. This is private property."

He shoved his key into the lock.

A bearded man with unkempt, greasy hair, who was holding a notebook, shouted, "If you're looking for your wife, she's not here. She left half an hour ago with three suitcases and the cat. I heard it mewing inside the pet carrier and she called it, Simba. She put the carrier with the cat inside it on the back seat and drove off in a little red car."

Reiss turned to stare at them all in dismayed disbelief as cameras flashed again.

"What? What did you say?"

"Your wife has left you, Dr Reiss, otherwise why would she take the cat with her as well?"

He yelled, "Get off my drive! This is private property!"

"Do you know where she's gone? Any idea? We'd like to speak to her, too."

"Leave me alone, will you?"

There was a further flash of photographs as they crowded round him. "What have you got to say about the allegations in the New York Globe that you suppressed evidence and put patients at risk?"

"It is a lie and I deny it. I will prove these allegations are totally false in a court of law if necessary. There is a press statement by my employer, Forsyte International Pharmaceuticals plc which clearly states our position. Please read it."

"Did you really not know that your close colleague Dr David Devereaux had a girlfriend Did you know she was also his patient?"

"When did you find out about it? When did you know he secretly gave his girlfriend Reduktopan? Do you know where he got it from yet?"

"You *were* his boss, weren't you? And he worked in the next room to you, didn't he?"

"Why are you surprised your wife has left you?"

Some wit shouted, "The good doctor here was far too busy chasing after red-haired journalists and Swedish blondes to bother himself with what his colleague was getting up to!"

Reiss slammed the door to shut out the hateful cackling laughter.

Inside, everything looked much as usual. The answering machine was flashing with six messages. Three were his own for Sally, one was from Joanne and two were from reporters.

There was a sealed envelope on the table with his name on it in Sally's bold, black script. He ripped it open and read it with a howl of dismay and distress and pounded up the stairs.

In their bedroom her side of the cupboard had been largely emptied and her toiletries were gone from the bathroom. He found it hard to breathe and to take in. Sally had left him alone when he most needed her to be by his side. He did not try ringing her again. He knew it was useless. That Sally was never coming back. His rocky marriage was finally over.

EPILOGUE

London, March 2004

I

In Stanford it was the middle of the night, but when the day dawned it would most likely be sunny and warm. In London it was cloudy and cold and Reiss's Californian tan was fast fading. Had he made a terrible mistake by coming back to the UK? To once again walk the wards for the National Health Service? To practise what Chris Schwartz annoyingly insisted on calling "socialized medicine"?

Chris had been understandably upset and disappointed by Reiss's decision to resign his post after only two years there when it had all been going so well.

They would be meeting up again though in a couple of weeks. Chris was flying to London for a major conference where Reiss was presenting a paper entitled: *Viewing the pharmaceutical industry from two different perspectives.*

Chris had asked Reiss for an advance copy but he would have to wait until the day before. It would allow him enough time to work out the questions and challenges to put to his former colleague in the ensuing discussion which would spark a lively exchange.

Reiss, however, valued their friendship. Chris had been very supportive of him during the miserable months after Sally left him and petitioned for divorce at the same time as the false allegations in the New York Globe were still being fought in the wake of the collapse of the Reduktopan trials and ensuing litigation followed by FIP's take-over by Sion.

In this most miserable period of Reiss's adult life, both socially and professionally, Chris had proposed that Reiss move from Flat Acres to take over as Medical Director of the new merged firm's R & D compound in Stanford. Reiss had been glad to accept. The Cambridge family house had been sold in November and he had put his books and his few items of furniture in storage where they were still.

But now, after more than two years, Reiss was weary of living in furnished accommodation. In Stanford at least it had been luxurious but the same could not be said for this small flat. Glancing out through the window for a moment, he saw a man crossing the street who reminded him of Sir Robert Millington, the retired judge who had run FIP's own offical Enquiry. Reiss had still been working (and for the most part living) at Flat Acres then which was when the merger with Sion was in progress but not completed. The experience of giving evidence under oath had been stressful but at the same time strangely cathartic. He was relieved that nobody questioned him about his "moment of weakness" with Sarah Goodwin, which Pomeroy had assured him was not minuted at the horrible board meeting.

In his report, Sir Robert had been sympathetic to Reiss whom he said was being unfairly castigated for having trusted his most senior medical colleague who gone to great lengths to conceal what he had done. Indeed, he had praised Reiss for his "stubborn determination" to recover Dr Devereaux' notes made on the company's loaned computer.

Pomeroy was also exonerated.

By this time, there had been a series of specialist investigations conducted on patients who complained of symptoms and also on some who were randomly selected. Reiss's action in promptly "pausing" the last two A.C.E. trials was (regrettably from FIP's viewpoint) found to be justified. However, curiously and for reasons that Sion & Forsyte were still now trying to understand, it was still not possible to predict the outcome for any particular patient. Some people had suffered no symptoms while others had some very slight ulceration that resolved within days or weeks and some of these had remained unsymptomatic throughout the trial and since. Others fared worse and a small core group had developed such severe ulceration that they had required major surgery to remove the affected sections of bowel. Reiss knew all this only from seeing the records; following the end of the trial he had no direct involvement with any of the patients or their treatment.

Where he remained in touch, it was on a personal level. It was a relief to him that the Pemberton contingent did not include any of the seven worst cases. Fortunately, the majority had benefited and were getting on with their lives.

It was a relief too when the libel claim against the New York Globe was settled satisfactorily. An apology printed on the front page admitted that substantial compensatory damages had been paid. Penny Wilson's complaint to the GMC was dismissed the week before Christmas and Reiss, his professional integrity duly intact, had left to take up his new post in Stanford.

The group action against FIP was continuing but, with the most serious cases settled, the action was running out of steam and looked as if it might founder.

The breakdown of his marriage had impacted badly on his daughters as well as himself and Sally. Mandy and Joanne were angry to learn of his repeated infidelity but also felt let down by their mother's failure to declare in public that their father's professional integrity was beyond reproach. They were photographed standing on either side of him both before and after he had been exonerated by Sir Robert Millington's report to the Enquiry.

For Mandy at medical school it had been a difficult time. He had given her a hug: "I'm so sorry you've had to live with all the gossip and insinuations because of me?"

"Don't worry, I'm fine, Dad." Then she added, softly: "I know what David did was awful for you and everyone - but he was nice to me ... and I was fond of him ... are you cross?"

"No, darling." Reiss had held her close. "David had his good side, too. He could be kind at times, I know that."

She had looked a little sharply at him. "How do you mean, kind?"

"Oh, by some of his choices of trial patients. He wanted to help them have a better future."

Mandy, relaxing perceptibly, had snuggled against him.

"Will they?"

"Some will, yes."

Sipping his instant coffee, Reiss sat down to study the agent's particulars of the three houses he was to see that morning. Prices in London were higher than in Cambridge and he had only half of the sale proceeds of the family house but he had kept back a portion of his large salary to add to the deposit.

Their moving day had been in late November more than two years ago; Sally had already contracted to buy a smaller house in the area, but Reiss was shortly to leave for the USA. At the sight of all their possessions boxed up and ready to go to their different destinations, Joanne and Mandy had become tearful. Reiss had held them tightly and reminded them he would pay their (economy) air fares if they wanted to come to stay with him during the holidays. And they had done so, twice a year in spring and summer, sometimes travelling together but sometimes separately as their lives took different directions.

Reiss and Sally met up if occasion required it, but were mainly in contact by email. From their exchanges, Reiss knew Sally had met a divorced engineering don called Peter who was from a different college.

Reiss, having put his mug in the sink, planned his morning. He was the duty consultant on call that weekend, so he would call in at the hospital after he had viewed the three houses that were on his list. Hopefully he would not be detained there too long; he was looking forward to meeting Emma Koestler at the Flask pub at 2.30 that afternoon.

They had met indirectly through the late Dr Singer who had asked Reiss to be one of his executors and a trustee of the nascent medical research charity which Singer had been busy setting up before he died the previous October. As there was some documentation to be concluded with the trust's lawyers, Reiss had arranged to join them at a conference with counsel in Lincoln's Inn earlier that week.

Arriving a little too early, he had opened his laptop to read Chris Schwartz's long email in which he discussed the current situation with regard to Reduktopan's future.

Further research would continue for now. Chris's view was that R/P might still, with luck, be considered relatively "safe" for the short term for morbidly obese patients. Would they not do better to take it and reduce?

Unfortunately, the media frenzy prompted by the Globe's article and the collapse of the trials had created a mood of high anxiety. In consequence, many patients who said they had felt fine all through the trial began complaining of very unpleasant symptoms and it was these cases that were now foundering. In most cases their doctors' physical examinations revealed no organic cause. If they were not malingering (as some undoubtedly were) the causes were psychological and anxiety related. Expectation of monetary compensation meant the group action had initially surged.

As Chris had sourly pointed out to Reiss, a careful review of the claimants' medical records indicated that most had been prescribed psychiatric medication for similar symptoms long before they ingested Reduktopan.

Reiss was glad that Frank Miller was not among any of these litigants. He had kept up his exercise and healthy diet regime and trained to become a fitness instructor who specialised in obese clients. He had become friendly with Ronnie Orloff during the holiday in Scotland with Mrs Shane and for the last two years had been sharing Ronnie's late father's large Miami apartment where Ronnie had fitted out a small gym where Frank could bring his clients.

Mrs Shane also emailed Reiss now and then. She was still hoping to find wealthy husband number four.

Sharon, now bleached platinum blonde, had reduced her weight further and had started a college course to study sociology. Her friend Bella had an apprenticeship in the fashion industry.

The Dower House had been bought by Sion from Lord Pemberton's mortgagees. Duly modernised, it had been swiftly absorbed into Pemberton Manor Health Farm that was later sold off by Sion & Forsyte inc. Cecil Pemberton was reported to have moved in with an old school friend on the Suffolk coast whose wealthy wife had recently died. He had resigned from FIP's board immediately after the emergency meeting.

Bill wrote to Reiss from time to time. He had moved to Australia and was a specialist registrar in gastroenterology in a Melbourne hospital. He and Jessica were "an item". Harriet was in New Zealand.

Sarah Goodwin, who had continued to attack Reiss until she had been silenced by the Globe's lawyers, was "let go" when the libel action was settled. She had married a
former boyfriend and they had a little girl of nearly two. She had a part time job as a features writer on a gossip magazine.

II

Reiss having closed the laptop, saw that a pretty young woman, dressed in a formal straight black skirt and black jacket, was standing in the doorway.

"Excuse me, but are you Dr Raymond Reiss?"

"Yes?"

She came forward and held out her hand and he stood up politely to shake it. The top of her head came a little way above his shoulder.

"I'm Emma Koestler. We don't know each other, but I was hoping I'd catch you before you went into con with Barry. He's my room-mate here in chambers. He mentioned you were coming in for a conference today. I wanted to meet you on account of my grandfather, Henry Koestler. Well, originally it was Heinrich, but he changed it to Henry. He thinks he was at school with your father in Vienna before the war. The gymnasium?"

Reiss corrected her pronunciation using the German hard g. "The *gymnasium*? Well, Dad did go there so it sounds more than likely, but I'm afraid I can't ask him as he died four years ago. What a shame they didn't meet up before; I'm sure Dad would have loved to talk about old times."

Reiss smiled apologetically, but also encouragingly, at this earnest young woman whose long dark hair framed her oval face. He put her age somewhere in the mid-thirties.

Emma smiled.

"Grandpa read about you in the papers and then he saw you interviewed on TV - it must be two years ago, now - and he said, "That must be Rudy's boy? He has that same expression and the tilt of his head. Rudy did a first year in medicine before he had to leave like we all did after 1938. I heard that he went on to become a doctor in England."

"My father's name was Rudolph and he was a doctor. Why didn't your grandfather get in touch with me then?"

"He said you had too much on your plate to be bothered with him and you were living in California."

Reiss grunted, "Yes, I was out there for two years. But I'm back now, I think for good. And I'd like very much to meet your grandfather, if he's still up for it?"

"He'd be delighted. He says your father was kind and stopped some bigger boys from bullying him in the street."

"I'm glad to hear it."

There was a pause, then Emma said, in her low, pleasant voice. "If you're too busy to visit, you could just speak to him on the phone? It would mean a lot to him. He's quite old now, but he was three years younger than your father. He says your father was always smartly dressed and that he liked pretty girls?"

Reiss laughed, genuinely amused, "That sounds like Dad. He

was vain about his appearance right to the end. Look, please tell your grandfather that I'd genuinely very much like to meet him."

Emma responded, smiling. "He'll be so thrilled to see Rudy's boy."

"Some boy. I've turned fifty." They both laughed. "What did your grandfather do?"

"He was a solicitor. Retired now. All of us Koestlers are lawyers, I'm afraid."

"Tell you what, Emma, why don't you come with me the first time. Would you? We could meet first and go on together?"

She nodded. "Yes, I'd like that." She added her private mobile and home telephone number to her business card and handed it to Reiss. "Grandpa moved to Highgate recently from Richmond. He has a flat in the Village. It's quite near a pub called the Flask. Do you know it?"

Reiss, smiling broadly, responded, "I do, Emma. I grew up in Highgate. I went to school there. Home territory for me."

He passed her one of his newly printed cards with his mobile number and thought for a moment. "I'll be on call this next weekend, but we can risk trying to meet up if you and your grandfather are free this Saturday afternoon?"

She checked her diary. She could be free then; her paperwork could wait.

They agreed to meet at the Flask at two thirty.

"I'll let you know if anything changes or I'm held up at the hospital."

Emma was about to leave when Toby, Singer's solicitor dealing with the trust appeared. He was a genial, plump young man who grasped Reiss's hand eagerly. They had met only once before.

"Dr Reiss, it's good to see you again. I saw Barry coming in. He's just taking off his robes ..." He glanced from Emma to Reiss a little puzzled. "You two look like you know each other?"

Emma replied quickly, "We recognised each others' surnames. Our families were friends years ago, in Vienna." She smiled at

Reiss, who nodded and smiled back.

"Yes, it seems they were."

"Quite a coincidence then?"

"Yes, it is. But a good one."

"Bye - er - Dr Reiss."

"Goodbye, Emma. Tell your grandfather, I'm looking forward to meeting him very soon."

Barry, who had just come in, exchanged a raised eyebrow with Toby. Reiss hoped the two of them would not warn Emma off.

Emma, however, had confirmed their arrangement and Reiss was looking forward to it in a few hours time.

He walked to see the three houses all of which were local. The first two were disappointing.

Feeling rather discouraged, he walked briskly for ten minutes and checking the number, rang the front door bell. He was outside a stucco-fronted house that was the last in a terrace of five. The agent had described it as "quietly situated in a sought-after county road within easy reach of East Finchley tube station, restaurants and shops and a local park".

An old woman opened the door.

The hall was small and a little dark and yet Reiss's spirits lifted a little as he walked in. It had a shabby charm along with its original fireplaces and the two living rooms, interconnected by folding doors, were bright and of a good size. There was a downstairs lavatory squeezed under the stairs. The old fashioned kitchen had a separate scullery from which a door led down to the cellar: "dry and useful for storage". Upstairs were three bedrooms, a bathroom and separate lavatory and above that were three large attic rooms. Reiss supposed they could be converted to provide a pair of bedrooms with a bathroom between that his daughters could stay when they came to visit.

The house appealed to him, but he hesitated; as a busy doctor, living on his own, it would be a major project for him to take on. It needed total renovation: rewiring, new plumbing, a new boiler and new central heating, a modern kitchen with a wall being removed and it was likely the roof would need work too. Notwithstanding, while he stood around outside in the garden, he rang the estate agent with his offer.

"I'll put it to them now."

Moments later, he saw the old woman pick up the telephone in the sitting room. She was obviously sharing the information with her husband, who stood close to her elbow. Then they both turned to look out of the window at him and smiled and waved and he waved back.

They would accept the offer.

III

Reiss was walking back to fetch his car to drive to town when his mobile rang. It was his registrar, Dr Rajiv Modi, apologising for disturbing him. A patient who had just been admitted from A & E was causing some concern.

"So sorry to disturb you like this on a Saturday."

"I was planning on coming in anyway. I'll be with you inside an hour."

It was nearly five years since Reiss had left his consultant post for "industry" and he was still feeling his way back. He was also adjusting to living in London, a city he had grown up in, but had left twenty-five years earlier. He had been cautious during these first ten weeks; careful not to rush relationships with his new colleagues and the stressed junior staff. He was made aware that his appointment was not universally welcomed or popular. Gossip surrounding the debacle over the Reduktopan trials and litigation and stories of his extra-marital relationships no doubt persisted. And he was regarded with a degree of suspicion arising from his decision to work for "Big Pharma" on both sides of the Atlantic.

At first, if he were honest with himself, Reiss found himself missing the perks: business class travel, good hotels, restaurants, wining and dining and the country club where his subscription was paid for by his employer. He also missed some of the friendships he had built with some of his former colleagues and it would take time to fill in some of the gaps these left.

But those moments were fewer now and he was adjusting to his changed life. His punctuality, meticulous thoroughness and underlying competence had been quickly recognised and much appreciated by the hard pressed junior and nursing staff. His opinion was increasingly sought first for tricky cases. This did not make him popular with all his consultant colleagues, but already most of them appeared more friendly and receptive than when he had first arrived in January.

Leaving his car in a side street, Reiss dashed up the flight of broad echoing stairs of the 1920's red brick building, then strode rapidly down the long linoleum corridors until he reached the medical wards. At the nurses' station, a harassed senior house officer, noticing him arrive, bleeped Modi, before approaching Reiss himself.

"It's an elderly gentleman. He says he knows you personally, Dr Reiss? Says he's an old friend of yours? He's asking to be transferred to a private room. I said you would talk to him about that. Ah, good, here's Raj, now. He has the notes; he can fill you in better than me."

Reiss frowned as he glanced over the thin sheaf of notes and exclaimed, "Good Heavens, what's he doing in here?"

Dr Modi said, nervously, "He was brought in by ambulance mid-morning. He collapsed in a computer shop, apparently. He vomited on the way over here and he was pyrexial as well. When he reached A & E he was poorly and moaning a lot and complaining of aches and pains and all over muscle weakness. He's got respiratory problems as well. I've made a provisional diagnosis of viral pneumonia, but I'm really not convinced that's right. We've taken the usual samples and sent them to the lab for testing. He's just come back yesterday from a foreign holiday somewhere with his wife. She's not here now - she's gone to fetch him some pyjamas and toiletries and stuff. A very vocal lady."

Reiss followed Dr Modi to the bed at the end of the ward which was opposite the door leading to the lavatories and shower rooms. In it, Marcus Pomeroy, looking pale, sweaty and very unwell, lay with his head raised a little and oxygen tubes in his nose. His eyes were closed and his steel framed spectacles lay abandoned on the bedside table.

Reiss waved away Dr Modi, who was hovering curiously, and pulled up a chair to sit down by the bed. "Hallo, Marcus. Fancy seeing you here?"

Pomeroy opened his eyes and reached out for his spectacles with trembling fingers. "Raymond, thank God, you've come at last. I'm feeling terrible." He sounded very breathless. "What's happening to me? I was alright at breakfast this morning."

"Dr Modi thinks you may have pneumonia, Marcus. We can treat it, don't worry. I gather you've been away on holiday?"

"We went on a three week cruise round South America. We flew back last night. We'd planned to spend a couple of nights up in London and I booked the company flat but I've ended up in here instead." Pomeroy, glanced around him disdainfully and moaned again, saying his head was hurting a lot.

Reiss put on his stethoscope.

"This place is in a shocking state, Raymond. The paint's peeling off the ceiling up there. They made me change into these horrible pyjamas because I was sick in the ambulance. I don't like to think of who was wearing them before me. I hope they've been boiled for hours on end."

Reiss smiled, faintly, "You're lucky, Marcus. You're in one of London's flagship teaching hospitals. A centre of excellence."

"I don't want to be in a noisy ward with twenty toothless, incontinent, demented old men, Raymond. I'm on BUPA and I want to be in a private room. That Indian doctor said I had to speak to you first. Can I be transferred? Will you arrange it for me?"

Reiss grunted, "I'll see what we can do later. Right now I need to listen to your chest." He helped Marcus open the buttons of the faded jacket. "Breathe in as deeply as you can, then out. Take

392

the deepest breath you can now then let it out slowly. That's right. Now, I'm going to tap your chest. Then I'll send you down for an x-ray, or has this been done, already?"

"No, not yet, Dr Reiss. He only came in a very short time ago and it is Saturday, remember."

Pomeroy whispered, "I don't understand you, coming back to work for peanuts in this crumbling dump. Chris Schwartz was really pissed off. He pulled out all the stops for you after that fiasco with Reduktopan and you left after just two years in the job. Why? You were earning three times as much with a nice easy life and all mod cons and it was all going well. Whatever possessed you to come back to this?" Pomeroy coughed and spluttered, painfully.

"Not the money, that's for sure."

He tapped Pomeroy's chest.

"You must have some of the damages left? I know you gave a lot away, but you did keep some back didn't you?"

"I've given half to Singer's medical charity of which I'm now a trustee. The other half is in a bond for my two daughters to use as a deposit when they buy their first flats."

Marcus moaned, "Raymond, please do something. My head is killing me and I feel like I've got weights pressing down on my chest. I'm finding it really hard to breathe."

"Your lungs are congested. Don't talk so much, now. Breathe as deeply as you can. Slowly and deeply. That's right... " He left the stethoscope hanging around his neck and made a note. "Any neck stiffness?" He felt the glands round Marcus's neck. They were swollen. Not a good sign, but he kept his face neutral.

"I ache everywhere. I feel awful."

"Do bright lights bother you?"

"I've got a splitting headache and everything bothers me." Pomeroy lay back weakly with his eyes closed.

Reiss said, "Brace yourself. I'm going to shine a torch into your eyes, now."

Marcus turned his head away. "No, don't. It makes things worse."

Reiss added another note. "Dr Modi has already tested your reflexes, but I'm going to do it again, now."

"You Germans are so thorough."

Reiss glared at him. "Don't go there, Marcus."

Pomeroy, spluttering, apologised, "Sorry, Raymond. Stupid in-joke. Bad taste. I'm glad you're thorough."

A nurse was now standing beside the two junior doctors, watching curiously from a few feet away.

Reiss turned to Modi, "Raj, Let me know as soon as you get the results back from the lab. Get an x-ray organised for him now. I know it's Saturday, but you can find someone to do it, can't you? Meantime, we'll start him on intravenous antibiotics. I don't think we need a lumbar puncture yet, but let me know if there's any change." He spoke again to Pomeroy. "When do you think Mary will be back?"

"She won't be long. She went to the flat to fetch my pyjamas and a dressing gown and slippers and a toilet bag, but they're still packed in our cases filled with dirty washing in the flat." Pomeroy sniffed cautiously at his sleeve. "I hate to think who last wore these. Mary booked us seats for one of those Lloyd Webber musicals. She loves them, but I don't suppose I'll be going with her, will I?"

"Not tonight, no. Tell her to sell the ticket."

Reiss tapped out the last of his notes and glanced at his watch and stood up. He did not want to be late for Emma, who would soon be waiting for him at the Flask.

Pomeroy grumbled again, "I want a private room, Raymond. Can you fix it? I'd like you to go on treating me privately. BUPA will pay you, of course."

"If you go into a private room it will be under a different consultant. I don't have any private sessions; I have too many research commitments for that."

Pomeroy groaned faintly, "Don't get pious on me, Raymond, please. All right, I'll stay here if you're looking after me. Just don't abandon me to the students."

Reiss bared his teeth. "This is a teaching hospital. They've got to learn on someone, haven't they?"

"Not on me, Raymond. Not on me, today, please. I'm really ill. I know I am." Marcus rolled around petulantly. "Where's Mary? Why isn't she back yet? She should be here by now? I hope she's not trying do the washing before she comes back here?"

Pomeroy looked increasingly unwell. He was feverish: sweating and shivering. He would probably develop rigors in the next couple of hours. Reiss felt concerned for him. He told the staff to move the bed so that it was next to the nurses' station. He would need regular monitoring. Reiss patted Marcus gently on the shoulder.

"I'll tell them they can call me day and night, how's that?"

Pomeroy said dolefully, "I feel lousy. I can hardly see out of my eyes and my whole body aches ... "

"Unsteady gait, it says here. You need to cut down on the Glenlivet."

"Very funny. Will I be here long?"

Reiss said evasively, "Can't say yet. We'll see how it goes. We won't keep you any longer than we have to. Can't spare the bed."

He moved away and said, quietly. "I want to know if there's any deterioration. Don't hesitate to call me, any time, night or day. I need to know."

His mobile rang again and he took the call in the corridor. It was the estate agent.

"It's definite. They've accepted your offer. You'll want a structural survey, but we can recommend you someone to do that."

Reiss agreed. It occurred to him that he should tell his girls of his plans. He went back to the ward and stood beside Marcus's bed for a few moments. He was snoring, his face flushed, but the medical staff were setting up the drip and parenteral antibiotics to infuse his veins. Reiss scribbled a note for Mary, leaving her his mobile number and then drove to the Flask in Highgate.

When he arrived, Emma was reading a novel and sipping a diet

Coke. Her dark hair was flopping forward, partly concealing her face. She looked up and smiled at his arrival. Reiss took the chair opposite.

"Sorry if I'm a little late. I was called in and the patient turned out to be an old friend of mine."

He tilted her book towards him to read the title. "All Quiet on the Western Front. It's a great book."

"Am I missing a lot, reading it in English do you think?"

"I've only read it in German, but I'm sure it's good in translation, too."

The weak winter sun slanted through the ancient glass panes picking out auburn glints in her dark hair. She was casually dressed in a cherry red sweater and blue jeans. She smiled at him again.

He smiled back and stretched out his hand to hers.

End.

ABOUT THE AUTHOR

Diana Brahams

 Diana Brahams practised as a barrister at Old Square Chambers, specialising in personal injury and clinical negligence cases. During her professional career and since retiring she has written numerous articles on a wide range of medico-legal and ethical issues. For twenty years she wrote a regular "Medicine and the Law" column for "The Lancet."

Diana is the Editor-in-Chief of the Medico-Legal Journal which is has an international readership. She lives with her husband Malcolm in North London.

ABOUT THIS BOOK

A slimming pill that really works! Just as it is due to be tested on patients the drug company's chief research physician David Devereaux dies in a car crash and its medical director, Raymond Reiss, is forced to take over in a hurry. He is alarmed by evidence he finds in David's house. And why is David's computer blocked?

As the drug is tested on patients all goes well at first. Sarah Goodwin, an attractive journalist visiting from New York, is initially impressed but senses that some data has been concealed. After starting an affair with Bill, Reiss's assistant and later with Reiss himself, she secretly probes deeper into the circumstances surrounding Dr Devereaux' death...

Printed in Great Britain
by Amazon

10960774R00231